THE FAMILY RETREAT

Bev Thomas was a clinical psychologist in the NHS for many years. She currently works as an organisational consultant in mental health and other services. She lives in London with her family. Her debut novel, *A Good Enough Mother*, was published in 2019.

'I raced through this beautifully written, emotionally intelligent thriller . . . The author was a clinical psychologist in the NHS for years and it shows. Gripping.' *Daily Mail*

'A gripping and smart thriller that kept me guessing . . . Sensitive but not sensationalist, a page turner with an important message, I was hooked.' Marisa Bate

'An evocative domestic noir that builds to a dramatic conclusion.' *The Sun*

'Bev's ability to excavate the complexities and intricacies of violence never ceases to amaze me, and her skill when it comes to offering a deep and comprehensive portrait of her character's psychological landscapes are second to none. You must read this book.' Lucia Osborne-Crowley

'No one describes complex feelings as nimbly as Bev Thomas . . . Packed with suspense, the story bristles with secrets and emotional insights. Powerful, intelligent writing that tells a timely story, and doesn't miss a beat.' Jane Bailey

'Thomas joins the ranks of first-rate masters of misdirection who delight in artfully distracting us readers from the terrible truths planted right before our eyes.' *Washington Post*

'I thought *The Family Retreat* was, quite simply, excellent – in style, subject matter, plot and character. I found it compelling, affecting and educational as well as totally entertaining. Don't miss this one.' Laura Hill

'Dark drama, big picture issues.' *Sainsbury's Magazine*

'*The Family Retreat* is the perfect summer thriller if you're looking for a smart, sophisticated read with superb characterisation and well-written suspense. It's a very human story with an unexpected twist in the tale, which I thoroughly appreciated.' Emma Welton, damppebbles.com

'To write such a captivating, clever, compassionate story and to stimulate readers is in my opinion the mark of an author with huge potential.' *Thriller Books Journal*

by the same author

A GOOD ENOUGH MOTHER

The Family Retreat

BEV THOMAS

faber

First published in the UK in 2022
by Faber & Faber Limited
The Bindery
51 Hatton Garden
London EC1N 8HN

This paperback edition first published in 2023

Typeset by Faber & Faber Limited
Printed and bound by CPI Group (UK) Ltd, Croydon, CR0 4YY

A CIP record for this book
is available from the British Library

ISBN 978–0–571–34957–9

2 4 6 8 10 9 7 5 3 1

In memory of my father

And the inimitable George Jeffrie
1964–2020

THE FAMILY RETREAT

ONE

It happened on the beach. A woman I hardly knew. A woman I didn't even really like. 'My sister's in trouble,' she said, as our children played on the sand. My eyes were fixed on the water, on a small pool of silver light, but I heard the desperation in her voice, the undertow of panic. This unexpected ripple in her sheen of self-restraint. The moment shifted between us, and this woman I hardly knew became a woman I wanted to help. I didn't wait to be asked. I was already straining forwards, a greyhound in a box; I knew all about rescuing, waving the red flag like a lifeguard on a beach. But that summer, I was so caught up in my heady rush of altruism, I didn't notice the real horror was happening somewhere else.

Helen wasn't the sort of person I'd ordinarily be drawn to. She was self-contained, with an organisational efficiency I found irritating. The type of person who had hand sanitiser long before it became an essential piece of armour for us all. From the outset, we were not a good match. If I remember anything about that first brief sight of her in the morning by her car, it was her poise, and her neatness. If I'm honest, the thing that interested me most about Helen was her kids. My eyes feasted on them greedily as they got into the car; their size, their age, and the rush of joy as I weighed up their compatibility to my own. And as predicted, the very next day, my two would home in on them in the crowd, like heat-seeking missiles in a warzone.

We met properly at the party next door. An event that was nothing like the 'small gathering' Joyce had described. She had

3

appeared at the door in muddy wellies and a large baggy green jumper with patches at the elbows. 'Welcome to Langton!' she said, handing over a homemade cake and fresh eggs. 'Are you the writer?' she asked, peering at me. I shook my head. 'Rob. My husband.' Joyce was overseeing the rental of the cottage in the owner's absence. I liked her straight away. Her warmth. Her cheerful weathered face. The speed of her words. The tight grey curls that bobbed as she spoke.

'We're having a little gathering – at the farm tomorrow,' she said, 'a fundraiser for the gardening project my son goes to. A few stalls. Stuff for the kids. The villagers are all coming to support. Green Shoots, it's under threat of closure. We need to make enough noise to get the local papers along. And it's Leo's birthday. His eighteenth,' she said with a proud smile. 'I believe you met last night,' she laughed. And I felt my face flush at the memory of being lit up on the picnic table, as if naked on a stage.

I'd gone outside to investigate the incongruent roar of a tractor. *Who ploughs a field at night?* I said, seizing the opportunity to get away from Rob and the doll's house. It was just after dusk, but it was night black. That deep and absolute darkness of the countryside that always takes me by surprise, and guided by the light on my phone, I picked my way across the lawn, then climbed up onto the table to try to see over the hedge into the field beyond. The tractor was some distance away. The headlamps were on full beam, and as it swung in my direction, there was a boy, or young man, I came to see as he got closer. He was running ahead of the tractor along the furrowed lines in the field. He was smiling and laughing, and I was struck by his running style; a strange robotic movement, stiff straight legs, and soldier-like arms by the side of his body. As the tractor got closer, I was momentarily illuminated by the beam of light and I felt exposed and faintly ridiculous. I

4

lifted my hand to wave, but the man in the tractor cabin simply nodded, a slight dip of his head. No smile. The boy seemed oblivious to me, or anything else around him. I jumped down, and as the light swished away, I was plunged into darkness. I stood still as my other senses rushed to compensate: the sweet smell of the honeysuckle, the feeling of the spongy grass underfoot and the roar of the tractor in the distance.

'He's autistic,' Joyce explains, on the doorstep. 'He's always loved straight lines. A run along the furrowed tracks is his equivalent of a bedtime story,' she says. 'Burns off energy at the end of the day. Helps him sleep. Though it's harder now he's older. All those hormones,' and she shakes her head, 'but it usually gets us a three-hour chunk of rest,' she adds brightly.

Joyce gives me the lowdown on my new neighbours, but she's talking too fast and I've had too little sleep to concentrate, so for the most part, they are a jumble of names. I hear about a Penny who keeps horses, and her father who's writing a book. Then she mentions the family with children. 'They're very nice,' she says, 'she's here with the kids during the week and her husband James comes at the weekend –' then she stops to squint at Sam and Ruby who have pushed their way through to the front door, '– look roughly the same age as yours.' And then she's off down the path. 'No mobile phone reception in the cottage,' she calls back, 'just a small patch by the picnic table in the garden. Gets better as you walk up the driveway to the farmhouse. So – in an emergency, just lean out of the bathroom window and yell,' she laughs. 'One of us will come running.' She waves a hand in the air. 'See you tomorrow.'

After lunch, I head over with the kids, leaving Rob to work and join us later. It's a sunny June afternoon. Clear blue sky and small wispy clouds with the streak of silvery sea in the distance.

The kids are giggling and I feel the warmth of the sun on my face. I stop for a moment, noticing something I haven't felt in a long while. The feeling of lightness. Like a lift. The unbuttoning and loosening of a thick and heavy coat around my neck.

As we cross the track from our cottage, the kids are excited by the sight of the candy-striped bunting in the trees and the row of stalls. As we get closer, we see a tombola, a bouncy castle, a guess-the-number-of-sweets-in-the-jar, a wire and buzzer game and skittles laid out in a carpeted alley on the grass. There's a huge crowd of people, and tables and chairs are set out in the sun around long trestle tables with tea and cakes and barrels of beer. It all feels a long way from East London.

We each have a go on the tombola and Sam is delighted by his win of green Radox bubble bath, and as we are milling through the crowd, I feel a tug on my sleeve. 'Look,' whispers Sam, 'that boy. He's got a Transformer.'

He points to a boy sitting at one of the tables by the cake stall, pulling me over, mesmerised by both the toy and the boy who's holding it.

It's the family I'd glimpsed earlier in the driveway. The woman is sitting next to him, tapping at her phone. She's wearing trousers and a crisp white long-sleeved t-shirt, her neat ponytail swishing from side to side as she taps.

Sam's now standing directly in front of the boy. There's a small girl, more like Ruby's age, hunched over some paper, doing a drawing with felt tips. She has a wide-eyed dreamy sort of face, her hair falling out of what were once neat plaits.

'I like your Transformer,' Sam says shyly.

The boy beams. 'It's Optimus Prime,' he says.

Sam nods knowledgeably. 'Does it flip from the back? Or front?'

'Both,' the boy says, and with a deft finger movement, the truck morphs into a robot. Then another swift sleight of hand the other way, and it's a vehicle again.

Sam is impressed.

'I'm Ollie,' the older boy says.

'I'm Sam.'

All the while I'm standing there, the woman doesn't look up from her phone.

'Hi,' I say eventually, 'I'm Jess. My son's obsessed. Transformers,' and I roll my eyes apologetically.

When the woman does glance up, it's enough of a delay for it to feel rude. She seems momentarily confused, then sees the boys. 'Oh – it's fine,' she says, looking back down at her phone.

There's something about her detachment that makes me feel nervous. And in my awkwardness, I start to talk too much, filling the silence with the sound of my own mindless chatter.

'We're here for a month,' I explain, 'having repairs done on our house in London,' and I can hear the people-pleaser tone of my voice. The woman stares back at me. 'Flood damage. A burst water tank in the loft . . .' and then my voice trails off.

'Do you live in the village?' I ask disingenuously, given I saw them yesterday.

The woman shakes her head. 'Just over there. The cottages,' she nods. 'Opposite yours. I saw you arrive last night,' she adds.

'Lived there long?'

'Just here for the summer,' she says, eyes back down on her phone, before I can ask anything else.

The woman is not nudged into reciprocity. She asks no questions in return. Offers no information. She's not interested in furthering or deepening the conversation. And I'm surprised by how much this irks me. We lapse into silence as the boys

7

are locked together in their mutual toy-admiration. Ruby slides onto the seat next to the little girl. The woman looks at least ten years younger than me, and comes across as self-sufficient, the grown-up in the face of my child-like neediness.

I stop talking. I try to escape the 'tyranny of niceness' I've been discussing in therapy. These new nuggets of learning, or of self-awareness, seem to pop up in real life unexpectedly. They stop me short. Leave me feeling momentarily self-conscious, like my features have suddenly become cumbersome and over-sized. I try to feel comfortable in the silence. I still can't work out whether it's the recent events that have made me so sensitive, or whether I've always been like this. It all feels muddled. I breathe in and out. I distract myself by watching the boys. Sam is as close as possible to the older boy, without actually sitting on his lap. Ollie has a small, furrowed brow and the wise serious face of an old man. He's talking as he moves parts of the toy. He doesn't offer it to Sam to hold. Sam, I can see, doesn't expect him to. He is just happy to simply circle the orbit of this cool older boy.

Just then, over on the other side of the garden, I catch sight of Rob, in animated conversation by the skittles. I can tell he's talking about his script. It's that strange new demeanour he's developed of late. A slightly puffed-up version of himself. He looks taller. Takes up more space. And he weaves his hands about in the air as he talks. Something he never used to do. Odd what success does to a person. I can't get used to it. All jaunty and optimistic. It's weirdly disconcerting.

'Look – there's Daddy!' I say to the kids, like he's a long-lost relative. 'Let's go over.' Ruby is happy to come, but I have to take Sam's hand briskly. Unsurprisingly, it's not the prospect of a father he saw half an hour ago, but the hissed promise of cake and a game of skittles that finally coaxes him away from Optimus Prime.

'—it's finding that moment,' I hear him say, as we come over, 'all drama is conflict—'

The woman he's talking to nods intensely and flicks her mane of swishy hair.

'This is Penny,' Rob says, as I approach. 'We're talking about dramatic tension,' he laughs.

Penny is the horse woman. She has an ageless quality about her, in the way that outdoorsy types often do.

'The script!' she says, turning to me like she's announcing a piece of news. 'How fantastic! So exciting.'

I nod. I wonder what Rob has said.

'The Jean-Paul Sartre device sounds brilliant,' she says. 'I do love Sartre.'

'Do you?' says Rob, rising up a bit taller. 'You can read it if you like?'

Penny beams.

'I'll drop a copy over.'

'I live in one of the cottages,' she says, pointing. 'My dad – Philip – he's staying with me for a while. He's writing a book. He's taken some time off work to get it finished. Non-fiction,' she says. 'Academic type thing.'

She looks between us like an eager child and we nod obligingly like proud parents. And it's something of a relief when the ice-cream van arrives with its loud tinny jangle of noise. The children stop in their tracks and look up in excitement. For me, it's a sound that always evokes a strange sense of longing. A reminder of the long hot summer when Gemma was ill. The school holiday I spent on the ward, my legs sticking to the plastic chairs, listening to the joy and laughter somewhere in the distance.

The van pulls up on the gravel track by the gate, and I'm about to walk the kids over when they both turn towards me.

'Can we just go with Ollie and Lexie?' they whisper. 'On. Our. Own.' I look at their pleading faces, then open my purse and fish out money that they fold tight into the palms of their hands.

It happens as they're on their way to the van. The four of them are racing across in hot excitement, and in their haste, Lexie trips over her flip-flop and sprawls forwards with a howl. Her mother leaps up and runs over, sweeping her up into her arms in an instant.

By the time I get there, Lexie is shuddering with great racking sobs and Sam is peering at the grazed bloody knee.

'My mum's a doctor,' I hear him say solemnly, 'she can help.'

All of a sudden, the woman swings round to look at me, like she's seeing me properly for the very first time.

'Are you?'

I look away, across the garden, but I can still feel the woman's eyes on me. It's a relief to see Rob crossing the path towards us.

'Oh – I don't think she needs medical input,' I say vaguely, waving at Rob.

'What sort of doctor?' the woman asks, stroking the little girl's hair as she wails on her lap.

I feel a snag of irritation. Of all the things we could have connected over, it's the job I'm currently not doing that has piqued the woman's interest. Rob arrives and lifts Ruby up onto his shoulders. Lexie's sobs have dwindled as she gets distracted by Sam leaping about making pig faces.

'Where do you work?' the woman persists.

I feel my face flush. It's not like I haven't had time to rehearse an answer. Hours spent in the basement in the beige consulting room in West Hampstead turning things over. But every time,

I'm like the clumsy kid at PE, fumbling for the ball. The mention of work is like a Pavlovian response. And I am back there again. The sudden swooping sensation of falling. *Perhaps you've made a mistake?* And I feel it like a burn, the hot flush of shame across my cheeks. *I don't like being made to look a fool.*

The woman is still staring at me.

'East London. Spitalfields,' I say eventually. 'I was a GP,' and I make an apologetic shrug. 'I mean – I *am* still a GP,' and I stumble over my words, 'it's just –' and I pause, '– I'm just off work at the moment.'

And that's when it happens. We lock eyes for the briefest of instants. A split second. And a look of something like recognition passes between us. Afterwards, I will come to wonder if it was that moment that sealed things for us.

'How come?' Her voice is pleasant, but persistent. I pretend I haven't heard her.

Rob is standing next to me now, and because I don't know what else to do, I leap forwards theatrically.

'Dr Jess Gibson,' I trill, 'coming through.' I know I sound ridiculous, but becoming a pantomime version of myself is the only thing I can think of doing to avoid answering her question. I find myself hamming it up completely. 'Where's the patient?' I say in a loud sing-song voice.

Rob is staring at me.

Lexie has now stopped crying and is awe-struck with the attention.

'A *real* doctor?' she asks.

'That's me,' I say, and I lean forwards to lift her leg and inspect it gently in my hands. I offer a diagnosis, and a treatment 'of antiseptic wipes and a plaster', both of which the woman miraculously produces from her bag.

'But –' and I hold my hand up dramatically, '– most important is the medicine . . .'

Lexie blinks back at me.

'. . . a big fat ice-cream. Preferably a double cone, with strawberry sauce and a flake.'

The little girl laughs, then wriggles off her mother's lap, slips her foot in the retrieved flip-flop and joins the others as they make their way slowly to the van. The woman stands up.

'I'm Helen,' she says, holding out her hand. And this time she's giving me her sole attention. 'And thank you for the medical input,' she smiles, her voice full of gratitude. I wave away her thanks and, just as she's about to say something else, Joyce steps onto a makeshift stage of hay bales and taps the microphone. There's a shushing sound in the crowd as the garden falls silent.

'As many of you know,' she begins, 'it's Leo's birthday,' and there are some claps and cheers. 'But unlike most other eighteen-year-olds, it's not the gateway to independence and adulthood.' She pauses to gather herself. 'He will never go to university, or live independently, or have many of the opportunities that others can enjoy –' her voice cracks a little, '– so as his mother, it's my job to advocate for the things he *can* do and the things he loves to do.'

It's then that I see Leo. He's at the end of the garden on his own, staring out over the field. In his hands there's a small silver object attached to a piece of string. It looks like a scrunched-up ball of baking foil. He's rocking back and forth, happily, I think, and as he weaves it in and out of his fingers, it catches the sun, sending little darts of light that flicker on the grass.

'Closure of the project would be devastating for my son, and for many other young people.' Rousing murmurs of agreement ripple through the crowd. 'With council funding withdrawn, we've been fundraising for a while now, and it's our last chance to keep this place open —' she stops for a moment as she looks round at the crowd, '— and continue to provide a place for our children where they feel a real sense of belonging.' She finishes by thanking everyone for coming, urging them to donate, and to sign the petition: 'It's up to us to give a voice to the voiceless.'

After the presentation, the crowd disperses and we all walk back to the stalls. I see Joyce and Leo by the edge of the field. She is standing near him, but not too close, and she's rocking back and forth in time to his rhythm. She holds a palm out towards him. Together they move in a kind of clumsy unison, until eventually, he places his hand on top of hers.

The kids are busy scanning for their new friends, and I can feel Rob looking at me. I know exactly what he's thinking. I look straight ahead. There's a longer silence, but in the end he can't help himself.

'Why don't you just say something?' he shrugs, 'Anything. Just make something up?'

I'm not sure if I'm imagining it, but I can hear that tone in his voice. The one that's been creeping in of late. Not quite irritation, but somewhere on the edge of dwindling patience. Perhaps it's a trace of regret. A wish for things to go back to how they were before. Before Keith and Nina. Before Jackson. Before I had to stop work. Before any of it.

He's trying to speak kindly, but I hear the nudge of something else.

'All that looking embarrassed and guilty. It sort of makes it worse,' he says, 'just draws more attention to it.' And he waves his hand like he's patting a ball in the air. 'You could just say something banal, you know. We talked about this before.'

We talked about this before. There it is. That edge of exasperation.

I don't know how to explain what happens to me in those moments. How it's something I can't control. That it all comes back at me. Fast and furious, like logs down a waterfall. And I am hit by the familiar paralysis. The shame of my mistakes.

And as time's gone on, the gap between my real, lived experience and my ability to explain it to him, or even to myself, is ever-widening, like a small boat untethered and drifting from a jetty.

'Mmm?'

I look back at him.

'Just say you're on a sabbatical or something?'

'A *sabbatical*?' I say, a bloom of fury in my chest.

I close my eyes briefly. 'Good idea,' I say. 'I'll try that next time.'

TWO

The cottage was Rob's idea. We were sitting at the kitchen table when he first mentioned it. 'Let's get away,' he said, 'while we get the repairs done on the house,' and he flipped open his laptop as if the idea had just popped into his head. 'With my first script payment, we could rent somewhere, maybe by the sea?' He looked up at me. '*A Month in the Country* – wasn't that a film?' he said, tapping at his keyboard.

I'd been avoiding thinking about the onslaught of the builders in our small, terraced house. The replastering of four walls on both floors as well as replacing the rotting flooring and units in the kitchen.

'It'll be chaos. Good to be out of the way,' he said, suddenly standing up. 'A chance to be expansive,' he said, flinging his arms out wide, 'to live outside the box!'

Expansive? I stared back at him as he moved around the kitchen. Light, like a dancer.

Success had changed him. His moods had always been extreme, but I was more used to the trenches of doom, his cynicism and his railing against the injustices of the world. This new upbeat positivity and uncharacteristic 'can-do' attitude in the wake of his success was becoming unbearable. He was like a self-inflating balloon that I had to keep pulling down by the string to stop him floating away entirely. He grew in size, and changed in other ways; the way he held himself, the tone of his voice, the animated waving of his hands. The way his voice got louder when he was on the phone to his agent or the film producer. And none of this would have mattered if I'd been able to shrink to accommodate him. If I had moved aside, as I might have done in the past. Waiting it out until he was punctured by the sharp edge of reality and normal life could be resumed.

But since February, things were different. The incident at work had altered things in a way I still didn't properly understand.

'Let's have a look.' It was his jaunty spontaneity along with the speed with which images popped up on the screen that made it obvious this was something he'd been mulling over for a while, but was perhaps unsure how to bring up, given my unpredictable mood. I know I should have felt grateful. But mostly, I felt wrong-footed.

'What about Dorset?' he said. 'Lovely beaches. Not far from London. Lovely June sunshine. I can finish my script in the mornings – then we can hang out with the kids. Fly a kite . . . play games . . . do all the things you say we never do. *Family time*,' he over-enunciated. There was a pause and, perhaps in response to my silence, he added, 'Come September we'll be locked into school holidays for the next fourteen years. We should, you know, *carpe diem* and all that, while we can.'

'Besides,' he mused, and I could see he was choosing his words carefully, 'might be good for you to get away. Fresh air . . . change of scene . . .'

His words were left hanging in the air, as he turned back to his laptop, typing in *West Country*, *Dorset* and *month long lets*.

And while he hadn't mentioned it, I knew he had noticed the hastily closed case folder that was still out on the table. The folder we'd already had one row about. And there was the house. Even by Rob's standards, it was a mess; washing-up in the sink, unwashed clothes and the kids' toys strewn over the floor. I could see it was taking all his willpower not to ask me what I'd been doing all day.

I didn't expect him to understand something I was still grappling with myself, and I knew he meant well, but there was something irksome about the notion that my personal and professional crisis might simply dissipate in a blast of fresh air.

Soon we were both scanning stone cottages, sandy beaches and cattle grazing on verdant green fields. Most were way out of our price range, and I began to drift away, to peer into the fridge and decide what could be assembled into lunch. Sometime later, he swivelled round. 'I've found somewhere. Come and see.'

I peered at a pretty stone cottage, dappled in sunlight, with tall white hollyhocks by the door.

'Look,' he said excitedly, jabbing at the screen, 'irises! You love irises!'

I lean over to look at the details.

'Why so cheap?'

He shook his head, scanning the rental details.

He flicked through the other linked pictures. It was one of a cluster of cottages, in a square around a shared patch of lawn with a picnic table. There were other pictures of coastal paths, rocky cliffs and rolling fields of rape.

'And what a pub,' he said, tapping at an old stone building, a sunny courtyard, rustic benches. 'It's right on the South West Coast Path. Look. At. That. View.'

'Expansive,' I said.

I was the limpet on a rock in the face of his rising tide of excitement. I couldn't explain my lethargy. My lack of enthusiasm. Perhaps my reluctance was due to the fact I was still smarting from yesterday's row. My flat joylessness, a weapon to pick away at the scab of our argument that had erupted after my session with Veronica earlier in the day.

It was my fifth session with Veronica. She sat very still, with her cropped grey hair and dash of red lipstick, in what was her uniform of stylish black trousers and cream shirt. I looked back at the nest of her elegant fingers. My mind felt empty of feelings. Empty of everything. But in my body, a constriction in my chest, as if bracing myself for an attack. The familiar burn of my cheeks, a feeling that I was somehow talking about the wrong thing. That heaped on top of my many failings, I hadn't even managed to grasp the rules of therapy.

I looked back at her blankly. I felt her words sliding over me. Hard to grasp. Until I realised she was now talking about something else, about the origins of the word shame, 'how its derivation can be traced back to the words *kam* and *kem*,' she said, 'meaning to cover, to veil,' and then she cupped one hand over the other, 'to hide.'

I blinked back at her.

'Shame can be paralysing,' she concluded. 'I wonder if perhaps it is time to come out of hiding. To not only show yourself. But perhaps try to understand how this piece of shame fits into the jigsaw of your life?'

I nodded enthusiastically, but in reality, I felt the sting of irritation. Anger towards her and her neat beige room. The oatmeal sofa. The nondescript pictures on the wall. Her smug observations that I'd initially thought were wise and skilled, but now felt patronising. But of course, when she signalled the end of the session, I didn't say any of this. When I noticed her slight shift forwards on the sofa, the small inclination of her head, 'it's time,' I simply stood up and thanked her, grinning like a fool as I left the room.

Before all this, my experience of therapy had been a few awkward family sessions as a child. They left no lasting memory other than the hot stuffy room, my mother's twitching fingers and my father gazing into the middle distance. As an adult, as far as I was concerned, therapy was something I was happy to refer my patients to, but its irrelevance to me or my life meant I had little interest in understanding what actually went on behind closed doors. Was it normal, I wondered, to feel so resentful of having to even be there?

For the rest of the day, my anger felt hot on my hands.

And then Rob came home.

It was late, he was back after his weekly teaching at Adult Education. He was opening the fridge for a beer when he mentioned it casually, like it had just occurred to him.

'I was thinking, we should make a plan for September,' he said, 'when Sam starts school.'

I looked back at him, confused.

'I need to sort my timetable out,' he said, 'for next term's teaching – so I thought we could think about the kids . . . pick-ups, drop-offs – who does what,' and he took a swig from the bottle. It was not an unreasonable request. He needed to look ahead and plan. But it landed badly.

In the immediate aftermath of my state of collapse, Rob had been brilliant. But almost overnight, it was as if the whole axis of our relationship shifted. Up until then, I'd been solid, dependable, then all of a sudden, I was floundering in a way he'd never seen before. And after I was signed off work, and my state of 'not-working' began to have a kind of open-ended quality about it, I felt his growing frustration. That while genuinely concerned for my welfare, there was, in the way he spoke about it, an undercurrent of it being in the past. Something to move on from. And while I had initially thought this myself, my continued difficulties suggested this wasn't the case at all. I tried to tell Rob in a language I thought he might understand. 'I thought

Keith was the *inciting incident*,' I said, 'but now I think things are a bit more complicated.' He nodded, waiting for me to elaborate. But at the time, I hadn't any more to offer, other than a sense of malaise. A block and a heavy impasse when I thought about work.

So, for the most part, Rob and I skirt around the whole issue. I don't mention it. Nor does he. There are a few no-go areas. My 'return to work' is one of them. I don't want to discuss it and I can see that he does. As it stands, we have until the end of August, after which, if I don't return, my pay, quite understandably, will be halved. In the early days, I'd see the question pass across his face. Trying to work out how to phrase it in a way I might find palatable. He starts, and there is a half-formed sentence on his lips, and then he sees the look on my face and he thinks better of it.

In the early weeks, he was stressed after a call with his ex-wife who was requesting funds for Nic's Geography field trip next year. I said nothing. And then, miraculously, the financial squall blew over with the unexpected news about his script. But that day, I could see that the college timetable was a convenient way to test the water again.

'Any thoughts,' he said, peering into the fridge, 'about whether you'll work the same hours and days?' He was trying to make his voice sound light. Casual.

'Not really,' I said. 'I've made no plans about work.'

He nodded, taking another swig from the bottle, before plunging a crust of bread into a tub of houmous.

And then before I quite understood what he was saying, I realised he was talking about GP locum jobs. And how much they paid.

I froze.

'Two or three a week,' he said, 'and we'd cover the cost of the mortgage.' He was peering into the fridge again, avoiding me.

'Just thought it's worth thinking about. You know,' he said, 'if you don't feel like going back to your surgery. If it's the place that's—'

'It's not the place,' I cut in quickly, and my words were clipped and furious.

'Wooah! OK,' and he did his strange head-wobble thing he does when he's really pissed off but trying to look all jokey and fun. And that was that.

So, I was still aggrieved about all this when the cottage conversation came up, and by then, Rob's exuberance and the mention of seaside and kites and holidays had drifted down the hallway to the kids, who were now hanging off Rob's shoulders as he peered at the screen.

'Will there be shells?' Sam wanted to know. Ruby was more interested in the journey. How many hours on a plane, she asked, hopeful for her first ever trip to the airport, then looked momentarily deflated when Rob told her we'd be going in the car.

Rob looked so disappointed by my lack of enthusiasm. I felt a stab of guilt, like I was furiously paddling upstream, just because I could.

'Why not?' he whispered, looking confused. 'What's the problem?'

We moved over to the sink, leaving the kids poring over the pictures.

I opened and closed my mouth. I had nothing to say.

'You're thinking of that holiday in Scotland, aren't you? When I had to go back to London to work and you were left in the cottage on your own with two small children?'

I wasn't.

'I promise. Not going to happen. Hardly anything left to do. It's a final polish. Then off it goes. Whooosh,' and he flew his hand in the air like a plane.

I still looked doubtful. I mentioned my dad's birthday lunch.

He shook his head. 'It's Dorset – not Denmark. Last time I checked, we can actually drive to Oxford from there.

'And I haven't forgotten about the boys,' he said, hands up in the air.

I had. But pretended I hadn't. The twins were coming to stay after their exams, while Carla, his ex-wife, was away for a week, on a yoga retreat in Portugal.

'They can just come there. They'll camp in the garden,' he said. 'They'd love that.'

I nodded.

What I was really thinking about were my twice weekly sessions with Veronica. After our last appointment, a part of me would have been delighted to find a reason to stop going. But I felt a fluttery kind of anxiety about taking a break from seeing her. But of course, I couldn't mention this. He'd already asked when they 'might be finishing?' – at the end of yesterday's feisty conversation, tentatively wondering whether they were making me worse not better, 'stoking things up,' he said, 'rather than calming things down.' 'Therapy's not all cosy chats and arm patting,' I'd said with irritation.

Then just in that moment, Rob reached across and took my hand. 'I was thinking about your appointments with Veronica. If we rent a place for a month, you could come up to London for a couple of the sessions. I can be here with the kids—'

And there it is. That's all it takes. A small gesture. Some words.

When I mentioned our plans at my next session with Veronica, she said that's fine, but she works internationally, has many clients she sees online. 'You're welcome to come in person,' she said, 'but it may be easier for us to work digitally for those weeks you are away. It's as you wish.'

I noticed myself bristle at the mention of her *other clients*, her *international* work. How glamorous her other clients must be. How dull I felt.

*

Two weeks later, we were walking up the path. We left London too late. Hit the traffic. The kids fell asleep in the car, heads back, mouths slack, catching flies. But as we turned off the motorway and weaved our way through the narrow country lanes, the evening sun was low in the sky. It spread a golden hue across the surrounding fields, and we both fell into a kind of trance, marvelling at the views. The buttery gold of the sun on the yellow fields. That first sight of the sea, a secret shimmer of silver in the distance.

From the outside, the cottage looked exactly like the printout. The grey stone. The hollyhocks in bloom. The small, shared garden with the picnic table. The fence of white jasmine.

But the bargain price became clear when we pushed open the door.

'Oh,' we both said.

It was tiny. Minute.

'It's the opposite of a Tardis,' Rob laughed, darting about. 'They must have taken the shots from here,' he said, crouching down, 'and used a special lens.'

'The furniture, though?' I said, but as I stepped forwards to reach my hand to the back of the navy sofa, it became obvious.

'It's undersized,' I said, 'that Ikea range. For teenagers. Or small kids.'

23

As Rob eased his six-foot-two-inch body down onto the sofa, his bottom hung cliff-like over the edge, his knees jutting out to the side like giant wings.

'One of the reviews said it was cosy,' he laughed.

'It's like a doll's house,' I said, taking the three steps to the kitchen which was the size of a large tea towel. 'Come in here,' I said. 'Fling your arms out wide. Be *expansive*.'

'A doll's house,' he said, slapping his thigh at the hilarity of it all, then found it a huge source of amusement to start calling me Nora.

He then got up, chuckling to himself, before folding himself over to negotiate his way up the narrow stairs. 'Nora,' he called down. 'I'm hungry, make me my dinner!' More laughter.

When he came down, I'd already seen the ceramic boat on the mantelpiece, with *You put the wind in my sails* inscribed on the hull, and I was now staring at the two enormous framed photo montages that dominated the room.

'There's two more upstairs,' he laughed, 'one in the bedroom, another on the landing.'

We both silently studied the poster-sized frames of cut-out family photos. A day at the beach. Cricket on the sand dunes. Glasses chinking in the sun. Dazzling white smiles. *Look at us and our marvellous lives!* There were groups of women in bright patterned swimsuits wearing pearls and pink lipstick on the beach. Children posed in front of complex turreted sand-castles that they couldn't possibly have built. There was a bald man who popped up in different outfits in various pictures. Most abhorrently, the one where he's wearing a chef's hat and a plastic apron with a naked woman's body on the front. He had one finger to his lips as he poked sausages on a barbecue. *Cheeky.*

'I mean, who does that?' I said, knowing Rob would be sharing my thoughts. 'Cutting up and making a collage. It's the kind of thing students did in the eighties. What kind of grown-ups do this?'

But instead of exchanging scathing comments, he simply laughed and said nonchalantly, 'Each to their own,' which is a phrase I have never heard him say in all our years together.

'Nora, you should wake the kids,' he said, 'or they'll be up till midnight.'

When we roused them, they startled awake, hands like small starfish. They were overcome with delight at the pint-sized home, whirling about the room like marbles in a jar.

THREE

When the doorbell rings, I'm surprised to see little Ollie on the step.

'We're going to Dancing Ledge,' he says, with his small, furrowed brow and serious expression. 'Mum said to ask if you wanted to come with us.'

Sam has pushed his way through to the front door. 'Dancing Ledge!' he shrieks, quivering with excitement.

'What's that?' I ask, as Sam frantically pulls his coat on over his pyjamas.

'It's a secret place. You get to it across the field,' and Ollie points behind the farmhouse. 'It's a big stone ledge by the sea. And there's a swimming pool in the rocks.'

Sam's eyes widen. 'Can we swim in it?'

Ollie nods. 'You can – but it's very cold. My dad does. But you might need a wetsuit. And it's very deep. We don't have any wetsuits, but we might get some soon. But when the tide is out there are rock pools, and we can take the fishing nets.' Sam is on the floor pulling on his boots, in a state of utter disbelief that this older boy, the owner of *The Transformer*, is standing at the front door, inviting him to a place called Dancing Ledge.

'It's really cool,' Ollie adds unnecessarily.

In the face of Sam's excitement, I feel a heaviness at the thought of spending time with Helen.

'It takes about half an hour to walk from here. The path is quite steep and we're taking a packed lunch to eat on the rocks,' he says, speaking like a tour guide.

Ollie looks at Sam buttoning up his coat.

'I'm ready,' he says.

Ollie blinks back at him. 'We're leaving at ten o'clock,' Ollie says.

I look between Ollie's expectant face and my son's that is ready to burst. 'OK,' I say, 'tell your mum thanks. We'll see you outside later.'

I have to show Sam the clock. 'One hour,' I say, pointing at the hands and eventually he's persuaded to take off his coat and boots and eat his breakfast first.

We meet in front of the cottages and I can see straight away that Helen's mood has shifted. 'Have you been to Dancing Ledge?' she says warmly, as we set off across the farm, telling me about an Enid Blyton book set in a boarding school.

'*Malory Towers?*'

She nods. 'Apparently the rocky swimming pool in the books was inspired by this place in Dorset.'

'I loved those books,' I say.

I don't tell her I went to the library to look up boarding schools to go to when I was twelve. How I sat for hours in the reference section researching schools. My favourite was one on the coast in the Outer Hebrides.

'I had no idea it was based on a real place.'

'It's wonderful. I used to swim there as a child.'

'You grew up round here?'

Helen shakes her head. 'Just holidays and stuff. The cottage was my grandmother's. Belongs to my mum now. She divides her time between here and a village just outside Bristol, where I grew up. But she's in New Zealand at the moment, staying with her sister. We're here for the summer. In between house-buying.'

We push open a cattle gate and turn onto a gravelly path with hedgerows either side. 'Priest's Way,' she says, and as the path twists to the left, I listen as Helen talks about relocating from Germany. How the place they were buying in London fell through. 'We're in the process of getting somewhere else,' she says. 'James, my husband, has a new job. He's starting up his own business. Renting a room in London,' she explains, 'cheaper – until we get ourselves sorted.'

To the right, another larger cattle gate leads into a wide stretch of hilly fields. Cows and sheep graze lazily in the sun, and the sky is full and wide and blue. We join the footpath as it slopes up the hill, chatting as we walk. Helen is friendlier than the day before. She points out local landmarks, tells me about places to visit with the kids. 'Chapman's Pool is lovely on a sunny day. And there's Corfe Castle. And I'm sure Joyce will show the kids round the farm.'

I warm to her, but there's something neat and polished about her. Something guarded. I can already tell that our conversation will hover on the surface of things. And I have an instant pang for my friends in London. The ability to quickly read a mood from the expression on each other's faces. That deep familiarity of people you know, and who, in turn, know you so well.

The kids are walking in a huddle, just ahead of us, listening as Ollie holds court about something or other.

All of a sudden, Sam swings round.

'Ollie doesn't go to school,' he says defiantly, hands on hips, 'and he's seven. So why do I have to?'

Momentarily thrown by this sudden demand, I open my mouth, then close it again. The response I usually give to this recurring and persistent question is the lazy and not altogether true statement that '*everyone goes to school*', and of course, it's the very one I can't use here. Before I have a chance to answer, Helen jumps in.

'He will be going –' she says, 'in September. He has a place then at the school we wanted in London. But not for the rest of this term. So, we decided to wait until then. He's keeping up with his studies every day. He'll soon be at school – just like you.'

As the children move out of earshot, I explain to Helen about my error. 'That school shooting in the States, at the beginning of the year?' I tell her how I thought I'd turned the television off, then came back in the lounge to find Sam sitting pale-faced on the sofa. 'It was pretty graphic,' I say, dropping my voice down low, 'screaming children . . . general carnage. Just awful,' I shake my head. 'He now associates school with guns. I feel bad. It was totally my fault.'

And in the space where I expect some kind of reassurance, or even a platitude of some kind, there is nothing. She just nods, as if agreeing with my parental failing.

I push ahead, and perhaps the scooter I'm dragging behind me takes the brunt of my annoyance, and it predictably comes apart, as it does on average several times a week. 'Shit,' I say under my breath as I scrabble round on the ground for the screw and makeshift repair I'd botched with a ballpoint pen lid.

Helen crouches down and inspects it. 'It just needs a new washer. And a longer screw. James will have one. He's coming up this weekend. He'll fix it for you.'

'I shouldn't have brought it with us. Ruby was insistent – and she's not a great walker, but clearly her new friend is a wonderful distraction,' I say, nodding over at the two girls, huddled together conspiratorially. 'If it was just the three of us, she'd be slumped on the path wailing by now.'

We pass a camping ground, the colourful pitched tents dotted over the hillside like lunar landings, and then, at the top of the hill, the view suddenly opens out in front of us. The solid chunky blocks of colour. The deep blue of the sky. The rising wedges of green and grey cliffs and the deeper navy of the sea. 'It's beautiful,' I say, breathing in the rush of salty air. The grass is a carpet of daisies. 'Like snow!' Ruby says clapping her hands and, wordlessly, the girls lie on the ground and roll themselves down. I can see Sam wants to join them, but he glances up at Ollie and, taking his cue from him, he keeps walking.

We follow the dirt track down to the bottom, then there are stone steps down to a large grassy ledge. Clumps of samphire are tucked in between the rocks; their thick paddle-like leaves are plump and succulent and the small yellow flowers look sprinkled on, like an afterthought. Above our heads, the skylarks dip and swoop.

'The pool is further down,' Helen points. 'It's a bit of a tricky climb.' At the edge, she goes first, easing her way down slowly backwards, her hands and feet feeling for the footholds in the rocks. I pass the bags down, and Ollie and Lexie go next. They are deft and skilled and have clearly done this many times before. Ollie shouts up instructions to Sam, who tries hard to hide his obvious caution. I go next, then catch Ruby as she jumps the last bit. The ledge is wide and pocked with holes, like a giant Ryvita. The rectangular pool is a dark gin-clear blue. The surface of the water is still. The place is quiet. We are the only people here.

'Do you see,' Helen says, 'just there,' pointing out to where the ledge meets the sea. I watch the waves roll in and lap gently on the rocky surface. It must be the combination of the pocked holes and the sun on the surface that creates the dancing silvery movement, the mesmerising illusion that the ledge itself is moving.

'It drops away,' she says, 'at the edge.' She tells me the water's very deep. Maybe 150 feet. Deep enough for big boats to come right in. 'Treacherous and beautiful,' she says. 'Deceptive, isn't it?' And I shudder as she speaks, and immediately turn and call out to the kids, 'Stay away from the edge, it's dangerous.'

I turn back to Helen. 'Can you swim from the ledge?' I ask, looking out at the wide, open sea.

'You can,' she says, caution in her voice, 'on a day like today, but when it's rough, there are undercurrents. People have been swept away—'

Just at that moment Lexie whispers something to Ruby, and the two of them begin to jig about. Swirling hand movements and hip sways from side to side. 'What are you doing?' Helen asks, a question that seems primed, one she's asked before.

'We're dancing on the ledge,' they both shriek in unison, then collapse with the hilarity of a well-worn joke.

With the kids engrossed in the rock pools, I change into my swimming costume.

'I'm just going to dip in the pool,' I say. 'That OK? Can you keep an eye –' I say, nodding over at the kids.

Helen nods. 'Brace yourself,' she smiles.

The surface is flat like glass and as I peer over, I can see to the bottom, the craggy rocky sides of purple and mauves and brown. The swirl of seagrass in the small crevices. The darting shoal of shimmering fish. I ease in, slipping my body under the surface. The trick is always to be swift. Not to linger. But still, it's an ice-cold hit that takes my breath away. And then I swim. Long strokes back and forth as if doing lengths of a pool. I feel the surge of energy. The tingle of my skin. My fingers and toes.

My arms pulling back and forth, my legs powering me through the seawater. I feel awake. Alive with the rush of my own blood in my veins. The pump of my heart as it echoes in my ears.

Afterwards, I wrap myself in a towel and sip at the coffee Helen has poured out. What strikes me most about Helen is her lack of curiosity. She doesn't really ask questions. When I speak, she listens or nods, but doesn't seem interested in further exploration. There are no layers. The information she offers about herself is superficial. She talks a lot, yet I know very little about her and her life. We stay, for the most part, on trivial stuff. The kids. The weather. Dorset. And as the morning wears on, I find myself feeling grateful for the lack of demand. For the ease of the conversation. We slip into a relaxed rhythm. Pond-skating on the surface of our lives. It's strangely calming. So, when the question comes, I'm startled. Not so much by the question itself, but by the fact she's asked it at all.

'So,' she says, 'what was it like working in the East End?'

'Busy,' I laugh. And perhaps because of my invigorating swim, and the fact that she's asking about the place, rather than my job, I find myself talking freely, unfettered by the events that triggered my departure. Much later, I will come to wonder if this was a calculated decision on her part.

As I talk, I paint a picture of the place I loved. The bustling streets of Tower Hamlets. The shops. The markets. A place that was bursting with life and energy.

'It was like nothing I'd experienced before,' I say. 'I started as a medical student at a hospital in Whitechapel. Over twenty-five years ago. It was like another world for me. It's changed now, of course, but I was so taken with the vibrancy, the noise. The mix of people. I loved it – and such a contrast to the place I grew up in.'

It couldn't have been more different to those wide silent streets

32

of my suburban childhood. The semi-detached houses. The neat front gardens and the patioed driveways for off-road parking. My father religiously putting the car away in the garage every evening. The weekly and slightly fraught ceremony of emptying the bins on a Tuesday night. The twitch of the net curtains when the couple at number nine started having a row on a Sunday afternoon.

And as I'm talking, I remember the first time I walked from Aldgate East tube as a student, past the warehouses with floor to ceiling rolls of material; silver and gold threaded fabric and silks in pinks and yellows and reds. The smell of spices, the rows of sticky sweets and pastries in the shop windows, the animated arguments on street corners in a language I didn't understand. Mr Begum who ran a fruit and veg stall at the market, selling vegetables I'd never seen before, and how, as I got to know him, he gave me recipes that I tried out on the weekend, reporting back the following week.

'I've never even been to the East End,' she says. 'It's probably different to what I imagine.' And she looks at me with admiration.

And perhaps because I have a captive audience, and there's something naïve about her, something slightly parochial, I find myself enjoying telling the story. I notice the bits I focus on, and the bits I leave out. I talk about the social deprivation, and the difficulties, and perhaps it's a wrong assumption, but I feel it's unlikely she will know much about the complexities of working in a multi-cultural community. But I'm aware that there are things I choose to amplify. And as I speak, sitting on a rocky cliff in the middle of Dorset, I can see that I am talking about it all with a backward glance of time passing, much like a challenging holiday that you regard with increasing fondness, as you flick through sunny pictures with the glow of nostalgia.

33

And I realise I like the sound of myself. The way I present. The 'good' work I did. Perhaps there's a hint of self-congratulation in the way I speak. Perhaps, given it's something I'm no longer doing at the moment, and because I feel I've messed up, I notice I'm hungry for praise, to be seen in a particular way. Eager to inflate myself through her eyes. I shudder to think what David and my other colleagues might have said if they were listening.

'Why a GP?' she asked.

'It was always what I'd planned,' I say. 'It suited me.'

In fact, I'd excelled in all my placements, and various consultants and mentors had tried to persuade me to specialise in their field. And I'd wavered only once, after six months in Paediatrics. But after I qualified, I elected for my two-year GP trainee placement in Spitalfields and I knew it was exactly where I wanted to work. I thrived on the workload, the pressure and the level of demand, and in my mind's eye, I likened it to batting in a rounders game, hitting the balls on target as they were bowled at me, one after the other. I found multi-tasking effortless, the referrals, results, follow-up calls, and the occasional home visits or hospital call outs. I thrived on the volume of work and the kind of order and efficiency I was able to frame around my day. And those cases that couldn't swiftly be knocked for six with a satisfying thwack of wood, ones that were more complex that required a more rigorous analysis and a careful kind of detective work, I loved these too, and rose to the challenge of searching for a diagnosis in these medical mysteries.

'You must need such a breadth of knowledge – as a GP?'

'Yes,' I say, 'but a lot of medicine is all about patterns. Clusters of symptoms that lead to a diagnosis. It's about probability,' I shrug. 'For example, most skin rashes are not meningitis. It's all

34

about the illumination of data. Identifying patterns was something I loved to do.'

She nods, and seems interested, eager for me to continue.

'I also liked the continuity of care,' I say, 'being involved in the trajectories of people's lives. It appealed to me, more than the short episodes of medical input in so many other specialties. The span of a person's life – I felt like I could really become part of something. Part of the community. Make a difference.'

She nods again, full of admiration. 'Is that why you became a doctor?' she asks. 'To make a difference?'

I feel a pull in my chest. 'Well – yes, maybe. I haven't really thought about it before,' I say, which isn't true given it had already come up in one of Veronica's sessions.

Again, I feel myself expand in the face of her naïvety. I can't help myself and I'm astonished at this self-aggrandising that takes place when no one else is looking. 'I definitely became known as the soft touch,' I laugh. 'The GP they'd come to for housing letters. The doctor who would go above and beyond, do the home visit.' And fleetingly, I think about the thank-you cards, the flowers and the feedback I got in return. 'I also took on the safeguarding role,' I continued, 'for the practice. Difficult cases. Hard at times. But rewarding.'

These are the things I focus on. Not my appraisal. Not the feedback from the senior partner. Not the reason why I left.

I look out over the sea. I can feel her eyes on me.

'Such responsibility,' she says. 'I can't imagine.'

I feel myself shift under the scrutiny, knowing we're in danger of straying somewhere I don't want to go. 'Well, mostly it was the years before I had other responsibilities,' I lie, waving my hand in the direction of the kids.

A brief silence falls between us.

We look over at the children. Their shrieks of joy. Their patience with the fishing nets has finally borne fruit. Lexie waves from the rock pool, her face beaming. 'A crab. A massive crab,' she says, jumping up and down, splaying her fingers wide open. We both wave back.

The whole debacle around Keith and Nina is never far from my thoughts, but suddenly, Keith's face looms into view. His tight and rigid expression. My confusion in response to his anger. Behaviour I interpreted as bullish and risky. Then, a few weeks later, when he came out of David's office, after my frantic visit to Jackson's school. A different kind of look. Triumphant in the face of my defeat.

'There must have been some patients you couldn't help – what was that like?' Helen asks quietly.

The moment seems heavy.

I feel a tightness in my throat as we move away from the generalisations that feel safe. Protected. I don't want to talk about the detail. The specifics of what happened next.

She's waiting. Expectant.

'Sure,' I say breezily. 'But it's part of the job. What you sign up for. You can't help everyone. I'm not Mother Teresa,' and I laugh, bringing my hands together in a clap.

She doesn't respond to my jovial tone.

'But still,' she persists, 'that must have been hard.' Then she leans over to refill my cup from the flask of coffee.

'Yes,' I say, finally meeting her gaze. 'Sometimes there are people you can't help. And sometimes you can miss things. And sometimes,' I say carefully, 'you can get things wrong,' and I keep my voice even, trying to express a nonchalance I don't feel.

It's hard to conceal it. The trace of regret in my voice. And I feel she's edging closer to a question I won't want to answer. Still don't quite know how to answer.

I feel exposed. Like it's one-sided. That she's probing and prodding for all this information, and I'm getting nothing in return, apart from the directions to Chapman's Pool and the ingredients of the dressing she made for her pasta salad the night before. I feel uncomfortable with this level of scrutiny. Like I've over-shared and feel a strange kind of vulnerability. And yet, somehow, it also feels good to have skirted on the edge of the difficult thing. To have been able to find some words. To not clam up. To not have resorted to a manic pantomime version of myself simply to get through the conversation. This in itself feels like a triumph.

'Anyway,' I say, standing up, 'it's good to be on holiday. To have this month away,' and I chop my hand decisively through the air between us, then call the kids for lunch.

We're unpacking the picnic, and I'm amazed by her dizzying array of food: a homemade quiche, pasta and pesto, salads. I feel embarrassed unwrapping my six-pack of crisps and houmous and cucumber sandwiches.

'Anyway – what about you? Living in Germany – how was that? Whereabouts were you?'

But somehow, whenever I ask a question, she brings it back to the moment. Something the kids are doing. How the sea looks different every time they come to the cliff. Or whether tuna mayonnaise is best on its own or with sweetcorn. I realise we are back to pond-skating and I decide, on balance, that it's the place I'd rather be.

After they've eaten, the kids rush back to their fishing nets, and it's as we're packing up the leftovers that Helen's phone rings.

She glances down. 'Sorry,' she says, a small crease of a frown on her forehead, 'I need to take this.'

I sit back on the blanket Helen has laid out over the rocks. The sky is a clear cloudless blue. I watch a fishing boat move beyond the cove, a flock of birds flapping around the sails and, as it motors ahead, it leaves behind a foamy wake that glints silver in the sun.

Helen's on the grassy hill behind the rocky pool. She's on the phone for a long time. And when I glance over at her, her expression is serious, intent. Mostly she looks like she's listening as the other person talks. But sometimes, she moves a hand as she speaks. It's not a happy call. She looks anxious. One time I see her shake her head briskly from side to side, with one arm hooked on her hip.

But in spite of the long and animated call, I notice how attentive and watchful she still is over the children. She's far enough away to be out of earshot, but her focus is on the kids. At one point, she cups her hand over the phone, and calls over to Lexie, 'Give the others a go. Share.' She gestures with her other hand, and then she is back to the caller. Then later on, 'Careful!' she calls out when Lexie swings the net. 'You nearly hit Sam!'

When she eventually returns, she's been away so long, she perhaps feels she needs to offer up some sort of explanation.

'My sister,' she says, waving the phone as she sits back down on the blanket. 'She's having a really hard time at the moment. She calls me a lot.'

'Oh,' I say, 'sorry to hear that.'

She reaches across for the flask of coffee.

And because of the awkward silence, and because I don't really know what else to say, I tell her I have a sister too. 'Gemma. She's two years younger. And yours?'

There's a brief hesitation.

'Mine's younger too. Polly,' she says. 'Her name is Polly.'

There is something about her hesitation. The way she glances over at the children before she speaks. The softer hushed tone of her voice. I know then that there is something secret about Polly. Something withheld. Something forbidden. Something risky. And in that pause, I have the feeling that the very mention of her name is like a door she has nudged ajar, just slightly, to let me come inside.

FOUR

I was surprised to discover Nina was in a relationship with Keith. And if I'm honest, a little disappointed. Nina told me she'd met someone when she came in to see me on a routine appointment for her IUD. She said she was experiencing discomfort, and was thinking of alternatives. 'I've met a lovely man,' was what she said. 'It was so odd,' she laughed, 'we met online six months ago, only to find we live a few streets away.' Her eyes were bright. She looked happy. And given what she'd been through, when she told me she was getting married eight months later, I was thrilled for her.

It was Sandra, one of the receptionists, who mentioned it was Keith.

'Keith Strutt?'

She nods. 'They got married in the spring.'

'Keith – the office contractor?'

'That's the one.'

We all knew Keith. He was a popular figure in the practice. Often found in reception, endlessly entertaining the admin staff. He was a fitness fanatic and one of those men who couldn't stand still. Slightly hyperactive, and would charge in, leaping about from one foot to the other as he told a joke. I found him likeable enough, if a little too much, but my attitude towards him changed dramatically after the fiasco over the office contract.

It came about when we were extending the surgery premises. We had planning permission to build a large meeting room, a kitchen and four more consulting rooms and an office for the practice manager. With notices up in the surgery informing the patients of the proposed work, Keith had seized the opportunity to offer his company up for the lighting and rewiring contracts. 'We also do water dispensers, vending machines if you need that sorted?'

His company was local. Carried out commercial work, mostly offices, but shops too. He came in showing the work he'd done on a large dental practice in Cable Street. 'Fiddly job. Lots of ceiling lights and moveable angular points.' He persuaded the partners to let his company put in a quote. I remember at the practice management meeting how David had held his hands up in supplication. 'I was browbeaten. He wore me down with his brochures,' he dropped his voice down low, 'he simply bored me into submission.' He sighed. 'I told him to submit a quote and we'd consider it with the rest.'

The problem was, Keith heard this differently and assumed he'd got the contract. In the end, after reviewing the quotes, David went with the building company with links to another firm, so Keith's proposal was turned down.

When the practice manager called to let him know, there was a scene. He came straight in to see David, who was adamant he'd requested a quote, with no guarantees. Keith was incensed, and the raised voices in reception drew me out of my room. Keith was at the front desk, pale and incandescent with rage. His hands were gripped onto the reception desk. A hard ridge of fury had settled in a line above his top lip, telling David he was on commission, that without this job, he wouldn't meet his target. His whole body was tight. 'I don't like being made to look a fool,' he spluttered. He looked mean in a way I'd never seen before and David tried to usher him away, into his office. Afterwards, David was astonished at the speed of his anger, 'like the flick of a switch,' was what he'd said.

After the fallout, we all assumed Keith would leave, and join another practice. But instead, he switched from David to seeing me. Every time he came, I'd have to endure the same comments about the lighting in my room. How dark the corridor was, and how they'd used the wrong kind of casing. 'The louvred mirror ones would have reflected the light better.' It was tedious. And every time I'd feel the heavy lurch of dread as I knew I'd have to listen to the loop of his mindless sales patter and be given pamphlets on water dispensers that were 'eco-friendly and sustainable'. Once he even drew the louvred design on a piece of paper that he pushed across my desk. He seemed unable to let it go, like a dog with a bone, returning over and over to what he perceived as a personal slight. 'Business is booming,' he'd say, clapping his hands together. 'You pay a little bit more for quality. But I think that's worth it. Don't you?'

It became something of a running joke in the surgery. Sometimes we'd switch the lights on in the group room for a meeting and we'd shake our heads gravely, 'if only we'd gone for those louvred ceiling lights.'

So, given I knew Nina well, I was surprised when I found out it was Keith she'd married. Nina was bright, worked long hours and had told me about her recent promotion, 'managing a team of eight now,' she'd said proudly. She was quieter, more cerebral than Keith. But after my initial surprise, I saw them in the street when I was picking the kids up from nursery. It was a fleeting glimpse, and she was looking back at Keith, laughing in response to something he was saying. And another time on a Saturday, they were walking along Brady Street, chatting as they swung a small boy between them. Both times she looked happy. And I felt a sudden lightness to see her obvious joy. The two of them laughing, sharing a joke in the street landed like an anchor in my busy week. And if anyone deserved happiness, it was Nina. Her first husband Mike had died tragically, nearly ten years ago. A waterskiing accident in Corsica on their honeymoon.

The first appointment with Keith and Nina came at a very busy time. Ruby had started at a new nursery and was unsettled at night. And with two GPs off, one on maternity leave and the other on sick leave, the senior team was depleted and we were managing on locums. There had also been no let-up in the unremitting demands of my safeguarding role.

At home, things were hectic; Rob was working all hours on the script and his availability and input into family life had receded to next to nothing. 'It's just a couple more months,' he said, as he was bombarded with an entirely new set of script changes. But it kept on coming. The 'couple more months' extended out across the year. More rewrites. More suggestions. More changes. A new exec. A different director. And then, just before Christmas, there was another extensive set of notes. When he mentioned them, they sounded familiar. 'Isn't that close to what you had in the first place? Way back when . . .?' and I wafted a hand behind my head.

Rob said not. But I knew it was a way of hiding his own exasperation with what we could both see was a ridiculous process. Six different decisions. Six different points of view. Then all fired back to the writer, who's back to square one. 'It's so nearly done, Jess. Seriously. They're drawing up a schedule for the shoot. An immoveable deadline.'

I didn't hold my breath. In the end, my response to the frustration with the whole process was simply to take myself out of the discussion. I let it roll on. And I kept the plates spinning. The demands of a full-time job. Childcare, food, laundry. Football for Sam. Dance classes for Ruby. Swimming lessons. Then there was the application form for Sam's school which had to be in by December. The nursery fees to pay. A new cleaner to find. The list was endless. And yet, I still found myself taking on more. Volunteering for the cake stall on my afternoon off. Offering to help run the Pimm's stall at the nursery fundraiser. It was as if I constantly wanted to prove I could outrun myself.

Then there were the additional responsibilities that came with working in a busy practice; the leaving present for the practice nurse, or the row that had broken out between two of the receptionists that needed me to intervene. David would pop his head round the door: 'Donna and Jane have had another bust up,' and he'd give a little head wobble. 'Can you maybe have a word?' In spite of his feedback at my appraisal, he continued to call on me when it suited him. With the two female GPs off, it somehow fell to me to pick up what he considered the 'nurturing' tasks. 'You're so diplomatic,' David said. I could have said no. Could have delegated, handed some of it back. But I liked to help. And when I was managing whatever was thrown at me, I liked the efficiency of it all. The sense of achievement. Smoothing my hand over a cleared empty desk at the end of the working day. The adrenalin rush of getting it all done. Of being in control. The truth was, I liked things being done well. And I liked the way I did things.

And then of course, in amidst all this, there were the patients. The endless flow of demand. Crammed surgeries. Emergency slots. And around this time, I had a couple of very tricky cases. I was supporting Mrs Chandra, who was terminally ill with stage 4 breast cancer. She wanted to be cared for at home and I had arranged the palliative care team to come in. I went in twice a week to see the family. I felt dented by the quiet dignity of it all. The unbearable sadness. Her four small desperate children.

And there were the safeguarding cases; one from an anonymous caller about her elderly neighbour and suspicions of financial abuse by his carer. The other was Terri Garner. Terri had come in to see me in the very early stages of pregnancy. She looked pale and thin, a yellowing bruise on her left cheek. She was hesitant, but eventually requested a referral for a termination of the pregnancy. After a difficult session, she made reference to her husband's 'volatile' behaviour. It was clear that she was at risk, but ambivalent, and I contacted the Multi Agency Safeguarding Hub to escalate my concerns both for her and the baby, should she decide to keep it.

Keith and Nina came to see me in the middle of all this. And I could make endless excuses, but the truth was, I took my eye off the ball.

Keith came in first. His characteristic jaunty walk. Full of bluster and banter as he pushed on the door, holding it open for Nina, who sat in the chair closest to my desk. I realised I hadn't seen Keith for ages. And for once, he made no comment about the lighting or the water dispenser, but I did notice his gaze lingering just a little too long over the anglepoise lamp that I had brought in from home.

He told me how they'd started running together. 'Nina had only ever run for a bus when I met her. Now she's out three times a week. Do you do any regular exercise?' he asked, and before I could speak, he was talking again. 'I said I can't marry a woman who doesn't do any exercise. In our first month together, I downloaded the Couch to 5k app for her – and she got the bug!'

I had a sense that he was filling the space. Covering up his nervousness. He stopped talking. His hands fell to his lap. There was a brief silence. A flicker of tension that I couldn't read.

'How can I help?'

He turned to Nina and gave her a nod of encouragement and

45

she went on to quietly outline their reason for coming.

'So, we wondered if there were any tests – a clinic you could refer us to?'

I nodded. And I then gave an overview of the approach. 'At least two years,' I said, 'before we'd usually start to investigate.'

'It's been two and a half,' Nina said quietly.

'Really? OK. My mistake,' and it seemed unfathomable that so much time had passed.

'I'm thirty-six,' she said. 'I know there's plenty of time. But I have a friend,' she said, 'who was in the same situation. But they left it –' and as she spoke, Keith reached for her hand and gave it a squeeze, '– and then all of a sudden, it was too late.' She looked down at her lap. 'It didn't happen for them. I don't want to be in that situation.'

She turned to him; they exchanged a brief glance. His look was full of a kind of adoration. The look of a man who can't quite believe his luck. And I felt bad for my judgement about what I saw as an ill-matched union. Who knew what went on in the confines of other people's relationships?

I pulled open the drawer and fished out some forms.

'I can make a referral for you to the fertility clinic. They'll need to see you both, for a separate range of different tests. Blood tests. Sperm samples. Hormone levels and various other checks.'

I looked at my screen. 'It can take up to eight weeks. If you haven't heard anything by then, let me know and I'll chase it up. But in fact, when I last referred a couple, they were seen quicker, in just over a month. I'll tell them to send all the results to me, and we can discuss them here together.'

Nina looked visibly more relaxed, her shoulders dropping with relief. Keith was shuffling forwards in his seat. He glanced at Nina, and she nodded.

'I've got a son from my first marriage,' he said. 'Jackson.'

He reached into his pocket and produced a photo. I peered in to see a picture of the two of them dressed as Stormtroopers. 'At his last birthday,' he said proudly, 'he's six.'

I nodded. And the memory of the two of them in the street with a small boy came back to me.

'Keith's a great dad,' offered Nina, 'and Jackson's a lovely boy. We have him every other weekend.'

As Keith picked up the photo, it dawned on me. 'I'm afraid that won't make a difference for the clinic. They'll still want to see you both. Fertility can change, for all sorts of reasons – they'll need to assess the situation. Have a clear baseline to start from—'

And before I finished speaking, Keith was nodding enthusiastically. 'Totally understand. No problemo, a full MOT,' he boomed. 'But it's got to be a good sign, hasn't it,' he said, 'if the old fishing tackle has caught something once before?'

Nina laughed.

And then, in a way I found vaguely patronising, he slung his arm around Nina's shoulder. 'We'll get through this together. I know we will.'

'Any other things I should know about? Any particular stress at the moment?'

They glanced at each other. 'Well, not really,' Nina said. 'Keith's mum's not doing so well. Bad back, acute arthritis. But we're managing. He's being fantastic. He's been taking her for her hospital appointments. And been sorting her garden out. He potted up bulbs last autumn and they're just beginning to come through. He's the Monty Don of Spitalfields,' she laughed proudly. 'Other than that, things are good. We're just so ready to have a child together.'

Again, she looked at him and smiled. He patted her hand. And again, I felt myself soften in the face of her happiness.

As they got up to go, I tried to reassure them. 'Please don't worry. Try and put it to one side.'

And as I added the referral letter to my list of things to do before I left, I didn't think much about it. It felt like a standard referral. In fact, around sixty per cent of couples who come in to discuss a referral to a fertility clinic got pregnant in the next few months, often while waiting for the appointment. This wasn't a scientific piece of research, but one based on my own anecdotal evidence. It was as if coming to talk about it, voicing the worry out loud, and having a referral in process, meant the anxiety dissipated. And they invariably got pregnant happily and naturally without any further intervention required. I had no reason to think this wouldn't be the case for Keith and Nina.

I remembered that day very well because it was the day Mrs Chandra died. I'd called in to see her on my way to work. I could see the end was near. I sat with her husband as the nurse busied around the bedside. He said little. He knew it too. As I looked at her thin face on the pillow, I remembered her laughter and joy. Her fierce demands for the needs of her children, and the speed with which she moved, sweeping in and out of reception in a swirl of gold and purple.

I felt the very thing that had drawn me to General Practice in the first place was also the thing, that day, that was so acutely painful. The continuity, the generational involvement in a family over the years, making a difference to the trajectory of someone's life. The good trajectories were so gratifying: supporting a couple through four rounds of IVF and then finally seeing the proud parents fuss over their plump baby in the waiting room, or seeing one of my patients with stage 3 ovarian cancer respond to treatment and go into remission, or Mrs Kenley, the ninety-two-year-old woman who reluctantly moved into sheltered accommodation and had a new lease of life 'looking after the old folk' after the death of her husband. These are the happy trajectories. The threads of other people's lives that unspool, then miraculously and sometimes unfathomably wind themselves up again. The life of the Chandra family was a trajectory that had unravelled and hadn't wound itself back up into a new shape, but just lay in a messy tangled heap.

I sat quietly, the nurse gently squeezing water onto Mrs Chandra's dry and cracked lips, and I felt a stab of envy for the surgeons. For the doctors who cut open bodies and sew people up. Brief and incisive interventions, and then they swiftly move on to the next. Small and task-focused snapshots of time with their patients, after which the long haul of recovery is passed over to nursing staff and then to us in General Practice.

As I got up to leave, Mr Chandra saw me to the door. 'Thank you for coming,' he said politely. I saw the defeat in his eyes. The flat inescapable resignation of what was to come.

The call came through at 3 p.m. Two hours later, there was a box of homemade sweets left at reception, with a thank-you card from the family. Signatures from the husband and each of the children in their neat swirly handwriting. I sat at my desk for a long time. Thinking about them. How the family would reconfigure without her. I thought about the dilapidated block they lived in. The damp. The discarded rubbish by the garage and the smell of urine in the stairwell.

Before I left that evening, I made calls about Mrs Chandra, spoke to the palliative care team. I did my referral letters quickly, including the one to the fertility clinic, and rushed home. Things were tight. Rob was away on a three-day read-through of the script and there was no time to linger. As it was, it was the third time I was late to nursery. Naomi wasn't happy. I muttered my excuses, tried to tell her the sort of day I'd had, hoping she'd make an exception, but she cut me off. 'If we made allowances for every parent, it would be impossible to run the place efficiently.' As she shook her head, she jangled the keys in her hand. 'It's not something we like to do – but there will be late charges this week. Please be on time next week.'

She pushed open the door to the now empty playroom, and Ruby and Sam ran over, clutching an assortment of paintings. 'I'm sorry,' I said to Naomi, 'it won't happen again.'

FIVE

Helen's husband James arrives late on Friday evening. I see the car pull up as I'm closing the curtains in the kids' bedroom. It's a small sporty vehicle, which he tucks in by the side of the cottage next to Helen's car. In the morning, they all set off early, getting back just before Rob returns from a big supermarket shop in Swanage. Ollie and Lexie are polishing the body work with chamois leather and wax from a tin. Rob's unpacking the bags of shopping when James waves and strolls over. I'm at the window washing up as I watch them shake hands. He's got dark curly hair, looks tanned and is wearing jeans and a red checked shirt. They exchange some words, then both walk over to James's car. I recognise it. An old boyfriend had one. An Austin Healey Sprite. Racing Green. Rare all those years ago, so rarer still to find one now in such good condition. The two men walk slowly round the car, James occasionally bending down and pointing things out. Rob has no interest in cars, vintage or otherwise. But given his recent affable personality transplant, he feigns enthusiasm and even asks a few questions, which James answers as he runs his hand over the gleaming bonnet. After more chat and laughter, Rob nods over to the shopping – and gathers up the bags and walks back to the cottage.

Recently, I've been paying attention to the way Rob does things around the house. How he puts his own inimitable stamp on tasks like bringing in the shopping. That day, I watch as he staggers in under the weight of it all, straining as he heaves the bulging bags up onto the table. It's like watching a cave man drag in a slaughtered deer, and as he hefts the bags up onto the table, small items, an apple and a tin, spill out, like entrails from the beast. Then once the spoils of his labour are on display, with a mixture of pride and triumph on his face, he retreats to the sofa, exhausted, but proud of his efforts. His job is done, his body says, as he seeks refuge and reward in coffee and the paper. The path is now left clear for me to step forward and perform my wifely duties: skinning the carcass and preparing the banquet. Or in our case, putting all the stuff away into the small dolly cupboards and picking out something to turn into the next meal.

'I know – I know,' he says, holding his hands up in surrender, 'but for a man with a convertible, he actually seems like a nice guy. Although, I could go on *Mastermind*,' he says, lying back on the tiny sofa, his legs dangling over the armrest. 'Specialist subject, James's car restoration project. What is it with men and cars? I did nod off a bit when he was talking about buying the third hub cap from a dealer in Macclesfield.'

He gets up to make coffee.

'The final thing is replacing the soft top – then it's done. The end of a seven-year project. There's a big rip – by the back seat—'

It's astonishing that Rob has not only retained the information, but is now repeating it to me. A person who couldn't be less interested in cars if I tried.

'He's patched it up with masking tape. Made quite a nice job of it. He's gutted he can't replace it. But they're a bit strapped for cash – what with the new job venture and everything.'

He reaches for two mugs. 'Did you know they've relocated from Germany?'

'I know. Helen told me.' Then I turn to face him. 'But I didn't know about the car. The soft top repair – that's all news to me.

Absolutely riveting,' I say, folding my fingers into a gun that I fire at my temple.

'OK – OK. He's a bit of a car nerd. But he's nice. Good fun. Twinkly blue eyes. You'll like him,' and as he pours the coffee, he tells me about the barbecue. 'He's invited us all over later.'

Rob finds social gatherings a burden. Deeply excruciating and a sheer waste of time. *The small talk. The chit-chat. The echo chamber of other people's lives . . .*

'Said around four? That OK? At least we don't have far to go,' he says merrily.

I stare back at my husband, warily, like he's a strange nocturnal animal.

Sam rushes down the stairs. 'Was that Ollie's dad? I saw you talking,' he says, breathless with anticipation. 'That sports car. It's sooo cool.'

'It's very cool, buddy,' Rob says. 'I'm sure he'll let you have a look. And you'll never guess what?'

Sam can barely contain his excitement.

'He built it from scratch,' and Rob glances up at me, 'he'll be able to tell you all about it.'

Thrilled at the very thought, Sam rushes off to find Ruby.

We head to the coast for the rest of the morning. Rob remains cheerful even after reversing into a bollard in the car park. By the time we get to the beach, the wind has picked up and clouds scud across the sky, eclipsing the sun in giant blinks. 'Perfect for the kite!' he says, as I shield my eyes from the sting of the wind-whipped sand.

Rob unwraps the kite with the kids. He talks as they open it up. 'You undo that end bit,' he says, 'I'll do this bit.' So, the three of them work together. It takes patience, this approach. It is a parenting style I aspire to, but often fail at, resorting in the end to simply doing it myself. He is so much better at this than me. When it's been unfolded, the main diamond of the kite is a bright vibrant red. Sam undoes the band wrapped around the tail and small darts of yellow and orange spill out over the sand. Rob places the kite down on the sand and hands the spool of thread to Sam. 'Unwind a little bit.' Sam unravels too much. 'Wind a little back up. I'll launch it,' he says, walking a few steps away. When Rob hurls it in the air, it catches, twists around in a spiral and then nosedives onto the sand. This happens four more times, and Sam is looking close to tears, and we're teetering on the point of a major tantrum.

'If it catches at all. Even a little bit,' Rob says, 'run like mad.'

Sam nods.

And this time it lifts. 'Run!' shouts Rob, and Sam tears along the sand. The kite climbs higher. Sam keeps running. The bright red diamond, the orange and yellow tail. It flies higher, twisting and turning. 'Look at me, Mummy!' Sam shrieks, his eyes ablaze with excitement. 'Look what I'm doing. I'm doing it. It's flying!' he says. And Ruby runs along beside him, clapping her hands. Rob catches up with him and gets Sam to stop. He steadies his hand and helps him as the kite rises up and pulls on his arm. Sam gazes up. 'Higher. Higher,' he says. 'Up with the planes and the birds,' he says. I feel almost euphoric watching. The flash of red and orange streaking across the wide blue sky.

This is the moment, I think. This is what we are here for. The dart of kite in the air. The blue of the sky. The joy on their faces. The kids running into the wind. These small moments of elation sandwiched between the tears and the tantrums and thwarted plans and disappointments. And they are worth it every time. Rob looks over at me. It's a kind of smug look. *You see. What did I tell you? I knew you'd love it. Four more weeks of this.* And I nod back at him. I smile. I allow it. Of course, he is right.

After the successful kite flight, Rob goes to the café, and returns with ice-creams. But as Ruby peels off the shiny Cornetto wrapper, it's lifted by a gust of wind. She runs after it over the banks of seaweed heaped up closer to the water. Just when it's within her reach, it curls away from her. The silver glints in the sun. 'I have to get it, Mummy,' she shrieks. 'The birds,' she says. 'Remember what you said about the birds. You said if they eat rubbish, they will die.'

The birds? Had I said that once? Probably. Was it true? Or simply a way of stopping them dropping litter in the park. But now I see her stricken face. Her desperation. Like she's holding the survival of all birdlife in the palm of her hand. She lurches over another bank of seaweed. The wrapper is now near the edge of the water, and the seaweed is wet and sludgy. She falls. When she stands up, her face is covered with black mud and debris, as are her trousers and sweatshirt. She's wailing. The mint choc chip Cornetto now upended on the sand.

'My ice-cream!' she howls. 'And my pants. They're all wet—'

She wants to go home.

'Is there anything for her to change into? Have we got spare clothes?' Rob asks, looking around him for the imaginary bag he might have packed.

I shake my head. 'No,' I say, '*we* don't.'

A hunt in my cavernous handbag produces an old pair of Batman pants and, unfathomably, a lime green football bib.

'Superhero pants!' Rob says, rescuing the situation before Ruby's look of disdain can become a stand-off. 'Come on, Bat-girl,' he says enthusiastically as he swiftly makes a cape out of the football bib, and the three of them dart away to catch villains on the sand dunes.

Rob buys chips and beer and more ice-cream from the café, and we sit in the lunchtime sun. Afterwards he builds a dam at the water's edge. I read a chapter of my book. Then I just close my eyes in the warmth, sleepy from the beer.

It's on the way home that I pick up the news about my father.

Several texts, missed calls and three voicemails from my mother. The first message is breathless and anxious, the last, calcified into a kind of fury, as she concludes my not picking up is some kind of conspiracy or personal vendetta.

'I need to call her back,' I say to Rob, waving my phone in the air, then I walk back up the driveway to find some reception.

'Oh. Thank you,' she says tightly when she answers.

I try to explain about the mobile phone reception, but she cuts in. 'Something's happened,' and then she pauses to relish the drama of it all.

When she tells me, I can't quite take in the information.

'What do you mean *gone*?'

My mother sounds skittish. And while I can hear the anxiety in her voice, as ever, it is displaced onto other things, like objects she scatters haphazardly in every direction. Getting through to her is like an obstacle course. A kind of verbal *It's a Knockout*, as I try to get the conversation back on track.

I find myself asking the same question again and again. I feel heavy. Waterlogged.

'I told you,' she says, 'he's gone – somewhere,' she says again, 'disappeared,' and she outlines the sequence of events; her difficult afternoon the day before putting up eight trestle tables on her own, her getting home late, *lightheaded with hunger* because Marie forgot to bring lunch, 'just a couple of Rich Tea biscuits all morning – then there was his note on the kitchen table.'

A pause. I wait.

'I nearly didn't see it at all,' she says, triumphantly, 'it was placed on a newspaper. Swept the whole pile up for recycling—'

'*Mum*. What did it say?'

'Two nights, it said. He'll be back on Monday.' A pause. '*I'm taking a short break*, was what it said.'

'A short break?'

She tells me he took a case. And it's this that floors me. The notion of my father selecting items to take with him: a change of clothes, a toothbrush, toiletries. To my knowledge he's never packed a bag in his life.

'The small brown leather one. The one we bought in Greece. It's missing,' she says. 'Do you remember that funny gift shop?' and then she retrieves a memory about the shopkeeper and my father's inability to find the right money given his confusion over the currency.

'Mum—' I try to interrupt, but my mother's still talking; she's telling me about the Silent Auction, and how they have the Sullivans coming for Sunday lunch. 'What will I say?' and the sound is muffled as I picture her moving about, the phone hooked under her chin as her hands flap uselessly around the kitchen.

'Apparently Tony has allergies. Eggs! I didn't know,' she says, like it's some kind of joke on her. 'I'm sure I've made my lemon meringue pie in the past.'

Her voice is speeding up. Manic. Avoidant.

'But where is he?' I say. 'Dad never goes anywhere.'

I think of my father's week. How he spends his time shuffling between four places: his college room, his study at home, his shed and the occasional trip to the Dog and Bone when coerced by Max. How he fought a credible case against having a mobile phone, given that he was 'only ever in one corner of a square'.

How every week he bought a Sunday paper, and every day he took one section to read on his way to work. How, ever since I was a child, he'd empty out the loose change from his pocket after work, stacking the coins into neat towers of silver and copper that he'd line up on his chest of drawers. My father likes his routines. He is not a man to embrace the unexpected. His aversion to trips abroad was a long-standing family joke. Once, he got so stressed by the non-arrival of a piece of luggage in Naples that, when it did appear a few days later, he left us all by the pool to collect it from the airport, at which point he got the next flight home to Heathrow, ringing my mother from Arrivals. To say he was a creature of habit was an understatement.

My mother says something else. A muffled muted sound as the receiver dips further and further from her mouth. There's the noise of a cupboard door opening then closing, then I hear her rifling through the tins and packets.

'What did you say? I can't hear you. Have you spoken to Max?'

There is more rustling and then sudden clarity as the phone is reunited with her mouth.

'I've left him a message,' she says. 'I'll try him again. He's bound to know something. Let's speak this evening.' And so we arrange to speak at eight.

'But text me,' I say, 'if there's any news in the meantime.'

Before she rings off, I wonder about calling the police. The words sound ludicrous as they come out of my mouth.

'*The police?*' she scoffs. 'He's not a missing child. He's a seventy-year-old college professor, what on earth do you think they'll say?'

But I can tell she's not horrified about the absurdity of the suggestion. About the fact that the departure of a seventy-year-old man, who's left a note, is hardly a police matter. What she's horrified about is the thought of any external involvement. The fear of judgement. It's not about him at all. It's about her. The indignity. The shame of it all. A suffocating and paralysing shame that has threaded through the fabric of our family life. *What will people think?* And in that moment, I too have that flicker from the past.

After I put the phone down, I feel something. A shift of unease. I call my sister. But it goes straight to voicemail. I don't leave a message because, as Gemma has repeatedly told me, she never listens to them.

SIX

When we cross the lawn just after four, James is warm and welcoming. He's put out an extra foldaway table and chairs and a box of toys on the grass next to the picnic table. The barbecue is set up on the path to their house and is already sizzling with the smell of food. 'I forgot to ask if there were any vegetarians? I've done some meat and some veg,' he says, offering us drinks. 'Beer, wine, juice?'

I'm not sure why, but I'm surprised by James – his handsome face and his affable and outgoing personality – and I can see that Rob is more than a little taken with him, chatting and laughing with him at the grill, drinking beer together, like new best mates. He's perhaps a little older than Helen, but has a crisp clean look about him in his white t-shirt and blue jeans. He cooks with efficiency; plates of corn on the cob, chicken marinated in ginger and garlic, and vegetable and halloumi kebabs.

Helen is characteristically reserved, and steps inside to fetch the salads, waving away my offer to help. She unpacks plates, bowls and cutlery from a picnic hamper. Everything is sensibly plastic for outdoor use, even the stemmed wine glasses.

James is generous and hospitable, and Rob is happy to find his drinks refreshed with the adeptness of a waiter. James talks about his new IT project. How he used to work for a company in Germany, but was looking forward to starting his own business, 'being my own boss,' he says. 'It's early days. And a crowded market, but so far, so good.'

I try to listen, but find myself zoning out, preoccupied with my father. I keep trying to picture him packing the small brown suitcase, selecting clothes from the wardrobe, items from the bathroom, and then walking along the street, case in hand. Glasses. Coat on. But no pictures come.

When I tune back in, James is talking about the paintballing company in the field beyond the farm. Says he bumped into a woman in the post office who'd taken her kids, 'apparently it was a disaster.' He pauses to take a swig of beer. 'Kids were really excited, but after they got divided into groups, there were two blokes on the other team, older guys, in their late fifties, who'd brought their own equipment with them. Had semi-automatics and just fired the crap out of them all.'

I'd seen men queuing in clusters at the gate. Their army gear; the combat trousers and the camouflaged hats and jackets. Joyce had told me the company had recently leased the empty field. There'd been resistance among the local farmers, but the land was council-owned and they'd approved it for the summer. She said the sign went up in May just before the half-term break. '*Collateral Damage*' splashed across a big wooden hoarding.

'One of her kids got hit on the forehead. Drew blood,' he shakes his head, 'what a shambles.'

Rob is nodding too. 'There's always one,' he shrugs, 'give him an army jacket and a gun and he thinks he's Rambo.'

James makes a face. 'Men running round like soldiers? What's that all about?'

The two of them nod away, appalled. I decide this might not be the moment to remind Rob about his friend Dom's stag week-end in April and the riotous paintballing on the South Downs.

The conversation drifts back and forth. James is delighted to hear Rob is a scriptwriter. 'Wow,' he says, 'amazing. What are you working on, Rob?'

It's music to Rob's ears. And in talking about the film script, he glosses over the years of failure and rejection. Before I rush to judge, I remember I pretty much did the same thing with Helen the day before. I get it. We all want to show the best versions of ourselves. Why wouldn't we? And listening to him talk, I feel a swell of pride for his achievements.

Later, I'm talking with Helen about a book I'd listened to on Audible. 'Such a different experience,' I say, 'hearing it read out. I've always been a bit rigid about needing to see the words on a page—' My voice is suddenly loud, falling as it does in a lull in the men's conversation. James's focus switches to me, swivelling his chair round to face me.

'Interesting you say that, Jess,' he says, and it's then that I notice how frequently he uses our names, in a way I find both disarming and intimate. 'How is it different?' he asks me, like he really wants to know the answer. And I see what Rob is drawn to. He asks questions. Pulls you in. There's something about the way he listens. He sits very still, fixing you with those astonishingly blue eyes. And in that moment, as I'm talking about my recent discovery of Audible, it's as if I'm imparting the meaning of life. I feel interesting and important, but it's disconcerting, and at first, I flounder under the scrutiny, but as the afternoon progresses and our glasses are topped up, I find I want more of that clear undivided attention. Soon Rob and I are vying for his attention. Who can be the funniest? Who has the most amusing anecdote? We are like children competing for our moment in the spotlight.

And because I've had two glasses of wine in the afternoon, I decide to tell my Alison Steadman story.

'I'm at the swimming pool in Muswell Hill, and I've just bought a ticket at the kiosk,' I say, talking a gulp of my wine, 'and then the woman who was ahead of me turns as she gets to the turnstile, then sees me and waves as she strides over.'

I pause. 'I looked at her blankly. No recognition,' I continue, 'then as she gets close up, right in front of me, she says, "Oh sorry, I thought you were someone else," and turns away.

'But now, I'm thinking, I *do* recognise the woman, I'm sure I do know her. And I'm wracking my brains, and I can't think how, or from where – but it's bugging me, so I find myself following her.'

Another swig of wine. '"Hi," I say in a loud voice. "I do know you – I just can't remember where."'

I look over at Rob. He's rolling his eyes. He's heard this so many times before.

'But she's already shuffling away as I speak. Shaking her head. But I can't let it go. I follow her. I don't give up. In the end, in the corridor to the changing room, she turns round. Her voice is a kind of hiss, as she drops her voice down low: "I'm an actress," she says, moving away.'

I look up, and see James and Helen exchange a glance.

'So, I'm left standing there like a fool,' I say, 'and then I think, is this what actresses do, when they need a little bit of attention? Feigning friendship – to prompt recognition? Then shuffling away, triumphant—' I'm laughing at myself as I speak. 'The next hour I have to pass her in the lanes as we swim up and down.'

There's a silence. James shifts uncomfortably in his seat. For one awful moment, I think he's going to tell me that he knows her. That she's a family friend.

But then I realise they have no idea who Alison Steadman is.

'She's an actress. Quite well known. Someone you might recognise—' I mutter something about *Abigail's Party*. More blank looks.

'I'm afraid we don't tend to watch much television,' he says, by way of explanation. 'Find it a bit of a waste of time to be honest.'

My face flushes, feeling suddenly foolish. 'Sure. I know what you mean.'

Helen is smiling.

And very quickly Rob comes to the rescue and sweeps in with talk about the location for the film. And soon there is a more relaxed conversation about towns in the South of France and holidays James and Helen had before they had children. 'The rolling fields of sunflowers,' he says, 'I'd never seen anything like it.'

When James asks about casting, Rob tells him they're planning to use unknowns for the main parts. 'People who are new to the screen. For the French student and possibly even the father – not sure. The director says he does his best work with new actors. People who aren't famous. No bias. No projections. Says the script can stand alone—'

James and Helen are nodding away.

'Lets the writing breathe.'

I almost choke on my wine.

'Excellent,' James says. 'Well, I'm impressed,' and he raises his beer. 'Here's to seeing *Bad Faith* at the cinema.'

'Well – if all goes well, there'll be a screening – you must come!' Rob says effusively.

Helen brings out fruit and ice-cream. There's a neatness and order about the whole barbecue, like it's been planned meticulously. That same brisk efficiency I have seen in Helen runs through the afternoon, and while this can evoke a desire in me to behave badly, that day, I notice I'm enjoying being project managed, being cooked for and looked after as we sit in the sun. And when I look over at the kids, the four heads huddled together laughing, I feel grateful for this moment.

A little later, James glances surreptitiously at his watch. And then, when he gets up and moves over to the barbecue, puts on a gardening glove and starts cleaning the grill, I get up too.

'No rush,' he says, 'please. Sit down. Finish up. This is much easier to do when it's still warm.'

'We always end up buying those throwaway ones,' says Rob, 'such a waste. That one's a perfect size,' and he turns his head to me. 'We should get one, Jess.'

This is another Rob-ism that has become magnified of late. It sits neatly alongside other phrases like 'we must get the coat hook repaired' or 'order a new hosepipe' or 'clear out the shed' or 'get the kids to eat more vegetables'. These often entirely astute observations of what's required come with such conviction, such enthusiasm, the thrust of 'we must' carrying such weight and such authority. To anyone listening, it would be hard to believe there would be no follow-through. That the energy lies exclusively in the idea, not the execution. But instead, I have come to know that these suggestions are simply left hanging in the air, like ripe fruit for someone else to pick. For *me* to pick. And early on in our relationship, I was too quick to reach up and do just that.

And as I watch James chatting as he cleans the grill, I feel a stab of envy. For the fact that a task would probably be done before Helen had time to notice. The rack in the hall wouldn't have to fall repeatedly and scatter the coats on the floor before he'd intervene. He's a man who would anticipate. He's a fixer. Someone who likes to head the crisis off at the pass. And if I'm not careful, I could let my warm glow of pride for my husband evaporate in the face of this efficient scraping of a greasy grill.

Helen is now standing up and the energy has shifted. It's as if the social activity has been a task, something to be completed, with a beginning, middle and end. And all of a sudden, I realise, we are most definitely at the end. There is no lolling about and drinking another beer or glass of wine. It's time to leave. Rob gathers up the empty bottles and I help Helen take in the salad bowls. Later, once the cleaned grill is packed away, they work together. I notice how well matched they are. James scraping plates, and handing them to Helen as she neatly and deftly stacks them into a pile. Their kids are polite and step up to help, and when I glance over at my two, Ruby is trying to make herself dizzy by doing cartwheels, and Sam is digging a tunnel in the dirt.

When I bring the glasses over, James asks about the scooter. 'Before you go,' he says, 'let me take a look. Helen says it's broken. I've got my tool-box here.'

By the time Rob's lifted it from the boot of the car, James is back with a rectangular box with complicated drawers and layers of screws and bolts in neat partitions.

The two men crouch down. Rob is again making the right noises and nods of his head. James reaches into his box. In minutes, it's fixed. Rob brings it over, proudly. 'Brilliant! And James has also fixed the fastening catch,' he says. 'The man's a genius. It's been broken for weeks.'

If Rob hadn't been so contented and affable, he might have found it infantilising. An assault on his masculinity. But given his geniality, and his camaraderie with his new best friend, he's whistling as he takes the fixed scooter back to the boot.

The two men do some backslapping, and we thank our hosts. 'Beach next week?' Helen says to me, as we move away. The kids wave goodbye. As we stroll back across the lawn to our cottage,

Rob slings an arm around my shoulder. I pull him closer. We're fuzzy and warm from drinking in the sun.

'*Allow the writing to breathe?* Who even are you?' I laugh, turning to inspect him closely.

He nods solemnly. 'RIP the Alison Steadman story,' he says, by way of an answer.

After bath time, Rob watches *The Lion King* with the kids. It's a favourite. They know most of the words and songs and relish the anticipation of what's to come. The predictability of knowing Mafusa will be destroyed and get his come-uppance in the end. That there will be life after death. And that good will prevail. There's a joy in the simplicity of it all. And as I am pottering about in the background, I smile as I listen to Rob explain the Three Act structure.

I pour a glass of wine and take my book outside; I sit on a chair by the hollyhocks, and I think how much better he is at the fun. The spontaneity. The play. How often I feel I am outside the moment. Looking ahead, anticipating. Carrying the respon- sibility. The one at the bottom of the roller coaster anxiously clutching onto the bags.

And I see my younger self, during those interminable meals at the table. Having to sit and witness the agony of my sister chase her fork after peas on her plate. My head busy with my calculations and bargains and complex trade-offs. By then, I knew all her tricks with the food, but I sat there willing her to just eat enough so we could all leave the table. The silence. The tick of the clock. My father's laboured, angry breathing and my mother's wringing hands and my own fists curled under the table, nails making moons into the flesh of my palms.

At the sound of a voice, I look up to see Joyce waving from the lane. I beckon her over, and as she hurries across clutching a stash of paper, I nip inside for another glass, just in time to see Rob and the kids acting out the denouement, with Ruby lifting one of her swaddled dolls high up to the sky as they sing 'Circle of Life'.

'Will you have one?' I ask Joyce, the bottle hovering over the glass I have grabbed.

'Oh, I can't stop,' she says, sitting down on the bench. 'Oh, go on then – half a glass. I'm on a mission,' she says, pushing one of the leaflets across the table. 'One of the parents set up a GoFundMe page, there's a link. I hate to ask – but I just wondered – would you send it round? To anyone who might feel able to contribute? Anything at all. It all helps.'

She tells me they have funds for two days a week until the end of June, and then they just have the local donations.

'Leo was used to going five days a week. And of course, with such limited communication, he doesn't understand. He's missing his sister too, Kirsty – she went away travelling last month. A late gap year, just landed in Thailand,' she says proudly. 'She was so good with him. Now he's just got us all week. He's getting more agitated. Frustrated,' she shrugs. 'It's hard for him.'

And it's only then that I notice her tired face. The dark lines under her eyes. 'I'm so sorry.'

There's a brief silence. She looks away.

'And at the end of those two weeks?' I ask. 'If there's no reprieve from the council? Or no more funds?'

'That'll be it,' she sighs, but before we can dwell on the implication of this, she says cheerily, 'but there's still time – we must keep up the fight.' And she raises a clenched fist. She sits back, taking a sip of wine. She looks in no hurry to leave.

'Pete's at a farm in Wareham,' she says. 'He's taken Leo. He's gone to borrow a grain distributor.'

And because it feels so comfortable, so easy with Joyce, I ask her if I can come over on Tuesday. 'I've got a meeting,' I say, deciding not to tell her it's therapy, 'but I can't get much quiet or privacy in the cottage – and is there any chance I could sit in a room at the farm? It's just for an hour. It's this Tuesday at 6 p.m.?'

She's nodding before I've finished. 'There's the empty cottage across the lane,' she says, 'but actually the wi-fi in Kirsty's room is much better. Use that. And Tuesday is perfect,' she nods, raising a glass to me. 'It's badger night. Pete runs a meeting for the local farmers.'

Seeing the confusion on my face she explains. 'Bovine TB. We lost a third of our herd last year. It's been on the news. You might have seen the posters in the village? The *Can the Cull* banners when you came off the motorway?'

I shake my head, embarrassed.

'Some farms were hit far worse. It's controversial,' she says, 'but most of the farmers are in favour of the culls. There's local opposition. And national. I understand it. But most of it comes from the holiday homeowners. People who wouldn't know one end of a cow from the other.'

Joyce tells me she's not entirely convinced. 'I mean there's evidence, but it's by no mean unequivocal. Pete seems to believe it's the way forward, though.'

She twists the glass in her hand. It catches the sun, and a cascade of rainbow colours dance a small shower across the table.

'Have you ever seen a badger,' she asks, 'up close?'

I shake my head again.

'They really are beautiful creatures,' she says, suddenly wistful, and then she sips at her wine. The pink in our glasses glows peachy in the sun.

I ask her about Pete's role in the meetings.

'Co-ordinates it all. Liaises with the council and holds regular meetings with the local farmers, then they all have a pint in the pub. He's in his element running something,' she says, 'it galvanises him. And I guess the badgers can't answer back. And like lots of men, Pete needs to find a way to channel his anger.'

'About the cattle?'

'Well, yes, but all this,' she says, waving at the leaflets.

I pick one up. A picture of a wide open space. Raised vegetable troughs and borders of flowers, and a green-painted work shed.

'It was the same when Leo was small, and it was clear he had severe developmental difficulties. Pete threw himself into court cases. Trying to prove medical negligence,' she shrugs. 'I'm at home with a tricky two-year-old and he's having endless furious meetings with solicitors. Pointless,' she says, taking a gulp of wine. 'Sometimes there simply isn't anyone to blame.'

As she speaks, I think of a patient I once had. She came in after the diagnosis of her son's rare genetic disease. 'One in twelve million,' she'd said flatly, 'that's some roll of a dice.'

Joyce continues. 'He's a good man. But his ability to handle stress is zero. It sidelines him. He's like a wrecking ball. Renders him angry. Incapable. I've learnt to protect him from the stress, otherwise it's just worse for me in the long run. But he's taken the news about Green Shoots pretty badly.'

I reach over to fill her glass. I think about his grim-set face in the tractor on the night we arrived.

'Hence the manic badger activity. Don't get me wrong,' she laughs, 'I'm very grateful for Tuesdays. Leo always goes along for the drive and hangs out there. He loves it. Big empty barn. Rolling fields. He's in seventh heaven –' she looks up and smiles, '– and I get to have an evening off. Next week, if you have time after, stay for a glass of wine. We can sit in the sun and chat.'

'I'd like that,' I say.

She looks down at her leaflets. 'While Pete pours his energy into culling the badgers, I'm focusing on the gardening project.' She tilts her glass to mine. 'Cheers,' she says.

'Funny really,' she muses, taking a sip of her wine, 'how men often put energy into fighting, or annihilating things or razing things to the ground, while we busy ourselves growing and creating and keeping things alive.'

We sit for a moment. The sun casting an orange glow across the grass. In the distance the field. A swirl of grasses. A ripple in the wind. And the sea, a far-off glint of silver.

'He seems good with Leo,' I say.

A look passes across her face. It's hard to read. 'Yes,' she laughs, 'in a pick 'n' mix kind of a way. Leo adores him. And he *is* good –' she says carefully, '– at some things. Like driving his tractor up and down in the dark endlessly, whatever the weather. He's good at that. But there are other things he can't – or won't – do. When Leo gets stressed, Pete doesn't cope.' She doesn't go into details, just says, 'I don't have that luxury. Most mothers don't,' she adds. 'Can you imagine – a mother being able to pick the bits she liked or was good at doing? Think of all the crap that would fall through the middle. And believe me, with Leo, much as I love him, there would be an awful lot of crap,' and she roars with laughter.

'Pete's less good at the battles we have to fight,' she explains, 'he just loses his temper. *I can't handle it.* Every time he's on the phone, he manages to upset the whole community nurse team, undermining all the good work I've built up.' She pushes a curl away from her face. 'It's not that I don't feel angry. I share it. *You don't have a monopoly on the anger,* I tell him all the time. But isn't it what women do, parcel it up? Put a frame around it to get things done. Make the best of things?'

'I guess,' I say, thinking of the hanging fruit that I seem unable to resist picking, but feel the sting of resentment when I do. 'But doesn't it bother you?'

'Not any more,' she says. 'If there are spills, we mop them up, don't we?'

*

Later that evening, I sit at the picnic table to call at the time we arranged. My mother picks up the phone on the first ring.

'It's all OK,' my mother says quickly. 'Everything's fine,' and she speaks over the top of my questions. 'He's back. He's fine,' her voice clipped. In a hurry. Impatient, like I'm the one who started the drama and need to calm myself down.

I look up and see Pete drive back to the farmhouse; the music's on, the windows are down and Leo's arm is out, waving in the wind.

My mother's distracted. She's clanking and crashing about in the kitchen. 'I'm making a hazelnut torte,' she says. 'Luckily I hadn't got around to phoning the Sullivans – it's all hands to the deck,' she says jauntily. 'Found one of Nigella's that doesn't need eggs,' she purrs; her words are rich and smooth, like melted chocolate.

This is her default position when she's stressed and anxious. It's what she did when Gemma was ill. The restless baking, the distraction of the recipe books and the endless array of dishes that appeared on the table, like an all-you-can-eat buffet.

Your father, she keeps saying, like he's something stuck to the bottom of her shoe.

'How is he?' I ask.

'Oh – he's fine,' she scoffs. The more I try to ask, the more desperate she is to get off the phone. As far as my mother is concerned, order has been restored, and the whole episode is to be folded away like a crisp piece of laundry. His return was the glassy flat sea after the unexpected squall of his sudden departure. There was no need to ponder on its epidemiology. It was gone. In the past.

When I ask to speak to my father, she hesitates. 'He's upstairs.'

There's a pause. I wait.

Dad's also reluctant to talk. He's evasive. Perhaps more so than usual, and he's quick to deflect the focus away from himself. 'How are the kids? How's Rob's script?' he booms.

He seems to have momentarily forgotten we are in Dorset. 'Ah yes,' he says enthusiastically. 'Are you near Corfe Castle? I had a great-aunt who lived out that way. I spent many summers in that area.'

'Dad – what happened?' I press. 'Are you OK?'

'I'm fine,' he says, and he refers to the whole thing as a 'rather silly distraction'. He laughs. 'Nothing to worry about. A longer pause. 'It's over,' is what he says.

My father was not a spontaneous man. That was the clue. The time to wave the red flag. And when I look back, I wish I'd pressed him further about his whereabouts. And how can I explain why I didn't? Was it because I was away myself? Displaced from the usual reactions and responses I might have had from my kitchen table? Instead, I simply followed the unwritten rule of our family life. That moments of high drama were swiftly cast to one side, like the sudden and distracting flurry of a magician's sleight of hand, drawing you away to look at something else.

But I came to realise that when someone wants to look away – and is determined to keep looking away – how easy it becomes to simply follow their gaze.

It's over. They were words that sounded dismissive; trivial and banal. Words I took to mean the end of his trip, his change of plan. I had no way of understanding their significance. But perhaps if I'd picked things over, just a little, I might have seen things for what they were. *Where did you go? What did you do?* I might have discovered the small ticking time bomb that was hidden underneath. Sometimes, I even imagine I might have been able to prevent what happened at his birthday lunch – and the terrible event that followed. On other days, I think there's an inevitability about such a calculated act of violence. An air bubble trapped underwater that eventually finds its way to the surface.

SEVEN

For the rest of the weekend, Rob finds little excuses to pop out-side and join James when he sees him in the garden. They have a coffee on Sunday morning by the car, and I find them chatting over a beer at lunchtime, before each of our families heads off for the rest of the day. And after the departure of his new best friend on Monday, he looks a little bereft. 'Perhaps we can invite them over next weekend. You know, return the favour?'

It's Tuesday morning when I come back from the shops with the kids to find Rob on the lawn, frowning as he talks on the phone. I can see something's happened. The phone's clamped to his ear. His shoulder hunched. His face angular with tension. He is silent, mostly just nodding and grimacing. If it wasn't for the mobile reception, he'd be pacing up and down; as it is, he is restricted to tight rectangular laps of the picnic table.

I catch his eye. 'What's up?' I mouth.

He gives a brief shake of his head. And then the flick. The thing I most detest. The dismissive hand flap that he might use for an insect on a humid day.

As I take out the bags from the car, I see Joyce with Leo in the corner of their garden. She's kneeling on the lawn next to a bag of compost, handing Leo a trowel. But he's rocking back and forth, pulling at his t-shirt, making a high-pitched noise, and then he hurls the trowel down. Joyce, endlessly patient, picks it up. She tries again, until he kicks over the row of terracotta pots she has laid out in readiness. A little later, from the kitchen win-dow, I see him running off down the track into the field.

By the time I've made coffee, Rob is finishing up. 'Sure. Sure. No problem. See you then.'

His face is white as he steps into the cottage.

'Jed said the studio have got some questions. In the light of #MeToo.' And he drags a hand through his hair.

'They're not sure if Amélie should be French,' he says, and as he turns in frustration, he slams his head against the beam. He swears. The kids look up from their Lego.

'They're talking about setting it in the US. So, Amélie becomes Cindy or Shelley. I mean, what the actual fuck,' he says, in a furious whisper as he stares down at Sam's Plasticine animals lined up on the chopping board.

'So, I said that would be tricky, that the whole point was the existential crisis with Sartre and Amélie,' he says, pacing around the small square of kitchen, his voice getting louder.

'Shall we go back out?' I suggest, nodding over at the kids.

I sit on the bench while he circles the table. I don't know what to say. I feel the weight of his mood roll back into position like a boulder.

'*Cindy?*' he scoffs. 'Instead of Amélie. Jesus. The whole script depends on it being a French exchange student.'

He rants and raves and I try to offer something. Small nuggets of support.

'Fucking #MeToo. Don't they get it? Irony. It's i-ron-ic.'

I sip my coffee.

'They keep going on about the sensitivity of "the affair",' he says, making dramatic air quotes. '*There is no affair*. That's the whole point. It's in his head. He's a fool—'

Over in the field, I can hear Joyce calling Leo. A gentle voice as she walks towards him on the far side by the outer fence.

'So, I try to say this, I tell them I'm not sure a character called

Cindy or Shelley or whatever the fuck they want to call her fits very well with the Sartre motif.'

'Exactly,' I nod, 'I mean, that's the whole point—'

'So, there's this long silence – and then Jed says, *well, we might have to think about losing Sartre.*'

He turns to me, hands open wide, aghast.

'*Losing Sartre?*' I repeat.

'Precisely.' He nods vigorously. 'Sartre *is* the screenplay. It's the whole point. Matt's midlife crisis. His existential angst. Bad Faith. The death of his father. His delusion. Amélie's obsession with Sartre. Don't they get it?' He runs his hands through his hair. 'There is no screenplay without Sartre.'

He looks away across the field, then jerks his head back.

'Apparently it came from the actors. They had "questions",' he says, with more violent air quotes. 'I mean, isn't the point of an actor to just say their lines? To do their job. Be good at that? Since when is it an actor's job to comment on content? On issues of sensitivity. Why does everyone have to get involved in everything? When did the personal become so bloody political?'

And that's when it comes. The bombshell that hasn't occurred to me. 'They want me to have a meeting on Thursday. I need to fly out as soon as I can. I'll have to go to London this afternoon—'

It takes me a moment to take it in. 'Fly to where?'

'LA,' he says. 'They want me to rework things. Rework? Jesus. Rework a film about an existential midlife crisis about a middle-aged bloke's ridiculous fantasy about a French exchange student. And take out Sartre. And set it in the US.'

He thumps his palm on the table. 'There. Is. No. Story.'

I say it before I think. Before I can help myself.

'You're leaving?' I am open-mouthed. 'When? For how long?'

He shrugs. 'I don't know. I mean, this isn't something I've

planned. I have no idea,' he says, brusquely. 'Jesus – what are you even asking me?'

'But your boys are coming,' I say, and I can hear the panic in my voice. 'When's that?'

'End of June,' he says, shaking his head. 'But this is a disaster. A project I've been working on for the last five years. Looks like it might get pulled – and you're worried about the twins coming?'

I feel stung. Then I have that familiar small feeling in the face of his anger. Being reduced by his big emotions and his wild and mercurial moods. And all the while, I am consumed by the prospect of being holed up alone, with two kids under five, in a cottage no bigger than a rat's nest.

*

Rob goes to get fish and chips for lunch, and when he returns, he looks up at the collage of photographs as if he's noticing them for the very first time. 'I mean, who does that?' he snaps. 'What the actual fuck? Who sits at a table with scissors and glue and makes something like that?'

He stands up and peers at the picture. 'Just look at that bloke cooking sausages. What a wanker.'

He looks again. 'Is he naked under that apron? What an utter tosser,' he says. 'Why do people feel the need to parade their joy like that?' and on he rants in a way that is familiar and weirdly comforting. 'Public displays of happiness are obscene.'

He jabs at his chips. Shovels in mouthfuls of fish. 'They're probably bankers. Or lawyers,' he says, waving a fork in the general direction. A piece of fish flies off and lands in his lap.

I listen. I keep quiet.

'I wonder which one is Amanda,' he says, 'the owner.'

I already know who Amanda is. Amanda is the one holding the camera, taking the pictures and documenting these family gatherings. Recording these moments of family joy that she can press into memories that she puts on a collage. On the day we arrived, I'd scanned the picture. There was a small snap in the corner. A woman with a neat blonde bob, her arms round the two blonde daughters. That's her, I thought. That's Amanda.

After lunch, Rob reads to the kids. Book after book. He lets them choose. He reads the same book over and over. Somewhere in between the fifth and sixth reading of *Green Eggs and Ham*, he tells them about the trip.

'On a plane?' says Ruby, wide-eyed. 'Eight hours?'

And she thinks about this for a moment, then asks how he will go to the toilet.

'When will you be back?' asks Sam.

'Hopefully in a week. But I'm not too sure,' he says.

A week? My heart sinks, already knowing it'll be longer.

We drop him at Dorchester station. 'Family hug,' he says, and he gathers us all up in a giant squeeze that makes the kids laugh.

'I'll ring from the train,' he says.

'Great,' I say, 'I'll be at the picnic table, waiting.'

On our way back we stop at a café for cake. I let the kids order what they like and then after the overcast morning, the sun breaks through and we sit outside in the garden. There's a soggy sandpit in the corner and they busy themselves with plastic scoops and spades as if they were on the beach.

As I drink my tea, I notice a couple arrive at the table near-by. The woman is pushing a double buggy. Baby twins. She looks tired, hair hanging down over her face. She's in joggers and a tracksuit top with a stain down the front. The man is wearing an estate agent blue suit. It's too small and stretches tight across his thighs. As their plates of food arrive, one of the babies starts to cry. She leans over and scoops him up. He nuzzles into her neck, getting suddenly frantic, fists flailing. She unzips her top and feeds him. Opposite, the man is feasting on his plate of bacon, beans and eggs, a hand reaching intermittently into the basket of toast.

When the baby is finished, she shifts him up in her arms, his head resting on her shoulder. She picks at her now cold plate of food. The man has pushed his plate away, wiped a sleeve across his face and is tapping at his phone and chuckling. The woman jabs at the food with her fork. The baby wriggles in her arm.

He chuckles again. I imagine he's watching YouTube videos – funny clips of dogs falling off planks or hilarious goalkeeper errors. Either way, it keeps him amused. It's only when the other baby in the buggy starts to fuss that he glances up. 'Just a sec,' he says, tapping into his phone. More laughter. Then eventually, he reaches across to take the baby she has fed, as she leans down to pick up the other.

He is slow to notice, even slower to help. She doesn't ask.

And I feel a rush of irritation for them both. But mostly, I realise, for her.

On our way back, we stop at the supermarket and the kids choose comics and Kinder Eggs from the toy machine. As we get in the car, there's a plane overhead.

'Is that Daddy?' Ruby asks.

'Yep, there he goes,' I say. 'Whooosh,' and I fly my hand through the air.

*

Back at the cottage, Philip, Penny's father, is at the picnic table reading the paper. He has earphones in and doesn't hear us come back. He looks startled when the kids clamber up onto the table. And it's clear he feels trapped by our arrival, that had he seen us coming, he'd have discreetly slipped back inside through the door that opens onto his small patch of lawn. I've seen him do it several times already, a flash of movement when we've come out into the garden, scurrying off before he gets embroiled in conversation. It's clear he's avoiding us. Or more likely avoiding the noise and exuberance of the children.

'Sorry,' I say to him, then try to usher the kids away. 'Philip's reading. Let him have some peace and quiet.'

Ruby makes a pouty face. 'But we have biscuits,' she says, pushing the plastic plate towards him. She has arranged the fingers of shortbread in a circle, like petals on a flower.

'How lovely,' he says, and he stays seated, clearly not wanting to offend her, and after further encouragement from Ruby, he helps himself to one.

He has a cup on the table and I point to the pot I've brought out on a tray, and this too he accepts. We've exchanged greetings over the fence, but this is the first time I've seen him properly. He has a solid handsome face. White hair cropped short, with a neat salt and pepper beard. He's wearing a soft wool navy jumper and jeans. He looks perhaps in his late sixties, but has a kind of distinguished youthful air about him.

We chat about the weather. The coastal walks. Rob's departure. Chit-chat as I pour the tea. He tells me he's staying with Penny for a month or so. 'She's recently got divorced. Said she wanted the company. But really,' he smiles, 'I think she wanted to keep an eye on me.'

When I ask about the book, he looks momentarily surprised, and blinks back at me, pushing his glasses up onto the bridge of his nose.

He goes on to explain how he took six months' study leave, that it was his first proper break in forty years. 'I wrote about thirty thousand words,' he says, then he sips his tea. 'But now I'm not sure if I want to write it after all.'

The children have eaten the petals of biscuits one by one and are now on the grass arguing over the toys they got from the machine.

He smiles at me. 'If I was a priest, I might say I was having a crisis of faith.'

His openness is disarming. Perhaps it's because I've been spending so much time with Helen. I'm taken aback, and for a moment, I'm not sure what to say.

'I'm a psychiatrist,' he says, helping me out, 'and a psycho-therapist. I work in addiction. Mainly drugs and alcohol.'

'NHS?'

He nods. Then after a pause, 'Joyce tells me you're a GP.'

'That's right,' I say, 'I'm on a sabbatical,' and the word feels lumpen in my mouth.

He looks away across the fields. 'It's a very difficult time to work in the NHS,' he says slowly. 'The National *Health* Service – the health bit sometimes feels the least of it. It's all the other stuff that drags people down.'

He turns back to me. 'Did you work in London?' he asks, and when I tell him Tower Hamlets, he smiles, 'Well, I'm sure you know what I mean.'

At first, I think he's alluding to the systems and red tape and the bureaucracy of work in the public sector, but he shakes his head. 'Oh no,' he says, 'I steered clear of all that. Never went into management. Just ran a specialist clinical team in South London.'

He goes on to say he had this desire to consolidate his work, to write about the case studies, the forty years of clinical practice.

'But the more I wrote, the more I concluded the circumstances of some people's lives are hard,' he says, 'right from the beginning. I felt overwhelmed . . .' his voice drifts off.

Fleetingly, I think of Mrs Chandra. The Robsons. Their damp squalid living conditions. The neglected estate.

I look back at his open face, his warm kind eyes, and I see he looks genuinely anguished. He tells me it wasn't a new revelation, one he's felt many times over the years, 'but there was something about the process of sifting through my work, selecting the cases I wanted to write about. I was struck by the power of that choice. It left me feeling very uncomfortable,' he says. 'There I was, in my nice middle-class life, writing a book about my patients' very difficult lives –' he pauses, '– I don't know. I felt a sense of guilt in the power and privilege I had. Or in the omnipotent belief that we can turn the tide, like it's an easy thing to do.'

I think of Keith. His angry words in my room. *You hold all the power. We're just the little people.*

'I'm sorry,' he smiles, 'my daughter thinks all the writing is making me far too introspective – perhaps she's right.'

He is silent for a moment, as if gathering his thoughts.

'But surely therapy helps?' I say. 'To understand what's happened? To make change? And anyway, addiction doesn't discriminate.'

'True,' he nods, 'but the hardest bit is always *sustaining* the change. That's so much trickier when you're poor. When you have no money. No resources.'

He talks about the other important things in someone's recovery. 'A nice place to live. Money to buy decent clothes,' he shrugs, 'a sense of self-worth, status and independence. I mean, some of the halfway houses that I've visited across the country

83

– simply indescribable. Not a great advert for the "life without drugs" is better message,' he laughs.

He reaches into his pocket and pulls out a white square of a handkerchief and flaps it open like a flag. He carefully takes off his glasses with the other hand.

'Sometimes it's just the roll of a dice, isn't it?' he says, as he cleans his glasses. 'Right from the beginning.'

'Yes,' I agree, 'it is.'

'I mean, human decency,' he smiles, 'it's not rocket science, is it?'

He places the clean glasses back on his nose.

I take in his earnest face. How he talks with such compassion about his work and his patients. I want to say something about the kindness I can feel, about all the people he must have helped. I want to say something about hope. But I, too, feel defeated.

He tells me he was left with some questions he struggled to answer. 'I felt in touch with the pointlessness of what I do.' He holds his hands out. 'My loss of faith laid bare,' and then he clears his throat. 'Speaking of which,' he says, slightly reeling back at his self-revelation, 'my apologies. I hadn't intended to be so confessional.'

I shake my head. 'It's interesting.'

He smiles. 'It makes a welcome change from having to talk enthusiastically with my daughter about a book I'm not even sure I want to finish.'

There's a moment of silence.

'Maybe you need to write a different sort of book,' I venture, 'about what you've been talking about. The guilt. The hopelessness. I'm sure it will resonate with other clinicians.'

He considers this briefly, looking back at me.

'Anyway,' he says, leaning forwards to pat his hand on the table in front of me, 'your turn. Tell me about your GP sabbatical.'

It's a relief, in that moment, to see Penny's car turn into the gravel track. He looks over in her direction and lifts his hand to wave. Then, turning back to me, he says, 'To be continued, another time.' Then he eases himself up from the picnic table and dips his head towards me. 'Thank you,' he says with real sincerity, 'for listening. And for the tea,' and then he makes a point of walking over to Ruby and thanking her for the shortbread, 'and its magnificent presentation.'

She beams back at him.

And then he is gone, slipping back into the cottage.

*

When I tell Joyce the change of plan for that evening, she's delighted to have the kids; she says she'll take them to see the new piglets. 'We'll have a lovely time,' she says. 'Kirsty's room's at the top of the stairs, second on the right.'

I am a little early. I set up my computer, and I look around the teenage room. A map of the world. Her route drawn out in a thick red line on the poster. I think about Thailand where I once went travelling. The crystal-clear water. The white sand. I scan her shelves; books, jewellery, posters of bands and celebrities I don't recognise.

When we link up, it's weird at first, just to see Veronica's head and shoulders, not to be sitting on the soft oatmeal sofa. But I quickly adjust and I'm surprised to find myself talking about my father. I talk about his strange mini-break. His speedy return home. The mystery of it all. 'So odd,' I say, 'so unlike him.' I tell her he's reserved. Quiet. Repressed. 'But lately he's been different. More outgoing.'

85

I tell her all about his depression. His heavy weighty moods when I was a child. I didn't plan on talking about any of this. In fact, as I was climbing the stairs to Kirsty's room, my mind was blank. I had no idea – or even desire – to talk that day. But silence would have been intolerable. Especially on a Zoom call.

'We'd have to be really quiet,' I tell her, 'me and Gemma. Mum told us he was working. She'd tell us to keep the noise down, "play quietly," she'd say, a finger on her lips.

'But I knew it wasn't work. I didn't know what it was, but I knew it was the opposite of activity. I'd peer at him through the crack of his study door. He'd be sitting neatly in his chair, hands folded in his lap, staring into space.

'I'd come back hours later, and check up on him. Creeping along the corridor. And his shape. His hands. The direction of his gaze. All unchanged.'

'What did you make of it at the time?' Veronica wants to know.

I shake my head. 'I don't know. I just felt the weight of it. Something I didn't understand.'

She thinks about this for a moment. 'I can feel the heaviness of it as you talk,' she says, 'it feels suffocating. Silencing.' She wants to know if we talked about it. 'Your mother and you girls?'

'Not that I can remember. I just had a sense of us accommodating him. This giant elephant of a mood. It was something to co-exist with. We tiptoed around him. We were quiet, inconspicuous. We got smaller. It was as if the black mood had fallen from the sky. There was no sense that he had any control over it.' I pause for a moment. 'There was a kind of passivity about it. Like it was a giant hand pressing down on him.'

She asks when I first noticed it. 'Was it before your sister got ill?'

I'd mentioned a little about Gemma in passing, and several times Veronica has returned to it. And I'm aware that, every time, I feel a resistance. A pull away.

I think about this for a moment. Casting my mind back over those blurry two years. 'Afterwards, I think,' and then I nod, remembering that when Gemma went into hospital, Dad rarely came. 'It was mainly me and Mum,' I say, 'he must have been at home. Sitting in his chair.'

She nods.

'But you know,' I say, 'it's so strange that his mood, something so passive and inactive, could wield such power.'

It's towards the end of the session that she talks about the different theories of depression. 'There are many,' she says, doing that twirl of her hand. 'But there is one I have found to be helpful. And one that may explain the weight, the force. One theory understands depression as anger turned inwards.'

There's a pause. I think about this.

'It may explain why it emanates such power. Such fear,' she says, 'and can feel so immobilising. And your mother? What did she do? How was she with him?'

'She fussed about. Mollified, accommodated. Appeased. Perhaps it's how I learnt to do the same,' and I know, as soon as I say this, she will ask me to elaborate and so I find myself filling the space in order to block the question. 'But you know, I believe my mother was angry too. I think she felt a kind of concealed vitriol for his weakness. And when he got better, it came out. Like well-aimed poisoned darts.'

And at the end of the session, she comes back to my sister.

'A child that doesn't eat. A child that refuses the most basic of human functioning, the withholding of nourishment needed to survive. This must evoke a deep sadness. But also,' she considers, 'a kind of rage. And I find my thoughts returning to this, and how little we have talked about it here.'

*

Joyce is picking me some beans from her vegetable patch when we hear a shriek. Sam comes hurtling out of the kitchen.

'There's a gun,' he sobs, 'in the kitchen,' and he runs at me, flinging himself into my arms.

Startled, I look up at Joyce.

She crouches down next to him. 'The one up on the wall?'

He nods, his eyes wide and fearful. He's trying very hard not to cry.

'Is it for the bad people? Are there bad people here?' he gulps. 'Dad said there can be bad people everywhere. But not here?' He looks stricken. 'By the seaside—'

His body shudders. I realise he's referring to the 'stranger danger' chat we'd all had a few months back, which was prompted by Sam's fervent belief that 'bad people' only lived in big cities.

Joyce sits down on the grass and pats the space next to her. Still clinging onto my hand, he drops down by her side.

'So,' she says, 'because you're a big man, I'm going to tell you the truth. It would be a lie for me to tell you that you can't find bad people at the seaside. Your dad is right, there are bad people everywhere. But, and this is a *very big* but – there are very few bad people. A tiny amount,' and she puts her hands up, her thumb and forefinger a minuscule space apart. 'There are many more good people than bad people – it's like the good ones squash out all the bad ones with their loveliness and kindness.'

He seems to like this. I feel the grip of his hand relax in mine.

'The next thing to tell you is that gun on the wall is not for people.'

He blinks back at her.

'It's to scare off pests who might kill or harm our animals. All farmers have to have a gun. That's a rifle, and Pete sometimes uses it when the foxes come to worry the lambs. He fires it in the air to scare them away—'

'What would a fox do to the lambs?'

'Well – it might really hurt them – and the lambs are very small. They need to be protected, until they get bigger.'

He thinks about this for a minute. 'So, the gun can save the lambs?'

'Exactly.'

'By the noise?'

'Exactly. And you see where it was – high up, in that special case?'

He nods.

'It's up there, out of reach, because it's just for Pete to use. No one else. OK?'

'OK.'

EIGHT

Seeing Keith's name at the top of my list on that Thursday morning landed like a heavy stone. I was exhausted. Ruby had woken with a nightmare and when she'd eventually fallen asleep in my bed, I'd lain awake for the duration, willing myself to go back to sleep, and ruminating about how dreadful I'd feel if I didn't. Rob was away again, and having to do all the nursery pick-ups and drop-offs was eating into my non-patient time. Admin was piling up, including the stack of out-patient letters I had yet to review before they were uploaded onto patient files. So, that day, before I pressed the buzzer to reception, I closed my eyes, bracing myself for the sensory overload of what was to come; the jaunty energy, the jokey banter and the barrage of irrelevant detail.

But when Keith knocked on the door, he was slow to come in, and when he did, his movements were muted, in sharp contrast to his usual Tigger-like entry. He was muttering about the appointment system. 'What do you have to do these days,' he asked, 'sell your soul to the devil?'

I said I was sorry if he had to wait. 'It's been exceptionally busy.'

He rolled his eyes. 'We're all busy,' he said, as he sat down in the chair by my desk.

He was wearing a grey hoodie, shorts and a black baseball cap. He explained he'd come straight from the gym. 'Go every morning before work. Nina thinks I'm nuts. But you've got to look after yourself, don't you? Keep everything in good working order, eh?' and he clapped his hands together. His upbeat stance seemed strained. A little tried for.

'What can I do for you today?'

He said he'd had a 'funny turn' and told me about the dizziness and the breathing difficulty, 'like I couldn't get enough air into my lungs.'

He told me he was at Power Gym in Bethnal Green, how he was training for a marathon.

'Can you describe what happened?' I said with a tight smile.

'Suddenly woozy and lightheaded,' he said. 'But then an odd feeling. Like an out-of-body experience, as if I was floating somewhere up above, watching myself,' he said, shaking his head. 'And my heart was going like the clappers. And I was really hot. Pouring with sweat, hadn't even started my workout,' he laughed, and went on to give me details about his cross-training programme. 'It was day two, so it was squats and bench presses. A hundred of each—'

'So, all this was happening *before* you'd stated exercising?' I cut in.

He nodded. 'I was just standing in reception, chatting to Bob, he was telling me about some big family party. Talking about his grandkids or something – and then bang. That's when it started.'

'OK, talk me through it,' I said.

'I think I started to feel hot at first. Then it was the racing heart – out of nowhere. Then the breathing problem after that. My legs felt wobbly, like jelly. Thought I might keel over. Bob had to get me a chair. Then there was a pain in my chest.'

When I asked him to describe the pain, he hesitated, thinking back.

'Was it a sharp stabbing pain, or more of a dull heavy pressure?'

'More of a stabbing one, I think,' he said. 'Like lots of little needles, right across here,' and he stroked his hand across his upper torso.

'Had anything like this before?' I asked.

He shook his head. 'I thought about going straight to A&E – but then it got better. I skipped the training session and went home. I felt fine. Tried to book an appointment here. *Three weeks*, I was told, if I wanted to see you. So, when I got the racing heart thing again as I was walking home just now, I phoned in, and they said there was one emergency slot left.' He picked at his fingernail, then looked up at me, his gaze meeting mine. 'Lucky,' he nodded, 'it was you I wanted to see,' and as he spoke, a strange look passed across his face. One I couldn't read.

'So, the "funny turn" you describe, when things were really bad – when was this?'

He thought for a moment. 'It was day two . . . so . . . it would have been Tuesday.'

'Any chest pain since?'

He shook his head.

I told him I'd do a few checks, and as I reached for the blood pressure monitor, I asked some more general questions. 'Had you had breakfast that morning? Plenty of fluids?'

He nodded.

'Anything different about that morning? Anything happen this week?'

Again, a protracted pause. An odd stare. He shook his head again.

I unwrapped the arm band with the rasp of Velcro, and he peeled off his hoodie to the sudden smell of sweat and after-shave. He was wearing a black singlet, tight over his obviously toned upper body. His arms and biceps looked comical, almost cartoon-like in their sculpted contours.

As I wrapped it around the top of his arm, his hand curled into a tight fist. He flexed his arm. The muscles strained against the material. I stopped. Felt an involuntary flinch inside.

'You'll need to relax your arm,' I said, neutrally.

'Ah, reflex reaction,' he said. 'All those blood tests. I've been needing to pump up my fist to get a vein.'

In that moment, I clocked that he was referring to his tests at the fertility clinic. But I chose not to pick up on it. Partly because it was something that concerned them as a couple and separate from his presenting problem that day, but mostly because I always knew I had to keep Keith Strutt on track. That if I let him deviate, even a little, we'd get hopelessly lost and distracted and I'd be running over time, before I'd even finished my first patient of the day.

There was a silence as I pumped up the air. Then waited. I jotted down the figures (119/70). 'That's good,' I said. 'Very good in fact.'

We sat in silence. The slow wheeze as the air released. I unclasped the band. Another rasp of Velcro. I wound it back up and placed it on the shelf. Then reaching for the stethoscope, I got him to breathe in and out, taking deep breaths as I moved the diaphragm around to listen. 'All good,' I said, as I folded it up and put it in my drawer.

As I turned back to face him, he told me he thought he was having a heart attack. 'It was pretty scary,' he said slowly.

I nodded. Then I went on to reassure him. Told him everything looked fine. 'I'm not picking up anything to worry about. If anything, I'd say you were very much in the healthy category of normal,' I smiled.

He didn't respond. There was something in the room between us. Something that jarred. Felt off. But I couldn't work out what it was.

'As a precaution, I can send you for an ECG,' I continued. 'That will monitor resting heart rate. They keep it on for a few hours. Shows up any signs of abnormality. But as I say, it's more to put your mind at rest, rather than anything else. I can't see anything wrong with your heart. All looks and sounds good.'

Still nothing. A sheen of sweat had formed above his upper lip.

'So, what was it then?' he said.

'Well, it's hard to be completely certain. Sometimes these things can arise from being dehydrated . . . or exercising without eating. Stuff like that. But from what you describe,' I said carefully, 'your symptoms sound very much like some sort of stress reaction. Like a minor panic attack—'

He reeled back dramatically, puffing up his chest as he did so.

'A *what*?' he said, a look of disdain on his face.

I told him it was a physiological reaction, the body's response to stress. 'An increased heart rate, then you start to over-breathe. Take too much air into your lungs. Then it makes you start to hyperventilate. This can make you feel dizzy – and then it can sometimes trigger pain in—'

'No,' he said, shaking his head briskly, cutting me off mid-explanation.

I sat back.

'Definitely not. Why would I be *panicky*?' he said, raising his voice slightly. 'What have I got to be stressed about?' He looked around the room in mock exaggeration. 'I'm fine.'

I began to try to explain how the body can sometimes be out of sync with the feelings and thoughts we might be aware of. 'Some stress reactions can feel like they come out of nowhere—'

'I'd like to be referred to a specialist,' he said emphatically. 'My quick Google search suggests these symptoms are similar to those of a heart attack.'

Inwardly, I sighed. I kept my voice calm, even. 'Pain for a heart attack would have continued after the initial episode last Tuesday. And it would have been a different type of pain,' I said. 'The racing heart and difficulty breathing are more indicative of a panic reaction.'

'Perhaps you've missed something,' he said, his face fixed on mine. 'Glossed over something important?' His tone was firm. Hardening as he spoke. But mostly, it was the way he fixed me with his eyes. The unnerving stillness of his sweaty face. 'Mistakes happen,' he said tightly. 'It wouldn't be the first time.'

I stared back at him, confused. 'We don't refer to Cardiology unless there are grounds to,' I said. 'And at the moment, based on what you've told me, and the investigations I've just done, there aren't any reasons to refer.'

He didn't speak.

'My suggestion would be to refer you for an ECG, which, as I already explained, is a cautionary measure. I can do that now.'

I typed into my computer, then printed out the form.

He edged his chair closer.

I told him he could go in anytime to the Royal London. 'You could go across now, if you have time? They see people on a drop-in basis.'

I handed the paper across to him. He didn't move. My hand hung in the air. Eventually I put it on the desk.

'The heart is a pretty important organ in the body, wouldn't you say?' he said, leaning forwards. 'I'd like to get it checked out.'

His gaze was still on my face. He smiled. A strange smile. Lips slightly parted. His mouth looked small, tight. And then, he sat back in his chair, as if relaxing into an armchair, stretching his arms above his head, his legs falling open.

I blinked back at him.

Fleetingly, I thought of Dr Levenson, the cardiologist, his strict referral criteria. Our recent altercation over a previous patient he deemed a 'waste of my time'.

If I'm honest, I was struggling to focus. I'd already had two coffees, but my head was still foggy. When I think back to the appointment, it was as if we'd spent it underwater. Swirling about in a murky underworld. The struggle to communicate. The sense of disconnection. The exchange of words back and forth felt like bubbles of air. I had a strong feeling of wanting to get out. Like I was flailing about wildly, looking for the chink of light to swim to.

'Let's see the results of the ECG first. We can take it from there,' and I nudged the paper towards him. And as I did so, he carefully placed his hand on the desk, palm down, fingers splayed. Our hands were almost touching.

'Oh, you people,' he said with quiet contempt, 'sitting in judgement . . . holding all the power. Having information that can affect a person's whole life. I guess we're the little people. We don't really matter.'

I frowned. Was he still talking about the bloody lights? *Really?*

'You're making a mistake here,' he said, his voice cold. Clinical. His eyes glittered with anger. 'And this isn't the first time I've been on the receiving end of such shoddy treatment.'

I felt it then. The bristling of his rage. Under that careful measured sense of stillness and control was something else. Something wild and unpredictable. Something that could rise up and snap. It was something I didn't want to see. I felt my stomach contract. I moved my hand away.

But as I did so, he curled his fingers into a fist that he thumped on my desk. 'What kind of an operation are you running here?'

he shouted as my pen rolled to the floor. 'This place is a joke. The whole of the NHS is one big joke.'

As I reached down to pick up my pen, my head was pounding. My throat was dry. My overriding feeling was of wanting to end the session. So, I pulled back. I retreated. It was a feeling I knew well. A familiar reflex response, like moving a hand away from a boiling kettle.

I did what he wanted. I agreed to the referral.

'Good,' he said triumphantly. 'You'll do it today,' he said. It was a statement, not a question.

I stood up abruptly.

He stood too.

Having moved his chair slightly forwards, he was now standing a bit too close. I shuffled back. With my office chair now wedged against the wall, I felt trapped.

'You'll get the initial feedback from the ECG straight away,' I explained, 'and a copy of the results will be sent here. I don't know how long the out-patient appointment will take, but you should get a letter in the next two weeks. You may have to wait. Most departments are still struggling with the post-Covid backlog.'

A grunt of ridicule. 'Perhaps they should employ more doctors,' he suggested, 'if they can't keep up with referrals?'

Employ more doctors? I thought, as if we were van drivers delivering water filters.

Still he didn't move. So, in the end, I stepped past and walked round him to the door.

'Was there anything else?' I said, my fingers pushing down on the handle.

He was lingering by my desk, and nodded towards the picture on my shelf. 'Your kids,' he said, 'must be coming up to school age?' He nodded to himself. 'Nice.'

I felt a flutter of something in my chest.

Then he grabbed the form for the ECG and stormed out of my office.

I was unnerved by what had happened. I went over to the sink, and my fingers were trembling as I splashed water on my face. In the mirror, my cheeks were red and blotchy. I sat down at my desk and took some long slow breaths to calm myself down.

After the initial shock, I then felt furious with myself for how I'd behaved, or how I hadn't behaved. For allowing myself to be bullied and coerced by this small puffed-up man and his un-necessary request. I felt appalled by my formless shape, and the way I annihilated my professional knowledge and accountabil-ity. Already I was anticipating the letter I'd have to write to Dr Levenson, the fawning gratitude and the explanations. Perhaps I'd have to exaggerate Keith's anxiety symptoms to explain it away. What else could I say? That I felt bullied by a man with a tight angry mouth? That my husband was away and I was tired from sleepless nights with small children? That I had no idea what was going on in the appointment? That I really wanted him to leave, so I caved in? It was a complete waste of time and money to refer Keith Strutt to Cardiology. I knew it, and Dr Levenson would know it. The only thing I felt grateful for was that Erica, my trainee, hadn't been sitting in. *Come and watch how **not** to do a patient consultation.* But of course, I also knew it would have rolled out very differently for both of us, had I not been on my own.

It was later on, mid-morning, when I went out to get some more sample bottles from reception, that Sandra stepped back from the desk. 'Was everything OK,' she asked, 'with Keith Strutt?' I was startled by the question. 'It's just that he made a point of coming to the desk after his appointment and asking about the complaints procedure. Wanted to know if it was through the practice? Or the local CCG?'

I blinked back at her. '*He* wanted to complain?' I said, frowning. My voice was loud, indignant. Melanie and Fatima both looked up from their computers. I lowered my voice. 'Should be *me* putting in a complaint,' I hissed. 'What about? What did he say?'

She shook her head. 'He really just mentioned something about some kind of procedural issue. Talking about how one mistake can lead to another,' and she then dropped her voice to a whisper. 'To be honest, I didn't want to get involved. I just directed him to the details on the website. I thought it best not to get into it – you know,' and she nodded out to the waiting room, 'out here.'

'Quite,' I said. 'You did the right thing.'

As I walked back to my room, it was my turn to feel incandescent with rage. *A complaint about me?*

At lunchtime, after a long surgery, my eyes were gritty with tiredness. I swallowed the rest of the remaining coffee, took two bites from the egg and cress sandwich I'd bought yesterday, and joined the Zoom meeting with Sarita, the domestic abuse advocate, to follow up about Terri Garner. Terri was still pregnant and we were concerned about her safety, and the safety of the baby. We discussed the case, and as always, Sarita was calm, but very clear about her concerns. 'Pregnancy is high risk. A very dangerous time for both mother and child. If he finds out, the perpetrator can feel a loss of control. And the mere fact of being pregnant, means she has something that he doesn't.' She went on to talk about other warning factors, possible triggers to the escalation of violence. 'If Terri agrees, she needs to be referred to the Multi Agency Risk Assessment Conference.' I nodded, and confirmed that as far as I knew, she hadn't told her partner about the pregnancy, 'but that may have changed.' I also confirmed that while exploring the option of a termination, she also expressed a desire to keep the baby and leave her partner. 'She wasn't sure what she wanted to do,' I said, 'she was very emotional.' Sarita went on to say what I already knew, what I have already seen with countless women, that leaving, or the intention to leave, is a red flag, 'a time of increased danger that cannot be underestimated.' We ended the session with my agreeing I'd phone Terri to see if she'd be willing for Sarita to talk to her about safety planning, and that I'd email Sarita with an update when I had news.

By the end of afternoon surgery, the weekly stack of untouched out-patient letters still loomed on the shelf, waiting for me to read and hand over to the receptionist to upload them to the respective patient notes. Melanie had already put her head round the door to gently remind me that it had to be done by Friday. I had to leave on time to get to nursery, so I put them in my bag to review at home.

I was round the corner from the kids' nursery, in the narrow street which is used as a cut-through to the main road. That day I was some way down, when a car appeared at the other end and sped up. I noticed the acceleration, the swiftness of the driver to get beyond the small red zone by the pub that they could have pulled into to let me pass. Instead, the driver drove closer to my car. I watched the man sit back in his seat. It was a slight movement. But it told me everything. It told me he was waiting for me to move.

Ordinarily, I'd wait it out for a bit, then in the face of the cool hard stare of the opposing driver (usually male), I'd cave in, crunch my gears into reverse, then crane my neck behind me, before shifting the car backwards. It was a very narrow street, so it was always a slow and careful manoeuvre to avoid clipping the wing mirrors of the parked cars, until I reached the one gap in the street, by the offices, where I could pull in. I'd sigh heavily, cursing under my breath. And usually, if the driver was a man, I'd watch the car thunder by, without so much as a nod or wave of thanks. Mostly, they looked straight ahead. As if they expected me to back down and reverse. As if it was my role. Their right of way, so there was no need to thank me. And somehow, by being the first to lock my car into reverse, I allowed them this right. I did it all the time. My supplication was like a kind of muscle memory. I did it instinctively.

That day, I didn't move. My face blank. Even then I had no sense of what I might do. The man sat forwards. Peered back at me. As if giving me a double take. A look that seemed to say, *I'm waiting*. Neither of us moved. The man's nonchalance soon morphed into a glare. I simply looked back at him. And then he did what often came next in the face of any kind of delay. A slowness of response. He made a small gesture. A flick of his hand. Usually, if I managed to hold out until this point, this was the moment I gave in, acquiesced, usually with a deep sigh. The rumble of irritation, the swear words, before reversing reluctantly in the face of this stalemate. But that day, I sat still. The door and windows locked.

He shook his head and opened his window. 'You need to back up,' he said. He was perhaps in his thirties. A shirt and black anorak. Still, I didn't move. His face darkened. I felt the small slide of fear. Slick, like oil at the back of my neck. 'Hey!' he said. Another flick of his hand. Still, I didn't move. My breath misted up the front windscreen. Beads of sweat were collecting along my hairline. I could smell the tension on my body. Under my armpits. He swung his car door open.

'What's the matter with you?' he yelled. 'You need to back up.'
You need to back up.

You need to make the referral.

I didn't move. He got out of the car. A small reedy man, with his pot belly bulging over his trousers. At that point, I noticed a woman outside the pub opposite, sweeping up a broken glass from the pavement; she looked up. The man stopped. He realised there were witnesses. Whatever he was going to do, he checked himself. Thought better of it. He got back in the car. My response was to put my foot on the accelerator. I drove my car forwards, until it was close, perhaps just six feet away from his. I was near enough to see the twist of fury on his face. The curl of his mean lips. And I felt a kind of thrill. A sudden rush of adrenalin. A kind of excitement watching the rage on his face. I could see he was speaking out loud. Expletives, no doubt, aimed at me, but finally, he reversed.

I kept moving. He pulled into the pub layby. The place where the brewery lorries unloaded. As I drove past, I kept my eyes on the road ahead. He was leering out of his open window.

Cunt was the word that followed me up the street.

I drove on, my face ablaze with triumph. My heart thumping. My hands gripping the wheel in victory.

But by the time I picked up the kids and got home, my rush of euphoria had dissipated. I felt defeated.

I still had to write an obsequious letter to Dr Levenson. I'd still caved into the whims and demands of a weaselly patient I didn't like. Keith Strutt had still got his own way. When I told Rob about the appointment, the whole event sounded flimsy and inconsequential.

He took in my pale face. 'What an arsehole,' he said, trying to be sympathetic, but I could see he was distracted. He was reading through his evening teaching plan. I'd already lost his full attention.

'So now you're going to have to grovel to this consultant,' he said, missing the point entirely.

'It's not about the consultant,' I said, but when I tried to explain what it was about, I couldn't find the right words. And then he tried to pull me into a hug that I didn't really want. I resisted, and told him about the road rage incident. He listened as I began the story. 'What a wanker,' he said, shaking his head. But as my story gathered momentum, with all its fine dramatic detail, I noticed he was frowning. He then told me to be careful. 'Especially if you had the kids in the car. You could get yourself into a situation,' he said, 'you know. Something tricky.'

I felt the surge of fury.

'Do you remember,' I said, 'that time when we were away in Brittany? When you had to go into town to find an internet café?'

He was reaching into the fridge for a beer. Perhaps I imagined it, but I thought I saw his shoulders sink. Already preparing himself for the unknown weight of what was to come. I carried on. 'I'd taken the kids to the woods behind the house. Do you remember those woods? Those enormous fir trees – pine cones the size of grenades?'

He nodded, taking a swig from the bottle.

'It was quiet. No one about. We'd passed this guy on the way. I remembered him because he was wearing a yellow baseball cap. And not long after, he'd doubled back and was behind us. He seemed to be following us. Getting closer. Do you remember, I told you about it at the time?'

He nodded, vaguely. He clearly didn't remember.

I pressed on. 'Sam was two. Ruby just a baby – and so we

were moving slowly. There was no one else around. It was eerily quiet. I suddenly felt vulnerable. Ruby was strapped in the buggy, but I picked up Sam and moved fast. Moving towards the clearing. The open space where people were on the grass.'

'God, yes, I do remember. Awful,' he said, shaking his head.

I was nodding as he recollected the moment. 'But do you remember what you said when you got back?'

And that's when his face froze. The realisation that he knew he was heading into some kind of trap but had no idea what it was. When he spoke, his voice was tentative, a foot carefully feeling around a crumbling cliff edge.

'Umm – no – not really, it was a few years ago.'

'You were sympathetic,' I said, 'you were worried for me. For all of us. But you told me to *be careful*—'

He looks confused. 'So?'

I could see he was tired. But still, I ploughed on. 'Me being careful? Don't you see how significant that is? Just merely saying that. The fact that it was the thing that came most naturally for you to say.'

He stared back at me. 'You were on your own in the middle of a wood. With a man who was being weird. You were telling me you didn't feel safe. That you were scared. That the kids might have been in danger. Of course I was fucking telling you to be careful—' and he dragged his hands through his hair in exasperation.

'But that's the point, isn't it?' I said, triumphantly. '*I'm* the one who has to be careful. To watch where I'm going. To be mindful of a strange man lurking about. The point is – the responsibility is *on me*. The responsibility is always *on women*.'

He opened his mouth to speak, then thought better of it. Surprised by my outburst.

'It's become our responsibility to avoid the rapists and the murderers. To be mindful of all the weird fuckers out in the world. It's the angry men that have no boundaries. They're like cushions with the stuffing falling out – and we're the ones who have to stuff it back in again. It's up to us to say, no, you can't do that. That's not OK. It's *on us*,' I said again, jabbing at my chest. 'I mean, for fuck's sake – why can't men just keep their own fucking cushions in shape?'

He blinked back at me, startled by the tirade. He seemed to take a moment to try to find the right words.

'I don't know what to say,' he said, sounding defeated. Then he took a breath. 'This job – all the safeguarding stuff – I'm not sure it's a good thing. I mean, for you. For us. I feel like it's really getting to you. All these awful cases. Maybe you should take a break?'

I can't quite remember how I responded. But the row was short and explosive. Soon after, he left for his teaching course, and when the kids were in bed, I finally got out the stack of out-patient letters from my bag and flicked through them quickly. Mr Kahn's follow up at Dermatology. Angela Riley's biopsy showed her lump was benign. A visit to A&E for Pat Wilson. I paused, sifting this one out, putting it to one side to follow up. It was then I saw the letter from the fertility clinic. Nina Compton and Keith Strutt. I glanced at the date. Three days ago. I scanned quickly. The colour draining from my face. The results were there, in black and white. Clear and unequivocal.

NINE

My appraisal at work took place a few months before I had the first appointment with Nina and Keith. It had been delayed by the post-pandemic backlog of work, and I immediately noticed a different tone to the meeting. David was his usual jocular self. Kind and questioning, wanting to know if I had any problems. 'Anything you'd like to discuss?' and he asked about the safe-guarding role, commenting on how well I'd risen to the challenges in such unprecedented times. He then went on to talk about how he admired my dedication and my conscientiousness, my commitment to the team and the local community.

There was a pause.

'But,' he said carefully, 'the way you work can sometimes be a problem for the team.'

I was taken aback. Never before had my work been called into question. If anything, my conscientious nature and work ethic had always been seen as an example, something aspir-ational. Over the years, some supervisors have highlighted the importance of work/life balance, but they were the very same people who piled on more work when it suited them. When I joined the practice as a salaried GP, I worked hard, always put-ting myself forward when tasks were delegated. At the time, the two female partners had young children and were often mouthing 'childcare issues' as they rushed from evening sur-gery. I didn't have kids then. I hadn't even met Rob, but I found it irritating, and vowed, if ever I was in that situation, I'd not use motherhood as some kind of get-out-of-jail-free card.

Several years later, when I was pregnant with Sam, I was the GP rep at the locality forum. The chair, Michael Tompkins, was a retired GP, and at the end of the last meeting before my maternity leave, he sidled up to me as I was gathering up the discarded sheets of minutes. 'Just wanted to thank you for all you've done. And to wish you well,' he said, patting my arm. We exchanged pleasantries but still he lingered. 'You've been such an asset,' he said. 'I saw your talent right from the beginning. Youngest female partner in our hub. And you've made a fantastic contribution to the forum. We put our trust in you. I do hope we can count on that commitment and rigour returning. Don't want to see that fine brain of yours turn to mush.'

'I'm sorry?'

'All that training and hard work down the drain,' and he whirled his hand around to mimic the swirl of water.

I looked at him, not understanding.

'Baby brain,' he said. 'That's what we called it back in my wife's day. Probably can't say that now, can I? Might get *cancelled*,' and he roared with laughter, making a point of drawing his thumb and forefinger across his lips like a zip.

When I did come back to work, I worked harder than ever before, and a few weeks after my return David suggested I took on the safeguarding role.

'With Amy now on her secondment, we need a safe pair of hands,' he said. 'I know it might be hard at first – but I wondered if it was something you'd consider?'

He flattered me with comments about my attention to detail, my knowledge of the community, and how he thought I'd be the person staff would be able to approach. He paused. 'Amy was thorough. Excellent on the policies and procedures, but –' and he paused to make a face, '– her manner could be a little ferocious.

Not always the best response to sensitive safeguarding issues. People want to feel listened to. Contained. Have their worries taken seriously and in a sensitive manner. I really think it would be perfect for you.'

David was right in thinking it was the right role for me. I was both interested and suited to it. Managing safety and risk was hard work, and my learning curve was steep when I became part of the local Safeguarding Forum. The cases were often very disturbing. And in retrospect, what was I thinking taking on this role with a small baby? Most weeks I went home with my head full of the lives of neglected and abused children. And there was no let up. The next couple of years saw me working harder than ever, and in the midst of all this, I had another baby.

Then, when we were hit by Covid-19, along with many boroughs, our community and health care systems struggled to adjust. But we more than rose to the occasion. We accommodated the work, we navigated the chaotic government messages, the lack of PPE. We provided an excellent service to a community in turmoil and fear, and when the vaccine rolled out, we rotated shifts at the local vaccine hub. On top of all this, for me, the safeguarding role was busier than ever, with each of the three lockdowns exponentially raising the risk to both women and children.

As the crisis receded, we were burnt out. My trainee had gone off on long-term sick leave and, at the same time, we were bombarded with questionnaires about our mental wellbeing, advice about finding 'joy at work' as well as information about mandatory workshops on stamina and resilience. All the emphasis on 'building resilience' made me think of the construction of a wall. A defence against bad weather. Something that might look solid but would ultimately come down in the eye of a storm. All in all, I felt I'd managed exceptionally well under difficult circumstances, which was why my meeting with David came as such a shock.

I blinked back at him.

He pressed his hands together. 'This is a busy practice. Six partners, four salaried GPs and three trainees at any one time. To say nothing of the rest of the team.'

I waited.

'It's a large practice,' and he spread his hands out wide. 'It's not *Doc Martin*.'

'I don't understand,' I said, shaking my head.

'While we have patients that are registered with us as individuals, as you know, it's irrelevant, we will all see any patient. And we frequently do. And while General Practice is about developing your own style, keeping a sense of individuation, there are limits.'

Another pause.

'Sometime the stance you take,' he said carefully, 'can set a precedent for us. One that is not realistic or feasible for us all to adhere to.'

'What do you mean?'

'Often when I or one of the other partners explain why we are unable to meet a particular patient demand, we are told *Dr Gibson does that*, or *Dr Gibson has done that for me in the past*.'

I felt my cheeks flush.

With his head tilted to one side, he was speaking in a soothing tone that seemed out of sync with the content of his conversation.

'Don't get me wrong,' he said, 'I have full and unreserved admiration for your dedication. After all, it was me who fought for you to join the practice two months into your GP traineeship.'

I frowned at his empty flattery. 'What sort of things?' I wanted to know. My voice sounded tight and defensive.

'The housing letters. The home visits. Your insistence on

reviewing your own outpatient results,' he said, without hesitation. 'The extra time you spend. The number of double appointments you give out, the general tendency to go "above and beyond", your tendency to get *over-involved*,' he said, enunciating slowly, 'it causes difficulties.'

I was shocked. 'I meet all my targets,' I said defensively.

He shook his head. 'It's not about the targets. You *more than* meet your targets. It's about raising expectation in the practice. Setting a bar that we cannot – or simply do not want to – meet,' he said pointedly. Another broad smile.

Over-involved when? With whom? I wanted to know.

He was swift with his list. The Choudhurys, the Robsons and the Chandra family are the ones I hear first. But there are more. 'Sometimes we feel you cross a professional line.'

The mention of 'we' was crushing. The notion that I had been the focus of discussions among the partners.

'Have you seen the conditions in that block? The damp?'

He nodded.

'And we merrily carry on treating the bronchitis . . . the chronic asthma . . . all the health problems associated with that kind of living situation—'

He shook his head. 'It's not our job. It's not what we do. We're not responsible for their lives, any more than we're responsible for their health.'

'So, in our privileged position, we simply sit back and do nothing?'

He leant back in his chair and laced his fingers together. 'Do I think it's my job to save the community? To try and reduce the socio-economic divisions in the borough? No, I do not.'

A brief pause, and then he said, 'When you find yourself in these situations, I urge caution. A moment to think – is this really going to be constructive? Or is it simply for me? To make myself feel better?'

I went to speak, but he held his hand up. 'I believe it's misguided for you to assuage your guilt and sense of privilege by putting energy into doing some of the things you do.'

I stared back at him.

'As I have discussed with you on multiple occasions, in my capacity as CCG rep, I know how the housing process works in the council. It's a fantasy to think these letters have any impact. And raising the families' hopes and expectations is wrong.'

'Maybe I just care more?' It was a ridiculous thing to say. I regretted it as soon as the words came out of my mouth. It was a knee-jerk response to feeling criticised.

To his credit, he ignored it. He didn't deem it worthy of a response. 'If it makes you feel better about yourself to do all this, then that's a different matter. But to do it believing you're making a difference is delusional. And from now on, as senior partner, it's my job to help you understand it causes a problem for the rest of us.'

David worked very hard. He always left on time. He was efficient, but rigid. Was I envious of his male boundaries? His refusal to be pulled into the emotional undertow of his patients' lives? A responsibility I noticed he was happy to offload onto me when it suited.

He steepled his fingers under his chin. 'All this hand holding and brow mopping,' he said. 'They're patients. Not family members. You're a GP, not Mother Teresa. You need to rein things in a bit. Pull back.'

'Right,' I said, blinking hard.

What I didn't say was that I *did* feel responsible for my patients and for their lives. And that this was a role I liked and valued.

It was as simple as that. That small pinprick of something like satisfaction when I had been able to help. The joy of being able to make someone's life a tiny bit better. Was that so wrong?

It was sometime later that Veronica gave this tendency a name. Drew attention to its role in my working life. But also showing how the compulsion went much deeper, threading its way through every other area of my life.

TEN

'We're on the M3,' is the jaunty message I pick up from my mother. I call back and get her voicemail. On the second ring, she answers.

'We're about an hour away,' she says.

There's music in the car. It's hard to hear.

'An hour away from where?'

'From you!' she shouts over the music. 'Dad's driving. We're going to come to you first. Then on to the restaurant later this afternoon.'

'What restaurant?'

'The one we've booked for his birthday,' she says. She sounds exasperated. 'Didn't Gemma tell you?'

'No—'

I start to say something, but she cuts across me. 'We'll be there in an hour or so.'

In the background I hear my father saying something about a walk. But the music is too loud. She rings off before I can reply.

As I glance out of the window, I see James and the kids laughing as they load up the car. Buckets and spades, towels and packed bags in a trail of neatness. I look over at our small lounge area. Discarded clothes. A pack of wet wipes. The crust of last night's sandwich. Two empty juice cartons.

I walk over to the picnic table and call Gemma.

She yawns as she answers the phone.

When I ask her, she's vaguely apologetic about forgetting to tell me. 'I was going to call you this morning,' she says.

'What's going on?'

She tells me that Dad has changed his birthday plan, cancelling the long-standing arrangement to have a dinner in his college at Oxford.

'Why?'

'Dunno,' she says, 'but he seems pretty happy about it. He's found somewhere else. Out near you. One of the telly chefs. Really nice place,' she says, 'I've looked it up.'

I don't know what to say. My irritation at Gemma forgetting to tell me is eclipsed by a general state of confusion. And a kind of horror that my parents will be arriving in an hour.

'Oh – did you have plans?' she says.

And then I hear rustling and shuffling sounds. The sound of a duvet being moved. It's half past ten and she's still in bed.

Another yawn.

'Apparently the place does a set menu, but you can go off-piste for special occasions,' she says. 'Mum asked if I'd help with the menu.'

I bet she did.

'I don't understand,' I say, 'he was really looking forward to the dinner. He's been planning it for months.'

I can imagine her shaking her head. Tossing her beautiful hair over her beautiful shoulders.

'Well, it's a new plan. *His* new plan,' she says.

'But Max was going to do the speech. Some of his students were going to be there – I just don't get it—'

'Does it matter where he has it? It's just a birthday,' she says. I'm surprised by her clipped offhand tone and I imagine her disengaging, picking up a book or leafing through the pages of a magazine.

It's then that I think about the ceremony. The accolade he didn't receive.

'You don't think it's got anything to do with him not getting the Emeritus award?' and as soon as I've asked the question, I wish I hadn't.

She sighs and I can picture her slightly glazed expression as she inspects her skin. It's what she always does when she's bored. I've never known anyone inspect their body like my sister does. Peering at her forearms. The freckles. The blemishes. The skin around her knee bone. This habit she has of talking to you while poring over her body constantly. She does it with everyone. I remember her ex-boyfriend Marcus watching in a kind of wonder. I thought perhaps he found it some sort of turn-on. The idea of her body, her skin, under constant examination. Like quality control at a factory. Continuing to talk to him as her fingers prodded, inspected and scanned. For a person whose body was once the focus of such neglect and punishment, a body that became so malnourished and skeletal, she now routinely gives it an almost mesmeric kind of scrutiny.

'As I say, he's allowed to change his mind, isn't he?'

There's a heavy moment of silence.

'And anyway, it's his birthday. And he sounds happy and excited. Good for him,' she says, her tone short.

'OK. Sure,' I say.

'I'll text you the name of the place,' she says. 'It's got a beautiful garden.'

'Great.'

There's the difference between us. Her lack of curiosity. Helen reminds me of her in that way. No analysis. Gemma is unconcerned by this sudden 'change of mind'. She simply doesn't get involved. She's always taken a one step removed position in relation to family events and decisions. She detaches. Simply takes things at face value. Sometimes I envy this. I am the opposite. Overanalytical. Trying to understand and find a reason. Where there is space and absence, I dive in. I fill. I soak up. I overcompensate, and do the worrying and the thinking for the two of us.

After I put the phone down, I think back to the day we went over to my parents' house not long after the Emeritus ceremony.

We'd made a special trip over for Sunday lunch, just after Christmas, a belated meal for my mother's birthday. It was a bright crisp day, and we were in the garden, wrapped up against the chill. The kids were poking sticks in the mole hills on the lawn and my father was pottering about in his shed, clearing old pots and busying himself doing nothing. The kind of mindless activity that infuriated my mother.

Gemma was due to come, but she'd cancelled at the last minute. In itself, her sudden change of plan wasn't unusual, but my parents' inconsistent explanation about her non-arrival was. My mother said something about a social thing, while my father said it was work. *What work?* I scoffed, given her relationship with employment had always been tenuous to say the least. But either way, it was dropped and the conversation drifted on to something else.

We'd all been surprised by the turn of events. It was an award he was widely tipped to get. He's been told as much by two of the other professors. Max even told him to 'feign surprise' when his name was called out at the college dinner. But there was no announcement. Two dons were granted their professorship, but there was no recipient for the Emeritus. I imagined my father sitting at the table, peering through his glasses, waiting expectantly, hands arched in a steeple. Until it was clear there was nothing else forthcoming. No more awards. I imagined him blinking. Then swallowing his wine. Then reaching down calmly for his pipe and pressing a small scoop of tobacco into its bowl, feeling the softness of the strands under his fingers.

Mum had told me on the phone. Brisk sharing of information, as opposed to any engagement or conversation. And that day in the garden, I'd tried to press her for more information. But instead, she was preoccupied with Sheila Mason. 'Just a bout of constipation,' she said, 'only to find she's riddled with cancer. *Riddled*,' she said again, her eyes shining with the tragedy of it all.

Other people's traumas had always somehow been a comfort to her. A distraction perhaps from her own difficulties. At times I felt she revelled in them. A hobby, like others might take up knitting or bridge.

'Dreadful.' She shook her head. 'Those poor children.' She stopped for a moment, her mind busy with altruistic plans, her fingers twitching, and then she rushed inside. Later, I found her rifling through the unwanted present cupboard, wrapping things in shiny paper for the family.

'Sometimes that's the way it goes,' my dad explained. 'Last year there were two: Professor Watson and Professor Varma. Perhaps they needed a year off,' and he waved his hand dismissively, looking out over the fields beyond the house.

'But, Dad,' I said, 'they practically promised it. What happened? Max said as much—'

Perhaps it was my imagination, but at the mention of his closest friend, he seemed to cloud over.

'Yes – well,' he said, with a flash of irritation. 'It happens,' he said again curtly. 'Of course I'm disappointed. But we move on.' He pressed his hands together, then brushed them briskly on the sides of his trousers before getting up and strolling across the lawn. When he was still in earshot, my mother said, 'Lucky I didn't come along. If it wasn't for the music recital, I would have done. It is rather odd, don't you think? I've told him to take it up with them, but you know your father. Doesn't want to make a fuss. Forty years of work and dedication. I'd make a fuss. It's not right. Unsavoury,' she said stiffly.

My mind lingered on the word *unsavoury*. It's a word she often used. She also frequently found things *unpalatable*. And it occurred to me in that moment how frequently her expressions or judgements about behaviour were food-related.

I watched my father. Perhaps he was avoiding the skewer-like focus of my mother. But he seemed unable to sit still. Constantly on the move. I was sleepy. The afternoon sunshine was surprisingly sharp and bright. I closed my eyes, tired.

Instead of retreating to his potting shed, which he always did in times of tension or conflict, that day, in an unprecedented move, he joined the kids on the lawn, leaping about pretending to be a mole for them to whack.

My mother said nothing, got up with the tea tray and disappeared into the house.

*

When the car draws up, there's no sign of Dad.

Mum's waving a hello, but then gets distracted looking for something in the back of the car.

'Where's Dad?'

'He wanted to walk the last bit. He'll be here in a minute.'

And then she swings around. 'Where are they?' she says, peering round as if the kids will suddenly materialise. She is skittish as she talks about the traffic and how they stopped in Dorchester for a coffee. 'Lovely market town,' she says, 'have you been?'

'Mum – what's this about the restaurant? The new plan?'

And she wafts a hand through the air. An exasperated movement, like I'm slow to catch on. 'Gemma was supposed to call you. Did she not? Perhaps she couldn't get through? I would have done it myself, but Alicia Featherstone is very ill.'

She mistakes my confusion about Dad for confusion about Alicia.

'Our neighbour's sister? Brain tumour. She was getting a bit forgetful. Dropped the occasional word here and there. All a bit odd. Now we know why—'

'I've just spoken to Gemma—'

'Ah good. It's so close to here. One of the telly chefs. Can't remember which one. Hugo or Hugh – or something or other? Anyway, Dad thought it would make a nice change.'

I stare back at her. She's still avoiding meeting my gaze.

'Let me see my grandchildren,' she says. 'Where are they?' and she calls their names out loudly until they appear at the door.

'Nana!' Sam shrieks. She pretends she hasn't seen him.

'Sam? Ruby? Where are you?'

'Here!' they shout, and she looks the other way. They jump up and down and so it continues.

They love this ritual. This pantomime. And usually, I love it too. But not today. I see it for what it is. The smoke screen to avoid meeting my gaze or answering my questions. She's behaving like a cartoon villain throwing out drawing pins, or a smoke bomb to throw me off course. The longer it goes on, the more exasperated I feel. I go inside to make coffee, with the sound of the near hysterical laughter ringing in my ears.

As I bring the tray out to the garden, in the distance I see a figure striding towards us across the field. As it gets closer, it turns into my father. I walk down the path to meet him.

'I met your neighbour,' he says, kissing me with an unexpected flourish on both cheeks. 'Philip. The doctor? What a lovely chap,' and he waves his arms at the countryside. 'This is wonderful!' he says. 'Did I tell you I spent my summers out here when I was a boy? Staying with my Great-Aunt Elsie? She had a little cottage near Corfe Castle.'

As we push through the gate into the garden, my mother and the kids walk towards us. 'I seem to remember there was a huge rectangular rock pool. Fills up with water, like a swimming pool.'

'Dancing Ledge,' the kids say in unison.

'It was in the Enid Blyton books, you know,' he says, with an ebullient gesture of his hand.

I nod.

'Shall we go?' he says excitedly.

'We went there,' Sam says, leaping about. 'The other day—'

And all of a sudden, my father looks distraught, like a child with a broken toy.

'Can we go again?' Sam says, pulling on my hand. 'Can we take Grandad today?'

My father waves his hands in excitement. Sam tries to high-five him and after several missed connections, they manage a sort of half-connected fist-on-palm interaction, which Sam finds hilarious.

'Seventy is the new forty!' he says inexplicably and this time they bump fists.

Sam laughs. He is besotted with this new energised version of his grandfather.

'Let me get my binos,' my father says, rushing to the car. 'Shall we?' he says, when he returns, hovering on the doorstep.

I haven't brushed my teeth yet, and Sam is still in his pyjamas. 'Five minutes. Just hold on – I have to get a few things together.'

From the upstairs window as I get changed and grab sun cream and spare clothes for the kids, I see he is outside in the garden. Then, spotting Penny in her front garden, he strolls over, the binoculars slung round his neck. There looks to be an animated one-sided conversation. Lots of hand waving and then he is back in the garden. My mother is sitting at the picnic table.

We all set off together, crossing the road, then opening the gate onto the coast path. My father doesn't take a breath. 'I used to cycle here,' he says, 'when I was a boy. Me and Martin Fellowes, we'd set off with a packed lunch and go cycling all day. Looking for birds and wildlife. We kept a record of everything we saw. We set up our own birdwatching club,' and he grins. 'Different sort of birds now, eh?' he says, thumping Sam on the back. 'And I don't mean the feathered kind,' and he roars with laughter.

I stare back at him. Then look over at my mother. I am scanning for something on her face. Checking her out. What is this new version of my father? This mysteriously good mood, the ebullience, it's baffling. She doesn't look at me. She keeps her gaze fixed ahead. Then digs around in her handbag, keeping her head down low.

Sam has no idea what he's talking about, but he is enjoying the boisterousness and the animation of a man who had barely shown him much attention in the past.

'What a beautiful day!' Mum says to no one in particular. Then she talks about Rob. 'Poor thing, having to dash off like that. How stressful. Where will he stay? And what about meals?'

'They'll put him up in a nice hotel, Mum. He'll be fine.'

'But still – no homecooked meals – I hope he had something nice before he got on the plane. Airline food,' and she grimaces.

In my mind's eye, I have a fleeting thought about my father.

There is something about the cancelled college dinner, his recent absence and this new plan for his birthday celebration. The hastily rearranged restaurant meal. They seem like small separate bursts of light that don't quite string together. And similarly, there is no space. No opportunity to talk. He is moving too quickly and talking too much and too fast. I feel dizzy around him. And, in a thought that I will come to remember to my shame, part of me feels glad that he is a bit further up ahead. That he is entertaining Sam with the dizzying chatter. The pace. The wonder. The new-found interest in everything.

It isn't long before they peel away, the two of them moving out in front. I can hear the rumble of my father's voice, followed by Sam's hysterical laughter.

'Dad,' I call out, 'slow down. So we can catch up—'

I watch as my father waves in my direction. If I am thinking anything at that point, it's that whatever they're talking about, Sam is finding it amusing. He is happy.

I am walking with Mum, dictated by the slower pace of a three-and-a-half-year-old. Sometimes Ruby wants to swing between us; sometimes she slows down to pick up small things on the way: an odd-shaped stone or dandelions that she collects in a bunch in her fingers. The sun is warm on our faces. Further ahead is the blue of the sea, and the sunlight casting a pool of silver on the surface.

When I try to talk about this birthday change of plan, I am made to feel the fool.

'He decided he didn't want the fuss,' she says crisply, 'just wants to have drinks at the college instead. And this meal.'

It's as if these last-minute changes to long-planned events happen all the time in my family. That it's me who is rigid. Inflexible. I can almost hear Gemma on the phone now. 'It's his choice. Why does it matter?' And in this fog is something I can't articulate. And the more I am made to feel this is my difficulty, my problem, the more inclined I am to drop it. Looking back, of course, I wish I'd asked more questions. Wish I'd pushed her further. But even if I had, I'm not sure it would have made any difference in the end.

'Who is he inviting?' I ask.

'What?' she says, feigning confusion.

'The birthday lunch.'

'Oh,' she says wearily, like she's got to get something back out that she's already neatly folded away. 'Might be just family. A few others. He's not sure yet. Gemma's seeing someone. She might bring him. He sounds nice. Hope it works out. She's been unlucky with men – don't you think?' And then before she takes a breath, 'Look, Ruby! Look at those sleepy cows!'

Just family?

Already I can hear Rob's response. 'Just family? Jesus fucking Christ.'

She points up at the rolling clouds. 'Looks like we might get some rain,' she says. 'Ten minutes ago, it was bright sunshine!' She looks down at Ruby. 'Lucky you've got your raincoat, and what a lovely one. Those big white daisies – is it new?'

I look away. When I glance up ahead, my father and Sam are climbing the hillside. They are moving apace, then stopping every now and then. I watch as my father points things out to Sam, occasionally stopping to let him look through the binoculars. I see the dance of my father's hair, wispy and white, like the swirl of an ice-cream. He is striding ahead, with Sam happily running alongside, trying to keep up.

My mother seems twitchy. Anxious, talking incessantly about Gemma and the plans she wants to make about the menu. 'We're

123

going to discuss them this afternoon. Gemma always has good ideas about food and what goes together. So terribly creative with all that culinary stuff.'

I chew on the inside of my cheek to stop myself saying anything.

'Apparently, we can construct a special menu – "off-piste", was what Gemma said. We have an appointment at 2 p.m. We're going to have a spot of lunch while we're there.'

'I know, Mum,' I say, 'you told me.'

The wind whips through our hair as we walk. When we get to the decline on the hillside, the path up ahead is hidden. It's only when we finally get to the brow of the hill that I can see how far ahead they are. Two small dots side by side on the hillside. I notice a heavy lurch in my chest. I feel myself wanting to speed up. To close the gap between us. Ruby drops back to inspect a large stag beetle that has scuttled into the path.

'Hey, Ruby,' I say, 'can you hold hands with Nana? Take her on a little nature walk. You can point some stuff out to her, maybe do a bug hunt along the way?'

Ruby is delighted by the idea and barely notices as I gently slip my hand from hers and stride off.

'I'm going on ahead. To catch up with Grandpa.'

'Oh, leave them,' my mother purrs. 'They're probably having a high old time.'

'I'll see you at the pool,' I say, walking off purposefully.

I can move so much faster without a toddler and my mother – and I quicken my pace as I see them climb the final hill that leads down the long slope to the stone steps to Dancing Ledge. When they reach the top and drop down over the other side, they disappear from view. I push on. I feel hot from the pace of my walking. I want to take off my jacket, but I don't want to waste time. I feel an urgency to catch up with them that feels impossible to explain.

Birds, and I don't mean the feathered kind.

It's this phrase that's circling around my head. It's such an odd thing for my father to say. It sounds like something from a *Carry On* film. Something I can imagine Sid James saying to Hattie Jacques. It seems so unlike him. It pulls at me.

I push up the hill. It's steep and I feel the strain on my calf muscles. I remember what Rob says to the kids when we walk, 'small baby steps. In a zigzag up the hill.' It helps, it stops me from falling and I feel a stronger grip against the steepness of the incline. The change in the weather here is instant. The clouds that were scudding across have now gathered in a dark mass of grey.

I stamp my feet into the last few steps to the top of the hill, bracing myself for the final steep incline. The wind snaps at my face, small slaps against my cheeks. The view suddenly falls away, the grassy incline. The wide expanse of the sea. It looks different. A deep navy blue with curls of white as the wind whips over the surface. It's clouded over now, with just patches of blue and blinks of sunshine. One last step and I am at the top.

I look down. On the grassy ledge where we ate lunch with Helen and her kids, I can see my father chatting to two female walkers. One hand cupped above his eyes, the other gesturing towards his binoculars. I don't see Sam. I look again. I swing my head from side to side. There is no sign of my son. My eyes search as I start to hurry down the hill. I'm calling as I run.

As I get to the rocky steps, I'm shouting now, more urgently. 'Dad!' I call out. But he's still talking and laughing. When the two young women move away, I shout again, more fiercely, and all the while my eyes are darting, picking over the rocks and grass for any sign of Sam. The tide is in and the swimming pool is full. Blue-grey water sloshing back and forth as the waves roll in from the sea in great thunderous roars. I'm calling out. But with the thrash of the wind, and the cry of the gulls circling round the cliff edge, he doesn't hear me.

ELEVEN

I'm scanning as I run. I hope to see Sam on the near side of the rocky pool. The place we sat and had lunch when we came with Helen and the kids. The place that's hidden from view. But in three more steps, I can see the whole undercliff. There is no Sam. I'm running and screaming down towards my father. Eyes combing the rocks and the undergrowth, trying hard to avoid looking at the edge of the cliff, the rocky edge and the dark grey waves as they crash over the boulders.

'Where's Sam?' I shout.

Finally, my father swings round. The end of a smile. A slightly glazed expression on his face.

'What?'

Momentarily, he seems to have no idea where he is, or what he's doing. He pats at his pockets. He looks startled or perhaps lost.

'Dad? Where's Sam?' My voice comes out like a rasp. Sand-papery with terror.

'He was just here,' he says, looking around by his feet. 'Just a minute ago.'

I run towards the edge, where you drop down to the swim-ming pool. I'm looking everywhere as I run. I'm taking in the rocks, the hillside, the cliff edge. My heart is thumping in my chest. I'm gulping in air. I'm struggling to breathe. When I call his name, no sound comes out.

I try to slow my breathing down. I try again. 'Sam!'

When I have run the length and back of the grassy headland,

I return to my father. 'Was he with you at the end of the cliff path?' I say. 'When you got to this bit, was he with you?'

He looks confused. Disoriented. His pale wispy hair is whipped up in the wind. 'I was talking to the walkers. One's going to study medicine at Oxford.'

'Dad?' His helpless vagueness is familiar and I fight the urge to reach my cold terrified hand up, and strike it hard across his face.

'Yes,' he says, clasping his hands together, 'I think so.'

'You *think* so?'

I have a hollow scoop of fear. The panic is like a rock, pushing up from my chest into my throat. I can't breathe. There is no space for tears. For emotion. I feel my body freeze with dread.

I pick my way carefully down the rocky path to the ledge, by the swimming pool, calling out my son's name as I go. It's unfathomable to me that he would have been able to climb down this alone. Hands on the cliff edge, I climb down backwards, my feet trying to find the footholds. In my haste, I slip down the last bit, hitting my knee against the rock and grazing my palm. But I feel nothing. All my energy is going on trying to ignore the swirl of the water as it crashes over into the pool and then is sucked back out to sea. The loud slapping noise as it hammers against the rocks. The wind bites against my cheek. I try not to think about what Helen told me about the sheer drop at the rocky shelf. The deep water. So deep that boats can come right in.

Her comment about the beauty of the dance right up against the treacherousness and danger.

It's then I see the flash of red. His coat, discarded on the rocks. I hurry towards it, slipping on the wet rocks and the slime of the seaweed. 'Sam. Sammy. Where are you?' I call, trying not to look down at the slick swirl of dark water.

And then all of a sudden, there it is. His small voice surging up through the sounds of the wind and the waves. 'Muuum-mmy. Over here! Look at me,' he says, 'look what I found!'

He sounds excited. Not scared. I feel my heart lurch as I edge round towards his voice. Then I see him, perched at the far end, on the cliff edge with a fishing net in his hand. Below him is a sheer drop into the sea. The terror shoots through me. Searing and ice cold. My throat is dry.

'Look what I found!' and he swings round to me. His small body swivelling dangerously on the edge. 'I spotted it from right up there. It was here! Someone left it on the rocks,' he says, swinging back round clumsily. 'Can I keep it? Can I take it home? Is it mine now?'

I try to keep my voice calm as I continue to edge my way towards him. The wind is strong. There's a surging wave that crashes against the rock and lurches up into the air, and the sea spray is on my face, my lips, my cheeks.

Sam is swishing the net in the rock pools at the side. He's dangling it over the edge.

'Maybe a fish will jump in,' he says, lungeing his arm out, 'when the waves come in?'

'Sam,' I say firmly, but keeping my voice calm, so I don't scare him, 'can you please shuffle back a bit. Away from the edge.'

But he can't hear me. He's scooping and swirling the net in the air, then lurching forwards when the waves crash up, chuck-ling and shrieking as he catches the sea spray in the net. I'm moving closer now. The path is narrow. I keep my eyes on him. Not on what I know is to the left. The sudden drop away to the foaming crash and roar of the waves.

He is three steps away from me now. I make a run for it. I come behind him and grab the back of his hoodie, pulling him

backwards onto the grassy slope with me. He cries out in surprise as he falls against me and the net topples from his hand
and crashes down into the water. He struggles to get up. To
look over the edge to see where it's gone. But I have both hands
around him now, pressing him into my tummy. He wrestles in
my grasp.

'My net!' and he tries to wriggle away. To try and retrieve this
lost thing. 'My new blue net,' he sobs.

I'm crying now too. Pressing him to me. Holding onto him
too tightly. Sobbing quietly into the back of his hoodie. Then I
whisper very calmly, 'I'm really sorry about your net, Sam. But
it's dangerous here. We need to go back to the path—'

'No!' he wails. 'My net—'

'We're going to go back home now. And you can buy another
from the shop.'

'But I want that one,' he cries. 'I found it. It was blue.'

'I know. And I'm very sorry. But we have to move away.'

I decide it's too dangerous while he is wriggling. So, I sit with
my back against the rock. It's an opportunity to catch my breath.
I curl my fingers round his waist. I breathe into the smell of his
hair. The feel of his cheek on my own, the soft curve of his neck.
He wriggles in my grasp.

'Sam,' I say, wiping my face on my sleeve. 'You can choose a
new net. And you can also choose a bucket and a spade as well.
They will be yours.'

A beat.

'Not to share with Ruby?'

'Not to share. Just for you.'

It's this. This idea of sole possession that seems to distract
him, at least momentarily. As we slowly shuffle round the cliff
edge, I can see he is still struggling and mourning the loss of this

thing that he has found. This secret treasure that he spotted and retrieved. This thing that has incrementally increased in its preciousness, by the very fact that he alone has found it. And now the thing has gone, crashing away, out of sight. And as we pick our way carefully along the Ryvita ledge back to the swimming pool, we are both totally and utterly preoccupied with the same things; for him, the finding, then losing something so precious. And me, the same, just in reverse order.

He climbs up first, me behind, guiding his feet into the rocky footholds, and it's only then, my hand on the rock, that I feel the sting of pain on my palm. Once up on the grassy ledge, he complains, 'Too tight,' protesting at the hand that encases his own. 'I want to walk by myself,' he says, 'I'm not a baby.'

I shake my head, and in that moment, it feels inconceivable that I will ever let him go again. 'No. Not until we're back up on the main path.' And only now do I allow myself to look back along the edge. To peer down at the crack and swirl of the grey churning water. The waves that thunder and roar against the rocks.

As we walk back up to the grassy ledge and away from the cliff, I feel a heavy drop. The wave of relief. My legs feel unsteady under me. Jelly-like. Thrown off-kilter by the aftermath of danger. But also, the feeling of terror, which I have held in abeyance in order to do the job of saving my son, now hits me with the force of a truck. Is this what it is to be a mother, I think? To have to freeze-frame your emotions at the worst moments in life? Suspend everything, until it is safe to breathe again.

My hands are looser around Sam's and then, when we are back on the grassy area, I let him go. I am trembling as we approach my father. He is standing exactly where I left him. He sees us, and there is relief on his face. And then something else, perhaps he takes in the state of me. The upheaval that has transformed my body and my cold white face.

I shake my head. 'I don't know what to say—' Then, almost immediately, 'What were you thinking?' I follow up, in a furious whisper.

'I got carried away. I was distracted,' he says, and he seems to be looking around on the ground as if searching for something he's lost. 'I got talking to the walkers. One of them is going to Oxford. The red-haired one in shorts. She's doing Medicine in October at St John's—'

I'm staring back at him. And he stops when he sees my face. 'I thought Sam was there – just next to me—'

I bend down to help Sam on with his coat. The sight of it discarded on the rocks makes my heart thump. He is telling his grandpa about the net. 'It was blue. My favourite. Did you see it? I found it all by myself. But Mummy grabbed me and made it fall into the sea.'

I kneel in front of him and do the zipper up. His sweet hopeful face. His small peachy cheeks. I smooth my hands over his skin. His hair. I am crying freely now. I can't stop the tears. They are falling from my cheeks.

'Mummy – are you crying about the net?'

I shake my head and he reaches a small hand up to my wet cheeks. 'It's OK, Mummy.'

Behind me, I can hear my father. 'I was thinking about coming here when I was a boy. Just like Sam. We were alone,' he says, 'cycling along the coast path.'

I feel the pull of something so familiar. His absorption in his own moment. His obliviousness.

I can see Ruby and my mother coming down the hillside path.

'Sam, why don't you run up and meet them on the hill.'

I swing round. 'Dad – how old were you when you came for

the summer and went cycling with Martin Fellowes?' I can feel my face is burning. My voice is getting louder.

'Not sure. Nine. Ten perhaps,' and then he falters. 'I guess it's different now – with kids. What they can and can't do – I—'

I look back at him, aghast. 'Sam is four, Dad. Four years old. He'll be five in September.'

He looks distracted. Drags a hand through his hair. It seems a struggle for him to focus on what I'm saying.

'I'm sorry,' he says eventually, as though after searching through every alternative response, he's finally landed on the right one.

And in that moment, I feel ablaze with the heat of my rage, as if the event is like the touchpaper to ignite my feelings about all the other episodes of thoughtlessness over the years.

But I simply turn away.

Of course, given what will happen at his birthday lunch, I will look back on this incident. I will see his distraction, his confusion, his self-absorption and his inability to focus in a very different light. But at the time, I am angry. And for the most part, I am struggling to think of anything but my small sandy-haired boy. I just want to hold him close. To drink him in. To smell the top of his sea-salty hair. To press his hand in between my own. I cannot think beyond the fragility of his small body. His sweet face that trusts entirely that the natural world is a safe and risk-free place, and one that will look after him.

But I also know that my brush with death will leave a scar. And I already know that later on, and for a very long time to come, when I close my eyes in the dark I will see his small body dipping and weaving in the waves, his hands thrashing in the water. Then there will be a stillness, his body face down, arms out like a starfish. And I will sit upright in the bed. My face hot and slick with fear, I will have to take long slow breaths. I know I will have to get up in the night and go to him. I will have to press my hand lightly on his back and feel his breathing. And it will be this slight movement of his back, the gentle sound of his breathing that will begin to still my own thudding heart. I know this is what I will be doing. On many nights in the months and years to come. Perhaps – forever. And I know what this is. This is motherhood.

*

At the village shop, Sam stares at me in disbelief. 'Can I really?' he says, not quite believing the conversation we had on the cliff still stands.

I nod. And as I hold my purse open, I feel it's like I could so easily be opening a vein, letting him drink from my blood. I know he has no concept of how close he came. How close we all came to slipping through that gossamer-thin barrier between life and death. And I am grateful for his obliviousness. Just one small slip on the stones. A clumsy or excited lurch over the edge and how, in a second, all our lives would have been dashed on the rocks. Altered irrevocably. And just the thought of this makes me feel shaky all over again.

His face is shiny with the excitement of the fishing net. But I can see he is torn. Unbridled joy for the new net might look like he has forgotten the one that clattered down into the sea. Still mourning the one he lost, he says with gravity, 'It's not the same as the one I found. But I do like this one too,' he says. He wants both to embrace the excitement, and to hold onto the loss too. The thing that was so much more special, just by the very act of finding it.

When we get back to the cottage, the kids take the box of toy cars out to the garden. I shut the gate and sit near them on the picnic bench. I close my eyes and feel myself breathe for the first time.

'Shall I make coffee?' my mother says. 'I brought some biscuits. We can have those.'

'I'll stay here,' says my father. He sits on the bench near me, and I have the feeling that he doesn't quite know how to be. How to arrange his face. He stares blankly into the distance. Desperate for some sort of distraction. And soon it comes, in the form of Penny as she steps out of her front door. He waves exuberantly.

I get up and go into the house.

My mother is talking as I walk into the kitchen. I watch the kids from the window. Their two blond heads locked together as they make traffic jams on the path.

'Such a shame,' she says.

'What?'

'The hedge. If it wasn't so high, you'd be able to see more of the sea. What a shame,' she says again. 'Perhaps you could ask them to cut it back?'

I say nothing as I get the milk and the cups from the cupboard.

'It's such a diddy place, isn't it?' she witters on. 'Poor Rob! I bet he bumped his head on those stairs. How *did* he manage?'

I stare at the kettle, the swirls of steam as it clicks itself off.

'Must have been hard for him to work here,' she says. 'Difficult for him – with the children. The noise . . .' and her voice trails away.

'And that Baby Belling!' she starts again. 'Hard to cook a proper meal on that. Poor Rob, he does like his food.'

I feel a stab of irritation for her constant deference for Rob. For all men. Their needs. Their wishes. *Can he manage the kids' tea?*

she'd fret, on the days I was doing evening surgery and Rob had to pick the kids up from nursery. It reminds me of how she was when we were small. How she spent her days and weeks ushering us around the needs of my father, navigating his moods, his whims. 'Your father's doing *his research*,' she'd say, dragging us away, a finger on her lips. How she perpetuated his special status. And I, in turn, learnt to do the same.

I can see her looking around for things for her conversation to land on. Like a bird on the beach, looking for scraps. But she is not hungry to entertain or amuse. She is desperate to distract. To divert. To find ways for us to look away. And I know this feeling well. This is what she always does in times of crisis. I place cups and milk onto the tray and I walk out of the back door. 'I love these pictures. What fun!' I hear her say, as she peers at the photo montage as I step outside. 'Which one's the owner?'

And as I walk across the grass, there is a familiarity about all this. The whole incident has been filed away. Like an important document hastily shoved in the shredder. And I do what I always do. I say nothing. I eat my biscuits with my jaw tight. Swallow down the tea. Pebbles in my throat. I am twelve years old again, sitting at the dinner table.

My father is talking to Penny, over her small fence. They are laughing as she points to something in the distance. Already I can see the incident has gone from his face. And I marvel at his inability to keep Sam in mind. How in the face of a better, alternative distraction, my son has been dropped like a stone.

*

And what about me? What do I do? In spite of my incomprehension at his ineptitude, I am speechless. I withdraw. My fury is turned on myself. *I took my eye off the ball,* is what I think. I relaxed for a moment and entrusted someone else, someone I thought I could depend on, with the welfare of my son, and how this wrong assumption could have been fatal. I blame myself entirely.

And as I sit there pouring out cups of tea for us all, I resolve never to rely on him again. His habitual distractedness is legendary. But never like this. Never in a way that has put others' lives at risk. If anything, his tendency towards distraction is something of a family joke. Stories that we have woven into family mythology and linked to a kind of benign eccentricity. The absent-minded professor. The brilliant academic. How much he got away with; but how much, it occurs to me now, we let him get away with.

We drink our tea, and my hands are still shaking as I lift my cup. I have no energy for words. For polite chatter. When my mother updates me about Alicia's brain tumour, I look away. 'Just three weeks, they say.' And as always, a reminder, that however awful things might be, there is always someone worse off. 'What will happen?' she asks. 'From a medical point of view? Will it be painful – or will she just slip away?'

'Slip away probably,' I say, 'if she's given enough morphine.'

She asks some more questions and I simply cannot help myself. My default position, answering, engaging – even though I have no interest or inclination. What I do pull back from is finding placatory words to frame around what's happened. I want the horror to remain, laid bare in front of them. It's too soon to move away from it. Too raw. I want to remember. If anything, I want to move towards it, not away. To wave a banner like a protester on the street.

I have felt fear before. I think fleetingly of Keith. The flash of rage and tension in the room. But today's fear was coated with the heaviness of loss. Of responsibility. Of guilt. I never want to taste it again, but I want to remember that dull metallic taste of death. I want to turn it over in my hands. Like a sharp object in my fingers. I want to feel the pain of those jagged edges. And I want to give it to my mother, and fold her fingers around the edges, so she can feel it too.

I don't want to listen to talk about hedges and biscuits and brain tumours and menus for my father's birthday. I want to remember the fragility of life. Its brittleness. The momentary quicksilver of a decision. But, as ever, I am unable to express my anger. Because I know it will simply bounce off them both, and roll off down the hillside.

The kids are happy to be back in the garden with the box of cars. Sam has taken his new net and bucket and spade inside and hidden them under the bed, and when he comes back out, he asks about the beach. 'Can we go later – to the sandy one?'

I shudder at the thought. 'Tomorrow,' I say, 'we'll go tomorrow with Ollie and Lexie.'

After we have finished our tea, I stand up. 'Nana and Grandad are going now,' I announce to their surprise. I haven't consulted my parents about their departure time. I know they aren't due at the restaurant until 2 p.m. 'There's a lovely garden nearby,' I say, 'or you could have a drink at a pub on the way. The Royal Oak looks nice.'

My mother goes to speak, but decides against it, then stands up too.

She gathers up her coat and bag. 'Right then, we'll head off for the restaurant now,' she says, like it's her own idea.

My father is walking towards the car and stops to speak to Philip who is in a deckchair by their back door. 'Hello again,' he says cheerily, extending his hand, and they have a brief conversation I'm glad I cannot hear.

'Shall we pop back with a takeaway? Fish and chips perhaps?' she says. 'There's a good one in Swanage—'

'No, thanks,' I say, 'we're fine.'

'We'll practically be passing—'

I just want to be here, alone with the kids. I just want them to leave. But in the silence that follows, I can't keep quiet. Feel compelled to give a reason. I am like the default setting on my own phone that I don't know how to turn off.

'Feel a bit shattered after the events of the morning. Just need to rest. Chill out a bit.'

And of course, my mother seizes on the hook I have inadvertently thrown out. 'Won't it be a help then? Getting fish and chips, so you won't have to cook?' She looks around. 'And the kids love fish and chips, don't they?' raising her voice so they can hear.

I shake my head.

'We've got some bits and pieces to finish up – we're fine.'

'Really? What? I didn't see much in the fridge—'

'Pancakes,' I say, 'we're having pancakes.'

'Oh? Where are the eggs?' she says, looking around as if they might miraculously appear.

'We get them from Joyce—'

'But won't it save you the trip? If we bring food? Just trying to help,' she says, 'make things easier—'

'I've got to pop over to Joyce's anyway,' I lie.

Finally, with a disappointed twitch of her lips, it stops.

And then they are gone. I get crisps and snacks for us all. Juice for the kids and wine for me. The sun is on the grass. The path is a giddying array of traffic. 'It's a car park,' Sam says when I look over. The heat is warm on my face. There's the hum of bees on the lavender. I close my eyes. I sip at my glass of rosé. The kids are laughing, playing quietly for a moment. And I allow myself to relish the peace. And having brushed up against danger, I feel the preciousness of life. I feel it in my heart and want to hold on tight.

My mind drifts to Terri Garner and the conversation I had with Sarita about the risk for pregnant women. 'A very dangerous time for both mother and child.' And I think about how Terri had no children, but was already thinking like a mother. Of the sacrifices she had to make, knowing she couldn't bring a baby into an unsafe house. 'I can't have a baby with Danny,' was what she said the next time I spoke to her, as she asked for a termination and a referral to the clinic. Telling me she had to go at the weekend, while he was away. She already knew she wouldn't be able to protect a child. She knew what she had to do.

As I look out across the fields, the clouds have now gone, and the sky is a bright brilliant blue. The sun is on the cornfields, lighting them up in a golden hue.

The phone rings. I look down. It's Rob. I switch it to silent, turn it over, and close my eyes. I can't speak to him at the moment. I am not ready to say what's happened out loud. But mostly, I realise, I'm not ready to manage his emotion. I can't listen and accommodate his response, the swirl of his panic and outrage, as he sits on his beach in Los Angeles. I know I can only tell him when I feel better, when my own emotions are safely beached.

TWELVE

Not long after we get to the beach, Helen's phone rings. 'My sister,' she mouths to me, before moving away along the sand to answer the call. She always feels the need to tell me who it is, even though it's always her sister. Occasionally James, but never anyone else. We have set up our blankets and towels on the dry sand and the kids are a little further down towards the water's edge where the sand is damp, and apparently the perfect consistency for their construction of a complex set of moats they hope will be filled by the incoming tide.

I watch them, and feel my mind drift. My eyes casting over our bags. The jumble of my own, stuffed in haphazardly. And Helen's. Neat. All Tupperwared up, with folded clothes and emergency essentials. As a family, I could see the Dunstables were neat. James and Helen, and the kids too, especially Ollie. In fact, in a flat sea of calm and order, it's Lexie's day-dreamy stares and her unwieldy hair that offer the only ripple of disarray. But since Rob has left, I feel grateful for Helen and her family. There's something appealing about her shape. Her organised place in the world. Their definiteness as a family. And I start to like this. I start to feel spending time with them might make us all shape up, and morph into something more solid.

Helen is the sort of mother who has tissues, plasters and a change of dry clothes for both children always at the ready. She is prepared for all eventualities. The kind of mother who exposes my chaotic kind of mothering. A mother who I cannot imagine bent double and nauseous with panic as she searches for her lost child on a cliff. And if you looked at my previous organisational skills and abilities at work, she's exactly the sort of mother I thought I'd be. Earlier, Sam was proudly showing off his new blue net. I said nothing. I did not want to talk about the drama. Nor did I want to see the horror of it reflected on her face. The flash of judgement she would have done her best to hide.

In spite of my ability to multi-task at work, unfathomably, I was unable, or unwilling, to translate this work efficiency into my domestic life. I was not the mother who puréed carrots into ice cubes when the babies were small. I did not batch cook trays of fish pie and chilli that I put in the freezer. I didn't seem to manage to arrange online deliveries before the cupboards were empty. Nor did I schedule the washing and the ironing around the kids' naps or start organising childcare in preparation for my return to work after maternity leave.

Instead, I found myself repeatedly surprised by the need for certain essentials, in the same quantity, every single day. I seemed in a perpetual state of shock at the repetition of it all, especially in those early years with two children only fourteen months apart (*what was I thinking?*). I lacked the drive for anticipatory behaviour. The truth was, I found the daily need to look ahead on the rail tracks of motherhood boring. The tedium of anticipating arrivals, in spite of the fact that the timetable didn't change and each day was a repetition of the last. And perhaps it was precisely because it rarely altered that I seemed unable to succumb to it. Unable to hand myself over, simply to find the only person it ultimately rebounded on was me. To the outside observer, this might seem odd, given my liking for order and patterns.

I used to wonder if the forgetting and disorganisation was an act of rebellion against the tedium, providing small pinpricks of drama to fend off the monotony. The excitement of the late-night dash to the Turkish corner shop for milk or nappies or wipes. A spontaneous chat with the lovely Ali, arm on the counter, talking about everything and nothing. The creation of little pockets of choppy chaos in the otherwise predictable sea.

I loved the babies. I loved them instantly, with a fierceness I had not foreseen. It was a clean and pure kind of feeling that I'd never felt before. And if being a mother was just about loving your babies, it would be easy. But sometimes, it felt that loving your kids was just a small cork bobbing in the ocean of motherhood. There was the constant flotsam and jetsam of everything else. The feeding. The washing. The shopping. The cleaning. The tidying. Now I wonder, with a burn of shame, whether it was less about rebellion, and more about the thankless nature of the repetition. No thanks. No glory. No prizes. It felt like a tidal wave of domesticity. And it washed up on my shore.

Rob's riotous bay was full of fun. Spontaneous and in the moment. The wild hysteria before bed. The choppy hilarity before a bath. Plunging his face underwater, balancing a boat on his head. The hysterical laughter as he pretended to be a character from a series they'd just watched on the telly. His funny voices. Their red laughing faces. Me laughing too – but all the while keeping an eye on the sloshing water on the bathroom floor. Surreptitiously mopping it up so I didn't look like the kill-joy that I was. The fun-police.

And while I was on maternity leave, we muddled along in our state of happy and haphazard chaos. But my return to work was less a car crash, more a motorway pile-up on the domestic front. Was it then I began to look ahead and anticipate?

And now, here in Dorset for this month, life feels easier. Obviously, the days are free of work, but that is no different from the last few months in London. But being away, there is simply so much less to have to do. Fewer clothes to wash. A smaller number of toys to clear up. Fewer people to see and arrangements to make. Less rushing about to classes and pick-ups, including the weekly stressful dash to yoga where I pay an exorbitant fee to force myself to lie down on a mat and breathe. Life has got smaller and more manageable. My head is less busy. Less full of the 'to do' list I never seem to get to the end of. It feels unbelievably light and freeing. Like the pressing of a giant pause button on my life. I can't quite imagine how I will ever press 'play' again.

*

I watch the kids, as their heads bob in the sand. The faces of determination. The intense concentration. The way they nego-tiate their plans. Someone speaks, usually Ollie, and their heads jolt up. There are small snatches of conversation; plans, deci-sions, ideas. The pointing. The nods of agreement. Then more furious collective digging.

I am now used to the calls from Polly. The first few times, I felt a sense of irritation. Given the length of time Helen spent on the phone, I experienced a weird sense of feeling excluded. Of rejec-tion. A sense of my own isolation, abandoned on the blanket. But now, I expect them. And I have come to welcome them. Polly calls at least once a day. Sometimes twice, and every time, I wave a hand. *Of course, off you go.* And I sink into the time alone. I look at the sea. The clouds. The changing colour of the water and the sun as it hits the waves. Sometimes my eyes focus on the shimmer of silver. Glittery gems that sparkle on the surface. I watch almost mesmerised. And perhaps one of the reasons I find it relaxing when Helen goes is that these rare moments are gifts.

A time when my mind doesn't drift, or race to cluster around the worries that preoccupied me in London. It simply hangs, as though suspended, and that day, when she returns after her phone call, I realise I am still there, the unopened book in my hand, sitting very still and staring out at the sea at the small shots of silver on the horizon.

Unusually that day, Helen's not on the phone for that long. But when she comes to join me back on the blanket, she is obviously distressed. Her face is red. She looks tearful.

I hesitate before saying anything. I still often feel nervous with Helen, wary of saying the wrong thing. Of overstepping the mark.

'Are you OK?' I ask.

She shakes her head, chewing on her lip. She reaches for her water and takes a long drink. I can see she is trying to swallow away her distress. It sits like a lump in her throat. I know that feeling. The upsurge of sadness, the swallowing down. I look away as she battles to gain the composure that I know she wants to find. I dig into my bag for the flask of coffee and pour her out a cup and place it on the sand on front of her. She's searching for tissues and then dabs at her face.

For a while, we sit in silence. It is not my way. Not how I would usually respond. But I have got used to Helen. How she likes to be left. How sometimes even an innocuous question can feel like an intrusion and she not only reels back, but something closes down on her face, like the snap of a shutter at a kiosk window. And I feel propelled back. Like I have been rude to ask. To say anything. Sometimes it's a look, but it can land like a slap, and when it happens, it's a reminder that for all the time we spend on the beach with the kids, we hardly know each other at all.

But that day, I bite my lip; it's hard not to comment on her obvious shift of mood. Her sadness and her distress. I take a risk.

'Do you want to talk about it? Is there anything I can do?'

My voice is gentle and, in spite of herself, she weeps into her tissue that is pressed against her face. Given how neat and shiny she usually presents, it's a shock to see her raw emotion. Her red blotchy skin, like a tarnish on her sheen.

I wait. I pour more coffee, digging a little indentation in the sand to place the cup inside. As I move back to my place, I put my hand on her shoulder. Give a gentle squeeze.

'It's difficult,' she says, after a while. There's something about the way she says it, the hesitancy. The reluctance she has in even putting it into words. She looks up, twisting her fingers. 'I'm sorry—' and she starts to cry again.

We sit together in silence.

'I'm here,' I say, 'if you want to talk . . . if there's anything I can do?'

After some moments, she wipes her face. 'I just feel so helpless. My sister's in trouble,' she says, 'having such a hard time. I don't know how to help her.'

Again, I feel that invisible barrier. Like an electric fence that if I touched, moved too close, I would get sent suddenly reeling backwards. The shock of electricity tingling at the end of my fingers.

And as if she has read my thoughts, she says, 'I'm sorry – but I can't talk about it. It's Polly's business. It would feel a betrayal. I promised her I wouldn't.'

I nod.

And because there is now clarity – I am not to push, I am not to ask – there is a kind of relief. I don't need to approach the fence after all. I can step away. Take a different path. Find a different way in. It isn't something I have considered before. It isn't something I have planned. But seeing her sadness, her helplessness, there is something resonant. Something I connect with. Something I perhaps feel might be useful to share.

'I don't know what your sister's going through,' I say, 'but it doesn't matter really. But I do feel for you. And I do know the pain of watching something difficult happen to a sibling. The helplessness of it all,' and without thinking much about it, I find myself telling her all about Gemma.

'It started when she was ten,' I say. 'I was two years older.' And as we sip our coffee, I tell her about how sick she got. How it started suddenly, when she came back from a summer camp. It began with food fads. Things she would eat, things she wouldn't touch.

Vegetarian? my mother would repeat, aghast, simply not comprehending. Then, as she looked down at the tray of lasagne, 'It's just a little bit of mince. Mostly tomato,' she'd say, heaping a spoonful onto Gemma's plate.

I tell her how mealtimes became tense. A battleground. How we all had to stay at the table until she had finished. 'My dad's rule. It became interminable,' I say.

And as I talk, I am back there again. The tick of the clock. The silence. Then the jittery conversation of my mother. Filling the time with an endless stream of consciousness; recipes, ailments of the neighbours, her charity work. And there was my father's dark mood. The tightness of his knuckles as he gripped his knife and fork. The rigidity of his jaw. The stiffness of his body. Like a boiling pot, with the lid pressed firmly down. And my twelve-year-old self, and my own desperate attempts to help. And I see now how we were all hungry for something. Sitting like small birds open-mouthed, as we huddled around the table.

'We watched her disappear in front of us,' I say. 'The clothes got baggier, but her limbs and body got smaller and smaller. She was like a feathery creature. Her skin almost translucent in the light.'

Helen looks stricken. 'What happened?'

'She went into hospital,' I say, and I drift to the heat and boredom of that long summer holiday. 'I spent it mainly in the canteen. Reading books and sitting by her bedside.

'She was an ice skater,' I say. 'Really talented. In line for a place in the British squad.' I roll my hand out in front of me. 'It was all ahead of her: the British Championships, the Winter Olympics. Mum tried to use that as an incentive when she was in hospital. She brought in her pink and purple sequinned skating leotards, one of her trophies. A reminder, I guess, of what she was missing. The girl she was before,' I shrug. 'The next day Gemma took a pair of scissors to one of the outfits. Told Mum to take the rest away.'

Helen is still. The emotion on her face.

'I felt, as her older sister,' I say carefully, 'that I should be able to help. Should be able to make a difference somehow. Should be able to have some kind of influence on the situation.'

Helen nods.

'I don't know how much of this was my stuff, or something we all felt in the chronic state of powerlessness. My dad particularly. They were desperate. But paralysed.' I look over at the kids. 'Watching your child fade away. Refusing to eat.' I shake my head. 'I look at Ruby – I simply can't imagine—'

I tell her how I went in every day, 'told her stories. Found self-help books. Read out stories from the magazines we had at that time.'

I pause for a moment remembering that long summer. How I missed the fun we had. How I wanted it back.

'I felt elated when she put on weight, when she seemed better. Then full of despair when she got worse. It was like an emotional see-saw,' I say, 'and one we were all caught up on. The eating problem was like an interloper. An uninvited guest at the table. It took over.'

'What happened?'

'She got better,' I say simply.

In the weeks before, she had repeatedly pulled out the feeding tube that went into her stomach. It was then I thought, perhaps for the first time, that she might die. Then something changed. Her friends were moving up a school year. Life was carrying on. There was no breakthrough moment. No epiphany. As far as I could tell, no soul searching that uncovered the root cause of her illness.

'She started eating again. Slowly at first. But little by little, she got better.'

'How?' Helen asks.

I shrug. 'I don't know. Much later, in her mid-twenties, she published a book. *The Disappearing Act*, it was called. It was about her descent into her illness. Pretty graphic. But it also covered her road to recovery. What helped her. Mainly, she said, she chose life. She wanted hope. The book went to auction. Five publishers fighting over her memoir. It was a big deal at the time.' I laugh. I try to make it sound jokey, upbeat. 'It was beautifully written. Haunting. But empty somehow. I realise I was hoping for something else.'

'Like what?'

'Some answers maybe. A reason why it happened. Instead, it just all seemed so random. I wanted to understand. To see a pattern.'

What I don't say, what I pull back from saying, is that I was also looking for something else. That I scanned pages greedily, devouring her words. Searching for something else that, in the end, simply wasn't there. I was mentioned just once, in passing. Once in the whole book. My parents twice. But only in relation to finding the residential unit she stayed at for a while. There was nothing about me. I'd been erased. But as I speak, I remember the incredulity. The burn of rage. Remember how I smiled so hard at her book launch that my face ached for weeks.

'My parents were so proud. Like it marked the end of her recovery.'

'And did it?'

I pause for a moment as I think about this. And I feel a sudden and unexpected sadness.

'I'm not sure. Yes, in a way. But it never felt like she was the same person. I thought she would go back to who she was before. But she didn't.' I stop. 'She was –' and then I correct myself, '– she's complicated.'

We sit for a moment in silence. Then Helen says, 'Is that ever really possible, I wonder, either for her – or you? After something as terrible and life threatening as that?'

And I am surprised by the comment. I feel it in my gut. I've never really thought about this before.

We sit for a moment in silence. Perhaps both contemplating our sisters, their difficulties. Our role, or not, in their recovery.

'It was a kind of lesson—'

'A lesson?'

'That you can't help everyone. That people get help in their own way. And in their own time. That perhaps we can't help as much as we think we can. Sometimes helping is just being there. Bearing it. That the best thing we can do is step back.'

But of course, as I am saying this, I know very well this isn't a lesson I have learnt at all. If I'd learnt this lesson, I wouldn't be off work. I wouldn't be seeing Veronica. But somehow, in the face of Helen's fragility, I feel our roles reverse. I want to appear the one who is wise. Who has clear foresight. The one who knows. The one who isn't a mess.

'And what about your patients,' she asks, 'ones who don't follow what you thought they should do? How did you manage that?'

I talk about people whose physical health issues are dire. The ones who need to give up smoking or drastically change their diet. 'The drinker with liver disease.' But they don't, or simply can't and this is hard. 'As a doctor, the trajectory is clear. And frustrating they can't see it. But I also learnt that the process of change is hard. Behaviour change isn't linear.'

'What do you mean?' she asks.

'People do things in their own time and pace.'

'What about patients who don't do what's in their best interests, for other reasons? What do you do then?'

'Well,' I say, 'it depends what it is – but I've learnt from bitter experience that you can't make people do things that either they're not ready to do, or can't do. Sometimes, life, or other people, can get in the way. They don't get better just because we want them to. Our desire for change has no bearing on their ability to change.'

There's a pause, as she seems to be contemplating this.

'Even if they might be at risk? Might be harmed – if they stay where they are?'

The air seems to shift between us. I turn to look at her. But she is looking straight ahead. At the children. Or the sea, or the sand. At anything but me.

'Yes,' I say very carefully, 'even then.'

I wait for a moment before adding, 'Except of course with children – or those deemed vulnerable. Then there is a legal duty to intervene.'

Just then, there are whoops from the kids. Ollie runs up for a bucket. 'It's coming in. The water's coming into the moat. Come and see,' and he claps his hands. All four of them have turned round and are waving us down.

'We'll come now!' she calls out.

When she turns back to me, she has gathered herself. She looks seamless again. 'Please,' she says, 'don't mention my sister in front of the kids.'

'Of course,' I say, 'you said already.'

'I know,' she nods. 'But even her name. If she phones. Not in front of the children. My sister's kids – their cousins,' and she waves a vague hand down the beach. 'Anything. I don't trust myself when she's mentioned,' and her voice sounds suddenly breathless and panicky. 'And I must be thinking very clearly,' she says, 'if she needs my help.' And as I nod, I feel it too, in the quickening thud in my chest.

*

I settle the kids in front of the telly for my morning session with Veronica. 'The back door's locked,' I say, 'just come up if you need anything,' and I leave the bedroom door ajar.

I had planned to talk about my dad. The incident on the cliff. I don't think I've even told her that Rob has flown to LA. But instead, I find myself talking about Gemma.

'I wanted to be happy about her book,' I say. 'But I wasn't. I felt full of fury.'

I tell her how I'd frantically skimmed the pages, looking for something about myself. 'Looking for me, in her book. In her life—'

I'm surprised to feel the sudden well of tears.

'We were mentioned in the acknowledgements. But there was a great list. Effusive and detailed thank-yous to people I didn't even know. The author of a book she'd read. Someone on the ward,' I throw my hands up, 'I mean she probably never even saw these people again.'

More tears.

Veronica asks what I was hoping for. 'What would you have liked to see in the book?'

I shrug. 'I don't know. Some recognition of what I did.'

'And what did you do?' she asks gently.

'Sit there with her. Read her magazines out loud. Sacrificing a chunk of my childhood. Not going on school trips. Not doing the fun stuff—'

She nods. Her voice is kind, gentle. 'And how do you think these things helped with her recovery?'

There's a silence. I shift in my seat. I feel a sudden venomous feeling towards Veronica.

'Well – I cared. I was there. Day in, day out – the ups and downs of her recovery. It wasn't a barrel of laughs.'

'I'm sure it wasn't. I'm sure it was an awful time –' she pauses, '– but it sounds like your happiness became very bound up with her recovery?'

'Of course. How could it not? She was my sister. She was fading away. At one point, I thought she was going to die. We all thought she was going to die.'

Veronica thinks for a moment, moves her hands.

'Getting better, coming back from the brink like she did –' she says, '– many people don't manage it.'

'I know.'

'There is pain and anguish in watching from the sidelines. Having no control over *someone else's* recovery.'

I note the emphasis. I blink back at her.

'I wonder where those feelings went?'

'Well,' I say, 'my parents retreated. Cooking and flapping. And being depressed.'

'And you?'

'I worried. I felt responsible – I bargained.'

'With who?'

'I don't know. God, maybe. I bargained with someone. I made pacts. Things I would do. Things that needed to happen—'

'Like what?'

'Silly things. Grades I needed to get in my tests. Plants I had to keep alive. Good turns I needed to do for neighbours. Other staff and patients on the ward. Looking back – all sorts of things.'

'And if you did these things – she'd get better?'

I nod.

I sit for a moment. *Her recovery* is the phrase that's ringing in my ears.

'A child's way of making order out of chaos,' she says, and she tells me she feels such a poignant sadness for my younger self, 'the busy twelve-year-old. Trying so hard to make things better.'

Again, I feel the tears. The surge of emotion.

'When people are ill, in this way, it's very easy to get caught up in the web of their behaviour. And for our emotions to follow suit. The pinballed emotions of elation and despair. It's exhausting. But the recovery is theirs. And theirs alone, however much you might will it or want it and make all sorts of pacts and bargains. Sometimes helping is not *doing* anything,' she says, 'it's simply bearing witness. Sometimes the best thing to do is to take yourself out of the way.'

I nod.

'And perhaps,' she gently suggests, 'you felt disappointment with her recovery. And her book. Because your efforts, your sacrifices had not been acknowledged. Not been seen for what they were.'

'I feel ashamed,' I say, 'that I was so preoccupied with myself. She probably had a lot on, all that trying to stay alive,' I say flippantly, 'yet, there I was, jumping up and down saying, *what about me?*'

She looks at me kindly. 'More shame,' she comments. And then she surprises me with the next question. 'Did you ever feel envy towards Gemma?'

'Envy? For that life?' I shake my head, shocked. 'She had no life.'

'Of course,' she says. 'I'm not suggesting you wanted *her life* – but it was a life that sucked up all the energy. She was in the spotlight of the family. Used up all the electricity. There can't have been much light left to shine in your direction. It sounds like you were the planets in the orbit of her anorexia.'

The moment hangs between us.

'Co-dependency is complex,' she says, and tells me the term arose from work in addiction. The addict takes up all the focus in the family and the pull to fix them, to get them well, is strong. 'The compulsion to help becomes like a kind of drug,' she says, 'helping becomes addictive. And in turn, the emotions of family members get linked to the recovery, or not, of the other person.' She clasps her hands tightly, knotting the fingers together. 'Everything gets very enmeshed. It's easy to lose yourself.'

She goes on to say that this is equally applicable to an eating

155

disorder in a family. 'To any chronic compulsive behaviour in a loved one that feels out of our control.'

I sit still. To my right, I can see the twitch of a bird in the eaves outside the window. But I keep my eyes fixed on hers.

'I think perhaps there is something here to return to. This relationship between the helper and the person being helped,' she says, 'and how it might have played out more recently, in your life as an adult. And as a doctor to your patients.'

I glance at the time on my computer. But I already know it's time to finish, by the cue of her movement, her small edge forwards in her seat.

THIRTEEN

The day after I'd read the letter from the fertility clinic, I dropped the kids off early at nursery and went straight into work. I sat at my desk and frantically clicked the mouse, scrolling down for the referral letter I had sent to the clinic. There was no note from me. No highlighting the sensitivity. No mention of Keith's six-year-old son from a previous marriage. But most significantly, no request to send the result to me to discuss with the patients before sending the letter out.

When I spoke to the receptionist, she put me through to one of the nurses. He confirmed what was in the letter.

'Azoospermia.'

'No sperm at all?'

'Correct.'

'Historical – or a recent thing?'

A pause. 'Why do you ask?'

'He has a son. A six-year-old,' I said.

There was another pause, when I imagined he was scanning his computer screen.

'There's nothing in the notes.'

'I know,' I said, and I felt my cheeks flush.

'Well, they can do a DNA – but I'd say it's ninety-nine per cent likely not to be his. I see from his case notes he had cancer as a child. A brain tumour. Some chemo can cause infertility. That's a possible cause. But we'd have to investigate further. If we'd known at the time—'

In the background a phone started to ring.

'What's his partner saying about it?'

'Ex-partner.'

Another pause.

'Is he involved? In the boy's life?'

'Yep,' I say.

He made a kind of whistling sound.

The phone was still ringing. It became loud. Almost deafening in my ear.

I thought of him in the reception area. *I don't like being made to look a fool.* And then, much later, the thump of his fist on my desk. *Mistakes happen, it wouldn't be the first time. This place is a joke.*

He scanned the file. Then told me Keith had told them he was booked to have another test at a private clinic. 'Most do,' he said, 'if they can afford it. Results will be the same. But I guess you pay for the sensitivity of a one-on-one consultation. The tissues and the squashy sofa.'

I felt the sting of shame imagining him receiving the bomb-shell of a letter through the post.

I sat for a while, then collected my post and admin from reception. There were three calls from a Carol Marshall. Two were left on Monday evening, and one that morning. 'Is she a patient?' I asked. When I was told no, I put the messages at the bottom of my already hefty pile.

I felt jittery. On edge for the rest of the day. Concerned about Keith and Nina, but as the day went on, increasingly concerned for his ex-partner and Jackson. It was hard to explain what feelings I was left with.

David was on leave for a fortnight, so in his absence I sought out Stephen, one of the other long-standing partners. 'Can I have a word?' I asked.

When I ran through the details, he was wading in before I'd finished.

'So, he pushed for a referral to Cardiology – and you caved in?' He shrugged. 'We've all been there, over the years. Sometimes it's the only way they'll leave—'

I was shaking my head. 'He'd already had his results. He was angry. He was talking about a mistake. Now I realise he was talking about something else entirely. Something I didn't know about.'

Stephen nodded.

'So, you hadn't seen the results?'

'No.'

A pause.

'We were at cross-purposes. I could see he was annoyed. Was ostensibly focused on this breathlessness. The "funny turn" he'd had, but now I see it was about this huge revelation.'

'The infertility?'

I nodded.

'So, I didn't agree to the referral because I was in a hurry. I did it because I felt bullied into it.'

Stephen didn't nod. Didn't seem to understand. I wondered how the conversation might have played out if it was one of the other female GPs I was talking to. What she would have made of it. How she might have related to the scenario I described.

'Ah, you can't let yourself be bullied by the likes of Keith Strutt. Do you remember the office lighting debacle?' and he rolled his eyes.

I felt alienated by his lightness, his frivolity. I stared back at him.

'I did it because I was afraid,' I said, and it's only then, as the feeling made its way into words, that I felt it most acutely. 'I was afraid of him,' I said again.

And it's this comment that fired Stephen into action. 'Did something happen? What did he do?' he said, suddenly animated, puffing himself up in readiness for something. 'Did he threaten you in any way?'

Did he threaten me? Did I find him threatening? They seemed very different questions.

Brash one-dimensional Stephen. The GP who always refers patients to our resident psychologist whenever they cry in his session. His eyes were attentive, fixed on me.

'What did he do?' he asked again.

And I was floored for a moment. I didn't know how to answer this question. How could I explain that there is a cavernous divide between feeling afraid and a tangible act of intimidation?

I could see Stephen was trying to understand. He took my hesitancy for reticence. He shuffled his chair forwards, in a gesture of concern. But I realised I had nothing to give him. Nothing tangible at all. No clear and identifiable act of intimidation that he could grab with his big fat hands.

'He was clearly very angry. His fist on my desk. But other than that, he didn't *do* anything,' I said eventually, ' I felt there was –' and I hesitated, '– something going on, in the room—'

But already Stephen's demeanour had changed to a look of relief. And there was an imperceptible shift, like the tension had receded. It was a small moment. Something insignificant that at the time I wasn't able to pinpoint. But a sense of his concern dropping away, as if somehow my narrative was something irrelevant. My experience had been inadvertently brushed aside, by Stephen, and earlier by Rob. An event that to me felt seismic. Difficult. But because it was hard to put into words, to produce something observable, something to show, it appeared small and unimportant.

'The thing is,' I said, 'I'm worried about the implications. For Nina. For his ex-partner. For Jackson. The fallout from all this—'

'Sure.' He was nodding, but he looked distracted. A little bored. A surreptitious glance up at the clock.

Not long after I left Stephen's office, I picked up a further message from Carol Marshall, but this time in brackets after her name were the words *Jackson Strutt's mother*.

I called her back immediately, but it went straight to voicemail.

As I turned over the sequence of events, I began to feel that Keith held some risk. The feelings crept up on me gradually. It started with checking the NHS EMIS digital record system for any new details on any of them. I did it occasionally for patients I was concerned about; we all did from time to time. But while it started as a casual check-in, scanning for any contacts with services, admissions to A&E, it became like a nervous tic. It was obsessive. I refreshed the search several times an hour, looking for updates on either Keith, Carol or Jackson. There were none for any of them. I'm not sure what I was expecting, but I felt full of nervous anticipation. Waiting for something to happen. My mind scrolled through my recent safeguarding cases. Fixating on the different tragic outcomes that loomed large in my mind.

Every morning I felt it as soon as I drove into the car park. A kind of heaviness. A tightening of my chest. The moment I pushed open the door, everything felt louder. The sudden weight of need. The pulsating demand of the patients. The stressed mothers. The pale whiny children. What I previously found a challenge, the satisfying thwack of my well-aimed bat, now felt leaden. All that week, I muddled along. My sleep was poor and erratic. In between patients, I checked EMIS for updates. One day, I checked between twenty and thirty times. In the time I'd ordinarily be firing off referral letters before going home, I simply sat slumped at my desk.

While I knew I was obsessed, I didn't know how else to manage the worry I still felt about their safety. I became absolutely convinced that Keith could do harm to Jackson or Carol. Or both. That they were likely to be on the receiving end of his anger. And that it was somehow my fault.

On Friday, I felt my grasp of things, my sense of perspective, was slipping. I noticed I had difficulties making decisions, found myself buying time with my patients, while I anxiously consulted the MIMS prescription guide on my shelf.

It was mid-morning when I got the call about Terri Garner's A&E admission from the Urgent Care registrar. He was thoughtful, considered. Explained she'd been treated for a broken jaw, and, having checked the file, and given my role, he wanted to keep me in the loop.

My panic about Keith Strutt escalated very quickly after that. I behaved as if on autopilot. I made a safeguarding referral. But I also knew we wouldn't be able to meet until Monday. I barely slept at all that night. My mind was racing. It was on Saturday afternoon, while I was in the park with the kids, that I called Carol's number. This time, I left a message. It was only when it was played back to me several weeks later that I could hear how rambling and chaotic I sounded. I called a few more times. I left another message. Carol not answering or picking up served to intensify my anxiety. I felt entirely responsible for the way this had rolled out.

On Monday, it didn't take more than a few calls to find out what school Jackson went to, and obviously, in retrospect, my turning up at the playground on my lunch break was a gross error of professional judgement.

The following day, I was in David's office.

'What were you thinking?' he asked. And before I had a chance to reply he was shaking his head. 'How did you add two and two together and come up with five?'

'He was very angry,' I said, flatly. 'And you've seen him angry before. You know what he's like.'

'Jess,' he said carefully. 'A man has a child who he has no reason to think isn't his biological son, only to find, with the arrival of a set of results, this truth is blown apart.' He paused, laced his fingers together. 'Do you not think disbelief, hurt, betrayal and possibly anger might all be within the normal range of response?'

Another pause.

'Did it really warrant a safeguarding referral? Turning up at his kid's school?'

I didn't know what to say, suddenly haunted by the sight of Jackson's stricken face.

'Do you not think Keith was entitled to feel a little angry? How do you think most men might take this sort of news? How might your own husband respond to this kind of a bombshell?'

'Look – I—'

'Medicine is all about facts. Evidence. We look for a pattern in a collection of symptoms. But we can't make a pattern out of feelings alone. A whimsical gut feeling. It's simply not professional.' He shook his head.

I said nothing. But I also knew he was wrong. My time in safeguarding had taught me that much of the work *is* about gut feeling. That while you cannot act on this alone, in cases of risk, you can't always wait for hard evidence. Waiting for hard evidence can sometimes mean it's too late.

'I felt something in the room – I know what I felt.'

'Not all angry men are violent,' he said.

'I know that,' I said, 'but I felt something—'

He was exasperated. 'Is it possible that your role, the terrible stories you hear week in week out have perhaps contaminated your view of men? And what they are capable of?' He drew his hands together. 'Perhaps I was wrong to give you this role. Perhaps it was too soon. Too much for you.'

I felt the sting of shame. Of humiliation. And of fury.

'I know I acted rashly. I'm sorry.'

Was he right, I wondered? Had all the awful stories skewed my view of the world? Of men. Was I seeing things that simply weren't there?

He leant forwards in his chair. 'As you know, Keith and Nina came in to see me yesterday evening. They have requested a referral to Counselling and Family Mediation. They want to go together with Carol. There's talk of formal adoption. Keith is very keen to remain a part of Jackson's life. I gather the biological father is not on the scene. A one-night stand, apparently.'

I stared back at him. *Counselling and Family Mediation?*

'Is that the Keith you know?' I said. 'Don't you think he's maybe just going through the motions? Making himself look like one of the good guys. Making all the right noises?'

Had I really got this so badly wrong?

'Jess,' he said firmly. 'That's enough. It probably won't surprise you to hear that they are moving surgeries. To Bethnal Green and he has made an official complaint.'

I blinked back at him.

'Harassment. You are of course named, but it is the practice that will be under scrutiny.'

'Harassment? *Really?*'

He nodded. 'Carol has twelve missed calls and two incoherent voicemails and then there was the school incident—'

I looked down.

'You picked the wrong guy,' he said. 'Remember what happened before with the surgery contract?' He shook his head. 'A dog with a bone. This one is not going to go away.'

'Can't you see what's going on here?' I said. 'What he's doing? All the fury about the infertility is all coming my way. You know Keith, he'll want someone else to blame,' I shrug, 'shoot the messenger—'

'Except you weren't the messenger,' he said pointedly.

'OK, but it's a way of channelling his frustration. His fury about the situation. Landing it all on me.'

David sat still for a moment.

'I'm listening to you, and I don't get the sense that you feel you have done anything wrong—'

I tried to interrupt, but he held his hand up.

'You've made a mistake, and it worries me that you don't seem able to accept it. This concerns me a lot.'

Much later I would hear the same from Rob. An exasperated argument after my refusal to believe I'd got it wrong meant I was continuing to search for evidence to prove myself right.

'Just face it,' he said, in frustration, 'you messed up. We all do.'

David then said he felt like it might be advisable to have a few weeks off, 'a bit of a break. Take a breather.'

'Are you suspending me?'

'Of course not. I just think, with the official complaint, there will be an investigation—'

'I'd rather be at work,' I said emphatically.

He nodded. I could tell he wasn't happy with my decision.

But when I came in the next day, everything felt different. I felt small, weak and intimidated by my patients; their need, their hopes and expectation that I could help. I saw several patients in quick succession. The appointments were a blurry haze, had an underwatery quality about them.

It was just before lunch when I saw Mary Jones, a woman in her early seventies, who came in intermittently for housing letters. 'This weather. So damp,' she said, clutching onto her bag on her lap. 'My chest,' she said, and her papery hands fluttered in front of her body.

'I can't help you,' I found myself saying, more briskly than I'd intended.

Mary Jones looked startled. Her hands froze on her bag. She looked up at me, bird-like.

'I'm sorry,' I said, 'I can't write you another letter,' and then, 'I can't write any more letters. I write letters all the time.' I flicked back over her file on the computer. 'One. Two. Three. Four . . . five . . .' and I counted them all out. 'I've written seven housing letters. They don't do any good. Nothing. Nothing changes.'

Much later, I will think back to this defining moment. One which I will come to talk about with Veronica. The sudden realisation of the illusion of control. The shattering of the notion that I could help. The pointlessness of it all. The thought that I could make a difference. It was as if the image I'd wanted to project of myself was false. And once I had seen this, I felt useless. The tsunami of need that I had somehow been bracing myself against, like holding a door against a giant curling wave. And suddenly it all crashed down on me. It began to affect my clinical judgement. I felt wracked with indecision.

My last patient that morning was Fiona Watson who brought in her baby Mollie with a vivid rash on her tummy and arms. I liked Fiona. She'd had a difficult early few months with Mollie. An emergency caesarean after a sixteen-hour labour that had left her shell-shocked. At one of the visits in those early weeks, she told me she'd caught sight of her face in the mirror at the hospital: 'I looked like I'd been in a car crash.' But seeing her regularly over the next eight months, I watched her transformation as she grew confidently into motherhood.

I placed Mollie on the examination bed and gently unbuttoned her Babygro. I peered at her body, pressing my fingers on her skin. 'It looks fine,' I said, 'most likely a heat rash or allergic reaction.' But I found myself looking again, peering at the underside of her arms. Her tummy. *What if it wasn't?* Mollie watched me with her blue-grey eyes, wide and blinking. I turned her arm over in my hands. *It looked fine. But was it really? How could I be sure?*

I felt a cloudy fuzzy sensation. Like I was struggling for air. Losing my sense of clarity and focus. Like I was adrift. At sea in my own consulting room. While I was inspecting Mollie, my thoughts were scattering: the cases I was worried about, Terri Garner and Pat Wilson. I thought about Mrs Chandra, but my thinking also clustered around other things: the leaking washing machine, the parking ticket I'd forgotten to pay, the fees I owed for nursery, the football course at Easter that I wanted to book for Sam and the birthday present to buy for Ruby's friend Lola. All these demands competed for my attention, jumping up and down, like eager children. Things I usually held compartmentalised in my head were falling through. And then, all of a sudden, there was Mollie's startled face as my tears splashed onto her cheeks.

The following morning, I saw my own GP. When I sketched out the details of what had happened, I remember her kind face. Her soothing words.

'Keith Strutt was angry with me,' I went on to tell her, 'and perhaps if I hadn't seen him lose his temper in the past – I might not have acted so rashly,' I said, by way of explanation. I could still see it clearly in my mind's eye. That tight-lipped grimace as he gripped onto the reception desk. 'It influenced my decision,' I said, 'it seemed like a pattern.'

She nodded sympathetically. 'You need a break,' she said. 'Take some time off, until this blows over. What a difficult situation to have found yourself in.'

Found yourself in? She made it sound like I had fallen down a well. It sounded so detached. I heard it as a criticism. A comment on me. What I really wanted from her was some kind of reassurance. Some indication that, given the circumstance I'd described, she might have done the same. But she didn't. And somehow I felt worse. The flush of shame on my cheeks as she scanned my notes and made observations about my busy life; the full-time job, the two small kids and comments about my career trajectory. 'Youngest female partner . . . and weren't you the GP forum rep before you took on the safeguarding role?'

Perhaps on another day, I might have heard her tone as congratulatory. But that day, it felt accusatory. It took me back to the humiliating conversation at my appraisal. *The way you work can sometimes be a problem for the team.*

'You've had a few very busy years,' she said, mentioning something about burn-out and stress, and she signed me off for two weeks.

And for someone who had never had a sick day in their life, it seemed self-indulgent and wrong. An ocean of time I had no idea how to bob about in. But something strange happened when I got home. It was two in the afternoon when I got into bed. I rested my head on the pillow and pulled the duvet up. I felt the softness on my face and my body. I sank down deeper and lay very still. And I found I had no desire to get up again.

Fiona and Mollie turned out to be the last patients I would see for a very long time.

FOURTEEN

In the days following the conversation I had with Helen on the beach, I find myself thinking about Polly, turning over the words in my head. *Might be at risk. Might be harmed*, are the phrases I keep coming back to. We meet up again on Tuesday and it's as if the conversation hasn't happened. We're in the church hall. A singing group and play session for pre-school children. Ollie is not happy. 'There'll be loads of babies,' he'd said on the way, his voice full of disdain, but given the rainy weather, and his general level of acquiescence, his objections went no further.

The church hall is chilly, paint peeling off the walls, and with a red bucket in the porch to catch the rainwater.

There's a woman taking money and serving teas from a hatch by the door. She's wearing a big wide smile and a polka dot pink hairband.

'It's a pound per child. That includes squash and a biscuit. And Julian will be doing yoga at ten thirty.'

The man next to her is wearing a beaded necklace and a black t-shirt with *Can the Cull* written across the face of a badger. 'Namaste,' he says, nodding as he makes the prayer sign. 'It's for the kids, but everyone's welcome,' he beams.

I fish about in my purse and put money in for all four kids. 'It's sorted,' I call back to Helen, and we shuffle through.

The woman in the hairband coughs, '– then it's five pence for every biscuit you have after that.'

'Right. Great. Thanks,' and I start to edge away but her face has locked onto mine. She does the weird smile again.

'Sorry – is there something—?'

And then in a strange sing-songy voice, 'I think there might be a little boy who's had another bicky,' and she's nodding over towards Sam, who has his mouth full. 'Another five pence,' she sings. 'Just pop it in the basket. No rush.'

I dig around in my pocket. I chuck in a fifty-pence piece. 'Fill your boots, kids,' I say, and to her horror, Sam comes back for another handful of jammy dodgers and custard creams. Ollie and Lexie are characteristically restrained.

The kids find two large boxes of Duplo bricks that they hive off for themselves into a corner. I am secretly relishing the possibility of 'biscuit woman' coming over to encourage them to share with the others, telling them *the toys are here for everyone*. We watch the kids reach for the blocks in fistfuls. Sam tentatively suggests a castle 'with a red tower on each corner'. There's a pause, as they look to Ollie.

'Good idea,' he says, and I can see Sam glow, as they all set about hunting around in the boxes for more red bricks. 'And let's make two green walls and two yellow walls.'

When we are settled on chairs with our stewed tea and biscuit, Helen mentions Gemma. 'I've been thinking about your sister,' she says.

I nod. 'And I've been thinking about yours,' I say, carefully.

'I was thinking how difficult it must have been,' she continues, 'her being so ill. I mean, I don't understand something like that. But I look at Lexie – it's funny how differently you think about these things when you have kids of your own,' she waves a hand in the air, 'things they may have to deal with. Things when we were their age, we had no idea what life would bring.' She sounds obtuse. Hard to read. 'And obviously, I know something about the difficulties of feeling helpless. Not being able to intervene. There are similarities in our situations.'

I wait. She says nothing more.

I think about my session with Veronica, what she said about co-dependency. 'It was very difficult not to get enmeshed,' I say. 'Her pain became mine. It was very hard to separate things out.'

'Of course,' she concurs, 'if you love someone. It's difficult.'

The sound of the rain drumming on the corrugated roof is strangely soothing.

After a while, I venture an observation. 'But the big difference is that Gemma's risk was in the past. A long time ago – and it sounds,' I say cautiously, again the sensation of my foot inching gingerly on the cliff edge, 'from what you were saying the other day, that Polly's is very much in the present. It's still alight with some degree of danger.'

She sits still.

We watch the walls rising up. Green is obviously in greater abundance than yellow, I think as I survey the completed walls. I notice that Lexie and Ruby have been assigned the job of searching through the other boxes for the required yellow bricks, while the boys do the important construction work.

'I want to talk about it,' she says, into the silence. 'To speak about it out loud. But it feels –' and she stops, twisting her fingers, '– such a betrayal.'

I nod.

'To my sister –' she says, '– to sit here talking to someone. Someone I barely know. A relative stranger in my life – about something so intimate. So revealing.'

I listen. And I notice she doesn't say friend. *A relative stranger*, is what she calls me. And it feels right. It comes as a relief, in a way.

'I – I promised not to tell anyone. Sworn to secrecy. She feels –'

and as she speaks, she looks down at the jammy dodger and idly picks off the grains of sugar with her finger. 'She made me promise I wouldn't tell anyone. She feels –' and again, she struggles to find the right word and looks down at her lap, '– such humiliation.'

I nod again.

'So, if I shared it with you, I'd be breaking a promise. And while it feels hard to break a promise, it feels harder still to watch someone you love feeling so unhappy –' and then she drops her voice down low, '– and possibly come to harm.'

I feel the shift of unease. It's not unexpected, I have been prepared for this. I already know to some degree what she is likely to tell me about Polly. I have read and been involved in enough case histories to know that while the details are different, the fear and humiliation and the paralysis at the heart of it are resoundingly similar. I understand both her nervousness and also the potential risk and danger of not sharing the information. I'm also aware that, as neighbours go, I'm the best person to share this with. But perhaps she knows this too.

'I can probably already predict what you're going to tell me,' I say. 'I worked in a busy inner London practice. I know the statistics. I know a lot about this.' I pause. 'But I also know it can be good to talk. Not to manage the worry all by yourself.'

But I can feel her need to talk is somehow stifled by the promise she has made. This feeling of betrayal. Which is why I say what I do. 'Perhaps we can think of this time – these conversations – as beyond those rules,' I suggest. 'We're not part of each other's lives – we are, as you say, relative strangers. We have been drawn together by this moment in time, where we are living, for a brief period. That's all.'

Afterwards, I wonder if any of this was necessary, if she was planning to confide in me anyway. But still, I felt she wanted to be sure of the confidentiality. That I was someone she could trust.

She looks up.

'In two weeks, I'll be gone,' I say. 'I'll be back in my life. And you'll be here, in yours, before you go to London. Then later on, we'll be in different parts of the city. Our lives will be separate.' I shrug. 'And by that I mean, you don't have to worry that what you tell me will contaminate you, or her life. You can choose not to see me again. Perhaps the normal rules can be suspended. Holiday rules?' I offer. 'And who knows? Maybe having a conversation here will make it easier for you to help her. After we've both gone back to our lives.'

I already feel it's unlikely our paths would cross. Even if we were in the same part of London, I can't imagine our lives entwining, our friendship deepening. It's not a mean thing. It's just what I think. It's not that I haven't come to like her more, but it's the guardedness. The walls she seems to put up. She is so different from what I'm used to with my other friends.

'Different rules,' I say, 'like the feeling that once you're in an airport, en route to your holiday, everything's free. It's part of the holiday.'

She looks confused.

I smile. 'Just me then.'

'Oh – sorry. That's a joke, right?'

But Helen is nodding, she seems to like the idea. Pressing pause on a promise she has made.

'And you'll keep it to yourself?' she asks.

'Of course,' and I gently dip my head.

And so she starts to tell her sister's story, and the narrative begins as they all do. 'They were so good together at first. My sister was happy, really happy,' she reflects.

And I keep my focus on the kids, as she talks. Lexie and Ruby running back, their skirts full of piles of yellow bricks. The boys growing the walls. It's taking shape. The high walls of yellow and green.

As I listen, it's a kind of monologue. As if having decided to speak about it, she's telling the whole story. And it is entirely and depressingly predictable in its trajectory. 'Polly had had these disastrous relationships, and when Alan came along, he seemed great. Attentive, kind, thoughtful. I mean, Polly was bowled over. Always making sure she got home OK. Hatching these innovative plans for dates. It wasn't like he spent loads of money. It was just the way he remembered something she'd liked or wanted to do, and he kind of wove these dates around them. Once, after she'd mentioned she liked outdoor swimming, he drove her out to Hurley, a place by the river in Berkshire where they could swim. He'd packed a picnic lunch. I mean, what men pack picnic lunches with homemade tortilla? I remember how I'd laughed, *that man's a keeper*, I told her.' Then Helen pauses. 'I feel bad, looking back. I realise I felt a little jealous. Why didn't I have someone so attentive? Ironic, now, of course.'

She watches the children. I look too and we both linger over the sight of them. The furious building and hunting for bricks. The whole operation under the eagle-eye of captain Ollie. Lexie seems distracted by something she has unearthed in one of the boxes. A pink feathery thing that she smooths across her arm.

'The way things are now. It seems mad to think I was jealous. Jealous of what they had.'

I nod. I'm already full of the weighty feeling of knowing what's to come. How so many of the women describe the attentiveness. The thoughtfulness. The feeling of being the centre of the universe. Until you realised that the universe was governed by the man. That the most important bit of the universe was their place in it. They were the planet that everything else revolved around.

'It started slowly,' she says, 'little things. Him being over-attentive. Him turning up at nights out she had with friends,' she laughs. 'It was right in that first flush of love. *I missed you*, he'd say, turning up unexpectedly. And at first, she and her friends thought it was sweet. Endearing.'

Biscuit woman makes an announcement about the yoga. 'Ten minutes,' she chirps, 'in the book corner.'

Helen tells me Polly was working as a teacher at the time, when things started to shift. 'Alan began checking her phone. Querying who she was with. Ringing her when she was out. At first it was nice and friendly. Then it became intrusive. *Who were you with? Who was there? How much did you have to drink? Why are you wearing that skirt?*' And she stops for a moment, as if remembering. 'Then accusing her of things she hadn't done.'

I think fleetingly of Terri Garner. How she had talked about her partner's sudden anger.

'At this point she mentioned a few things to me. Not much. But just that she was finding it a bit full-on. Then she had a birthday party—'

She takes a sip of tea. We survey the work-in-progress. The three sides of the castle are now at Lexie's waist height.

'They'd been together about a year, and at the party – he did this poem. It was amazing. With cards and pictures and record-ings of funny things. How they met. I mean,' she says, 'it was great. But then suddenly, it wasn't. Like although it was about her, it was really about him, you know?' and she looks over at me. 'A chance for him to talk. To demonstrate how wonderful he was.

It was her birthday – but ultimately, it was as if he made it about him. It was subtle. It went on and on. Verse after verse. No sense of reading the room. Or reading Polly. I remember looking over at her. I knew her so well. I saw that frozen smile. That look on her face. It was awful. It was killing her. She looked skewered, like a piece of meat. She was grinning away like a fool. Praying for it to finish. To be over. But I realised no one else saw it. Everyone else thought it was fantastic. How lucky she was to have him. *What a great guy to spend so much time. So kind and thoughtful . . . charming . . . such good company.* But I sensed what she did. That it was too much. That it was all about him. I saw her face in that moment. Saw him for what he was. For what he was in danger of becoming. And had a glimpse of the implications for her. That night was the first time I felt worried about her. But when I brought it up, she was irritated. We had a row. She said I was spoiling things for her. *Couldn't I just let her be happy?'*

I listen as Helen talks. There are things I want to ask. But I am careful not to interrupt, so I nod from time to time. Make occasional murmurings. Small comments of agreement. But no questions. I have never heard Helen speak like this. About something so personal, and for so long. I want to keep things alive. I'm aware how quickly things could be shut down. I just listen to her monologue. But even though I am quiet, I am listening in a kind of slow-motion horror. Of course, the question I most want to ask hovers on my lips. But I stay silent. There's something about the way she's talking, almost trance-like about her sister, that leaves me not wanting to break the spell. I know how things work with Helen, that if you ask or pry, she shuts down clam-like, and the conversation is over.

'That was it.'

'What do you mean?'

'Nothing happened,' she says. 'She was a bit frosty with me. And then a couple of months later – she was pregnant,' she throws her hands open, 'and well, things changed. They moved to Nottingham. I feel it got more difficult for her to speak about things after that. Like she wanted to make it work. Try harder.'

I nod.

'Well, you're a GP. I'm sure you can guess where this is heading – sure you've come across cases like this.'

'What happened?' I ask softly.

'Alan became vicious. Mainly verbally – but occasionally physically too. But it was more the mental torment, I think. It –' she bites her lip and looks away, '– it took her a long time to tell me. To admit it to anyone. To admit it to herself. He calls her. Needs to know where she is all the time. It's been bad for the last four years. But things were,' and again, she hesitates, looking away, 'especially difficult for her over the lockdowns,' and I feel the goose bumps bloom across my arms. I feel her caution. Her hesitancy. Her choosing her words very carefully. 'The kids . . . the house . . . I mean, she has no money of her own. She's financially dependent on him. He gives her an allowance for food. But in the last few months, she's been talking really seriously about going – about leaving him. There's a readiness in her that I haven't heard before. She seems to be moving to a place of action. But then that can change—'

'In what way?'

'She's scared.'

'Of him?' and while it's no surprise, I still feel a constriction in my throat.

'Of course – but also,' and she looks away, 'I think she feels so crushed. Underconfident. He's a powerful man. He's been so critical, always telling her how useless she is, often calls her a "waste of space".' She pauses. 'Our mother had some mental health issues in the past. He uses this. Taunts her with it. *The apple never falls far from the tree*, and all that. He tells her she'd never manage on her own. Tells her she's hopeless with the kids. A terrible mother. That she'd fall apart if she was on her own. I mean, she's gone from being head of the English department to being scared of her own shadow. Believes she's a crap mother because he tells her she is so often.' She shrugs. 'She believes it. She believes she simply won't manage.'

'Has she talked to anyone else? A friend? Her GP?'

She shakes her head. 'I'm the only person she talks to.'

'You can't do anything until she's ready. Until she's really ready to go. That can take a long time. I read up on it. Case studies. You can't persuade her to go until she's ready.'

She nods. 'I know. I've tried. So many times. I know that.'

'Does he hurt the kids?'

She looks shocked. 'No. Of course not.'

There's a moment. Neither of us speaks.

'But – you know. I think that's why she's at a turning point. Last week she said she was worried about her eldest kid. She has three children. But now they're all getting older – she said she can imagine they will start questioning some of his ideas. His methods.'

'What do you mean?' and I feel a creeping sense of unease.

She pauses. 'Things that really aren't normal,' she says. 'Things that kids might accept when they're young. But the older they get, they might question. Answer back. Argue,' and she looks away.

I am holding my breath.

'What sort of things?' I ask.

'He has some odd ideas. She doesn't want the kids to be influenced. Contaminated by these things.'

A beat.

'He voted for Brexit,' she says.

I laugh. 'So did half the country.'

But she doesn't smile. Her face is tight.

'He had ideas about people. Groups of people.' And as she speaks, I feel the pull of anxiety.

'Ideas about the country. His sense of injustice.' She twists the top off the jammy dodger. Two halves of a whole, sticky in her fingers. 'He blames other people for things that have gone wrong for him.'

'What do you mean?'

There's a silence. Her voice drops down low. 'Certain groups,' she says carefully, 'people he doesn't think belong here.'

I take a sharp intake of breath.

'Since he lost his job, he's become more fervent. More obsessed. Blames other people. People he says are taking all the jobs. Last week Polly said he spends all his spare time online. Says it's work . . .' and she trails off.

'What does he do?'

'He was a teacher. Now he's joined an online tutoring organisation. Lots of opportunities post-Covid,' she says. 'Polly says she doesn't know who he is any more. She fears for the minds of her children. That his influence will mould them. But also, I think she is worried about the pushback. And how that might be received, how it will go down with him, if they start to question, or argue with his point of view.'

The implication of this hangs in the air. For a moment, I don't know what to say.

'There are risk factors. Safeguarding guidelines,' I start to say. She waves away my words. Irritable. Affronted.

'I said it wasn't an issue now. She's worried it might be. In the future, as they get older. In many ways, it's a good thing that she's talking about it. I can use it to help fuel her resolve to leave.'

'And you're sure,' I ask gently, 'that they are not coming to any harm. At risk at the moment?'

'No,' she says, more softly this time. 'I know Polly. I know she wouldn't stay if anything like that was happening.'

And there is another silence between us. The clatter of noise in the background, the trays. The cups being stacked up.

'You know what the worst thing is?' she says, looking out of the window. 'I always put the phone down thinking – if she's told me that awful and humiliating thing that he did, that's so hard to admit to –' and this is where her voice breaks moment- arily, '– then what isn't she telling me? What is simply too bad to say to another person?'

I nod.

'Not about the children,' she adds quickly, 'but what he's doing to her. The things she can't even begin to think about. Let alone say out loud.' She pauses. 'I think a lot about what she's not telling me. Not telling anyone.'

And it's this final statement that stays with me. The shiver as I think about Terri. How in those minutes we spent together in my room, I felt that too. That if you're telling me these things, giving me horrifying pictures that I now have in my head, what about the other things? The things that are too shameful to repeat. To tell anyone.

With all the safeguarding cases, it's reading between the lines. The things that can't be said. The gaps between the words. The place where there are no pictures. And I feel this, like a clenched ball in my stomach, as we sit side by side on the hard wooden chairs in the musty church hall.

FIFTEEN

James arrives on Friday afternoon, and I notice how pleased I am to see him. We have drinks early evening on the grass. He asks how I'm managing. 'How are you doing?' he says, with concern. 'I gather Rob had to leave. Give me a shout if there's anything I can do to help.' When he stands up, he tells me it's Fajita Friday. 'We're eating our way around the world,' he laughs, and his clear blue eyes twinkle in the sun.

They are out and about early the next day; family walks and trips to the beach and a big supermarket shop that the children diligently carry in bag after bag from the car to the kitchen. Late on Saturday afternoon, I see James outside with Ollie fixing the fence around the cottage by the driveway. I tell him we're expecting a call from Rob. He lifts his hand, 'Say hi from me.'

The connection is bad in the garden, so we walk up the lane to try again. When we eventually get through, the kids leap about and press their faces to the phone. 'Daddy! Daddy!' And then Rob shouts out their names and there's a lot of happy hysteria.

'Where are you?' I say. 'I can't really hear you?'

'Venice Beach.'

'What's that whirling noise?'

There's a muffled sound, some words I don't catch.

'Roller blades.'

'You're *roller blading*?'

'No. Just watching.'

And then there's a thump. The sound of the phone hitting the floor. Muffled voices and laughter. And then the connection goes.

Later that evening, when it starts to rain, I go out to bring in the washing from the line and see James and Ollie still huddled by the fence. I stroll over. 'Still at it?' I say, coming to inspect the work.

'Been a bit of a disaster,' James says. 'We were prepping it for varnishing tomorrow, then discovered four of the posts were rotten.' He gestures over to two splintered struts on the path. 'Had to fix them before we start. They've been a devil to get out. Ollie's been my wingman. Two done. Two to go . . .'

'Very impressed with your staying power,' I say, picking up my basket of washing. 'My two are sprawled on the sofa.'

'Ah,' he laughs, 'the Dunstables never get defeated. What do we do, Ollie?'

And they lean into a fist-bump. 'We put the *able* in Dunst-*able*,' and they both laugh.

I laugh too. Was that a joke, I wonder, as I stroll back across the lawn? Then find myself wishing I could turn either of our surnames into some kind of life-changing mantra.

On Sunday morning, the three of them are outside varnishing the now fixed wooden fence. When I glance over, I see Lexie making long dreamy strokes, her eyes drifting from the task, distracted by the swoop of a bird, or an ant on the floor, or sometimes by an intense fixation on something in front of her that only she can see. This, in contrast to Ollie, who seems to follow his father's lead. Tall, upright, focused. And then James, overseeing them both, with a gentle but firm parental style that I could only dream of.

As I watch, for the best part of an hour Sam and Ruby have been arguing over a small blue plastic dinosaur. It disappeared soon after we arrived at the cottage, and has just been found, by Sam, down the back of the sofa, and is now at the centre of a bitter custody battle.

'I found it!'

'But it was mine before you found it—'

'Finders-keepers,' says Sam decisively.

'But it was always mine, it was from the bubble,' Ruby wails, looking with such adoration at this pitiful bit of plastic that came from a slot-machine outside Asda for a quid. 'And I've *so* missed it,' she says with a woeful face, dredging up a level of emotional drama that I can't help but find impressive. It has become more prized because her older brother Sam wants it. If he hadn't, Ruby would have most likely left it languishing behind the cushion on the sofa.

'You only want it because he wants it,' I say. Like that's something ridiculous, or childish that she will grow out of. Knowing, of course, that it's something we all do. It's the way the world works. The weight and significance of a thing grows with interest. With what we bestow on it. We all want to like what other people like. The swarm mentality that buzzes around the latest thing in vogue. Books, films, art. And even small plastic toys. Sometimes, it can be warranted, this interest. But other times, it's not. It's empty. I think about my friend Lorna. Her beautiful pictures. Her time and dedication to her creativity. And I think of the work of other more celebrated artists. More fashionable. More connected? How the interest can inflate the thing itself, sending the balloon soaring higher. And that without this collective interest it would pop, or deflate, or never, in the case of Lorna, rise in the first place. And still she continues. How difficult it is, how brave, I think, to swim against the tide.

As I listen to the argument escalating to surreptitious shoving and prodding, I am weighing up whether to intervene. There's something about my neighbours' dizzying array of activities over the weekend that makes me want to wallow in my own slovenliness, slipping down slowly into a pool of inactivity. Like a hippo sinking into the mud, I want to glory in the mess and chaos of my own making. As was once pointed out by an ex-boyfriend, this has always been my response to competition. 'You pretend you're not competitive. But you are,' he said, 'you simply look at the competition, and if you don't have a chance to win, you just drop out.'

And of course, in this instance, there is no competing with the orderliness and organisation of the Duns*tables*. They will win, every time. And knowing this seems to push me to the other extreme. I marvel at the chaos that has descended, the lounge, the small strip of a hallway. The kitchen is a trail of undone washing-up and plates of half-eaten food. Half-played games and lumps of Plasticine that have been discarded, pressed in small shapes along the fridge door. The once bright rainbow blocks of pinks and greens and yellows have already become mashed together, making a colour that is a dull dingy brown.

As I pile the dirty dishes into the sink, I watch the varnishing troop move along the fence. James is inspecting the work, and Helen comes out with a tray of snacks and drinks. I can't see from here, but I imagine homemade cake, slices of healthy fruit, fresh juice. She peers at their workmanship. She smiles at James, her hand resting lightly on his shoulder. James says something and then they all down tools to gather round the tray.

If there was a semblance of order before Rob left, it has entirely vanished on his departure. Not because he played any meaningful contribution to the domestic chores, the washing, the cleaning and tidying, but more because he often had an opinion on it. He had a way of instilling a kind of order and discipline to the proceedings. In terms of ideas and activities for the kids, he is so much better at it than me. But he is, I have come to realise, also good at navigating the domestic arena without actually managing to lift a finger. The captain of a ship who rarely puts his hands on the wheel. His departure has meant that this view, this third eye over the domestic proceedings, has gone. I am overcome with a kind of sloth. Like the long-awaited sinking into a full bath. There is no one to call my slovenliness into line. To inspect the quota of vegetables the kids are eating. Any other adult barometer of my parenting standards disappeared when I dropped him at the station. But we have reached a limit, and so I continue to pick up the discarded clothes, the plates of half-eaten food, and start to restore a semblance of order to the chaos.

And as I do, I find myself thinking about Polly. I don't know what she looks like. But already I have formed a picture in my mind from the things that Helen has said.

'She was a teacher,' she'd told me. 'So thorough. So dedicated. But also, so much fun. She made the lessons full of laughter. That's what all the kids said.'

She became head of department. And I see her as tall, with dark hair. A laughing cheerful face.

'He ruined her,' was what Helen said on the beach, 'he stripped her life of fun.' Her voice was bitter. 'But he then replaced it with something else. With fear. With a kind of smallness. A reduced version of herself. A terror that she had never known before.'

She'd looked down, pressing her palm into the sand. 'What makes someone so apparently confident, so apparently self-assured, put up with that?'

I had looked back at her. The enormity of the question sat between us.

Just at the moment the bickering is going to escalate to the point that even I can't ignore it, I see James striding across the lawn. 'Here comes Ollie and Lexie's dad!' I say, hoping my announcement will stem the flow of the heated debate. It seems to work.

When I open the door, he tells me he'd promised Ollie a spin in the car. 'Wondered if Sam would like to come? I'll only be half an hour or so. Just along the coast road. I have to leave this afternoon, so we won't be very long—'

Sam is already pushing through the doorway, spluttering with excitement.

'Lexie wants to stay here and play on the lawn, if Ruby wants to join her?'

Helen and I sit in the sunshine drinking cups of tea, as the girls play with a house that Lexie has started making out of a cardboard box.

It's only after the boys have gone that I realise I feel so much more relaxed in the countryside. There's the ease of being outdoors on the beach with the kids. The shrinking of our world. But I feel my innate sense of mistrust has also loosened. I can't imagine I'd have so readily let Sam go off in the car with a new neighbour if we were in London. It's the same shift of temperament with a two-week holiday away. How things lighten in the sun. A new set of rules come into play. Ones that are more relaxed. Less rigid, and less threaded with the catastrophising I have with inner-city life. I don't say all this out loud to Helen, but I do tell her I keep forgetting to lock up. 'I can't imagine ever doing that at home. Yesterday, when I went to the beach, I left both the front and back door unlocked.'

She laughs. 'Same, whenever we're here. But that's how I grew up, in a village in Somerset. Wouldn't have dreamt of doing that where we lived in the town in Germany.'

Together, we stare out at the rolling hills, the golden field, the glinting sea beyond.

'Perhaps it's an illusion,' I say, in a mock-spooky voice. 'A false sense of security. All these chocolate box cottages – who really knows what goes on behind closed doors? And as for Pete's so-called "late-night badger culls",' I laugh, 'all sounds a bit *Wicker Man* to me.'

Helen laughs again. But it's her forced laugh. The one I've noticed she does when she doesn't really get what I'm saying. It's usually when I'm not being serious. Any jokey or light-hearted stuff always seems to land badly with her. She looks slightly quizzical, and a bit desperate as she tries to work out how to respond, and instantly, I regret having made the remark in the first place.

We sip our tea in silence, watching the girls playing.

They have got tired of playing with the box house and Lexie has suggested a game called 'Lego Mansion'. The two of them delight in this new venture, making up the set of unfathomable and increasingly complicated rules as they go along.

It's an hour before the boys return. I look up at the sound of the car on the track. The roof is down, the boys sitting in the back.

When Sam gets out, his face is red and flushed, his curls in a tangle from the wind. He runs across the lawn. Ollie gets out carefully. That familiar serious expression, and how often in the face of the animation and exuberance of the others, he looks more considered, picking his way through life with the caution of an old man.

'It was so cool. We went sooooo fast,' Sam says. Ollie nods and Helen draws him in for a hug and they head inside for lunch. 'Wash hands,' I hear her say, before the door closes behind them.

Seconds later, their door opens and James comes back out, fishing something out of his pocket.

'I forgot to say,' he says, waving an envelope in his hand. 'This was so kind of your father.'

I stare back at him.

'Michelin-starred!' he says. 'It sounds great. But unfortunately, I'll be away on Friday. In Brussels on a three-day course. Thursday to Saturday, so I'm afraid we won't be able to make it. Will you let him know for me? There was only the number of the restaurant. Not a contact number for him. Otherwise, I'd have replied myself. We have a card for him, for the big day. Helen will pass it on.'

'Sure,' I say. 'Will do. No worries.'

And as he closes the door, I stand there for a moment. My hands shielding my eyes from the sun. Trying to take in the information that my father has invited the Dunstables to his birthday lunch. If I feel anything, it is a kind of embarrassment.

I ring Gemma. As usual, straight to voicemail.

I get the houmous and pitta bread. And I think about Rob as I chop up carrots and peppers (two vegetables) and grab a handful of cherry tomatoes (which makes three). I open the back door. The sun is still warm. The patch of grass shines like a small green jewel. I lay out a blanket and carry out the food. 'We're having a picnic,' I announce to whoops of excitement and, as always, the food tastes better when eaten away from the table.

They eat while rolling the trucks and cars in the dirt. There are no hand wipes. No sanitisers. And I'm childishly amused by how horrified Helen would be.

*

James leaves at about 4 p.m., waving as he reverses his shiny green car out of the driveway. Helen comes out a little later. 'Do you want to go to the beach?' she asks. The kids jump up.

'Sure,' I say, slightly surprised, given she usually likes to be at home for tea.

'We can take food for the kids to have down there,' she says, 'it's such a lovely evening. I have some leftover pasta.'

Everything is easier outside. The space. The sand. The endless possibilities that the landscape of a beach and a bucket and spade continue to offer. 'It's the gift that keeps on giving,' I say as we watch the kids rush over the dunes as if they hadn't seen a beach for months.

The sea looks different. It changes every day. But that day it's a dark cobalt blue, dotted with white curls as the wind scuds over the surface. Further out towards the horizon, the sea looks like mercury, jostling metallic waves dancing under the sun.

We sit on the sand. I am tired and have no great desire to talk. And Helen always seems happy to sit quietly together. Never seems to need the comfort of incessant conversation, the balm of chit-chat and small talk.

When she brings up my dad's birthday lunch, I don't really want to discuss it.

'It was kind,' she says, 'to be invited. So sorry we can't be there – James has a course in Brussels. Marketing and publicity for new businesses.'

I wave away her words. I don't want to think about it. About who else he has invited. What odd configuration of people will be assembled round the table. The thought leaves me feeling uneasy. What I don't say is that I'd try to find an excuse if I could.

'Very friendly of him,' she says, 'he was very chatty the other day. Nice to see him throwing himself into the celebratory spirit. I'm not big on birthdays myself. Always admire people who can embrace the moment—'

'Yes,' I say.

Our roles have reversed. Now it's me who is the quiet one. The one who wants to close things down.

After a while, she asks about Rob. 'Will he be gone much longer?'

I shake my head. 'Who knows? He said a week, but that was twelve days ago. The whole film business,' I say, 'it's so precarious. So uncertain really.' Again, I feel too weary to begin to explain the whole thing. Sketch out the contours of a business that is unwieldy and unpredictable.

My thoughts drift to Rob and the job. I already feel a heaviness. A sense of dread about the script. We've been here before. The upsurge and flurry of excitement. Then the slow drag back down as the tide of interest, or finances or something else, ebbs away. This time, he pointed out, it was different. He has been paid some money upfront. It is on course. But I fear the worst, and that the conversations about my return to work will resurface. Will be dredged up from the silty depths. I can see already how we edge around it. Kicking it back and forth and then, one day, he will just walk into the kitchen and come out with it, that small twitch of something on his top lip. 'I think you should go back to work.' And then finally, the thing we have both danced around will suddenly be unavoidable. So, this is where my mind has drifted when Helen tells me the news about Polly.

'I spoke to her earlier,' she says, 'she's had a bad weekend—' and then she falters, her voice cracking with emotion. And she does the thing that's become like a tic. Her fingers at her bottom lip, folding it in two, like a fortune cookie. I don't know her well enough to know if it's to stop herself getting upset, or if it's a thing she does when she's nervous or trying to say something hard and difficult.

'She told me she's ready,' she says, and her voice is suddenly matter of fact. But there is an urgency. A breathlessness. 'She wants to go. To leave. And she's asked me to sort things out. Make all the arrangements.'

I turn to look at her. As she is speaking, she is looking straight out at the sea.

'She's worried that time is running out,' she says, her hands scooping and digging, letting the sand idly sift through her fingers.

'What do you—'

'She's going to come here,' she says. 'Well, obviously not here at the cottage. But to this area. She wants me to sort school places for her kids. There's no way she'll be able to do it from Nottingham. He monitors everything. Watches her every move. Her calls. Her emails. Where she goes. Who she speaks to. And she has no money of her own. She asked me to do it for her. To make the appointments at the school, on her behalf. Sort somewhere to live,' and she speaks like she's ticking off a list.

Just then, we're caught by the gulls, the glide of their enormous white bodies as they scream up towards the cliff. Then all of a sudden, there's another noise. An odd whirring sound. And when the drone appears above us, it startles Helen, and she leaps up, sloshing water over her trousers. 'Jeez,' she says. The two men are by the steps, one with a controller in his hand. She glares at them. 'What are they doing?' she says, affronted. Perhaps it's the tension with her sister, but she seems uncharacteristically rattled by it.

'Boys with toys,' I say. Then I pour her some tea from the flask, and she visibly relaxes when they pack up and go.

She picks up with Polly's story, telling me she's been talking about leaving for ages, 'especially after that last lockdown,' and it's then she turns to look at me. 'But this is the first time she's asked me to do this. To set the practicalities in motion. To get everything in place.'

Her face looks suddenly alive. Animated. 'I really think it's happening. I think she means it. She's ready to go.'

I can hear the excitement in her voice. There's nervousness and a kind of relief. But mostly there is an energy about her. And I feel it too. Like an opening in my chest. A desire to stand up and surge forwards. It's as if all the events of the past four months have propelled me to this point. That, with all my knowledge and skills from my job, and the mistake I made with Keith and Jackson, I have the chance to redeem myself. To make amends. To help someone else. To redirect my skills and expertise to a worthwhile cause. Somewhere I am needed. While I put my net out to try to catch the wrong person, I now have the chance to catch someone else. And the thought that the knowledge I have could somehow benefit Polly fills me with a kind of elation.

'I just don't know where to start,' she says, 'she wants to move quickly—'

And I know what she's going to say. I hear the question before she voices it. I am ready for it, my eyes on the water.

She turns to face me. 'Can you help?'

SIXTEEN

When Helen outlines the details, I'm surprised to hear how far advanced they are. There has clearly been a lot of thinking and discussion. I think about those endless phone calls, the plans they must have hatched while Helen has been pacing about on the beach.

She has identified a refuge in Swanage. I don't know why I was taken aback to hear mention of a refuge, but it must have shown on my face.

'She won't be able to come here,' she says quickly. 'It's the first place he'll come.'

'And you're sure he won't accept her wanting to leave? Wanting to end the relationship?'

A look crosses her face. A kind of horrified disbelief.

I hold a hand up. 'I just want to check. To be sure,' I qualify. 'I know a lot about what needs to happen in this situation. I just want to be clear that Polly feels her life would be in danger if he knew where she was—'

'Her life is already in danger,' she corrects me. 'This risk will increase when she tries to leave him.' She looks away. 'It's clear from what she's already told me.'

I nod.

'One of the things I need to do this week is sort out school places. Term breaks up soon, and there are three kids to get in somewhere – hopefully at the same school. There's one within walking distance of the refuge—'

And then, she's galloping ahead onto something else. Her

mind seems scattered, darting about all over the place. She says she doesn't know enough about the legal and financial stuff. 'I told Polly I'd find out. Do you know about all that stuff?'

Before I can answer, she's moved on to the GP, 'finding one to register with in Swanage.' These rambling thoughts are unusual, so unlike her ordered and methodical approach I have come to know so well.

'Helen,' I say, holding my hand up. She stops and looks at me, startled. 'I know all about this. I can help.'

But I am pretty sure she knows this already. That strange look we exchanged the first time we met. We have, I realise, been building towards this moment.

Looking back, did I think this through at all? Was I too quick to offer my help? Did I consider any of the potential problems? I don't think I was thinking of much at all. If I was focusing on anything, it was about how my previous attempts to help had been misguided. And the landslide of repercussions that followed. And how I had another chance to help. I had a chance to help Helen and Polly.

I'd be lying if I said I wasn't delighted to have this opportunity. I felt a charge of excitement. This conversation released a surge of hope. The chance to be useful. A trigger, to release my own silent roar of frustration. A chance perhaps to assuage my own shame. My own paralysis. My own sense of failure. Looking back, did it mean I had blinkers on? That while my attention was fixed on Polly, I was blind to what was going on elsewhere.

She drops her voice down. 'When I'm sorting all these things out, I can't take my kids in the schools – or anywhere. They'll ask questions. Especially Ollie. No one must know. It has to be a complete secret. I can't risk anything going wrong. Any of the plans leaking out.' Her words are speeding up now, tumbling out in a kind of heady rush. 'Polly's trusting me completely,' she says. 'She made me promise not to say anything to anyone. Anyone connected to us,' she adds.

Given what I know about the other cases I have worked on, this is something she doesn't need to say. This is something I know already.

'I totally understand—'

And then she turns to me. 'I haven't even told James,' she says, and perhaps I look surprised, because she adds, 'I mean, he knows about the whole situation, of course. But not about this sudden development. He'd only worry. Ask questions. Try to help. We can't have that. It needs to be very simple. You're the only person who can know.'

Her hands fidget in her lap. 'I just wondered if you'd come with me. Then you can keep an eye on the kids. Find a play-ground nearby, while I nip in for the meetings?'

'Of course,' I say. 'Anything you need.'

'At some point, she'll be able to come here. But not at first. It won't be safe. But at least she knows the area. And Mum will be back in the autumn. She will be a support. A help with the kids.'

'Three kids. Single mum,' I muse. 'It's not going to be easy.' I regret this instantly when I see the look on her face.

'It's nothing compared to what she's dealing with now,' she says curtly.

I simply nod again.

Helen seems both focused and distracted. And as she stops to think, she pulls nervously at her bottom lip. I think about Terri Garner. The plans the Local Authority had in place. I feel a snag of worry about Helen's certainty about her sister.

'You know,' I say, pausing as I try to find the right words. 'It can take a woman a long time to leave. I did some research,' I explain, 'for my safeguarding role. And a patient I had at work. The decision can be back and forth. Three steps forward, one step back. The decision is complex, it's not a linear journey.'

She stares at me for a moment.

'I've been on this journey with her for the last four years.'

'OK. It's just,' and I look away, out to sea, '– anything can happen. I just don't want you to get your hopes up. I know you want this for her. But not only does she need to want this for herself, which she clearly does, but she needs to feel, in that moment, brave enough to do it –' I pause again, trying to find the right words, '– after years of being told she can't do anything.'

I think about what we often used to talk about at work. The hope that nothing will get in the way. The obstacles a woman has to face in order to leave; her self-doubt, her fear. And perhaps, most dangerous, and most frequently of all, her abuser.

'I understand I can't be in control of her and what she does,' she says. 'I have learnt this, very painfully, over the years. But I'll get things sorted from my end. With your help. I'll do everything I can. I feel hopeful,' she nods. She turns to look at me. 'I *need* to feel hopeful.'

She looks away. There's a long moment of silence.

'She told me something happened over the weekend—'

The stillness is broken by the chatter from the children on the sand. The scream of the gulls.

'What happened?'

'I can't say,' she whispers. 'I just can't say it out loud.'

But I see it on her face. In the words she doesn't say.

And that's when I feel it. The horror I know nothing about. The unspoken terror that is Polly's life. Unspoken by Helen and unasked by me. I feel it in the air. Our eyes meet. And in that moment, I see the pain on her face. Her fear for her sister.

Again, I feel the surge. The rush to help.

'Her life is in danger. But more importantly, she now sees that her life is in danger.'

I nod. 'It's a big step,' I say, feeling concern that I don't express. 'And there are things I can help with. Information that might be helpful. The legal stuff. The grants. The finance, I know a bit about it.'

'And the patient?' she asks with a sudden eagerness. 'The one you mentioned? Did it go well for her? Did you help?'

A beat.

'Yes,' I said. 'It was all good.'

'Excellent,' she says, and her face lights up and she looks suddenly child-like with hope.

'I brought these,' she says, and she pulls out two beers from the cooler. Each I notice is wrapped in its own holder. She hands one to me and it is ice cold on my fingers.

'Cheers,' and we chink bottles.

'To Polly,' she says.

'To Polly.'

The sun is still hot. We call the kids up from the beach for more sun cream. They have been trawling through the rock pools, collecting shrimps, scooping them up with their small nets, then tipping them out into one of the buckets. Every now and then Ollie brings the bucket up proudly to show us the collection of transparent darting creatures. And we peer in at their long antennae and enormous black eyes.

The obedience of Helen's kids has an unexpected roll-out to the behaviour of my own, as I note how obligingly they stand in front as I spray them with lotion, turning round patiently as I rub it in on their sandy bodies.

'Ollie,' Helen says as he picks up the bucket, 'don't forget to tip them back out later. They'll die in that warm water. That small space. And besides, they'll feel lonely, away from their family,' she says, and then they all run back down the beach.

In one of her dreamy wanderings on the sand, Lexie finds a pink bucket. 'Can we keep it?' she asks excitedly, when she brings it back to show us.

Helen thinks for a moment. 'What if it was yours? What would you want to happen?'

Lexie wrestles with the answer she knows, but doesn't want to say out loud. 'I'd come back tomorrow and hope to find it,' she says sadly.

'Exactly.'

Lexie sighs, a resigned expression on her face.

'So, let's maybe leave it here, a bit further up the sand bank, towards the path. And then if no one comes for it, and it's still here tomorrow, it's yours.'

She nods, and while not really liking the outcome, she trudges up the dunes, leaving the bucket where it's visible to any passer-by.

We linger in the early evening sun. And unusually for Helen, she seems in no hurry to get back. Ordinarily, she is clock watching. Liking the routines of bath and bedtime. But that day, there is something carefree about her. Something I have never seen on her face before. I can only imagine it's the news of Polly that has transformed her mood. The sense that something so profound might be shifting for her sister. And I know that feeling. How the smallest movement of change or progress for them can leave you feeling elated, full of joy.

But I also know the feeling of disappointment. How quickly that hope can be suddenly dashed, like a flimsy life raft on the rocks.

It's still warm at 8 p.m. as we start gathering up our things and calling out 'five minutes' to the kids.

It's at that moment that I glance at the sea. 'Look!' I shout, pointing.

Helen looks up. And we call out to the children. They're in a pod of eight or maybe ten. Their dark sleek bodies curling in the silvery water. We watch silently, and they circle each other, taking turns to make crescents in the sea. And then, just as quickly as they arrived, they are gone.

I tell her that sailors said they brought good luck, 'were seen as a good omen for the voyage.'

She nods. And for a long time, her gaze lingers on the small patch of water.

As we gather up our things, Helen reminds the kids about the shrimps. 'Don't forget to pour them back!' she says, as she shakes out her sandy jumper.

I watch Ollie trail off with the bucket, waving a hand in response as he makes his way to the rock pools.

My kids are sandy and sun-kissed. Their hair in tangled balls of curls. I tip Ruby upside down on my lap. Her sticky gritty hands are pressed on my face. I bury my head in her hair. She smells of salt and sun cream. She laughs. The sun is a shower of silver on the water. And in that moment, I want to capture and bottle the feeling of contentment. Of not needing to be anywhere or do anything. No rush. No babysitter to get to. No nursery pick-up. I embrace the sudden smallness of my world, in a way that feels wholesome. This is happiness, I think. Living right now, in the ripeness of the moment. It feels delicious and complete. Like a small peach.

It's only when we're at the car that I notice Sam has left his hoodie somewhere.

'Maybe by the rock pool?' he says.

I've already strapped them into the car. 'Can you keep an eye for a sec,' I say to Helen, 'while I run back down?'

The tide is rushing in now. I spot the flash of red by the rocks. I take one last look at the beach. Just a few stragglers on an otherwise empty stretch of sand.

It's on the way back to the car that I notice it. The pink bucket is where Lexie wedged it. But when I walk past, I notice it's full of water. I peer in. The shrimps the kids had caught. The darting eyes. The long antennae. Some are swirling about slowly. But mainly there's a stillness. I peer closer. Several are lifeless, floating on the surface. Scorched by the sun. I dip my fingers in. The water is warm.

I feel confused as I pick it up and walk over to the rocky salt pools. I thought I saw Ollie tip it out. I feel a sudden pang of sadness for these small spindly translucent creatures. When I empty it out, the ones that are alive dart and spin with a kind of ecstasy. Free from the entrapment of the hot plastic bucket, they swim and dance in the wide expanse of cool water.

As I dig the empty bucket back into the sand, I feel a shift of something towards Ollie. That perhaps there's another side to the boy who seems so shiny and good and obedient. That the child who looks like a perfect cut-out boy isn't perhaps so perfect after all. It occurs to me he might have a hidden streak of disobedience. Or even cruelty. And that makes him come alive a bit more. Become a bit more real.

*

On our way home, as I turn off the main road towards the farm and our cottage, Pete roars up the lane in his blue truck. He doesn't look up or wave. As I park, Joyce is walking briskly up the lane. 'Did you see Pete?' she says, shielding her eyes from the evening sun as she stops to talk.

'Yes, just now, we passed him on the way in—'

She looks distracted.

'Are you OK?' I ask.

She hesitates. 'Well, we've been better – Pete lost his temper with the duty officer at the council earlier. They were on the phone. He said some things he shouldn't have. And they basically gave him a warning. Red rag to a bull,' she says. 'Then he just left, without a word. I'm hoping he doesn't do something stupid. It'll just make everything worse.'

'I'm so sorry, Joyce. Can I help at all?'

She shakes her head. 'Hopefully, he'll calm down and see sense after he drives about for a bit.'

She turns to go. 'Oh – I meant to say, it was very kind. The invite from your dad. But it's not for us,' she says, 'Pete would hate all that fancy stuff. Not his thing at all. Nor me, to be honest. Sorry –' and she pushes away a grey curl that has fallen across her face. 'But I was going to ask,' she says, 'were you planning to take the kids? If not, they can stay here with us and play.'

I haven't quite firmed up plans for the kids. We're due to have a birthday tea with my parents in their hotel garden at 5 p.m., which the kids are excited about because my mother has already told them about the giant maze. But the three-course table lunch was going to be less than ideal. They'd hate having to sit at the table for very long, and I've already accepted that either Rob or I will spend the bulk of the meal outside in the garden with them.

'That's really kind. I'll have a think. I'm sure they'd much prefer being with you to a table full of grown-ups. Can I let you know?'

And she nods and waves as she strides back up towards the house.

It's late when Pete gets home. I'm at the kitchen window when I hear the tyres and look up to see his truck return.

SEVENTEEN

We don't see much of Helen and the kids the next day, and on Tuesday they set off early in the morning. I remember she said something about shopping, so I think perhaps they've gone to Dorchester. After yesterday's sun, it's grey and overcast, so after breakfast, we drive out to Studland, and park in the café car park, take the cliff path, then loop back through the fields for cake. The kids want to play on the beach, so I bring what we've brought from the café down to the sand. We're all in our anoraks. It's not cold, but there's a slight drizzle in the air, and I sit on the damp sand on a plastic bag I found in the car, as the kids scamper off down to the shoreline.

The beach is empty. Just a man and his thin spindly dog, like small scratches in the distance. I sip at my polystyrene cup of tea and watch Sam and Ruby digging at the water's edge. A breeze ripples over the surface of the water, and moves over their heads, like fingers in their curls. They work hard, silently, with heads down low, stopping every now and then to inspect and exchange treasures they retrieve from the sand.

It's only when I squint further in the distance that I see them. It's Leo I recognise first. His tall gangly body, head and shoulders above his mother, but it's his giant jerky strides that give him away, marching ahead like an enormous wooden soldier. And following behind is Joyce. Her red coat, hands pushed down deep into her pockets, and her grey hair looking startled in the wind. They are by the café at the far end, moving along the beach. But their progress is slow, dictated as it is by Leo's complex sequence of walking. The striding forwards quickly, then suddenly coming to an abrupt halt, then backtracking, then the twirling for a while on the spot, and all the while Joyce hangs back, waiting patiently until her son is ready to move on again.

When I look back down to the shore, I see that Ruby has discarded her spade and is scanning the sand for things to collect in her bucket. I watch her reach down for something, then she runs up the beach towards me, her fist clutched tight. 'Look,' she says, uncurling her fingers to reveal a piece of green sea glass. I take it from her outstretched hand, rubbing the smooth edges between my fingers. 'Like a jewel,' I say, and she nods proudly, before taking it back, placing it carefully in her pocket and turning round to join her brother.

When I next glance up the beach, Leo and Joyce have stopped. Joyce is saying something to him, but Leo is rocking back and forth. He looks agitated, like he was that day when Joyce was trying to encourage him to do gardening on the farm. He's spinning round and round. She reaches for him, but he jerks back, away from her. He rocks on his heels, harder and faster. As she moves closer, he strides off. The bay carries the sound of his noises. The grunting and the high-pitched screams and whoops as he twirls around. Since being at the cottage, it's taken me some time to get used to and learn the meaning of these noises. To distinguish between the different sounds he makes. And the more high-pitched, the more agitated they are. The noise that day is piercing and loud, like one long continuous shriek.

Even though they are some distance away, it feels intrusive to watch. I look away, then glance up at the car to see if I can gather everything up and get to the car before they are close enough to spot us. The distance to the car is short. Ten strides up the sandy bank. I look down at the kids; they are digging furiously again, spraying sand behind them in a big wide arc. It would be like prising two limpets off a rock.

There's a louder noise. I look up to see Leo bring his fist down hard against the side of his face. Once. Twice. Three times. Joyce steps forwards and tries to intervene. She reaches for his hands. But he shakes her off, rocking more vigorously back and forth. She tries again, but he steps back. His fingers are pulling at his jumper. I feel a lurch forwards. I should stand up. Intervene, offer to help.

His hands are pecking at his body like hungry birds. Suddenly the jumper is off and over his head. There's a grey t-shirt underneath. And seconds later, this too is on the floor. Not over his head this time, but ripped from his body in several clawing grabs. It sits on the sand for a moment, then it's lifted in the wind, scampering off along the beach like a frightened rabbit.

I look back at the kids. They are laughing. Ruby is shrieking and holding something out to Sam.

Next, I hear Joyce call out, 'Stop it, now!' It's loud and abrupt. She says his name, several times. It's clear and firm. Then she says something else, but I can't make out the words. But it is no good, he spins away from her, undoing his trousers, peeling them down and pulling at his pants. She lunges forwards to stop him, but he twists away from her, his white naked body dancing wildly in the grey drizzle of the rain, his arms flapping with distress. She reaches for him again. He twists away. Then he pushes her. She is sent off balance. I put down my cup. I stand up. I must go and help. They are in a tussle together, his fists are now pummelling at her chest, her head, and she's trying to stop him, one hand up to protect her face, the other flailing out.

I slump back down as I hear the sound of her hand meeting his cheek. It's not a hard slap, and it's arisen as a consequence of the chaos and flailing limbs. But nonetheless, it is a slap and makes a loud sound that echoes round the empty bay. A cluster of gulls are startled by the noise and flap up into the air. The hem of my jacket catches the cup and the tea pools away into the sand, small swirls of steam rising up. My cheeks are burning as I look away.

At the water's edge, my children are digging and playing in the sand. I want to be down there with them. If I had been, I wouldn't have seen Joyce and Leo. I wouldn't have seen it happen. There's a loud howling noise, and when I turn to look, he has slumped against Joyce. He's sobbing and she draws him awkwardly to her with one arm, the other clutching his jumper around him like a towel. They are hugging now, and slowly and gently, she helps him back into his clothes. I can see she is crying too. Clutching him, and pulling him to her. Stroking his head. I know I have to move fast. If she sees me stand up, she'll know I've seen it. So, while she goes to retrieve his t-shirt, I move quickly down to the water's edge.

'We're making a swimming pool,' Sam says, handing me a spade, and I begin to hack at the sand. I curl my body round, so I'm facing the sea, my back to the beach. If Joyce comes by, she might not see us. And even if she does, she will see we are looking the other way, and she can choose to walk quickly by.

Ruby has amassed a small collection of finds: a feather, an old zip from a jacket, a dozen shells, a mermaid's purse, 'like a squishy pillow,' she says, and three more pieces of sea glass. 'Treasure things,' she says, handing them over proudly. I pick up each one in turn, twisting them in my fingers. I have never given an assortment of random objects such undivided attention. After careful inspection, I reach for the spade again. I am engrossed in the swimming pool excavation when Sam calls out.

'Mummy, look!'

I feel my body freeze. I keep digging.

'It's the lady from the farm,' he says, 'with Leo!'

'Shall we wave? Let's wave!' and the two of them flap their hands wildly in the air.

*

It's my evening session with Veronica. It's a regular arrangement, but I feel awkward going. But equally, not going would feel more pointed, and might somehow look worse.

Joyce is distracted when I arrive at the door. She looks for a moment like she's forgotten I was coming. I hesitate. 'I can do the meeting at home,' I say. 'It's no problem.' But she ushers the children in. 'We'll go over for the milking,' she says.

Joyce is friendly and welcoming to the kids, but she clearly doesn't really want to chat. She looks exhausted. Yet, it feels wrong not to mention anything or offer my support, and so just before I go upstairs, I say, 'I'm so sorry things are so tricky with Leo. I should have offered to help – today.'

She seems uncomfortable, finding it difficult to meet my gaze. A brief shake of her head. 'Other people getting involved –' and she hestitates, '– it can make it worse.'

'Well,' I say, feeling embarrassed in the uncharacteristic silence, 'if there's anything I can do. To help. If you need a break. I don't know what I can do – but you've been so helpful. So kind. If there's anything—'

'Thank you. I appreciate it. It has been a difficult few days,' she says carefully. 'But we'll manage.'

She doesn't seem herself. Her face is drawn. Pale. And more than wishing I'd helped, I simply wish I hadn't been on the beach at that time. Hadn't been a witness to their private moment of distress. I want to tell Joyce that I could see it was accidental. That I saw how it had happened.

As I'm walking up the stairs, my head is full of the different things to talk about: my father's invites to the neighbours, my unease about his birthday that I don't fully understand. Helen, and my plans to help with Polly. But as I click onto the session, I watch the children out of the window, as they march off to the cow shed with Joyce. She's in the middle, holding each of their hands, arms swinging and laughing.

'I felt a sense of paralysis,' I say, telling Veronica about the beach, 'wishing I wasn't there. But since I was, wanting to help. I felt terrible.'

She comments on my sense of over-responsibility. A recurring theme in our sessions. 'Like it's up to you to sort things – to spot the potential for disaster. To prevent it happening – understandable, perhaps,' she says, 'given your feelings as a child – with Gemma.'

And without planning to, I find myself telling her about the Sunday lunch. It's an afternoon I still see so clearly, nearly thirty years later, but it's one I have never spoken about, not even to Rob.

'Sunday meals were difficult then. Long and protracted,' I say. I tell her how we'd already sat through Gemma's rice and pea dance. The agonies as she chased two peas to simultaneously skewer onto her fork. The repetition of the chewing. The silence. And how there was something about my father that day, how he ate without a word, his rage was in the room, 'hovering over the table like a mallet.'

I picture the scene. My father's rigid face, my mother's forced jollity. My own stomach scrunched up like a piece of paper. By then, Gemma was so pale, just a wisp of a thing at the table.

'She never ate the puddings my mother made – and that day, she reached for an apple from the fruit bowl. She cut it in half and began slicing one of the halves into smaller segments.'

I remember the surgical precision as she fanned the slices around the plate. So thin they were luminous and transparent. Her movements were slow, almost balletic. The lifting of the knife. The reaching for the wafer-thin slice of apple that she danced up to her lips. The whole operation was mesmerising and strangely beautiful, while threaded with the tension of life-saving surgery. Then came the chewing. A full two minutes per mouthful. I knew all the routines. All the timings.

'For crying out loud,' my dad thundered, his fist landing heavily on the table, and for the first time, he broke his own rule, and left the table.

I tell Veronica how we could hear him in the kitchen, crashing about, opening cupboards and drawers. Gemma carried on chewing and slicing. My mother clattered the plates together and I remember sitting still, my body pressed to the back of my chair.

'What was the feeling?' she asks.

'Dread,' I say. 'Fear –' and then I think for a moment, '– but also a hint of something else. Relief maybe? That finally, something was going to happen. Something different. Something that might break the endless routine.'

I tell her how the kitchen door swung open and Dad came in with a tray. I remember it was the metal one with the picture of kittens on. He placed it on the table. 'It was piled high with food items. Chocolate biscuits. Sausage rolls. Marshmallows. Crisps.

Slices of bread and a slab of cheese and packets and tins of other things—'

As I speak, I hold my breath, recalling the shock. The feeling of anticipation.

'He grabbed Gemma.'

And even now, all these years later, it feels hard to return to that moment. How he seized her arm, as she tried to stand. Then he came behind her, his arms around her waist. She was feather-light and no match for him, and as he lifted her, the chair toppled over onto the carpet. The ineffectual and half-hearted protest from my mother, 'Geoffrey—' she said, her hands whirling in the air like whisks. The shock on Gemma's face.

'He half carried, half dragged her across the dining room to the bottom of the stairs. He told me to bring up the tray. *Now.* I did what I was told,' I say.

I did what he wanted.

There was scuffling and shouting on the stairs as she kicked at the walls as he carried her up. I brought up the tray. I set it down where he told me to. I left. I couldn't look at my sister. She called out for me. Twice. Then there was silence. I tell Veronica how, at first, I went and sat in my room. My chest was pounding. And then I crept back to see – I had to watch. Had to know what was happening. 'It was like something I wanted to see – but was terrified to look at.'

Peering through the crack of the door, I saw Gemma was sitting facing me, her back to the window; it looked like a belt was looped around her waist, fixing her to the chair. Her hands were behind her back. If she had struggled earlier, now, she had surrendered entirely to the process. Her head was leaning back, as he pushed food into her slack open mouth. Pieces of bread, a marshmallow, crisps that he poked into her mouth with his fingers. She shook her head at the cubes of cheese, but he persevered. 'Swallow,' he said, a bottle of water at her lips. And she did. And so, it went on, as he ploughed through the contents of the tray. Spoonfuls of sweetcorn. Chunks of tuna. Pieces of digestive biscuit.

My father was talking to her, lifting her hair from her face as he fed her. 'Good girl,' he said. Soothing words, like she was a baby. 'One more mouthful,' then intermittently wiping her face with a flannel, as if it was a bib.

I watched with a kind of horrified fascination. Appalled, I wanted it to stop. But then I was aware of another feeling. The joy of watching my sister eat. I realised a part of me would have liked to be in there too, pushing the food into her mouth and filling up her tiny, emaciated body. I wanted to look away. I wanted it to stop. But somehow, I also wanted it to continue. A part of me wanted the cruelty. The violence.

'As if filling her up with food would change everything. As though it would miraculously turn Gemma back into who she once was. That we'd sit and laugh and read magazines on her bed. That I'd have my sister back.'

Of course, her body couldn't possibly digest all that food, and in the middle of the night, I woke up to a loud intermittent guttural sound, what I first thought was the sound of a fox. But when I got up, in the dim glow of the night light in her room, I saw the hunched shape of Gemma kneeling on the carpet, retching and roaring up the contents of her stomach into the plastic bags my mother held out for her. 'She was tying up each one, before reaching for another. Six or seven of them lined up neatly on the floor.'

I tell Veronica that my father didn't go to work the next day. 'He didn't get out of bed. A week later – Gemma went into hospital. It was never spoken about again,' I say.

'That was the beginning of your father's first bout of depression?'

'I think so.'

Veronica sits quietly for a moment. She tells me she feels very moved by the story. 'Listening to you, I feel full of loss. I feel the pain of it,' she says.

And we end the session in silence. Sitting with the sadness.

After the session, I close the computer and walk down the stairs. The kids are ready to go. There's no offer of wine. Our regular seat in the sun for badger night.

'I can't stop tonight,' Joyce says, 'let's catch up later in the week.'

I'm not disappointed; I feel relieved to go straight home with the kids.

*

The next morning, a police car arrives at the farm. Two policewomen and another couple in a separate car. They are all inside for over an hour. The female officers leave first. Then after another half an hour, the other two get in their car and drive away.

A little later, there's a knock at the door. It's Joyce, her face tight with tension.

'The police. And social services. Someone called them.' Her voice is clipped. Furious. 'Someone rang them about me striking my son when I was on the beach. They want to make an assessment about my fitness to parent. *Fitness to parent?*' She is livid.

'Joyce,' I say, 'I didn't—'

'You were the only person there,' she says. 'Thank you very much,' and she turns and begins to walk away down the path. Then she swings round. Her face has changed. There are tears on her cheeks.

'It was unintentional. An accident in the scuffle. I have never once laid a finger on him in eighteen years. Not once. Never. And now this. And I didn't need them to come over to tell me it was wrong. Whether accidental or not. I have never felt so bad. I'll have to live with it for the rest of my life,' she says, jabbing at her chest, her face pained, 'it's on me.'

I stare back at her. I try to explain. To tell her I didn't make the call. But she's not listening.

'Is this your way of helping? You really have no idea what it's like. How we manage on a day to day basis. How Pete is at breaking point. You people,' and she shakes her head.

'What can I do to help? you asked yesterday. The best thing you can do is to go home,' she hisses. 'Leave us alone. Mind your own business.'

EIGHTEEN

I wake up thinking about Joyce, her anger – and then her tears at the door. I feel the burn of guilt for something I haven't done. I decide to go over and talk to her later, after Helen and I get back from Swanage.

We'd arranged to leave at ten. 'Shall we all go in your car?' she says, as we walk across the grass.

I'm surprised by the suggestion. Legally, I can't get four kids in the back. Helen will know this. It's so unlike her.

I hesitate. 'The car seats. The booster – I can only really get three in—'

'Of course,' she says, 'don't worry. I was thinking Ollie could squish up. But you're right. Just would have been fun to go together.'

Luckily, the kids are huddled out of earshot, otherwise I would have been outnumbered. It feels odd to have the tables turned with Helen. To be the one making the sensible decision, the one who feels like a killjoy.

We park in the main car park in the high street in Swanage, and when we're walking along, Helen tells Ollie and Lexie she has to go into one of the shops, and then has to talk to someone in an office, to sort something out for Granny's house. 'You can come with me,' she says, 'or go with Sam and Ruby to the playground?'

As expected, there's no contest. 'I'll meet you there in an hour or so,' she says, handing me over a bag, 'some snacks and drinks for them all.'

As they whirl about on the roundabout, my thoughts drift

to my father's birthday lunch. It's like a hole I have been walking round and avoiding peering in. In the end, I text Gemma. *Everything sorted for tomorrow? Rob's flight gets in early, he'll get the train and meet us there. How many will we be? Is Max coming?*

To my surprise, she rings me.

'Ten of us, I think.'

'*Ten?*' I say, trying to do a mental add-up.

'Apparently he fell in love with a large table in the window. The Lavender table. He had to have ten people to reserve it. It looks out over the garden—'

Gemma seems unsure who'll be there. 'Max and Barbara aren't coming. There's a couple I don't know coming. Faye and Jonathan—'

Faye and Jonathan? 'Who are they?'

'Not sure,' she says vaguely. And again, as ever, I am the one who feels I'm fussing. Making a drama out of nothing. Making problems when, apparently, there are none.

'– and your neighbours . . . you two . . . me and Gavin.'

'Gavin?'

'Yep.'

She doesn't elaborate. So, I don't ask.

'Excellent,' I say, 'see you tomorrow.'

'You'll say a few words?' she asks. 'Mum wants me to read a poem.'

Random people called Faye and Jonathan. And Gemma's new boyfriend, also random. Words and *a poem*? I slump back on the bench.

Thank God it's just lunch, is the text I send to Rob.

When Helen comes back, she brings us coffee from a café on the high street. And a bag of croissants for the kids.

She looks flushed. Elated. 'I have tons of forms to fill in,' she says, 'but they had places for all three. And the school looks great. Polly will love it.'

She sits down next to me, closes her eyes and takes a long breath out.

She looks at her watch. 'I'll give her a call in a while,' and then, a few minutes later, her phone rings. 'It's James,' she says as she gets up and strolls over to the edge of the playground. She leans against the railings as she speaks. It's a short call. 'He's just off to Belgium. All good,' she says, 'he's coming on Sunday afternoon.'

She smooths her hands over her face. 'Well, one thing done. Fifty million other things to do. But it's a start. I've got an appointment later, with the solicitor. And I've got a meeting – at the refuge,' she says, lowering her voice, even though there's no one else around.

'That's fine,' I say. 'I can take the kids to Swanage beach. Just meet us there when you're done.'

'Thank you,' she says, turning to me, 'I *really* appreciate it. I just wouldn't be able to do this without your help with the kids.'

I wave away her words.

*

Shortly after we get back, I see Joyce walking over from the farmhouse. My heart sinks. I come out before she gets to the cottage and as I start to speak, she shakes her head, and reaches her hands out for mine.

'I'm so sorry –' she says, '– about yesterday. Can we talk?'

While the kids are watching telly, I make coffee and we sit outside by the front door next to the hollyhocks.

'It was Pete,' she says quietly. 'It was Pete who rang social services.'

There are tears in her eyes.

'I was very upset about the beach. When I told him what happened, he was – well, to put it mildly, in a bit of a state. He went out that afternoon. Didn't come back that night. Or the next. He sent a text, saying he was staying at the Thurloughs, the farm where he has the badger meetings. I suspect he'd had a few too many beers.' She pauses to sip at her coffee. 'At some point, he made the call. Left a rambling message. He had no idea this would happen. He came back an hour ago. He only just told me.' She hangs her head in shame. 'I jumped to conclusions, and I can only apologise.'

I feel the flood of relief. 'It really doesn't matter.'

'It does,' she says firmly, 'and I'm very sorry.'

I shake my head. 'Tell me about Pete.'

She sighs. 'The difficulties with Leo. The lack of support. The imminent closure of the gardening project, well . . . he was already struggling. And the beach incident scared him. The thought of me not coping,' she sighs, 'I shouldn't have told him. I should have kept it to myself. I'm the rock,' she says, 'I'm the one who holds things together. He panicked. Was worried for all of us. Things have really escalated. Leo hates change. He doesn't understand why he can't go to Green Shoots every day like he did before. He takes it out on us. And Pete – well, he's not –' and her voice cracks, '– he's really not coping at all.'

She drinks her coffee, swallowing down the grief, the tiredness, the relentlessness of it all.

'I think it was Pete's way of asking for help.'

We sit for a moment in silence.

'It's not ideal,' she says with a smile, 'but whatever he said did the trick. I've never seen them move so fast. Amazing, really. We struggle to get a response for almost anything over the years, and now I see, all you have to do is shout about risk and safety. Ha! If only I'd known,' and she laughs. 'Anyway, it's done now. I told him there were less dangerous ways of getting help – and he looked at me and said, *yeah well, we've tried all the others.*' She places her cup down. 'And I know what he means. I do see the logic. You do the right thing. You ask. You plead. You campaign. You raise money. You write letters. You sign petitions. But no one actually listens. No one *actually* takes any notice. No one actually *does* anything. *I didn't know what else to do*, was what he said.'

'I'm so sorry.'

'I haven't seen him so angry and upset since – well, since it all began. I'm worried about him really. He keeps it all in. It's all clenched tight,' she says, making a fist of her fingers.

'But so hard for you too,' I say.

She throws a hand in the air, 'Exactly! *He's* at the end of his tether. I wanted to say, try living in my head for a week,' and then she laughs. Her big throaty laugh that I have come to know so well.

Then, more seriously, she says, 'But maybe that's how things change. Maybe it's only drastic action. Maybe that's what we have to resort to, in the end. I did tell him to speak to me first before he hatches another plan. I said, if you're planning on setting off a bomb at the council offices, can you give me the heads-up first?' and she laughs again.

'What will happen now?'

'Well, there will be a series of assessments and meetings, but already all Leo's key workers from the project and all his clinical support workers have come forward to back us up. It's hard to say, but I am hopeful this will blow over. Pete was very clear it was accidental. But he did keep saying on the phone, *this is a warning sign. A red flag.* That's the only reason they raced over. They've got to cover themselves,' she shrugs, 'in case something else happened. But I'm not really worried about them taking him. And anyway, where will they take him? They'll take him into care over my dead body.'

I pass her the packet of ginger biscuits and she dunks one in her coffee. We sit and watch a long line of geese head out towards the sea.

'About tomorrow,' she says, 'it's Leo's day at the project. He'll be out all afternoon. That is –' and she pauses, '– if you're still happy to leave the kids with me?'

'Joyce? *Really?* There's no one I'd rather leave them with,' I say without hesitation.

'It's due to be sunny,' she says. 'I'm going to get the paddling pool out. Will Helen be going to the lunch? Her two would be really welcome.'

'I'll check,' I say. 'Last time she said she wasn't. But I'll try and persuade her. I think she could do with a break.'

'It's easier with all four. They get on so well,' she says.

*

I bring it up when Helen comes over later after pegging out the washing. The kids are all outside on the lawn playing on the blanket with the Lego.

I tell her what Joyce had said.

'I know you said you weren't going to come – but how about it?'

'Oh, no, I don't think so,' she says, nodding over towards the kids.

And I feel a feel a sudden flash of irritation. For her overprotectiveness. Her carefulness. Her lack of fun. The ordered and methodical way she lives her life. And how, in that moment, I want to see her drop her guard. Drink a bit too much. Maybe say something she might regret. Just be a bit disorganised. I want her to be someone she's not. I'm ashamed to say, but in that moment, her careful planning and total lack of spontaneity irk me.

Afterwards, I might tell myself a lot of things. I might say I did it for the kids. That they would have a better time if they were playing all together. Or that it was for Joyce; a real show of support and solidarity after what she'd been through. But neither of these would really have been true. The honest truth was that I was irritated with her rigidity. And I wanted to have my way, and a part of me wanted to simply crush her into some kind of submission.

'It's only ten minutes' drive away,' I say, 'you could just come for an hour. It might be good to have a break. I know James is away – but I'm sure you could have a nice time without him too. Apparently, the food is delicious.'

She looks unsure.

And then, perhaps most abhorrent of all, I use a tactic my mother employs when she wants to get her own way. I use the children as ammunition.

'Joyce told me she's going to put the paddling pool up,' I say, raising my voice. 'She's got one of those water slides you lay on the grass. It's going to be sunny. Thought the kids would love it.'

Lexie looks up. 'Can we?'

'Sure,' Helen says, 'we can pop over.'

'Can't we go by ourselves? With Sam and Ruby? Their mummy isn't going to be there, why don't you go to the grown-ups' party?'

Helen is thrown.

'And we can have our own party.'

There's a pause.

'Joyce would so love to have them all – go on,' I urge, 'just come for a bit.'

Afterwards, of course, I will think about this moment. How it's my behaviour that manipulates her into sitting around the ghastly lunch table, while her kids are at the farmhouse with Joyce and Pete. It's something I will think about and regret for the rest of my life.

It's Ollie's look that perhaps does it. 'Go on, Mum,' he nods. 'It's fine.'

'Well – OK. But I'll just come for a bit. And I'll drive myself, so I can nip back early. I'll check with Joyce, OK?'

All four kids cheer.

'Great! That'll make eleven of us. Philip and Penny are coming too. And my sister and her new boyfriend. Rob will be all mad and jetlagged. And there's a couple of others I don't know,' I say with a cheeriness I don't feel. 'If nothing else, it'll be entertaining . . .'

Helen smiles, the reluctant smile of someone who's been bamboozled into making up the numbers for a game she doesn't know how to play.

NINETEEN

Rob and I are introduced to Faye and Jonathan in the car park.

'Jonny,' he says, reaching his hand forwards, then pumping my arm up and down.

'And *you are*?'

'Jess,' I say, 'one of his daughters.'

'Ah . . . the author?'

'No. The other one. The doctor.'

'So charming of Geoffrey to invite us,' he says, turning towards the hotel. 'This used to be a manor house. Restaurant's Michelin-starred,' he says, winking at me.

Faye trots after him. 'We met your father at the marina last time they came up. Jonny has a boat here,' she says. 'It's a time-share. He has it for the whole of June. They'd just come from your cottage when we met them, said they'd had a lovely cliff walk with the grandchildren. Are the little ones here?' she asks, peering around.

'No,' I say and we head inside and make our way to the table. The Lavender table is appropriately named. I can see why my father liked it. It's in a separate alcove, with doors opening out onto a courtyard garden. I walk over to the doorway to look out. Pale paving slabs are arranged in a giant circle, and surrounding the stone patio are huge banks of lavender bushes. They are in full glorious bloom in the sunshine, their purple heads swaying in the gentle breeze, filling the air with their fresh intoxicating scent. I stand for a moment, breathing slowly in and out.

Dad is wearing a lurid lime green shirt and a pair of trousers

I haven't seen before. He is ushering people to seats and asking about drinks. My mother is chatting to Philip and Penny. 'Yes, yes,' I hear her say. The loud anxious voice quelling anything that could turn into a conversation.

Our waitress has short cropped black hair and a small elfin face.

'Very Audrey Hepburn,' my father says as she stands by the table.

'Sorry?'

'Your hair. Like Audrey Hepburn.'

'Oh,' she says, smiling politely as she offers him a menu.

My father smiles back, reaches out for the menu, but lingers too long before taking it from her hand.

'Dad –' I say, when she's gone. 'She looks about fifteen. She probably doesn't even know who Audrey Hepburn is.'

Hurt flashes across his face and he looks shaken for a moment.

I try to backtrack. 'Although, *Breakfast at Tiffany's* – I suppose everyone's seen that, haven't they, Rob?'

'What's that?' Rob says, looking up from his menu. 'Oh yes. Absolutely. A classic.'

Seconds later, he and my father are leaning together listing out all the Audrey Hepburn films on a napkin.

'Let's put them in chronological order,' Rob suggests excitedly.

My father retrieves films I didn't think he'd even heard of. My mother rolls her eyes. Her inability to contribute leaves her with a detached look of mild displeasure. Rob and my father begin discussing which character the waitress most resembles.

After listening for a while, I shake my head. 'She has long hair in *Breakfast at Tiffany's*.' Rob makes to disagree, but I plough on. 'There's a scene, towards the end – just before she's planning to leave, she's wearing a pale jumper and Capri pants and her hair's in bunches.'

'*Bunches?* Audrey Hepburn in bunches,' and Rob is shaking his head.

I nod. 'Long bunches down to here,' and I tap at my shoulders, 'not ones like a three-year-old. The cropped hair look is more *Roman Holiday.*'

There's a pause. My mother looks up with a dreamy sigh. 'That scene in *Breakfast at Tiffany's.* At the end when George Peppard finds the cat.' She sighs again. 'It's just wonderful,' she says, lifting her arms up to give herself a hug.

'Bonus point for the name of the cat?' Rob says, looking round.

'*Cat,*' my dad says, and they fist-bump.

Rob is delighted by his new father-in-law. They'd always had a rather distant stilted relationship. Rob always (correctly) felt Geoffrey found his job in film and television frivolous and referred to it with a hint of condescension. It had long been a point of tension and last Christmas Rob had snapped, pacing around their kitchen as he replayed the conversation in hushed furious whispers. '*How's work? Must be such good fun.* Jesus Christ, he talks about my job like I'm heading up to the park for a kickaround with the kids. Excuse me for not inhabiting the earnest world of aca-dem-ia.'

It hardly seems possible that six months later, they are huddled together in riotous uproar.

Helen arrives just as Rob is reading the Audrey Hepburn list out to the table.

She sits in the chair next to me. 'Sorry to be late,' she says, and I introduce her to the rest of the table.

'Where's your father?' she asks.

I shrug. 'He was here. But now he seems to be wandering about like Lord of the Manor.'

Rob stands up to pour wine. Helen declines.

'My advice?' he says, eyebrows raised. 'Drink heavily.'

She laughs, shaking her head. 'I've got the car,' and she reaches for the bottle of mineral water.

'Bad luck.'

'Is your sister here?' she asks.

'Not yet,' I say, and I can see my mother is doing her best to ignore the ever-widening two-seated gap on the other side of the table. She turns to Penny and Philip.

'So, what brought you to Dorset?'

Penny shifts uncomfortably in her seat. Philip clears his throat. 'I'm staying with my lovely daughter,' he says, smiling at Penny, 'and I'm trying to write a book.'

We exchange a glance. I smile back at him.

'I've recently moved from France,' Penny says, 'after my divorce.'

My mother is soon nodding anxiously into the silence before Penny rescues her and moves the conversation on.

When the waitress returns with wine, my father slips back into his seat, staring at her intently.

'Thank you, Audrey,' he says pointedly, curving his hands into a cup of gratitude.

'Dad –' I hiss, 'leave her alone. And stop calling her Audrey.'

His overattentiveness is starting to bother me. Even when she isn't serving at our table, I watch him tracking her as she moves across the restaurant. I find myself talking too much, trying to engage him in conversation, but each time, he looks back at me, reluctantly, his eyes sliding to the left of my face.

'Dad? Are you listening?'

I turn round. He's gazing at her as she reaches across the table by the window. He is transfixed. Like a child coveting a new toy. Or a forbidden bag of sweets. There is something about the look that unsettles me. It isn't the look itself. Or even the desire behind the look. It's the fact that he makes no attempt to hide it. That he has somehow lost the level of self-awareness required to conceal it.

On the other side of the table, my mother is asking Jonny where they live, 'when you're not on the boat?' then follows it up swiftly and incomprehensibly with, 'Do you have a garden?' and then I realise she probably wants to talk about her own. But Jonny also likes the sound of his own voice. He talks about the sunny aspect. The plants. The dimensions, 'small but perfectly formed,' he says with a wink.

'And do you like gardening?'

'We divide it up,' he says proudly. 'Pruning and weeding – *pink jobs*,' and he nods over in Faye's direction. 'I mow the lawn. Definitely a *blue job*.'

I stare at him.

My mother is nodding, then turns to Penny. 'What do you do here?'

She explains that her ex-husband bred horses. 'Thorough-breds mainly. Racehorses to sell,' and how while she fell out of love with her husband, it hasn't put her off horses. 'I'm planning to set up a stable here to teach riding. It's a new project,' she adds, 'something exciting to focus on.'

My mother gazes at Penny, watching her mouth move. She's nodding vigorously and inappropriately, but I can see she's not listening, just desperately scanning the conversation for a way to bring it back around to her. And when Penny reaches over for the wine, she seizes her moment. 'I went on a donkey once,' she says. 'In Margate. When I was a child.'

The selection of starters that Gemma has organised arrives. There are plates of crispy salt and peppered calamari, giant prawns with sorrel and cucumber, fried courgette chips with a garlic mayonnaise dressing, pan-fried scallops with asparagus spears, and a fennel and orange salad. The waitress announces each plate as she sets them down, and each time, my mother gazes at the plates in wonder, clapping her hands like her absent daughter has won a prize. 'Marvellous,' she says repeatedly. It's clearly a way of distracting the attention away from my father, who is staring at the waitress, enrapt.

As we reach for the dishes and pass them round, Jonny is telling Helen about his timeshare boat. 'Every June for the past eighteen years!' he says, as if startled by the news.

Helen is polite and makes the mistake of asking a question and this is just the cue he needs to reach down into his bag for a large envelope, from which he pulls a series of A4 photographs that he fans out on the table. All different images of a sailing boat tilting over in bright sunny water.

'Look at that angle,' he says, tracing his finger over the crest of a wave, 'we're almost at forty-five degrees,' and he slowly shakes his head in wonder.

'This is Andy Lawrence,' he says, pointing at a man in a white cap, 'and Michael Armstrong and Tony Wiseman.'

Helen and I nod inanely.

'And this,' he says, as his hovering finger moves across the picture, 'is Matt Rathbone.' He looks at us. Eyes flicking from one to the other.

'Right. Great,' I say.

'All five of us went to school together! And we've sailed for a week in June, every single year!'

He leans back, as if waiting for applause. 'How great is that?'

'Very great,' I say. And Helen nods.

I pass the bread to her, trying to catch her eye.

'We've raced at Cowes a few times. Came in third last year!'

Faye has now leant over and is listening in with adoration.

'The lads have been together every year, bar one. Do you remember?' he says, turning to Faye.

She nods. 'That time Matt had his leg in plaster.'

'Fractured his ankle doing the Tough Mudder. Bloody idiot,' he chuckles.

While my mother is telling Penny about Alicia Featherstone, Gemma and Gavin arrive. 'Just days now,' and she shakes her head sadly, 'she's been moved to a hospice. Religious, but non-denominational. Bit too happy-clappy for my liking. But perhaps it's a comfort for the children. Four of them,' she adds, 'simply dreadful—'

Gemma waves apologetically as she and Gavin slip into their seats.

My father seems unable to sit still at the table for longer than a few minutes. Philip, I notice, is watching him. He remarks on his restlessness. His voice is kindly, but I hear concern in his tone.

I find myself laughing nervously. 'Birthdays,' I say, twirling my fingers by my temples, 'that's what they do to you.'

Gavin is tall with dark curly hair. He is smiley and friendly and makes a point of coming over to introduce himself, asking about our holiday. We chat for a while. He seems nice, and I feel bad that this comes as a surprise. They order their main course quickly, and later, when the food arrives, I can't help myself. Years later, I'm still drawn to her plate. Anticipating what she might order. Noticing what she eats. What she might play with, or push to one side. I've already noticed she took a bread roll, but declined the butter. I would have been able to guess at her choices. That she'd avoid the beef with the rich creamy sauce and go for the low-carb option of grilled swordfish with steamed vegetables.

This running commentary, this roll call in my head is automatic.

And just in that moment, it occurs to me that we are all still doing this, nearly thirty years later. Worrying, inspecting and monitoring with a proprietorial scrutiny. And it slams into me, all of a sudden. For the first time, I wonder, *what must that feel like for her?* Hawk-eyes on her, scanning and assessing, so many years after her illness. Being watched like a child.

And it makes me think that my noticing, my worrying and my scrutiny are not only intrusive, but have no benefit at all. That it's about me, not her. It reminds me of the conversation with Veronica, about Gemma's recovery.

When she steps outside into the garden for a cigarette, I follow her.

'Gem,' I start, 'I just want to say –' and in that moment I catch the look on her face. Already bracing herself for some admonishment. Some subtle criticism about the way she lives her life. I feel suddenly ashamed.

'– I'm really proud of you.'

She looks surprised.

'I know it was a long time ago – but I don't think I ever really said how proud I was of you. How you turned things around when you were so ill. It was amazing what you did, it must have been some journey. I can't begin to understand—'

It comes out in a rush, and for a moment, she stops short, taken aback.

'Wow. OK. Sure. Thanks. I mean – it was a long time ago.' She pauses, lost for words, taking a drag of her cigarette. 'I mean, even the book and everything. It feels,' and she stops to flick the ash, 'a really long time ago.'

I nod. 'I know. But I just wanted to say how well you did to come through it.'

She is quiet for a moment and looks out over the banks of lavender. 'It was difficult,' she says, 'and I also accept it will always be part of me. Like a pattern of thinking I can retreat back into. It's something I still manage, in a way,' she says carefully, 'but I know the dark place so well now. I can see it coming. Can get back on track. So, I guess, I'm still a work-in-progress.'

'Ha,' I say, 'aren't we all?'

She turns to face me. 'But thanks anyway. Appreciate it.' She presses the cigarette to her lips.

'I think it was hard for me to accept you got better by yourself,' I say. 'To let you find your own way. I think I was holding onto something. And I'm sorry—'

Then the moment opens out. A bloom of something like joy on her face. And instinctively we move towards each other, and for the first time in a long time, we properly embrace.

It's a deep tight hug. Not one of those embraces that feel cursory and brief. This one is fulsome. I feel her body against mine. And as we hug, I allow myself to focus on the hug. The feeling of embracing my sister. Without my fingers itching to trace the contours of her body. Or prise at the flesh on her bones. To assess the weight she may have gained or lost. I hug my sister. Her whole self. And I grab onto her and hold her tight.

Sometimes the best thing to do is to take yourself out of the way.

'I've missed you.'

'Me too.'

We pull back. And look at each other for a moment. Then she jabs her cigarette in the direction of the restaurant. 'All a bit nuts in there, isn't it?' she laughs. 'Even for our family. And we set the bar high.'

I smile, and then she turns to me. 'There's something I need to tell you,' and her voice sounds urgent. Serious.

But just at that moment, our mother appears at the French windows, waving us over.

'He's disappeared again,' she calls out. 'Can you come? Quickly?' She's twisting the rings on her fingers.

Gemma nods at me. 'Let's go. We'll catch up later.'

I find my father at the bar talking with the manager. We walk back to the table together.

'I was asking about Hugh,' he explains in a loud voice when he's back at the table.

'Who's Hugh?' whispers my mother.

'That chef,' I hiss. 'Hugh Fearnley-Whittingstall.'

'Do you know him?' she asks, slightly affronted.

'No.'

'Is he here?'

'No. He owns the other place. The one we didn't book.'

'Why didn't we?'

'Because it was in Devon.'

'Oh, I love Devon,' she says, 'what a shame.'

But my father doesn't seem to hear her, or waves away the comment.

When I go to the toilet, I rest my head against the mirror and feel the coolness of the glass on my forehead.

Back at the table, my mother has made a small bonfire of broken toothpicks by the side of her plate.

'He's gone again,' she says. 'Ordered the dessert wine, then disappeared – we haven't even ordered dessert yet,' she says tightly. 'Did you see him on your way back?'

I shake my head, suddenly irritated by her child-like helpless panic.

'Please –' she urges, snapping another stick between her fingers, '– go and get him and let's go. We can do the birthday cake back at our hotel, when you come over later with the kids.'

As I get up from the table to search for him, Helen seizes the moment to leave.

'Sorry – I'm going to head off,' she says, looking a little agitated. 'I can't seem to get phone reception here. Can't get hold of Joyce. I need to head back,' she says apologetically.

'Go for it. I'm sorry,' I make a face, 'I'd join you if I could. The paddling pool party was by far the better option. I'll be coming to pick up the kids,' I call after her, 'I'll see you in a bit.'

My father isn't up by the bar or in the kitchen nor is he out smoking on the back terrace. I stand for a moment in the bright sunshine. The clear blue. The breeze on my face and the smell of the lavender. As I turn back, I can hear the small explosions of laughter coming from inside the restaurant and I feel suddenly deflated by the turn of events at the lunch.

It's on my way back that I think I hear his voice. I stop, hovering outside a door by the side of the bar, and reach for the handle and push it open. It leads into a vast wine cellar. A musty-smelling room with wooden shelves laid out in rows. Shiny bottles are stacked floor to ceiling on racks either side. The voice is his, but too far away for me to make out what he's saying. As I move along the rows, he sounds loud and ebullient, like he's giving a speech.

I find the two of them in the last row; my father is leaning against the wall at the end. He has a bottle in his hand and is holding it out to her, pointing at the label.

'Go on,' he urges.

The waitress shakes her urchin hair.

'Eight hundred and seventy-five pounds,' he purrs.

I quicken my step as I turn down the row towards them.

'*Feel it*,' I think I hear him say.

The waitress hesitates, then slowly unfolds the arms that are tight across her chest. I can see in that moment how it is all going to end. Like flicking quickly to the last page of a book. But it is like watching gestures and movements that belong to someone else. Someone other than my father.

As she reaches out, his other hand comes quickly.

'Dad –' I call out, but the word is thick in my throat.

It's a calculated movement forwards, fingers reaching for her breast like he's testing the ripeness of a peach. At the same time, his mouth comes searching, fish-like, for her lips.

The waitress gasps and backs away. The bottle falls to the floor. By the time I reach them, she is staring down at her apron, pressing at the wine stains as though stemming the flow of blood. My father is slumped against the wall, his hand still cupped forwards, like a beggar on the street.

For a moment, we all stare at each other, then, eventually, I lead the girl away.

'He ordered dessert wine –' she stammers, '– I came here to get it. He – he followed me in here. I didn't do anything—' and her eyes have filled with tears.

'It's OK,' I say gently.

'I need this job,' she says, suddenly panicking. 'If my boss were to think—'

'I'll tell him it was nothing to do with you. Do you understand?' and I turn her shoulders so she is looking right at me. 'You did nothing. Do you hear me? It was not your fault.'

The girl stares back at me.

'I'll tell your boss it wasn't your fault. But it's very important that *you* know. Do you understand?' I'm almost shouting now.

I lower my voice. 'My father –' I say, my voice catching with emotion, '– my father is not well.'

'*Not well?*' she says, sharply, her eyes suddenly dry. 'He's a pervert. That's what he is—'

I open my mouth to speak, then change my mind.

'I need this job,' and with that, she steps back into the restaurant.

I find my father on his hands and knees collecting up the bits of glass. Dark gashes of wine across his lime green shirt. His hair is wild and wispy but flattened at the back, like he's been slapped repeatedly on the back of his head. When he sees me, he lifts his hand into a feeble wave and for a moment he looks bereft, like a child with a broken toy.

'You go –' I say, '– back to the table. I'll do this.'

By the time he's up on his feet, he is smoothing down his hair. 'Ah,' he says seizing another bottle of wine from the rack, 'this will do,' and his voice is jaunty again, elated almost as he swings the bottle between his fingers.

'Dad, I—' but he is already gone along the rows of bottles towards the door.

When I get back to the table, Gemma and Gavin are engrossed in conversation, their shiny faces pressed up against each other. My mother is very much as I left her, bleached by the wait, with an untouched plate of raspberry panna cotta at the side. Now it's Rob and Philip who are hunched over the table.

Rob glances up as I sit down.

'Top ten filmic scenes with a therapist,' Rob says, head down again, scribbling away. He tots up the notes with his pen.

'We're up to eight and it's a tie between *Ordinary People* and *Good Will Hunting*. We're taking it to the table for a vote.'

Then he slaps Philip on the back. 'The man's a genius. A hidden talent.'

My father has been talking to the manager at the bar and as he makes his way back, I watch as he stops at a table of strangers, bending his head down low, peering at the guests and scooping his hands together in a gesture of abundance.

Back at the table, he clears his throat. 'I'm afraid,' he announces, making a steeple of his fingers, 'Audrey has had to go home. She is unwell,' he says, nodding with empathy.

There is a stunned silence. We are like fish flip-flapping on dry land, as we stare at his wine-stained shirt.

'Right,' I say, abruptly standing up, 'it's time to go.'

Everyone is hastily ushered to their feet. 'You can have your coffee in the lounge,' I say to Jonny and Faye.

Jonny looks disgruntled as he shuffles his photographs together. After I explain things to Gemma, she offers to sort things out with the restaurant, while I go back to get the kids. 'I'll meet you back at their hotel,' I say. 'Rob can go with you all now.'

I see Philip leaning in to speak to Penny as he gets up. 'Penny's got a meeting at one of the local stables. I can drive you back – be good to have a chat,' he says.

As I walk to his car, my hands are shaking from the sight of my father in the basement cellar. My cheeks sting with the shame and confusion. But in a short time, the incident in the restaurant will not be the worst thing. It will fall away to make room for something so much more terrible. And in those brief moments, I am blissfully unaware of what's to come.

TWENTY

When Philip and I come out into the car park, we find Helen looking flustered. 'I'm boxed in,' she says, pointing at the grey Vauxhall, 'reception keep trying to find the owner . . . I just want to get back,' and she looks close to tears.

'Jump in with us. Philip's driving. We can pick your car up later,' and whatever conversation he wanted to have with me will have to wait. The seats are hot from the sun. No one knows quite what to say, least of all me, so we sit in sticky silence on the short drive back.

I call Rob just before we get to the farmhouse. 'Pete might be able to drop me back. If not, I'll wait for you.' I hesitate. 'Have you left yet?'

'Um – not quite. Soon, hopefully—' He sounds stressed.

'Just get them back to the hotel as soon as you can. I'll see you in a bit.'

Back at the farmhouse, Joyce is shaking out a mat on the porch; she waves and as we get closer, I can see she's frowning slightly, a hand by her forehead, shielding her eyes from the sun. Perhaps Helen notices the confusion on Joyce's face. 'It's very quiet,' she says, closing the car door and striding purposefully down the path. 'Where are the kids?' she calls out to Joyce.

Just at this moment, Philip steps forwards, a hand on my arm. 'Can we have a word?' he says, his face thoughtful. I hang back by the car. And Helen quickens her pace across a lawn that is littered with the detritus of the afternoon entertainment; the paddling pool filled with discarded plastic beakers, the bright turquoise water slide, a space-hopper. Somewhere in the distance, I can hear Sam laughing.

Afterwards, Joyce will tell me she was surprised to see us back so early. And then a bit baffled about the timing, 'you must have passed each other on the road,' and she'll fling her hands up in mock exasperation. 'Didn't James call you?' she says, when she sees the confusion on Helen's face. But then she stops when the look becomes something else. 'Contorted,' she will tell me later, 'like she was in pain.'

I don't hear any of this because Philip is talking to me about my father. His hand is gentle, on my elbow, leading me forwards, 'some things that might be helpful to discuss—'

I'm nodding, but all of a sudden, I'm distracted by a strange noise, and when I look up I see Joyce standing very still, and Helen moving about in front of her.

And this is when things slow right down. And the next few moments feel like a concertina of events all strung together. Some moments are short, sharp and brutal – others feel long and stretched out, in a slow and hazy revelation. I place a hand on Philip's arm. 'Just a minute,' I say, moving quickly across the lawn.

As I get closer, I am looking between Helen and Joyce. I am confused. I scan their faces for information. For any kind of clues. Helen is moving in a circle, on the spot. Her fingers pressed to her temples. She is turning round and round, as if trapped in a small transparent cylinder. Her face is shockingly pale.

'What's happened?' I say, running towards her. My thoughts are immediately on her sister.

'Is it Polly?' I ask. 'Has something happened?'

It's then that Pete thunders out through the front door. 'Who opened the cabinet?' he yells. 'The gun is gone.'

All three of us stare back at him.

I feel the thud of panic. 'Where are the kids?' I say to Joyce.

She says something about ice-cream and the kitchen and we both run to the window and see my two at the table, waving their cones with toppling multi-coloured scoops. There's no sign of Ollie and Lexie. I'm just about to ask, when the noise comes. It comes from Helen's mouth. She is saying *No*. But it comes out like a howl. Like an animal. It's a sound that I have never heard coming from a human before. And then, like a jug being poured, she suddenly tips forwards at the waist and vomits on the grass.

I rush over.

She's wiping her mouth with her sleeve, while still moving in a tight circle. Her feet taking small steps as she circles a small patch of grass on the lawn. Her eyes are wild and fast-blinking. Beads of sweat glisten along her hairline. One arm is flailing to the side, as if, like a person falling, she is trying to catch hold of something to hold onto.

'What is it? Is it Polly? What's happened?'

I feel the quickening of my heart. The conversation we'd had yesterday. Her elation at the plans we'd managed to put in place. Her face in the sun on the beach. The feeling of lightness on behalf of her sister that we'd both shared.

'Is it your sister?' I say again, my voice louder, more urgent, placing my hands on her forearms to stop her spinning round.

'*Sister?*' Joyce says, frowning with confusion.

A look passes across Helen's face. Something fleeting. Irritation? Impatience? It's hard to say, but just as she goes to speak, things shift into place in front of me, and it all becomes shockingly clear.

'ThereisnoPollythereisnoPollythereisnoPolly,' she says. Her voice is breathless, quick. She is pressing the sides of her head with her fingers. 'I am Polly. It's *me*,' are the words she is saying as she starts to spin around again in her small, terrified circle.

And there it is. The realisation. The truth. The true horror of the situation becomes dazzlingly and piercingly clear. Like a blinding white light shining on my stupidity. And the realisation lands like a punch to the stomach. The story I have listened to, been a part of, for the last two weeks has a totally different central character.

I freeze.

There are many things I want to say. Things I don't understand. The phone calls from Polly . . . the arrangements.

'What—'

She waves away my words.

'Be quiet,' she says. 'It doesn't matter.'

There is no Polly. I am Polly.

And of course, she is right. It is not the time for questions.

Afterwards, I will remember the sensation of something dropping. Of something falling into position. A coin in a slot. How perfectly it fits into the space I have made for someone else.

The hours of conversations on the beach. The details she shared about Polly and Alan. The pictures I have built up in my mind. Alan with his pinched weaselly face, tight jaw and neat slacks. Thick-set, tall. Big controlling hands. Polly with her long dark hair and nervous smile. And now, I need to lift these images and apply them to other people. Onto faces I know already. Onto faces I have spent time with, faces they don't seem to fit. Helen. A model of efficient competence. Her neat shoulder-length hair. Helen and James, and their lovely kids.

Memories swim up. Words and phrases from the details she has given me. The *fuck you* conversations. *A waste of space.* Her incompetence as a mother. Her inability to cope. To manage social situations. And so, I follow these memories. These snippets. Breadcrumbs on a trail I don't want to follow. Until I arrive at a place I don't want to be. *He's a different person with other people. Her friends all love him. He's charming. So kind and thoughtful.*

Lovely helpful James. Nothing is too much trouble for James. He does the shopping, cooks up a delicious barbecue, washes the car. He can fix a fence. He'll persevere until it's finished. He'll hunt around for the perfect screw to fix a scooter. James with the focus and efficiency that Rob lacks. James who puts the *able* in Duns*table*. James who gets the job done. James who built his car from scratch. James is the man who likes to eat around the world; Tacos Tuesday, Fajita Friday. James is neat and tidy. He is also obsessive. A man who likes rules. Discipline. *He blames other people. Other groups for the things that haven't worked in his life. He thinks his wife is useless. A terrible mother.*

Helen is standing still now. Her mouth is open. She is drumming her fingers at the side of her temples. 'Where would he go . . . where would he go . . .' she mutters.

And then she suddenly stops. 'Quiet,' she says into the silence. 'I need to think.'

The pain on her face is unbearable. I wince at how I found her guardedness so irritating. Her caution. Her sense of control and efficiency. How I have tried to chip away at it. Mocked it silently. Sometimes even smiling at an item of clothing she's inadvertently left at home when we've been out. Celebrating this small sign of her fallibility. I think about times that I have cruelly rejoiced in a small sign of her imperfection and I feel deep shame.

There is no Polly. I am Polly.

Joyce is standing open-mouthed, Pete by her side. Philip has now joined us. They are confused. They have no sense of what is happening. And of course, there is no time for questions. For trying to understand how this has happened. There is no time for anything.

I turn to them. I tell them Helen was making plans to leave James. That he is a violent man. That he has taken the children. I don't need to say anything else. I don't need to mention the gun.

For a moment, we all stand. We are like a film on pause. We are immobilised by the fear. By the horror that is slowly dawning on all of us.

Helen turns to Joyce. Her face sharp, focused. 'What exactly did he say?'

Joyce tells us how he turned up, out of the blue. Said he'd got an early flight back from Belgium. 'He seemed cheery. Said he wanted to surprise you – and then he asked about the restaurant. I told him it had a lovely garden. That the kids could play—' and then she breaks off. 'I'm so sorry,' she says, the tears falling. 'I'm so sorry I let them go. I had no idea—' and she's wringing her hands. Pete appears next to her, an arm around her shoulder.

'It's not your fault,' Helen says, quickly and dismissively.

'What can we do?' he asks.

Afterwards, I will think about this time. How these long moments will seem to stretch and contract like several slow and gluey hours, but in reality, they were short. Not more than a few minutes between getting out of the car and getting back into it again. I will think about what James was doing while we spent those moments on the grass absorbing the horror of what was happening. I imagine him, thundering around the car, the blue vein on his neck pulsating like a hard ridge, straining with the pure energy of his rage. Channelling his frustration into a series of automatic movements.

It was the way he did everything. Methodical. Clear and focused. His refusal to be distracted or deterred. His eye on the end result. The finishing line. His determination for the completion of the task. *The Dunstables never get defeated.* But what I don't want to think about is his project that day. The purpose? The outcome he is hurtling towards? The task that must be finished?

Helen is still muttering to herself, fingers pressing against her temples. She then checks her phone again.

She closes her eyes for a moment. 'He will go to a place I love,' she murmurs, as though speaking to herself, 'somewhere we've liked going. Somewhere to spite me—'

Helen's body is moving with a kind of frenzy. Her face in a frozen howl. Muttered words on her lips. And then she jabs herself, hard, on the forehead. *Think. Think.* And she stands still.

There is no time for horror. To languish in the fear. The terror.

'Let's go,' Helen says, suddenly decisive. 'Let's just get in the car and go. We need to find my children.'

Philip takes his keys out of his pocket and runs towards the car and Helen follows.

I instruct Joyce to call an ambulance and the police. 'Get them here,' I say. 'Give them my number. Do you have James's?' She shakes her head. 'I'll send it when we're in the car. Give it to the police. Maybe they can track it? Tell them everything,' I say. 'Make sure they know it's an emergency. The risk . . .' I tail off, 'the children. That he's dangerous. That he has a gun,' and then I start to move away. Then run back. 'Keep Sam and Ruby inside,' I say. 'Please. Look after them. I'll tell Rob to come here.'

She's nodding. I don't need to say any of this. She's already pushing me away. 'Go,' she urges.

In the front of the car, Helen checks her phone again, her fingers trembling. 'This would be the ultimate punishment. The very worst thing he could do. Me alive. And my children gone. How does any mother live with that? He knew that. He knew.'

I blink back at her. I feel confused. It still takes me a while to comprehend what she's saying. To understand what she believes he could be capable of.

While Philip drives, Helen scans the fields and tracks and lay-bys for a glimpse of the green colour of James's car.

'Try Dancing Ledge,' Helen suddenly says, 'the pool in the rocks. He knows I love it there.'

We sit frozen in our seats. No one daring to speak. To voice the images that are clouding our thoughts. There is nothing to say. I ring Joyce with James's number. 'The reception is going to be patchy,' I tell her. 'Make sure they have all our numbers. So they can track them. Find us. Can they do mobile phone tracking?'

Helen is silent, head forwards, eyes scanning the windscreen. She has called his phone repeatedly. Each time it goes straight to voicemail. That cheery efficient message. *James Dunstable. Please leave a message and I'll get back to you very soon.*

I want to feel hopeful. But there is a deep fear in me. Being hopeful means not thinking about the gun. Being hopeful is not thinking about all the things I already know about Polly's husband. Fear makes my hands shake. I can't stop the images and information from scrolling through my mind. I don't want to see the violence that I thought was lurking in someone else's house. A long way from here, in Nottingham. But most of all, I don't want to think about the other things. The things that Helen didn't tell me about what happened to Polly. The things that were painful to talk about. How I saw Helen wince on behalf of her non-existent sister as she spoke. And I think about all the women with things that happen to them that remain unsaid. Dark secrets that will never be spoken out loud, even in a whisper. Too humiliating and too shameful to tell another living person. These are the things my mind curls around. Not the things I know, but the things I don't know. The things I know will be far worse than I want to imagine.

In the sticky heat of the back of the car, I think about my urging Helen to come. My wanting her to 'lighten up'. To have a few hours off, 'some time for yourself,' was what I think I said, internally rolling my eyes at her inability to be spontaneous. Her lack of fun. Her neat tight efficiency. I feel the burn of shame on my face. That this is the life of someone who is constantly vigilant. Constantly on her guard. Constantly set in readiness. *The kids would love it*. The horror I feel as I recall my persuasion. My deliberately raised voice about the paddling pool.

Everything looks different. The twist of a kaleidoscope. And all the shapes reshuffle into a new pattern. Ollie and Lexie appear different through this new filter. They were good and obedient because they learnt from an early age that doing what they were told, making themselves small and neat, was for the best. The path of least resistance. And very quickly, this became second nature. Oliver, with his serious furrowed brow, always looking ahead, anticipating possible rocks and bumps in the road and smoothing them out long before they had a chance to fly up and hit them in the face.

'I don't understand how he found out what I was planning,' Helen says, to no one in particular. 'I was so careful. So careful.'

'Left or right?' Philip says at the T-junction towards Swanage.

'Right,' she says, pointing towards the coast.

The road narrows. The wild flowers by the side of the road

swirl in a haze of pink and blue. The high hedgerows on the way to the cliff path. The golden hue of the sun on the green hills is the wrong backdrop for our desperate fears. Momentarily, we sink down, buried deep inside the hedgerows. I open the window. It feels hard to breathe. I want to feel the wind on my face.

Philip takes the left turn leading to the cliff path. It's a narrow one-lane track. The fields are a coat of yellow. The bright sky. The sun. The grasses in the fields that are dancing in the breeze.

'Cars can't go past here, but let's drive on,' Helen says, 'as far as we can.'

At the cattle grid by the kissing gate, Philip leaps out. 'It's padlocked,' he calls back.

The gate has never been locked before.

'The farmers use this track. Why would it be locked?' I query. But Helen is already out, whip-fast, inspecting the chain around the gate.

She says James had ordered a padlock like this. 'I'm sure it's his.' And with that, she is jumping over the gate. Running across the field towards the bottom of the hill. We both follow. After the grassy slope, we run onto the small dirt track.

It's cut with jagged rocks and flint. The gorse bushes over-hang, cutting into the path, and they scrape against my arms as I run. I think about the sound the spiky branches would have made as they scratched against the car. I think of the smart green shiny paintwork. The car low down on the road, juddering and jarring over the sharp flint stones. And it comes to me all of a sudden that the only explanation as to why James would have driven along this track, why he wouldn't have minded his car getting damaged and destroyed, would be if he wasn't intend-ing to drive it back. That it was a one-way trip. And then, the thought becomes an image I can't get rid of. A furious man, at the wheel of his sports car, hurtling down an unmarked track towards a cliff edge.

There's a cry out from Helen up ahead; she's waving something blue in her hand.

'Ollie's baseball cap,' she shouts. 'They definitely came this way—'

Philip is surprisingly fast and deft on the rocky track. Several times, I slip on the gravel, and once, I trip and manage to steady myself and rebalance before falling forwards. And as I reach the end of the track which opens out onto the grassy slope, I think of the last time we came, when Lexie and Ruby rolled down from the top. Small spirals that cascaded in laughter down the hillside. Lexie's attempt was a force of nature, rolled up tight and shooting down like a bullet.

When we approach the brow of the hill, Helen is up ahead. She turns and points. 'Over there,' she shouts. She has spotted the flash of green below us. It's parked on the left-hand side, tucked under the yellow gorse bushes, high above the ledge we used to picnic on. I can see it's the last place he can take the car before the path heads to the hillside, where the grassy slope opens out, then drops down to the stone steps to the ledge, where the walkers and rock climbers gather. Helen is tearing down towards the car. There's no one else in sight. She is yelling out. Words. Noise. Nothing that makes any sense. I hold my breath. I run faster.

I ring Joyce as I run. The reception dips in and out. We are cut off twice. I call 999. I direct them to the location. 'Dancing Ledge,' I shout, and I explain about the padlock. The need to hurry.

At first it looks like the car is caught in a shimmer of heat in the June sunshine. It takes a while to realise it is not a hazy mirage, but that the car is actually moving, juddering slightly in its stationary position. Then as I get nearer, it becomes obvious that the engine is running.

I keep on moving forwards. None of this is making any sense until I see something is hanging from the back window. And closer still, I see that the hanging thing is a black hosepipe, and that the other end of this pipe is attached to the exhaust.

The operator is cool and calm. Trained for these emergencies. When I say carbon monoxide poisoning, she wants to know the ages of the children. 'And their status?' 'I don't know,' I yell back. 'Please hurry,' I say. 'I'm a doctor,' I shout, as I charge down towards them.

Helen is sprinting down the path. Her hair flying in the wind. Philip is behind her. But keeping up. And I think about all his patients. His loss of faith. And I see all of this pumping through his body as he runs. And Helen. I can see she is running with the ferocity of a woman being chased. In danger. She is running for her life.

TWENTY-ONE

Afterwards I would wonder at what point the children realised that they weren't going to meet their mother at the restaurant after all. And at what point did the 'adventure' James promised become the sort of adventure neither of them could possibly have imagined. At what point did the 'game' he wanted them to play stop being any fun.

I try not to think about them in the car, but I can't help it; my thoughts pool there of their own accord, like water down a drain. I imagine Lexie, dressed in her pink tutu, the sparkly tiara on her head, her hair falling in messy waves about her face. I imagine her thoughts drifting as she stared out of the window. Her dreamy expression as she watched the green of the fields race by. Counting the cows and sheep in the fields. The grasses on the narrow lanes that brushed against the side of the car. Remembering the times when the roof was down, and she could feel them like feathers on the palm of her hand. And how she felt the flicker of disappointment when he said no, 'the roof will stay up today,' so she just rolled down the window to feel the wind on her face. She knew not to object, or to plead for him to change his mind. That never went well. *Are you arguing with me?*

I try to picture Ollie's face. His small serious expression. The furrowing brow when he might have realised something wasn't right. Was it when his father took the coast road? Or was it before then, when he noticed his father muttering at the wheel, his erratic driving and the strange bitter smell and the half-empty bottle on the passenger seat that rolled as he drove and the amber brown liquid that sloshed back and forth?

I don't like to imagine the scene when they turned towards the track to Dancing Ledge. The astonishment that Ollie felt when his father drove over the cattle grid and then locked the gate behind him. Perhaps Ollie didn't think fast enough. Perhaps he blurted out his surprise. 'You can't take cars along the track.' Or perhaps this was something he said in his head, already knowing it was a bad idea to say this thing out loud. The two of them in the back as the car scraped over the flints and rocks, listening to the sound of the bushes scratching against the paintwork. Was it then, perhaps, that Ollie slowly slipped his blue cap from his head and let it drop from his fingers through the opened window? A small sign. This way. *Help us.*

And when they do eventually stop, tucked away, up on the hill above the path down to Dancing Ledge, he watches his father get out of the car. Opening the boot, striding up and down in his neat jeans. The crisply pressed white shirt. His stiff movements. His face taut as he mutters under his breath. The vein on his neck, blue and livid with rage. And I can only imagine the two of them, sitting still and quiet in their terror and confusion.

It would have been Oliver, little Ollie, the wise man on the shoulders of a seven-year-old who would have seen where this was going. A small face that had probably already witnessed more than some men have in a lifetime. It would have been Oliver, in his measured and watchful state, who would have noticed the grim face of his father. That focus and determination. The one I saw myself that day in the rain as he fixed the fence. The face of a man who would not be defeated. Defeat and failure were not words in the vocabulary of the Dunstable household. *We put the 'able' in Dunstable.* Ollie would have seen that look before. That hard-set expression he wore in the light of an insurmountable task. *Defeat?* A task is an opportunity. *A challenge. The stuff that separates the men from the boys. Eh, Ollie?* Only sometimes when he slapped him on the back, it was too hard and it sent Ollie tumbling forwards, and made him feel stupid and weak and puny and all the other words his father didn't like. Ollie understood there was a task to complete that day. But the only thing Ollie didn't know was what it was. What would it look like when it was done?

At some point Oliver must have realised this task was different. That there was something in his father's mood he had never seen before. And he must have begun to feel a slow uncurling of unease. Perhaps he saw how his father was turned inwards. His twitching fingers, the words he caught under his breath. Was it the blazing eyes? Dark. Hooded. Full of fury? His face, tight-lipped and focused, that mostly seemed to have forgotten that the two of them were there at all. There were the snatched phrases he caught, the bad words he'd heard before. The ones Mummy said were bad. *Bitch.* And the other word that Mummy once said to forget he'd ever heard. He watched as his father took giant strides in front of the car, back and forth, like he was giving a talk. He mentioned family values. '*Great* Britain,' he said. 'The greatness of Britain,' he said, waving his hands towards the sea. 'An island,' and then something about commitment and families. *It's all fucked up.*

Oliver would have realised very quickly that it was not a time to talk to his father. To try to help. He would have done what he always did in times like that. He would have retreated. Tried not to get in the way. Be seen as an inconvenience. Lexie too would have picked this up. Sensed it from her brother. It was not a time to speak. To complain. To ask questions. It was not a time to even glance at his face. *What are you looking at?*

Perhaps this was when little Lexie started crying. Full plump tears that ran down her cheeks. There would have been a look from Ollie. An ability he has to convey both a kindness and a warning all in one glance. She would have seen this. She would know what he was saying. Would have read the sign. And she would have chewed on her bottom lip, to stop it wobbling, willing herself to stop the flow of the tears. By now, Lexie would know to keep quiet. But she is too small and frightened to help herself. She wants to go home. She wants to see her mummy. Again, another brisk shake of Ollie's head. Perhaps she then curled her fists round. It was the time to make themselves as small as possible. It was the time to disappear.

I have no doubt, when I picture the scene, that Oliver would have sensed, without fully understanding how or what was happening, that things were very bad. *Pretend you're in the army.* He would have noticed, at some point, that it wasn't one of the usual 'toughen up' or endurance games. That this was something real. Something with the edge of danger.

'Wind up all the windows,' their father told them, and carefully and slowly, they did as they were told. Oliver stole a glance over his shoulder as his father disappeared behind the car. He saw the coil of black rubber tubing. A snake-like spiral that his father slung over his shoulder. He asked Ollie to grab one end as he fed it through the small triangular side window by the back seat on his side of the car.

'We're going to play a game,' their father said. 'Like sardines,' he said. 'But we need to keep the windows closed.'

And when his father disappeared behind the back of the car, it was Oliver who whispered to his sister. 'Copy me. When I pretend to be asleep.'

'Sleep?' she repeated.

'Yes,' he said, 'when I say so.'

Sometimes when Ollie told her to do things, she wanted to argue. To not be bossed around by her older brother. Sometimes she wanted to disagree, stick her bottom lip out and not always acquiesce to him. But that day, in the fearful confines of the car, she simply nodded.

'It's OK,' he said. 'It's all going to be OK.'

Then when their father got back into the driver's seat and switched the engine on, Lexie was confused. 'Are we going somewhere?'

'Yes,' he said, getting out of the car. 'We're all going on an adventure.'

Ollie watched his father stuff a towel around the black pipe that he hooked in the window. And very soon he noticed the smell. And how quickly it got stronger. He could see the growing agitation of his father. The opening and closing of the boot. The glint of the metal on the rifle.

And all the while, Oliver sat immobile, his small hand gripped on the handle of the window. He stared at the green interior. The car that he and Lexie had washed so many times before. He knew every inch of it. The leather seats. The weave on the mat. The criss-cross patterns on the leather steering wheel. The small triangular corner windows that flipped open with a silver catch that he polished with Silvo and the blue cloth that his father liked him to fold in a special way before it was put back in its pouch. As the engine of the car turned over, he thought about the hours he had spent on the car; washing, shining, polishing. Doing what he was told. Keeping his father happy. That day, the windows shone, and he was thankful for the gleaming glass. From his position, he could see the sea. The swimming pool was tucked away, under the ledge, but he could see the wide expanse of blue. The swirl and call of the gulls. A small fishing boat on the horizon.

Ollie didn't understand what was happening. But he knew the adventure wasn't a good one and he knew he didn't want to go to sleep. He didn't like the smell. He also knew that keeping the windows closed made the smell very bad and that this was not a good thing either. Very slowly, he lifted his arm behind him, and moved his hand gingerly along the back of the seat, until his fingers found the small tear at the back of the hood. The patch that had been mended with masking tape. The patch that his father hated. The hole that wouldn't be there if he hadn't lost his job. The patch that 'spoilt everything'. *Ugly . . . unsightly . . .* and all the other words he didn't like. The new roof he had been planning to buy, if he had got that job that went to someone else. All the jobs he applied for and hadn't got. The job that had been taken by those other people. Those people who didn't belong. *Great* Britain, he muttered again, under his breath.

Keep the windows closed.

And while Ollie didn't quite know what was happening, he knew, above all else, that he needed to let the air in.

Slowly, without turning his head, Ollie scrabbled for a small edge of the masking tape, a piece to hold onto. But his father had sealed it well. It was smooth, wrinkle free, and his hands were sticky in the heat. There was no traction. His fingers were slippy and sweaty. He tried again, until he picked an edge free with his nail. He pulled, very slowly, and then stopped. It made too much noise. He waited until his father was muttering again. Until he had the bottle of brown liquid to his lips. And then he tried again. He prised it all the way along the bottom of the window. Digging away, poking at the fraying edges, until it gave way. He felt the fear in his fingers. On his face. The pounding in his chest at the thought of what might happen if his father turned round and saw him. *Built from scratch. My pride and joy.* Ollie waited until his father had gone around to the front of the car. He pulled again. Teasing it away carefully, so it made no noise. Then once it had peeled off completely, he rolled the tape into a ball that he stuffed into the pocket of his shorts.

It was at this point that perhaps Lexie looked over, staring at him wide-eyed as he tore at the masking tape. She watched what Ollie did, as she sat still, her fingers twisting in her lap. A slight shake of her head. Her brother nodded. *It's OK*, he re-assured her.

Ollie glanced up at his father. He was near the bonnet of the car. He was drinking from the bottle. Great gulps that dribbled down his chin. The back of the seat was hot now in the sun. And the smell was getting stronger. As he turned his head, he felt a heady dizzying feeling. And when he looked down at his lap, for a moment before he focused, he saw everything as a blur, like his hands were made of jelly.

While his father was busy at the front, Ollie's fingers found the small hole between the soft top and the bar. He had to choose his moment and do it very slowly, and once he had found the tear, he burrowed his fingers along, widening it, making it bigger under his fingers. Lexie stared in a kind of horror. He walked his fingers along, as far as his arm could reach, then pulled the canvas hood straight down, so it still looked closed, hidden from view.

The sun was high in the sky and when his father was at the front, he was in the glare of the sun, and it was hard to see what he was doing.

Carefully, Ollie tried the door. It was locked.

'Is your door locked?' he whispered to Lexie.

She didn't answer. He asked again. 'Lexie,' he whispered urgently. She turned to him slowly, her head lolling on her shoulder. Her eyes were drooping and heavy.

'Stay awake!' he hissed. 'And try the door.'

She did as she was told. Opening her heavy-lidded eyes. Then shook her head. The door was locked. All the doors were locked.

'You must undo your seat belt. But keep it stretched across you.'

But Lexie was sleepy, closing her eyes again.

'Lexie?' Then after glancing up at his father, he unclipped his own belt – and quickly reached over to unclip hers. Then tucked it under her legs. He shook her shoulders. 'Stay awake,' he said. 'Look up,' he said. 'Count the birds.'

And she opened her eyes and focused her attention on the gulls that swooped on the cliff, circling the nests that were perched at the top.

There was a noise at the back of the car. Oliver froze. Thinking about what the hole might look like from the outside. But when he saw his father in the wing mirror, he was preoccupied. Muttering and yelling. And barking out angry instructions to himself.

Oliver felt the smell in his nostrils. In his throat. On his face, thick and heavy, like a mask. He felt rocked by the gentle rhythm of the car. The soothing chug-chug of the engine as it turned over in the sunshine. He felt dizzy. A small throb at the back of his head and neck. But he fought against the fuzziness. It was threatening to fold him up – like a warm blanket. There was a moment when Oliver felt that it would be easier to hand himself over to the softness. It was warm and cosy, and he felt it calling to him. It made him think of his mother. Her soft wide arms when she wrapped him in a hug. His eyes felt leaden. He forced them open, they felt thick like glue.

James was around the front of the car now. The rifle swinging wildly on his shoulder. Ollie sat very still. The heat. The smell. And he felt the river of sweat on the back of his neck and a line collecting on his forehead, dripping down into his lap. The sun was in a wide glare on the right-hand side of the car. Ollie sat very still.

Keep the windows closed.

As he watched the ranting and yelling at the front of the car, he pulled in the towel that was stuffed into the small triangular window. It fell onto the floor. A rush of air. He tried to reach for the pipe, but it was too far away. His hands scrabbled uselessly in the air. His head ached. He felt dizzy. So he pushed at the window. It was half open when he heard the roar. His father. Like a battle cry. The sound of his fists thumping against his chest. Then the crack of the gun. His eyes were blurry now.

Then there was a loud thud. The slump of his father's body on the front of the car. His face against the glass. A small river of red running down the windscreen in a wide fan.

'Close your eyes,' he ordered Lexie. But when he managed to turn his heavy lumpen head to the side, he saw that her eyes were already shut. Lexie was unmoving. Her head lolling back. Mouth wide open.

'Lex,' he shouted. But his voice came out like a small rasping whisper.

Oliver's eyes were heavy now. He was confused by what he was seeing. He tried to move an arm, a hand. But his hand was heavy too, like lead. He looked at it. He couldn't make it move. He reached across to Lexie, grabbed her arm and pulled her over towards him. Then with the towel in his hand, he punched open the flap he had torn in the roof and stuffed in the towel, jamming it open. And squeezing his sister close, he felt the rush of fresh clean air on his face as he closed his eyes.

And this is how they found them. The older boy with his arm draped round his little sister, pulling her tight to him. Their cheeks pressed up close together, faces turned towards the sky.

TWENTY-TWO

As I run, all I can think about is that the smaller you are, the more quickly you are affected by carbon monoxide poisoning. Smaller lungs. Smaller immunity. Smaller chances. Smaller everything. I think about Ollie, at seven, and small feathery Lexie, just four years old.

Helen is at the window of the car and Philip is pulling on the door. Then I see him searching on the ground. And I will remember what happens next as a series of images. Philip with the rock in his hand. Holding it high above his head, then bringing it down against the driver's window. The sound of smashing glass. The doors being wrenched open. And each of them reaching in, pulling the children from the car. Philip carrying Ollie and Helen cradling Lexie.

I'm calling out instructions as I get to them. Waving them away from the car. 'The engine. Turn it off.' And Philip runs back to turn the key. There is a sudden deathly quiet as it cuts out. They lay them gently down on a grassy verge, some way from the car. I can see they are not moving. Apart from their too pale faces, they look asleep. Peaceful.

Philip is on the phone. Helen is all over them. Her hands on their cheeks, pressing them. Pulling at their hands. She looks up at me. A look of unbearable unremitting pain.

I drop to the grass in between the children. My hands are shaking as I press two fingers to Oliver's neck; with my other hand, I reach for Lexie's wrist. Little Lexie in her pink tutu. The small sparkly tiara now fallen from her head, and tangled up in the side of her hair. Helen carefully picks it out, gently unravelling the hair.

There is a still, empty silence. The terrible weight of it. Without looking up, I can see Helen's face. Pinched and pale. Desperate. Philip holds the phone to my cheek.

I search again. My two fingers of each hand on each of their necks. I wait. I try again. I sit very still.

'Unconscious,' I say into the phone. 'I have a pulse. For both. Faint.'

Helen drops forwards. The sound of a heaving sob. Once only. And then she lifts her head up.

He puts the phone on speaker, but also repeats the instructions carefully.

There's the screech of the gulls as I work on the bodies of the two children. I move with a quickness. I use my coat as a pillow, and Helen does the same. 'Tilt her head back,' I say, 'like this,' as I rest Ollie's head and move his chin upwards. Helen does as I say.

Philip is on the phone. Directing the ambulance. He explains about the gate. The narrow track. 'You'll have to drive across the field,' he says. We hear the scream of the siren in the distance. They are close.

The ambulance arrives in a flash of efficiency. Did they break the gate to get through, I wonder? Or did they have some implement to cut the lock? Either way, their arrival is calm and measured. Stretchers appear. Tank of oxygen. Face masks. A cannula for each. A drip. An injection. Proficient and wordless they each focus on one of the children. They check them over. Lifting eyelids. Checking pulses. Temperature. Heart rate. Helen has to move away. But she sits still, on the grass, her head bowed, her hands clasped together, as if in prayer. It's only when I speak to one of the paramedics that my voice starts to break. When I tell her about James. She glances over, then nods.

They both wake several minutes later. It's Ollie who opens his eyes first. Several gluey blinks before he is able to focus. Then Lexie too. They are dizzy and confused, but riotously and most gloriously alive. Ollie struggles to sit up, but, disoriented, he slumps back down. And after blinking several times, when Lexie's eyes can finally focus on her mother's face, she starts to cry. Helen is now sitting between the two of them, pressing their hands against her face; the three of them are crying together. I look away, biting at my lip.

One of the paramedics walks to the bonnet of the car. Then shakes her head to her colleague. It's a few minutes later that one of them gives the all-clear for them to be taken. 'Dorchester General,' she says, when I ask.

As they are carried inside the ambulance, Helen turns to me. Pulling me to her in a fierce and brief hug.

As she pulls away, I tell her I'll meet her there. She nods, then turns and climbs into the back of the vehicle.

In the moments after the ambulance screams off into the distance. In the moments before the police arrive. I whirl about. And in my rage, I grab the farm rifle. I've never held a gun before. I am surprised by its heaviness. I lift it onto my shoulder, and aim it at James. Even though the contents of his head, a strange pink and red mush, are covering the windscreen, I have a sudden urge for all of him to be destroyed. To make him disappear. To obliterate everything that's left of him.

'Put it down.' Philip's voice is calm, but firm. I don't move. 'Put. It. Down,' he says again.

I stare back at him for a moment. Then let the barrel swing down towards the floor. Slowly, he lifts the rifle from my hands and drops it onto the grass.

He steps forwards, but I don't want his comfort. I want my rage. My face burns with a white-hot heat.

I run along to the cliff edge, to the place that drops down to Dancing Ledge, and I fall to my knees. I take a deep breath and roar out into the ocean. I do it again. Over and over, deep guttural yells that I hurl over the cliff. The sounds of my voice getting lost in the scream of the circling gulls.

TWENTY-THREE

On the way to the hospital, my hands are shaking as I call Rob. I have a need to tell the story, to keep picking over the small horrifying details. The smell of the fumes. The mess on the windscreen. Their bodies huddled together by the window. I find myself going over and over it. I repeat the same words. As if trying to find a way to believe it myself. I know this is shock. And I know this is what I need to do; the repetition, the recall – but it makes no difference. There is no dilution, no absorption of the news. It sits steadfast, intact, like a blob of glue on blotting paper.

As Philip takes the turn-off towards the hospital, I ask about my father. 'Is he OK?' I say. Rob is reassuring, and tells me everything is fine. But I notice he doesn't offer any further information. He doesn't tell me about the complaint made by the waitress. Or about the events of their journey home. When I hear all about it later, I am so grateful he decided to keep it all from me at a time when my head was so full. My mind still trying to press the full horror of the events to memory, like knuckles kneading bread. Rob said nothing, because he knew there was no room for anything else. I also receive no communication from my mother, so he must have told her to refrain from calling too. And afterwards, I can't help wondering how this landed. The news that the bigger tragedy was happening somewhere else. That I was caught up in a much more pressing drama than her own.

In the hospital car park, Philip delicately broaches the subject of my father. And the incident at the restaurant. 'I don't want to interfere,' he says, 'or step out of line – but I'm assuming this was out of character?'

I nod.

We sit for a moment in silence. His hands are drawn neatly in his lap.

'Has he had mood swings in the past – erratic phases? Highs and lows?'

I shake my head. 'Lows, yes. But nothing like this.'

And I close my eyes, mortified all over again when I think about the wine cellar.

I tell Philip a little about my father's depression. 'It was something we got used to,' I say, 'over the years. But this version of him. This exuberance. These past few months – it's so unlike him . . .' and my voice trails off.

If anything, when I think about the shape of him in my life, I feel absence. Not just the retreat of his depression, but also a more general emotional distance, a difficulty staying rooted in the present, like an untethered tent lifting gently in the wind.

I look out across the car park. My eyes fall upon a father pushing a child in a buggy. The child drops a toy, and immediately starts to cry out and kick her legs. The father is on his phone, then he looks round, and rushes back to retrieve it, crouching down in front of the buggy as he places it carefully in her hands.

I turn to look at Philip.

'Is he having a breakdown? Is that what this is?'

'I don't know,' he says. 'Maybe. I wouldn't like to speculate. But it sounds like it would be good for him to see a doctor, when he gets back to Oxford. I have a colleague there,' he says. 'I can call her, if you like?'

'Thank you,' I nod, 'but if it is – what do we do? How can we help him?' I have so many questions.

Philip reaches a hand over and he rests it on my arm. It feels calm, steadying.

'Let's wait and see,' he says. 'And for all those questions, there are so many different answers. Some psychiatrists favour a very biological model, chemical imbalances in the brain,' he says and then dips his head. 'I myself prefer to see any psychological imbalance as something more relational. More a response, a defence against reality, if you like. A way of retreating from a situation that is too hard to manage.'

And perhaps in response to the confusion on my face, he says it doesn't have to be a specific trigger, 'more often, it's something more intangible; like old age. An escape from life.' He tells me that working in addiction and rehab, he has found diagnostic language unhelpful. Limiting to patients. He says it sometimes made him unpopular with his colleagues, 'but I think the question to always ask is *why this? Why now?*'

I think about some of my father's baffling and random behaviour; the weekend away, his distraction, the way he was the day Sam got lost, his exuberance at talking to the walkers, the birthday party. These odd incidents start to shuffle together in a line, like reluctant children.

We sit for a moment in silence.

I look back at this man's face. His kindness. His care.

'I know you have to go,' he says gently, patting my arm, 'but we can talk more, when you have time. I'll call my colleague. She's excellent.'

'Thank you,' I nod as I reach for the door handle. And then, just before I go, he says something about Helen and the children and about strength and courage, and it makes me cry.

I open the door, and turn back towards him. 'Your patients were so lucky to have you,' I say.

*

They are on the ICU of the children's ward. They have a large four-bedded room near the nurses' station. There are two police-women, one policeman and Julie, a family liaison officer. I see very little of Helen: she is back and forth with the kids as they undergo various tests. Sometimes they are wheeled away. Other times the curtains are screeched around the bedside as doctors and nurses gather around. I give a statement to one of the policewomen, about what happened at the farmhouse when we got back and about what I saw when I arrived at Dancing Ledge. I tell them I picked up the rifle. 'I wasn't thinking,' I say, 'about the prints. That I shouldn't touch anything—'

As a clinician, life in hospital is fast-paced and speedy. But for a carer or relative of a patient, time slows right down. The bedside is a series of visits and tasks as the patient is on the conveyor belt for different kinds of treatment, while relatives sit, stirring around in a kind of soupy daze. It's a terminal of waiting and transition. Of immobility and hope and expectation. Every so often, I go down for snacks and drinks from the shop in the entrance hall, and I leave the purchases on the spare bed for them while I sit in the waiting room next door.

At around 6 p.m., Helen appears at the door and says she needs to go with Ollie for another scan. 'Could you maybe take Lexie down to the café?' She looks suddenly stricken. 'I don't want to leave her on her own on the ward, even with the nurses,' and she's twisting her hands together in panic. I see then, how the terror of the life she has led is something she has internalised.

Something that's become so familiar, it's now a part of her. Something she will live with for a long time to come.

Lexie has her bag of colouring books and pens and holds tightly onto my hand in the lift. I get hot chocolate for her and a coffee for me. We sit at a table by the window. She watches as a heavily pregnant woman walks past us to the till.

'My mummy had a baby in her tummy. But it died when she fell down the stairs.'

I hold my breath. There is no emotion on her face. Her voice is flat, matter of fact.

But in the chilly silence, I feel it on my face. The fear in my bones. The quiet hidden secrets of another person's life.

I think about what to say, but Lexie's interest has moved on. She is opening one of her colouring books and picking up her pens.

'Shall we do one together?' she says, tapping a felt tip on the page. 'I like this one with the rabbits.'

*

An hour later, I am back in the waiting area. It reminds me of that summer with Gemma. The sticky heat of the ward. The hours spent by her bedside. Watching her pale face in the bed. My mother puffing up her pillows when Gemma took the long agonising walk to the toilet. Then carefully arranging the fruit in a bowl, as if preparing for a still life drawing class. The specialist eating disorder unit imbued a very particular juxtaposition of frenzied activity, alongside sloth and inertia. But by the time Gemma came in, she had no energy for the relentless regime of running on the spot and push-ups that I saw from the other girls. She was too tired for any of that by then.

I spent hours on plastic chairs in the canteen, making bargains and pacts about people on the ward. Things I had to do. *Smile twice at the nurse with the ponytail. Read the boy a story in bed number six. If the girl in bed ten gets better, that will help us.* Then how I made sense of random events in the cafeteria. *If six people order a baked potato in the next hour . . . if I clear the plates on the table by the window . . . if I smile at the cashier . . . if . . . if . . . if.* Small scenarios and tasks I set up and linked to Gemma getting better. If they came true, '*. . . and she smiled back!*' I was elated. A small lift. Like an internal fist-bump. And for all the times the targets were not reached, which was most of the time, I simply let them fall away, casting them aside, while I set up new ones. It was, I understood now, a way of managing my deep fear. A way of trying to make order out of chaos. A way of trying to gain control over something that was rapidly running away from me.

At about 8.30 p.m., Helen steps out to join me in the corridor. 'They're watching cartoons,' and she sips at a bottle of water. 'Tests are all looking good. No lasting damage. They will have more checks. But so far, so good.'

I feel the sinking. The sudden collapse of relief. My body gives over to it. A slump in my chair.

'Earlier, they were so sleepy. But now they've just seen the doctor, and they're bouncing off the walls. I had to put the telly on to calm them down,' she laughs loudly. An explosion of joy. And then, all of a sudden, she drops her head down, and is sobbing hard. She leans forwards, elbows on her knees, making a shelf for her head with her hands as the tears flow down her cheeks. I cry too. My hand resting gently on her back.

Neither of us speaks. There are no words.

After a while, she sits up. 'I must go back,' she says, wiping her face. 'I've given some information to the police, all the basics – but I have a full interview tomorrow morning At eleven. I'm allowed someone with me. Can you come?'

She asks if Rob can bring the kids in. 'It would be great for Ollie and Lexie. They can play together. Some normality,' she says.

'What do they know?'

'They know he's dead.'

I nod.

'I don't yet know what Ollie saw. What he understands. What either of them understand. But they will know it wasn't good—' She falters for a moment. 'I can't lie. But I can't tell the truth. At least not yet. It's a truth I can't believe myself—'

I reach for her hand.

'In spite of everything,' she says, 'he was still their dad. They were frightened of him sometimes. But they loved him. They are grieving. And I must honour that.'

*

When I finally get back home, the kids are fast asleep. Rob hugs me. He looks pale and stunned, like he's been run over by a truck. We go upstairs to the kids' bedroom, and stand by their tiny little beds. Sam, with his hands flung up above his head. Ruby, small and neat and curled up like a ball. We look at each other, then we stand there for a very long time, holding each other and staring at our children with a kind of wonder and gratitude.

268

TWENTY-FOUR

In the morning, we set off early and I pick up a few things for Helen in Dorchester, while Rob and the kids take a trip to Poundland, emerging with bags of dressing-up stuff and a mountain of plastic toys that he stuffs in the boot. All three of them are flushed and giddy with the excitement of the purchases.

Helen tells me they slept well. 'I was peering at them most of the night. But then I dropped off at around four,' she says.

She tells me they're allowed to go to the grassy play area in the hospital grounds, 'but I think they should stay on the ward,' she says, 'just for today,' and I nod. I can't imagine how she will let them out of her sight again, and as we take the lift up to the fourth floor to get coffee from the canteen, it's as if she's read my mind.

'It will take time,' she says. 'Even though the threat is over for us, I have to believe the world is a safe place – even though our house wasn't. At the moment, it's too soon. It's all mixed up.' She breathes out deeply. 'It's such a relief Rob and the kids are with them.'

We sit at a table by the window. It overlooks the car park. We watch for a moment, the comings and goings of people. Staff in uniforms hurrying back and forth with brisk efficiency. Then others, moving trance-like in hunched, hollowed-out shapes. And huddles of families each wrapped tight in their own private torments.

Helen fiddles with a sachet of sugar.

'It needed it to be a secret. For you not to know it was me,' she explains. 'I decided the plan was safer if no one knew. Of course, in the end,' she shrugs, 'it was neither here nor there.'

I nod.

'But also – I needed your clarity. Your knowledge. Your experience. And I needed it to be uncontaminated by any emotion. It was a forensic decision. If you knew it was me, it would have changed things.'

'I know. I understand.'

She pauses, shaking the sugar.

'It might have affected your willingness to help—'

She waves her hand to silence me.

'It's not a criticism. It's a fact. You liked James. Rob liked James. *Everyone liked James*. You might have been cautious? Even doubtful. I'm not saying it would have stopped you helping. But it may have. Or at the very least, it would have led to questions. The need for information. It was a risk I couldn't take.'

She puts the sugar sachet down.

'It's happened before,' she says, 'when I've needed help. A feeling of disbelief. A look of doubt. *James? Are you sure?* It was a mistake I wasn't going to make again. Sometimes the women you think will be allies are not. They are part of the problem. I understand it. They are drawn to the charm, like flowers leaning towards the sun,' she says, holding her hands out in a gesture of supplication. 'I mean, I was.'

I say nothing. I'm turning this over in my head. I think back to my shock of realising it was James. That Helen was Polly. *There is no Polly*. The seismic shift in my perception and expectation.

'I didn't plan to invent a sister, it just happened, that day on the beach. It came to me. As a way of explaining the phone calls – his constant need for attention. Wanting to know what I'm doing, who I'm with. Sometimes he called just to be angry.

To rant about his life. How it had gone wrong because of me. Because of other people.' She closes her eyes briefly.

And I see her on the cliff, pacing up and down, the phone at her ear. Tight-lipped. Shaking her head and saying very little.

'But very quickly, Polly helped me—'

I frown.

'Inventing Polly helped me take a step back. Seeing her life through your eyes. The horror on your face, it made a difference. It gave me objectivity. And you were so clear, so definite. It also gave me courage –' and she pauses for a moment, '– because Polly was believed.'

I feel an ache in my chest.

'You wouldn't have been able to do that if you knew it was me. You would have been scared. Worried for me. Your emotions would have got in the way.'

I nod. 'Maybe so, but I wouldn't have persuaded you to come to my father's birthday.'

'Sure,' she says, 'but I chose to come. There was a part of me that wanted a different life.'

She tells me about their life in Germany. 'I had no friends. People I talked to. It was just me and James. After a while, I began to believe his version of myself. Talking about Polly meant leaving became a possibility. Something she could do. Polly, short for Pollyanna,' she laughs. 'My alter ego.'

I smile.

'But also, if you knew it was me, you would have seen me differently.'

'How so?' I ask.

'I despised myself for being in this situation. I felt weak – I didn't want to see that mirrored back at me. I didn't want to see that on your face. To see your pity.' She shakes her head. 'It's not how I used to be. It's not the version of myself that I want to be reminded of. There are other versions of myself that I prefer. Other versions that have been buried. Over the years, I lost the belief in my own capabilities.'

She sits still for a moment.

'I wanted to be someone else. Polly gave me the chance to stop feeling like a victim.'

I sit with this, taking it in.

I take a breath. 'That patient I mentioned?'

She nods. 'I know she didn't leave him. It sounded too neat.'

'But when I told you, you looked – so relieved. So full of hope?'

'I needed to believe it in that moment,' she says, 'and I think you needed me to believe it too.'

She glances at her watch. We both stand. As we walk back to the lift, she asks about my father.

I tell her what Rob told me when I got back last night. How he was admitted to hospital in Oxford. 'On the way back home, they stopped at a bookshop.' I pause for a moment, trying to imagine the scene in my head. My father's flights of fancy. His grandiose plans. The glorious flames of his exuberance, my mother on the sidelines, trying to put out the fire with the flap of a damp tea towel.

'He wanted to make a purchase,' I say. 'But when the owner tried to help, my father said it was the bookshop he wanted to buy.' I surprise myself by laughing. Helen stares back at me. 'The owner said it wasn't for sale, but my father was very insistent. I know I shouldn't laugh, but it must have been a comedy moment, *how can I help you?* Only to be told *I've come to buy your shop.* Apparently, he was calling his bank. Writing cheques – even went back and forth to the cashpoint. I gather things got a little messy . . .'

I don't really need to say any more.

'I'm so sorry.'

I shake my head. 'It doesn't compare,' I say, 'to everything else.'

'Was it – was this a sudden thing?'

'Well, yes and no. In a way, it's a relief. Makes sense of the last few months. And hopefully, he'll get the help he needs.'

'Does he remember it all?'

'I'm not sure,' I say, shaking my head. 'I think he's been given some drugs to calm him down. But I'll find out tomorrow. I'm going to drive up to Oxford to see him in the morning.'

There's a pause.

'I just feel – I wished I'd joined things up. Seen the pattern – it's what I'm good at.'

She thinks about this for a moment. 'We all like patterns,' she says, 'they are neat. Easy on the eye. But sometimes, there's no pattern. And that's the most frightening thing of all.'

'Maybe I should have seen it coming?'

'Ah, yes,' she says, 'the *I-should-have-seen-it-coming* mantra. I know it well. I have berated myself with it for years. It sits neatly on the shelf along with other tomes of self-loathing,' she sighs, 'not helpful.'

As the lift doors open and we step inside, Helen says, 'It's hard to see what's right in front of us. Sometimes we are simply too close up. Too pressed up against it to see it for what it is. It's only when we retreat, step away, that things come into focus.'

TWENTY-FIVE

The interview takes place in the 'family room' along the corridor. All doctors refer to it as the 'breaking bad news' room. Attempts have been made to soften it. A bland poster in a frame. Blue chairs and a comfy sofa. But it still looks sterile. A room you don't want to stay in for long. I've been in so many versions of this room throughout my medical career. On a children's ward, it's the room where parents sit pale-faced, hand-wringing and clinging to each other, making whispered pacts with a God they've never previously believed in. It's the room where soft hushed words can collapse faces and break hearts. Phrases that parents will remember for the rest of their lives, and ones that make them fight the urge to reach a hand out and press it firmly over the talking mouth.

The family liaison officer, Julie, is there with the two detectives: an older man and a woman in her thirties. Julie has been with Helen and the kids since she arrived in hospital. Has slept in an empty side room on the ward. After enquiring about the children, the policeman asks how she is. 'I think I'm doing OK, given the circumstances,' Helen says. Julie pours water from a jug on the table. Next he asks Helen about her car.

'Can you confirm it's a red Ford Fiesta, registration number GD13 JDX?'

She nods.

He tells us about the mileage tracker. 'It was on your husband's phone. That was the car it was linked to. It tracks mileage, but also has a GPS system, so it can track and record the journeys a car has made. He kept a record of the details in a linked app.'

I feel my throat constricting as I hear this news. I reach for a glass of water.

'I see,' Helen says. It's clearly not so much of a surprise to her. 'I knew he tracked everything,' she says simply, 'but I hadn't got any evidence that he was monitoring the car. I looked repeatedly. I just hadn't found it.'

'It was a very small device, fitted behind the steering wheel.'

And then I remember Helen's unexpected request for us all to go in my car when she went to view the school. How surprised I was when she asked if we could squash all four kids in the back. How out of character it seemed at the time. How it was me that said no. Me that said it wasn't safe.

'From the notes, the evidence he recorded, we have reason to believe that he knew of your plans to relocate.'

Helen and I exchange a glance. And to my surprise, Helen does a brief semi-eyeroll. *No shit, Sherlock.* I have to look away, immediately. Perhaps it's the stress and tension, but I feel the rise of forbidden laughter, the sudden irrepressible hysteria that reminds me of childhood. But as I'm staring out the window, a thought occurs to me, something I haven't felt before. *Helen is funny*, is what I think, as I dig my nails into my palms.

'Your husband's phone records show he was in touch with Smithfield Primary School on Thursday 23rd June—'

This does come as a surprise to Helen.

'It would seem he spoke to a Mrs Cates in the admissions office.'

Helen nods. 'That's the woman I met earlier that day.'

'According to Mrs Cates, she had a call from James Dunstable that afternoon. He said he was ringing in on your behalf to say you'd forgotten to mention Lexie's allergies,' the man glances down at his notes, 'nut and egg, was what he said.'

I look over at Helen, frowning.

A brief shake of her head.

'I take it your daughter does not have these allergies.'

'No. She does not.'

'According to Mrs Cates, she recorded this new information in the file. She said they chatted for a while. She said how she was looking forward to meeting the children. Was sorry they couldn't come that day. When we asked her how he seemed, she said he was friendly.' He looks down at his notes. '*He was charming. Seemed very appreciative that we'd found the kids places at the school.* He said they were looking forward to September, *a new start for the family.*'

Helen is sitting very still as she listens.

'Can you confirm that James Dunstable was not aware of your plans to enrol the children in a new school? That your plans to relocate were a secret?'

She looks taken aback. 'Well – yes. For obvious reasons.'

'I'm sorry, Mrs Dunstable, I may be asking things that seem obvious, but this is a crime. It's important we establish the facts.'

She nods.

'It would seem therefore that James was testing out his hypothesis, and this telephone call was confirmation.'

'Did he go to Brussels?' she asks.

'No.'

The man leans forwards, clearing his throat as he glances down at his notes.

'We've been looking into incidents like this,' he says, and just before he speaks, I realise, of course, there will be a name for it. A name for the thing James has done.

'Family annihilation,' he announces, like it's the answer to a quiz question. 'It's a term first coined in the US, following a number of incidents there. But there have been some tragic examples here, in recent years. Domestic homicide – it's on the increase,' then adds unnecessarily, 'some very high-profile cases.' And while his careful words reflect the gravity of the situation, I also detect something else, the bristle of a kind of electricity. And I wonder what it must be like for this bomb of violence to drop here in the countryside, shattering the peace and calm of this small community. And how it must border on excitement for a rural Dorset police force bogged down by petty crime and disenfranchised teenage drug habits.

'Typically,' he informs us, 'it's a male response –'

No shit, Sherlock. I avoid looking at Helen.

He's reading from his notes, '– a controlling or abusive male response to his partner's impending or threatened departure. Usually, after the children, the perpetrator takes his own life. It is a violent response to a situation he perceives to be out of his control.'

I flinch. *A situation out of his control?*

Helen looks distracted. She doesn't need to hear any of this. The statistics, the predisposition. The signs and symptoms. The fact that men fall into one of four categories. She has lived it. She knows far more than they do.

But the man peers down at his notes again. He wants his categorisation.

'I see from my records your husband lost his job. Would you say that was difficult? A source of stress?'

Helen jerks her head up. 'Excuse me?'

There's a chilly silence.

'My husband's response to finding out I was planning to leave him was to try to *kill his own children* – do you want to put your pen down and just think about that for one moment? This was his response to his feeling rejected? I hope we're not going to spend the interview trying to come up with a reason to explain his behaviour?'

The man's cheeks flush. 'No – I—'

'And yes, he did lose his job. But he did so because he lost his temper with one of his colleagues. If we *are* going to talk about him, I'd prefer to focus on his coercive controlling behaviour over the last eight years. I imagine that men like my husband do these things precisely because it's the ultimate act of control. And the very worst possible punishment for the mother who is left behind.'

As she speaks, I can hear her voice is gathering momentum. 'The problem with the data,' she says, 'is that it focuses on men. The clusters of behaviour to look out for. None of this is helpful unless something changes for us. Otherwise, they are simply pieces of research. Reports that sit on shelves, that we get out and nod at with retrospective wisdom when the tragic cases hit the headlines.'

And as she speaks, I wonder how many tragedies happen before a name is given to something. Before it becomes a thing that you can google. A syndrome. How long before a pattern is detected in recurring signs and symptoms? How long does it take before a man's violent behaviour becomes categorised into a disorder and the warning signs for women become an eight-point plan?

'Did his behaviour conform to some identified pattern? Maybe,' she says. 'But the point is – it didn't start like that. It was slow, insidious and vicelike. And when it's taken control, and you feel isolated with two small children and no money, there is no clear pathway out. Imagine feeling so broken that you feel you can only breathe when you share the same air as your husband?'

The man is nodding, twisting his pen in his hand.

'And someone like James? *What a charmer,* everyone thinks. Sometimes, on the outside, there isn't anything to see. I didn't tell my friend Jess what was happening,' and she looks over at me, 'because she may not have believed me.'

My friend. And I feel my own face flush, as I recall my thoughts. *He's such good company. So kind and helpful.* How Rob and I flocked around him like moths to a flame. And when he declined the invite to Dad's birthday, how disappointed we were. *What a shame,* we both said, *he'd be good to have there. Great fun. The glue in what might be an awkward social occasion.* How painful it is to admit that both of us would have chosen him over her.

I look down at the carpet. My eyes are drawn to the weave of the blue thread. The swirl of a shape, a repeated motif, like a small undulating wave.

'From an early age, women learn that the world is not safe –' she switches her gaze between Julie and the policewoman, '– we risk assess all the time. The street that's well lit. The full carriage on the train. The cab we get into late at night. We live in a world where rape, child abuse and sexual assault are rife.' She is speaking fast. Her words speeding up. She sounds breathless. 'So much so, that we are bombarded with messages and advice about the things we need to do to protect ourselves. Last year it was "flag down a bus, if you don't trust a plainclothed policeman". I mean – *how fucked up is that?*' she asks, holding her hands out wide.

I realise I have never heard Helen swear before. Fleetingly, it occurs to me that perhaps this was another rule. A stipulation that James had enforced on family life.

'It's as if we're all just laid out, on a buffet table. A smorgasbord that men can simply reach over and help themselves to.'

Nobody speaks. I sense she is not expecting or wanting any dialogue. That there are things she simply wants to say.

'And even the services set up to help – *domestic* violence? It sounds so trivial. Like a Sunday night television drama. And *Violence Against Women and Girls*? I mean, *really*? It sounds like a statement of fact.'

She thumps a hand on the small coffee table. 'You see where the power is?' She shakes her head. 'It's not what do *we* need to do to feel safe, it's how society needs to address male violence and anger.'

She says she's always been vigilant. Always been aware of the risks out in the world. That she was always careful, 'but feeling fearful in your own home is a special kind of horror.'

The man is nodding. The policewoman, I notice, is staring at Helen, in a kind of paralysed disbelief. Not about what she is saying, but more about the fact that she is able to speak at all after what she has been through. But I can see how much Helen has to say. How these things are springing up, as if shaken awake from a kind of numbed hibernation.

She looks around and asks us to think of a time we've felt frightened, 'really frightened,' she emphasises, 'and then think about having that feeling in your own home. In the place where you should feel safe. My life was like balancing on a ledge of a very tall building, knowing that something would always happen to make me fall off, but never knowing, from one day to the next, or one moment to the next, what it might be.

'And of course, I wanted to leave. But it's difficult, emotionally – but logistically, if you live in fear and have small kids, I'd say it's brutal. Near impossible.'

The policeman, I notice, has put down his pen and closed his notepad. He is listening. He is giving her his full attention.

'We need big seismic changes. But smaller ones too,' she continues. 'I don't know either of you, but if anything comes out of this, I'd like to think if you ever get a call from a woman, who then backtracks and retracts her statement – write it down. Keep it in mind. It might be off your desk – but it won't ever be off hers.'

She stops to look around at us all, and when she speaks, her voice is loud and clear.

'People like James never stop. They get more possessive, more controlling over time. It *never* stops.'

There is a silence.

Her words are cut-glass clear. 'I'm lucky he's dead. Lucky there wasn't an alternative outcome. One of which might have seen me in court, fighting for custody over my children.'

The man draws back, a slight jerk of disbelief. Disagreement.

'You don't think so?' she says, the edge of anger in her voice. 'Take a look at the reporting of some of those high-profile cases. How the media tries to understand the behaviour of men who are violent to their partners.'

The man shifts in his seat. But her words keep coming. 'They compile a picture of a man under stress. They evidence the loss of his job. The debts. They will use words like *snapped, out of character* and *out of the blue*. They will paint a picture of *a loving father, struggling to cope,*' she leans forwards, '*a poor man who accidentally killed his wife.*'

The room is very quiet. No one speaks. Her words hang in the air.

After a while, the policeman glances over and nods at Julie. She opens her file and talks about the sessions she will set up for the kids. There will be play therapy, family and one-to-one sessions, 'but all at a time that's right for the children.'

Helen nods enthusiastically. 'Good. We'll take everything and anything,' she says.

'We have trained trauma therapists. And counsellors who are specialists in child bereavement,' Julie says quietly.

Helen nods. 'Every single time I close my eyes, I see it all. In full colour. I'm grateful Lexie was asleep when he fired the rifle, that she didn't witness it. I am grateful for many things. But mostly, I am grateful for the fact they are alive. And he is dead.'

She says she understands there will be grief and loss. That she's sorry they've lost their father. 'But I'm not sorry they will grow up without that father,' and her voice cracks with emotion.

She clears her throat. She is full of rage. She does not want to cry. She stops to take a sip of water. I can see how she wants to say these things out loud. To speak her truth. The reality of the life she lived.

Julie nods.

'When I booked the kids into the new school, made plans to leave, it was as if I was in a film, playing out some kind of fantasy. A part of me knew, I'd never really be free of him. That it would carry on, even if I left. That I'd always be waiting for something to happen,' and she holds her palms out.

'But I never, ever expected this,' she says, placing her hands back neatly in her lap.

'So, now, I have been released. And I know how lucky I am. If he'd done what he set out to do and my kids had died, I'd have killed myself,' she says matter of factly. 'And he would have won. He'd have wiped us all out.' She clicks her fingers in the air with a sharp snap. 'The whole family – annihilated.'

We sit for a moment in the silence.

The female officer then tells Helen they are clearing the London room he was renting. That there is some politically sensitive material. Helen looks neither surprised nor interested. She looks away, out of the window.

The officer asks about her plans. 'Where will you live, in the short term?'

Helen tells them she intends to stay for the summer in the cottage. 'I can't think about going anywhere else at the moment. The kids are happy here. My mum is away until the end of September.'

'Will she not come back?' I ask, without thinking, and my question sounds judgemental.

'No,' she says. And if she hears the note of surprise in my voice, she ignores it. She offers no explanation. And I think about her mother so far away in New Zealand, and how little I know about Helen's childhood and her life.

'I can settle them into school. After that, I don't know . . .' and her voice trails away.

Julie talks about finances and grants and some other details that I can see Helen can no longer focus on.

'I just want to learn to breathe without fear,' she says, 'how simple is that? To not make myself smaller. I've been annihilating myself for years. Erasing myself on a daily basis. In a way, the kids have too,' she says, 'moulding themselves around his moods. His demands. His unpredictability. Because they have seen me do it first. They have learnt it all from me. And I will have to bear that guilt. My hope is that they learn how to be kids again. To be naughty. To answer back and be rude. To not hand homework in on time when they go to school. To feel normal.'

When the policeman says something about the 'extreme' nature of this case, I imagine he thinks he's being supportive, trying to find a way of acknowledging the enormity of her ordeal, but Helen snaps her head.

'Ah yes, the nutter theory,' she says, 'the *one bad apple?*' She shakes her head with disdain. 'The whole orchard is rotting.'

All of a sudden, her body collapses in the chair and she looks deliriously tired. Then abruptly, she sits upright. 'I'd like to get back to my children now,' she says.

I can see the detectives have more questions, but Julie intervenes.

'Yes. That's enough for now. We can pick this up another day. The kids will be here for the next day or so. We can meet here again, or when they go home.'

*

When we get back to the ward, we peer in through the glass on the door. Rob and the kids have made a huge den by pushing two beds together and there's an elaborate arrangement of sheets and blankets. All five of them are wearing hats. Rob seems to be wearing two. Ollie's in a pirate hat. Sam's in a silver spacesuit. As we push open the door, they are all sitting on the floor giggling and enrapt at a story Rob is telling.

But our eyes are drawn to Ollie. The pirate hat is skew-whiff on his head and his face is flushed and glistening with sweat. He is rocking back on his heels, with his head back. He is laughing. A joyful burst of spontaneity. Helen and I exchange a glance. A brief smile.

I'm not naïve enough to think this won't be the beginning of a long and painful journey for them all. But in that moment, I feel such delight to hear his deep belly laugh, because it's a sound I've never heard before.

TWENTY-SIX

Max and Barbara live in a small village on the outskirts of Oxford. I call in to visit Max on my way to the hospital to see my father. Barbara is my godmother; I have known the two of them all my life. When she opens the door, she doesn't seem surprised to see me, but is instantly disappointed not to see the children.

'They're with Rob. I'm on my way to see Dad,' I explain. And she's nodding. I can see my mother has already told them what has happened.

'Max is in the garden,' she says, leading me to the back door. He's sitting at the small patio table, his trademark white floppy hat on, his face in a book.

He looks up. It's hard to decipher the look. He smiles, but he seems hesitant. Perhaps a little sheepish.

'I'll make coffee,' Barbara says and steps inside and closes the door.

After small talk that feels forced and awkward, I get to the point. 'I know you and Dad had a falling out – what happened?'

He pauses, fiddles with his fingers, looks out across the lawn. And in that moment, I see how alike he and my father are. How their friendship has been sealed over conversations unsaid. Words left unspoken as they sat together filling their pipes and talking about books. How together they are masters of the unspoken, sharing a tacit and mutual avoidance of conflict and difficulty.

'Max,' I hold my palms out, 'he's in hospital.'

'Yes, I'm sorry,' and he looks distraught for a moment. A beat. 'I don't think I've handled things well.'

Another pause.

And then, in a gentler voice, I add, 'Why don't you try and tell me what's happened?'

'It all started about six months ago,' he shrugs, 'it was just a student prank. Things are pushed under the doors all the time. It was after the Christmas exams. How can I say?' He steeples his fingers together. 'Spirits are always high at the end of that first term.'

He tells me some students had gone round and lifted all the call-girl and escort cards from the local bars and pubs and had taken them into college. Pushing them under the tutors' doors. 'One was pushed under Geoffrey's door.'

He stops. Barbara comes out with a tray. Cafetière, mugs, cake and biscuits. She places it down on the table. She doesn't join us, but slips back into the house.

I'm confused. I have no idea where this is going. 'Yes – and?'

He reaches for his pipe. I wait while he carefully unscrews the base and knocks out the charred contents into an ashtray before cleaning the base with a tissue.

'This is,' he says, looking up at me, 'a little difficult—'

'Please –' I say, '– go on.'

I pick up on his anxiety and I feel a twinge of unease. Instinctively, I find myself thinking about my children. I often do this, in panicky moments. I think about what they might be doing, where they are. My eyes scan over the lawn, as if searching for them. And in that moment, I wish they were here with me. With Rob.

'The lack of rain. It's parched,' he says, following the direction of my gaze. He seems keen to find things to distract.

'Max . . . ?'

He picks up his cleaned pipe and slowly draws out a fresh white pipe cleaner from a pouch in his jacket pocket.

'The card pushed under Geoffrey's door was from Sexy Sadie.'

'*Sexy Sadie?*' I snort.

And perhaps because of my anxiety, I laugh too loud and long at something that turns out not to be very funny at all.

'A small pink card. *I can make you happy*, in gold writing on the front.' He clears his throat. 'On the back, there was a picture of Sadie,' he says, waving a hand, 'I'm sure you can imagine . . .'

He threads the pipe cleaner in and out several times, then puts it to one side as he reaches for his tobacco pouch. As a child, I had loved this ritual. Had watched transfixed, at the small methodical details and tasks. Today, I feel irritated.

'And then?'

I can see he is choosing his words with care. 'I came to understand that Geoffrey saw it as some kind of a personal correspondence.'

I frown.

'He came to see me in January. He showed me the card. He believed it was written for him. That she had singled him out.'

There's a beat. A moment of silence. In the distance, there's a shriek, then laughter from a neighbouring garden.

'That she would make him happy. That they would make *each other* happy.' He looks up. 'That they were made for each other.'

'Oh God,' I whisper, a hand reaching up to my face.

He nods.

'He called her. To invite her on a date—'

He begins to shift uncomfortably in his seat. 'Perhaps you should ask him,' he says.

I feel a rush of irritation. Anger perhaps. 'Max – I'm asking you.'

'They had a date,' he says. 'And he told me he felt this connection. *The beginning of the rest of my life*, was what he said. They had quite a few more "dates". Over the last five months. Then they arranged to go away for the weekend.'

'Did you try to talk to him? I mean, he was clearly deluded. What about his marriage? His job?'

And that's when I remember. His disappearance. *His short break away*. The note he left my mother. The packing of the small brown suitcase.

It's over.

'I did try. Believe me,' Max says. 'It was difficult for him to listen. For him to hear anything that contradicted his very fixed view. I couldn't get through.'

He pauses for a moment, remembering.

'Things got a little tense,' Max says, 'between them at the hotel. Different expectations of the weekend. I imagine a two-night date is a costly business . . . I'm not sure your father thought he would have to pay up front. He was under this illusion that she wanted to be with him. Was choosing to be with him. He'd lost all sense that it was a *transaction*—'

He pauses. 'As I understand it, things got a little tricky.'

I nod for him to continue.

'She told him she had a husband. Kids –' again he looks away, '– that it was *a job*. He took it badly. Like it was the end of a relationship. Like he'd been betrayed in some way.'

I shake my head. 'Max. You should have said something. You should have seen he wasn't well. You should have told me.'

'I know,' he says. 'I'm sorry. I – I hadn't realised how seriously he took it, until after that weekend. How devastated he was. But then, I was reassured at how quickly he seemed to move on.'

'He seemed OK?'

'Well, yes. He recovered fast. I was surprised,' he sips at his coffee, 'until I realised he had moved on to someone else.'

'Someone else?'

'Someone who served at the canteen,' he says.

I close my eyes.

'There was always someone else.'

I think of the walkers on the cliff when Sam ran off.

He clears his throat. 'Is this sort of disinhibition a symptom? Of his breakdown?'

'I think so. Maybe. But I don't really know. I'm on my way to see him.'

'But in amidst all this, he was so full of life. I didn't want to—' and he falters, 'be the one to stop it. It was cowardly perhaps.'

He hesitates, sensing the feeling emanating from me.

'It *was* cowardly,' he says. 'But it felt like popping his balloon. Watching a child's face deflate. Perhaps I didn't want to be the one to do that.'

'So, it all started before Christmas?'

'Yes. There was something he mentioned. But I didn't understand. Something about Gemma. I thought he was referring back to that very difficult time, when she was younger. But he didn't go into details.' He looks awkward. 'I have known your father for a long time. And when you girls were young, his sudden depression was very shocking. And well –' his face is full of anguish, '– he was irretrievable for such a long period of time.'

He sips his coffee.

'And then this,' he waves his hand, 'for a while, he seemed so effusive. So happy. He drew people to him. He seemed so fun. So alive. So hard to resist. And I suppose, selfishly, I was relieved it was this mood, rather than the other.'

I nod.

'But I can see that things quickly got out of hand.'

'And the Emeritus?'

'Well, it was around that time,' he says. 'News travels fast in a small college. There were some complaints.'

'Will he keep his job?' I ask.

'I think so. If he gets well. If he gets help. I'm sure. But I don't know. It's not up to me,' and he presses the fresh tobacco deep into the bowl of the pipe. 'The Dean will have the final say. And as I'm sure you can imagine, the safety of the students is paramount.'

And as he says this, I think about the waitress at the restaurant. Her small face. Her youth. Her initial terror of not being believed. Of perhaps losing her job.

'Of course.'

'He asked me not to do anything until after his birthday. *Let me just have these two weeks*, was what he said. I said I wanted to intervene. To ring your mother. We had a falling-out of sorts – I'm sorry,' he says, 'I should have been a better friend.'

TWENTY-SEVEN

When I get to the hospital, my mother is fussing with some flowers.

'I didn't think they were allowed in hospitals any more – health and safety or something?'

She peers down at the mixed bunch of pink and orange blooms with disdain. 'From Barbara and Max.' There is outrage in her voice.

My father looks small in the bed. And somehow older. His white hair wispy on the pillow. His eyes are closed.

'He's sleeping,' she says. 'He had a very good night. More than I did,' she scoffs. 'They're digging out the basement in the house across the road. Start up so early. There was a fox in the road at three in the morning. Sounded like the scream of a baby. I was bolt upright. Couldn't sleep a wink.'

My mother rustles with the plastic wrapping. 'I'm surprised,' she says, 'Barbara, the eco-warrior. All her excessive recycling. This isn't exactly *eco*, is it?' More rustling. 'Did you see Gemma? On your way in?'

'She's here?'

'She went down for a cigarette. Said she'd texted you.'

I reach into my pocket for my phone. There's a message from her. *I'm outside, by the café, in the entrance.*

'Given he's asleep, I'll go and see her now. I'll pop back in a bit.'

My mother snips away at the stems with a pair of scissors. She looks affronted. Like I've insulted her.

'She'll be back in a minute.'

'I won't be long,' I say.

I find Gemma out in the courtyard by the café. It's a small grassy area with benches, and several patients in gowns are shuffling around with drips on wheels, smoking furiously.

'Hey,' she says, lifting her hand in a wave.

I sit down on the bench next to her. 'He's asleep,' I say.

She nods. 'He's still pretty knocked-off, even when he's awake. He must have had some fairly strong meds.'

I realise I'd meant to look at his chart before I came down.

'They should send some in Mum's direction,' she says, and we both laugh.

There's a pause, as she lights another cigarette and pulls on it hard.

'Did Mum say anything to you?'

I shake my head. 'I'd only just arrived. But she was pretty fixated on the flowers from Max and Barbara. Dreadful colour. Dreadful wrapping. All in all, a dreadful idea.'

There's a heavy moment of silence between us.

I look at her expectantly. 'Gem, what is it?'

She takes another drag of her cigarette. Crushes it under her shoe, then takes a long breath out, emptying her lungs. It's a jumble at first. She says something about a trial. About video testimonials and America. None of which makes any sense at all.

'I had to decide by July. And I've made up my mind.'

I stare at her for a moment.

'Do you remember? Years ago – that skating summer camp? The American coach who came to Manchester for six weeks? Our team were offered the *once-in-a-lifetime experience* to train with him?'

I feel the sudden and terrible pull of anxiety. For a moment, I want her to stop talking. I don't want to hear what I know she's going to say.

I close my eyes.

'Lance Silverton,' she says. 'That was his name. *World renowned* – we were so lucky to have the opportunity.'

And there it is. The missing piece of the jigsaw. The pattern I'd been looking for. The pattern that makes perfect sense. But it's a pattern I don't want to see.

I feel a sink and dip in my stomach. For a moment, I think I'm going to be sick. I lean forwards, dropping my head onto my knees. Breathing in and out until the moment passes. She rests her hand on the small of my back.

When I sit back up, I reach for her hand, and hold it tight.

'The first witness testimony was made last November. So far, a hundred and ten women have come forward to give video evidence about their experiences of training with him when they were children. The things that happened to them. The things he did to them. Some of them were as young as seven.' She pauses for a moment. 'I was ten.'

I am holding my breath and I'm squeezing her hand so tightly, she winces.

'Sorry,' I mumble, releasing my grip.

'I told Mum and Dad before Christmas. They kind of fell apart. Dad especially. I had until July to decide. They were against it—'

'Gem – why didn't you tell me?'

'They asked me not to. Pleaded. I think they were hoping it would go away. That I might drop it. You know what they're like. *Head down. Don't make a fuss.* But I've thought about it – and I just can't do that,' she says. 'Of course, I understand – they feel ashamed. Sending me there. Not knowing. I mean, I'm not a mother, but I get it. It's your job as a parent to protect your kids.

But I wanted their support – not their guilt.'

There's a silence that sits heavily between us. And I find myself drawn back to that awful Sunday lunch. I feel like my cheeks are on fire.

'Over the course of these six months, the evidence has gathered. There's been a group chat. An online support group. Most of the girls are American, he was their coach for years. But there are many of us from all over Europe, who came into contact with him on these special summer camps.'

'Oh Gem – I'm so sorry. I'm so sorry this happened.'

My tears are falling as I turn to her. We hug for a long time.

She is composed in the face of my emotions. She tells me she's been able to think about it for a very long time. 'If these other women are brave enough to come forward, then I can do it too.'

She tells me that when she first heard about it, she pulled away from it. It was a push-pull thing for a long time. But when she joined the group and read the stories, it all came rushing back to her. Things she'd shut away. Things she wanted to forget. She tells me for as long as she could remember, she felt like a bad person, 'rotten to the core. Like I'd done something to deserve it. I was so ashamed of myself. And then I listened to women who all felt the same, and it was—' and she struggles to find the right word. She shakes her head. 'I still can't explain how it felt.'

Again, I feel a wave of nausea.

'The pushback from Mum and Dad was hard,' she shrugs, 'but I've spent approximately a billion hours talking about it in therapy,' she laughs, 'shitloads. Costing a bloody fortune. And then I realised that when I'm with them, I'm like one of those mice in an animal experiment. Pressing the food lever time and time again,' and she holds her hands out, 'and each time, nothing comes out.'

I put both my hands over hers, encasing them in mine.

'I'd spent so many years feeling it was my fault. That I was to blame. He's a seventy-two-year-old monster. I think it's time some of that anger came his way.'

I have a fleeting image of her pale face on the pillow. Her feathery translucent skin. Thinning hair and hollow face. And next to her bed, her purple sequinned skating outfit cut up into shreds.

'I don't know what to say. I'm so sorry,' and suddenly, I'm crying all over again. 'Is there anything I can do?'

'When all this –' and she waves a hand upwards, '– has blown over and Dad's feeling better, tell them that I need their strength. Not their guilt. I've had spade loads of that myself. It's not helpful,' she says, and she lights another cigarette.

'I'm sorry I didn't tell you,' she says. 'I wanted to. But after telling Mum and Dad – it went so badly. I realised I just needed to sit with it myself. Work out what I wanted to do.'

I'm nodding. 'I get it. I understand.'

She squeezes my hand.

'And what about your video testimonial, when is it? Would you like me to be with you?'

She tells me Gavin is coming with her. 'He's been lovely,' she says, 'I really like him. He's surprised me.' She looks away, thinking for a moment. 'I feel like I can be myself with him, like I don't have to hide.' She turns back to face me. 'But maybe we can meet afterwards? With Rob too. I'd really like you both to meet him. Properly,' she adds, 'not like the Friday pantomime.'

'Of course.' And as I nod, some things fall into place.

'So, Dad's breakdown,' I say. 'Coming around Christmas. It makes sense now.'

She nods.

'My big revelation . . . my need for support – and he's the one

295

who falls apart.'

We both sit with this for a moment.

'And I felt very angry,' she says, 'after I told them. He didn't mention it again. Neither of them did.' And then she laughs. 'But every time I feel disappointed, I remind myself of the little mouse in the cage.'

*

When I go back to the ward, my father is awake. His head is still on the pillow. He is gazing up at the ceiling, his eyes gathering on the white tiles above his head. He looks tired, but calm, but there is sadness on his face.

Mum is bustling about on the ward, talking to a woman by the sink.

When she comes over, she tells me the woman's husband is in the bed by the window. 'He went a bit doolally,' she says, 'they thought it was a urine infection. Was on a medical ward first. Turns out he was having some kind of psychotic breakdown.' She throws her hands up in the air. 'Thinks the nurses are plotting to kill him. That there are rats in the wardrobe. Your father says there was quite a kerfuffle last night – apparently he—'

'Mum,' my voice is loud. Urgent. 'Can you just be quiet,' I say, 'can you just *stop talking*,' and she reels back, like I've slapped her.

She stares at me.

I sink down into the chair next to my father's bed. I turn round to face her. 'Can you give us a minute? I'd like some time on my own with Dad,' and I say these words with a clarity, a firm voice that I have never used with her before.

She doesn't move.

'Oh, don't mind me,' she says, 'I'm just pottering about.'

'Can you leave us? Perhaps go for a walk?'

'*A walk*?' Her face creases with scorn.

'Yes. Get a coffee? Have a walk? We're fine here for a moment.' And then I just sit tight and wait.

Her face looks bleached with fury. But reluctantly, she picks up her bag.

'Half an hour?' I say. 'Then we can get some lunch afterwards?'

'I'll see how I go,' she says, crisply.

When she has gone, my father turns to me. 'Ah, Jess,' he says, a flicker of a smile. When he talks, his words are thick and slow. It must be the medication. Idly, I glance down at his chart.

'I slept well last night. All night, for the first time in months.'

He looks small and sad. My anger dissipates. I reach for his hand. It feels cold, as I encase it between my own.

'I'm sorry, Dad,' I say, 'that I didn't see this.'

A pause.

'What's the point in having a daughter who's a doctor—'

He waves his other hand in the air. 'It would have done no good,' he says, generously. 'I think it had to take its course.'

We sit for a moment in silence.

'I didn't really want to take the medication—'

Perhaps he sees the alarm on my face, and he shakes his head and tells me not to worry. 'I'm taking it. I know I must. At least for now. And of course, as a result, my mind has settled,' he says. 'It's fair to say, I feel calmer – if somewhat duller.'

I squeeze his hand.

'There are alternatives to think about,' I say. 'Different ways to understand what's happened. How to help . . .'

He nods. 'It's hard to take something to suppress the goodness of those feelings. There was something so deliciously vibrant about the experience. So colourful. The world seemed –' and

297

he looks wistful for a moment, '– so brilliant and wonderful. Like anything was possible. For a small moment, I could do anything. I felt confident. Powerful. Like I could just seize whatever I wanted in life.'

I see his eyes are shining at the memory and I feel a lurch of anxiety. Remembering him in the wine cellar of the restaurant.

'I don't remember everything about these last couple of weeks, but I imagine I went rather overboard. I expect I was a little foolish.'

I nod, trying to be careful with my words. 'Yes, a little foolish,' I say gently, 'things got a bit out of hand. Losing a sense of reality can also be dangerous. To yourself . . . and other people.'

'When you see Max,' he says, 'don't be too hard on him. I don't remember the details, but if I had to describe it, it was like being in a wind-tunnel. Rushing ahead. It would have been hard for anyone to stop me,' he says. 'We had *an agreement* that he didn't really agree to – to say nothing until my birthday. I asked for this time. To be left alone. To see what it felt like. To be someone else, to live a different life. Just for a moment.'

I think about this. 'Living that different life must have felt like an escape,' I say, 'from the reality of your own.'

'Yes,' he says, and his face is glowing. 'But it was so wonderful to escape,' he says, with the excitement of a child.

I wait, hoping he will say more. Hoping he will say something about Gemma. But then his face turns on the pillow, a slight movement away, as if trying to move into the spotlight where he can shine again.

Then he closes his eyes.

I sit for a moment. My hand on his, listening to the sound of his breathing moving slowly in and out.

298

TWENTY-EIGHT

It was Pete's idea to organise a little party for their homecoming. 'Just a small gathering,' Joyce says, 'just us really. He thought it would be something nice for the kids.' She falters. 'He can't get over what James did. What it must have been like for the little ones . . .' her voice trails off.

'We all liked James,' I say, 'or the version of James he showed to us.'

'Actually,' she says, pushing the hair from her face, 'I didn't much care for him. Mr Helpful. All that bloody DIY. It's not normal, is it?'

I smile. 'Clearly not.'

'How will it be for them?' she says, suddenly desperate, tears springing to her eyes.

'I don't know,' I say. 'Hard. Easy. Lonely. Terrible. Peaceful. All of that. And more. All at the same time, I guess.' I shake my head. 'It will take a very long time.'

She reaches for my hand, and we stand in silence. It's such a recent horror, something so appalling, that we can still only flit around it, like butterflies, landing on it lightly and briefly, before we have to quickly fly away.

I see Pete in the distance on a ladder, stringing up some bunting; next to him Leo is tying long strips of silver paper in the bushes. He claps his hands and yells with delight as the silver catches the sun and showers the grass with darts of light.

'Leo looks cheerful,' I say.

'Of course he does,' and I notice she looks brighter, less tired.

'We all are,' she says, looking at me pointedly, widening her eyes. 'Something else to celebrate later.'

I frown. 'What? Am I missing something?'

She lurches forwards. 'The hundred thousand pounds,' she smiles, 'the *anonymous* donation.'

'What!'

She peers at my face, scanning my expression.

I start to laugh, when I realise she thinks it was me. In fact, I can't stop laughing. It's not just the fact that she thinks I might have that amount of spare cash, but the fact that she thinks I'd be donating anonymously. I slap a hand on my thigh. 'Do you not know me at all? I'd have been shouting it from the rooftops,' I laugh, 'milking all the attention, giving newspaper interviews. I'd have wanted all the glory.'

I shake my head. 'A hundred grand? That's fantastic,' I say, 'but who has that kind of money to spare?'

And just at that moment, the French windows of Philip and Penny's cottage open.

Philip steps out into the sunshine. He waves as he settles himself into a deckchair. There's a moment of silence as we look at each other, then back at Philip. I think about what he said about his guilt about his privilege. About his loss of faith.

'An anonymous donation is a true act of altruism,' I say. 'It's a kind and quiet thing to do.'

'Kind and quiet,' she nods. We watch him carefully open his glasses, and then his book. Then we stare back at one another.

Joyce tells me they now have funding for the rest of the year. And as a result, huge press coverage to shame the council into keeping the project open, 'especially after Pete's intervention, which seems to have been beneficial, rather than the train-wreck I thought it was going to be. The GoFundMe page . . . the level of support from all over has been amazing. It's enough to restore your faith in humanity.'

'And at least Pete didn't have to chain himself to the council offices,' I say.

She tells me how they took Leo over to Green Shoots the day before. 'They always use this picture board with the days of the week for the students. They showed him his photograph on the calendar, for every day next week. It's always hard to tell how much he understands, but his mood has changed. He seems happier.'

She tells me she's been clearing out the little farm cottage. 'You can take a look later if you like? How did Rob take the news?'

'Surprised at first. Then a bit freaked out. Now – we're all OK, I think.'

I'd told him the evening I got back from Oxford. At first, he looked stricken, worried about what I was saying. 'No,' I said, reaching for him, 'we're good. I just want to stay here for a little longer. Joyce said I – *we* – can use the cottage on the farm. All of us. I know you'll have to go back and forth to London a bit. But I'd like to stay on for a while. Be here for Helen – but also,' and I hesitated, 'sort myself out a bit more.'

He was nodding, trying to understand.

'It's a strange thing to say, given the unimaginably terrible things that have happened,' and I wave a hand in the air, 'but apart from all that, it was good for me. This time. Just staying still. Being quiet. Doing less. Hanging out with the kids. You were right,' I shrug.

'You look good,' he said. 'Better.'

I hesitated, trying to find the right words. In the end I just came out with it.

301

'I'm not going back to work in September. I'm taking some time out. A proper sabbatical. Unpaid.'

I saw the flash of panic on his face, then a struggle to look supportive.

'I've arranged it with David. I'm sorry I didn't discuss it with you before, but it had to be my decision. I spoke to him yesterday.'

'OK.'

'I've suggested they get a locum. For at least six months. While I decide what to do.' My voice was clear, decisive.

He nodded again, taking this in.

'It's what I need to do right now. I need to step back a bit. I've got too enmeshed. Too caught up.'

And in that moment, we didn't discuss the practicalities. We didn't talk about the bills and the mortgage and the finances. Nor did we talk about the uncertainty of his film project. It was an unspoken decision to save all this for another day.

'And there may be other things I want to do. At the local Domestic Violence forum. I just don't know yet.'

'It's fine. It sounds good. And I'm sorry if – I've been a bit of a wanker.'

There was a pause. 'I struggled to understand it all,' he said, admitting he didn't really know how to handle it. That he didn't want what happened to change things, 'to change you. To change us. I was scared.'

I nodded. 'I realise that when things happen, they do change us. Whether we like it or not. Even things that happened a very long time ago. It's more exhausting to pretend they don't. Holding a door against a tsunami and simply carrying on?' I shake my head. 'It doesn't work.'

And as I was speaking, I thought about Veronica. My session

with her the next day. And how I know I will continue to go back, week after week. And we will walk, like mudlarkers on the beach, side by side, sifting over the shingle and muddy silt, unearthing things to look at, piece by piece. The search to understand myself, my place in my family, and the effort it takes to pull away from the familiar, and what's been long ingrained in me. How I feel trapped into a conditioned response, doing the same things over and over, like pulling the string on a child's toy to activate one of the five programmed responses.

I told him I still felt all over the place, 'but the fog is clearing, just a bit.'

I glanced over to the kids on the lawn, heads hunched over the flower bed, the swirl of their curls, digging up cars they had buried in the soil.

I said I was confused, 'stuff about myself. Things I need to do differently.'

He shuffled closer and reached for my hand.

'I need to learn to be a different version of myself. One that doesn't get eclipsed by other people. Or rather, I need to not let myself be eclipsed by other people,' I paused, 'both at work – and at home.'

I paused for a moment, turning to look at him.

'I can't always be the one to pick the ripe fruit,' I said. 'You have to pick it too. Before it falls and makes a mess.'

He nodded, and just as he reached an arm around my shoulder, Sam grabbed something that Ruby wanted. She grabbed it back. A squabble broke out. An intense ownership battle that we listened to, until eventually, it passed.

*

Helen arrives back with the kids late afternoon. Joyce has baked chocolate cupcakes and a lemon drizzle cake. There is tea, and beer and wine. Lexie climbs onto Joyce's lap for a story, while Ollie and Sam run around playing Transformers.

Leo is over by the bushes. He is dancing about and waving his hands joyfully as the silver paper catches in the wind. He has hung a strip around his neck like a shiny garland.

Later, as the light fades, no one is in a hurry to go anywhere. Joyce lights a fire and Pete offers to take Rob, Sam and Ollie in the tractor trailer, and we watch them in the distance, the sweep of the headlights and Leo running along in front.

Joyce comes out of the kitchen with a bottle of champagne. 'I kept this back for us,' she says. 'It was from one of the parents at the project.' She passes it to Helen to open.

The embers in the fire pit glow orange in the dark. Lexie and Ruby are busy pressing marshmallows onto sticks.

After handing out the glasses, she leans forwards in her seat, looking directly at Helen. 'Families come in different shapes and sizes,' she says. 'And speaking from experience,' she nods towards Leo in the field, 'it hasn't always been our blood relatives that have held us up. When things have been difficult, my friends have been my towers.' Her voice wavers with emotion. 'Consider us a tower, if ever you should need one.'

Helen can only nod, biting at her lip.

'To you. And the little ones,' Joyce says, raising her glass.

We raise ours too and sip our drinks.

Helen says she wants to make a toast for Polly, and we silently lift our glasses again.

Lexie looks up. 'Who is Polly?' she wants to know.

Helen thinks for a moment. 'Polly is the name of every brave woman in the world,' she says, but Lexie is already distracted, bashing sticks with Ruby as they poke them in the embers.

The fire cracks and spits. Orange sparks fly into the air. Lexie's gaze follows them upwards.

'Look,' she says, pointing up at the stars, 'is that where Daddy is?'

I hear my sharp intake of breath. Joyce and I exchange a look. But Helen doesn't miss a beat.

'Yes,' she says, 'he's shining up there,' and she leans in towards her daughter. 'Do you see that one?' and she points to the brightest star in the sky. 'That's him. His big bright love for you. Watching down and looking after you.'

Lexie thinks about this for a moment as she stares up at the velvety sky. 'And he'll stay up there?' she whispers cautiously. 'That's where he lives now?'

'Yes,' her mother says, 'he'll stay there forever. And it's up to you when you want to see him. You can be the one to choose when you want to look up and find him.'

Lexie nods. She seems to like this. Then she picks up her stick again.

As I look up at the starry sky, I think of Helen. I think of all the women's stories I have heard. And I think of my sister. I see Gemma's small eager face. Her tiny body as it twirls in the air. The slice of the skates on the gleaming white ice. Her sequinned leotard, and the beam of her smile as she holds a trophy high above her head.

*

Pete drops off Rob and the boys, and returns to the field to give Leo his final run out before bed. We start to pack up our things, and I can see Helen has allowed herself to relax a little.

She moves slowly, taking her time. Tonight, feeling safe among friends, she has been able to let go of the clock watching and the rigidity of bedtime. Things I realise must have been some of the many rules instilled by James. As we leave, Joyce asks if I can pop over to the farmhouse. 'Just for a bit. Something to show you – while Pete is out with Leo?'

Rob carries Sam and I lift Ruby up into my arms and we take them to the cottage and up to bed. Once they are in their pyjamas, I leave Rob reading them a story, then wander across the track to the farm.

The house is dark when I knock. 'Come on through,' Joyce says, 'I've made tea,' and she ushers me into the back room off the kitchen with the swish of a small torch. In the distance, I can hear the hum of the tractor.

She presses a finger to her lips, gesturing me to a seat by the large patio windows, and points to the garden area outside. It takes a while for my eyes to adjust to the darkness. And then I see them. Two fully grown adults and five cubs. The low sensor light illuminates their small stealthy movements.

'It's the first week the cubs have ventured out of the dark tunnels. They spend the first twelve weeks underground, with their mother.'

I stare at them, mesmerised. I am in awe of their smooth bodies. Their full snouts and their shiny paws. The silky jet-black fur and the thick white stripes.

'First steps above ground,' she says proudly. 'There's a sett under the compost out the back. I feed them. They come out at this time. When Pete is driving the tractor.'

I blink back at her.

'Does he know?'

She shrugs. 'Maybe. Maybe not. Probably. We don't speak of it.'

We watch in silence. The mother snuffles in the undergrowth. Her snout rooting through the leaves, looking for grubs and insects. Her eyes are watchful, bright and shiny. Close by, two of her cubs charge into each other, cuffing heads as they roll play-fully on the grass.

We sit cradling our mugs of tea. The steam rising in the silence.

'We all need pockets of hope,' she says. 'And this is one of mine.'

Acknowledgements

As always, my thanks to Karolina Sutton and to the many others at Curtis Brown who work so hard on my behalf.

Thank you to my editor Louisa Joyner, and to all at Faber, especially Jordaine Kehinde, Jess Kim, Sophie Portas and Kate Ward, and a big thank you to the stellar sales team.

I was a clinical psychologist in primary care in Tower Hamlets for many years, and writing this novel reminded me of the dedication of the colleagues and GPs I worked with there. My thanks to Andy Powell for his help on medical matters, and to Shirley McNicholas for her support and advice on safeguarding. Any mistakes or inaccuracies are down to me.

Research for this book involved reading stories about the lives of many women. Heartfelt thanks for these shared experiences; I hope I've done them justice.

To quote my character Joyce, 'my friends have been my towers', and never more so than during the last couple of years. I'm so grateful to them all. Special thanks to Vicky Browning, Francesca Cardona, Fliff Carr, Sam Cook, Liz Cotton, Mary Anne Feil, Maggie Greene, Emily Hatchwell, Paul Harrison, Anna Jones, Rebecca Lacey, Simon Lacey, Emma Lilly, Megan Meredith, Claire McGlasson, Sally Norton, Carey Powell and Liz Stubbs.

Finally, love and thanks to my amazing mum – and above all, to Paul, Joe and Nate.